To:

St*

CW00968690

CROSS CUT

Lee Ellis

25 October 2008 .

CROSS CUT

Lee Ellis

Time Link

First published 2008 by Time Link Publications
PO Box 186, Exmouth. EX8 4WT

ISBN 978-0-9557928-0-9

A CIP catalogue record for this book is available from the British Library.

Typeset in Georgia 10/12

Prepared and printed by:
York Publishing Services Ltd
64 Hallfield Road
Layerthorpe
York YO31 7ZQ
Tel: 01904 431213
Website: www.yps-publishing.co.uk

Author's Note

Cross Cut is a work of fiction. Any similarity to real persons, living or dead is entirely coincidental. However, the 'Battle of Mapperley Fields' of August 1842 described in Chapter Five is based upon actual events as recorded by contemporary newspapers. For this I am indebted to 'Chartism in Nottingham' by Peter Wyncoll published by Nottingham Trades Council, 1966.

- 1 -

She had the dream again last night. The same woman she'd dreamt for so many years. The same woman of her childhood dreams, yet different for she ages as Ella Weston ages and something binds them, pulls them together. Is she too a nurse, is it the calling they share? Is that why Ella has always been fascinated by the medicine of the past? Before, she'd been unconcerned with what the woman said, but now deciphering her words intrigues and frustrates her. In the dream she turns and seems to speak, but the words are soundless. Yet there's a pleading entreaty, a frustrated disheartened demanding, her lips quivering in their clamour to be heard. She moves earnestly and dynamically, almost threatening with guilt overladen fear. This unnerves Ella as she's unable to receive and understand her words. Whatever she says, it must be important and always Ella wakes shaking and alarmed, a residual wondering if the woman might somehow rise from the depths of the dream, burst through the door and chastise her, or worse, for her failure. As Ella gets up she sees that forlorn figure transposed in the sunlight turning imploringly and balefully in her chair. If only she could understand her words...!

"I'm aware your transfer to us is not wholly voluntary. You'll have to get used to a different regime here to the Met."

Chief Inspector Jenner groaned inwardly. How many times had he heard such familiar phrases? Emmins appended his remark with a slightly gloating smirk, reflecting the undisguised schadenfreude. Ignoring it, Jenner contented himself with a neutrally oblique stare, though even this ruffled the chief superintendent, who coughed continually until he found slight solace, with a concentrated gaze at his desktop.

Jenner isn't pleased, but who is he to judge others? He'd earned his mixed reputation uncovering a criminal web, oscillating in the disjointed connection between past and present. If he told everything, not just Emmins would label him a crackpot. Yet he reminisces freely and indulging those memories provides some comfort. Had those things really happened? Perhaps the best policeman is the one who really knows few things are as they seem.

"I want you to tackle the Weston case first. It's been dormant for too long."

Jenner forced a smile.

"Surely there are more pressing ones? It's only a missing person and it's over two years since..."

"...three to be exact, which is precisely why I want some action. Besides the mother is insistent and she's sure...while the sister...well, we need to establish once and for all whether it's a simple case of a missing person or whether there's something more sinister. Personally, I've always been of the view..."

"I agree it's probably more sinister."

Sinister. The word hung ominously, bringing back unwanted memories. There was some truth in Emmins snide remark. Jenner had been glad to leave London. He couldn't have gone on, there had to be some relief, some change, even if it was only of scene. Such an unusual, not to say remarkable case could so easily have cemented his reputation. Perhaps it had, in the concrete of unbelievable lunacy. Yet the situation spoke for itself. However much the smart arsed clever dicks might mock, he'd solved a complicated and dangerous mystery. Such cases only come along once in a professional lifetime. Thank God! Yet it was an experience, of which others can only dream.

"After your previous ... more ... colourful investigations it's important to locate your feet firmly on the ground, keep your nose to the grindstone and get stuck in. Do I make myself clear?"

"Perfectly."

"Excellent. The only remotely unusual aspect of Bernard Weston's life, apart from his mysteriously sudden disappearance, was his involvement in the campaign to get the 'Cross Cut' canal reopened."

Jenner sits at one of the new 'way stations' on the Cross Cut, studying the visitor board with its illustrations of birds and plants. It seems tranquil enough, the murky, inert water, disturbed only by passing pebble tossing boys and the detritus of the nearby trees. All lightness and spontaneous fun, children playing, old men strolling, young women laughing, peace and stability. Yet peering into the water, unable to see the bottom he feels...a gloominess...even something... sinister? He can see the tunnel. It unnerves him. He wonders what it's like, but he's reluctant to go there. He looks away expectantly towards the valley, hoping perhaps to catch sight of some malevolent ne'r do wells who might be waylaid and forced to explain their evil intentions. Better that than go towards the tunnel.

The files gave no obvious lead, but he needed to acquaint himself with the area, soaking up whatever background data and atmospheric clues it might reveal. He started out with no particular objective. Continuing past the motorway interchange, he cursorily examined the old mining villages and market towns, heading for the Shearwell valley by accident rather than design. In the coal scarred country with its brooding low hills and sluggish streams he stopped short of the Derbyshire hills, drawn to where nature's green coverlet has gradually re-colonised the fields from their two hundred year industrial battering. The byways inevitably led him to the country park and its conflict ridden canal. The 'Cross Cut.'

3

He always likes to get the 'sense' of a case. Coming out here should make him feel better, but it's difficult when everything is 'cold.' As he sits by the canal, glancing nervously towards the tunnel, he detects a disturbing rapport between the environment and his own feelings. His initial sensation remains. The truth must be buried beneath the area's struggles, but he's disappointed. Time marches relentlessly like the verdant layer of grass and shrub encroaching on the old slag heaps, submerging events, hiding the past, destroying any hope of finding what really happened.

He gets up and re-crosses the canal at the lock. His thoughts embarrass and disturb. Embarrassed by their foolishness, disturbed by his inability to curb them. There was a time when he would never have thought like this. It may be of no matter. He'd rather avoid thinking about his own past. It opens up his mind to the inexplicable and the unbelievable. He grips the car roof, desperate to make contact with something immediately tangible, at least superficially real. Inside he shakes himself vigorously, hoping the physical activity will jerk and fire the brain from the locking trap of the past. It works, though a little boy passing by gives him a long, hard, critical look of mixed disbelief and ridicule.

"Could never see what all the fuss was about," Emmins had said, "An old disused canal out in the Shearwell valley, but there's no accounting for people's idiosyncracies. First thing, re-examine the family and his associates. You'll have a good team. An experienced detective sergeant and two reliable DCs."

With that Emmins returned his attention to the desktop, signalling the end of the interview. He didn't even look up as he said finally, "The mother's here. You can see her first. Keep me informed."

Janice Weston had been adamant about her son's fate.

"Bernard is dead."

"You're very sure."

"That's what I've been saying. I want something done. A mother feels these things, especially if you're a Traynor."

"A Traynor?"

"My maiden name. Bernard was as much a Traynor as a

4

Weston. Ella's the same. We feel things."

Despite persistent questioning, she failed to further enlighten him and her talk of 'feeling things' only reinforced his discomfort.

He's exhausted. A weekend in an accelerating learning curve of document digestion has consumed most of his waking hours. As the printed pages and scribbled notes jumped like dancing bears across the pages, he played one of his favourite CDs to ease his brain into wind down mode. He thought it might open up new lines of thought, just as from his vantage point on the touchline, the manager, usually sees the game better than the players. Then he reopened the files as the music enveloped the room, but Rimsky Korsakov's Antar Symphony only confused and disoriented him. After half an hour he finally admitted defeat, closed the files and went to bed. The after images of the documents continued to flicker irritatingly across his mind and he slept badly.

It's a different regime here, but not beyond your adaptability. Strength will return. You're still 'settling in.' Including sleep 'settling in' has involved an inadequate total of 27 hours and he's already suffering from information overload. All this is part of the transfer, he tells himself. He wonders about Emmins 'settling in.' He may have pursued a diverse career, equipping him with a veritable treasure chest of varied experience and expertise, but Jenner doubts it. Emmins' own 'settling in' has probably been taken at a leisurely pace spanning at least twenty years. The thought makes him feel better.

He concentrates on the group to be interviewed, all in their mid to late thirties, approximate contemporaries of Bernard Weston. By the time he's out of the valley and beyond the motorway, the old, reliable, rational man returns. Back at the station, he walks slowly along the corridor and up the stairs to his office. On the ground floor he acknowledges no one. After all, they're still strangers, though several officers speak to him. Upstairs he responds to a couple of 'morning sirs' and nodding 'guv's. They know *him* even if he doesn't know them. Even so, sinking into the sanctuary of his own chair, he won't allow soft centred thoughts of his new surroundings to intrude. He glances out of the window.

"Too bloody calm and peaceful," he snorts to himself, sitting back down.

He looks round anxiously, conscious he may have been overheard. As soon as appearance sake permits he must get an office on the other side of the building where there's traffic and people and reality. Will he ever get used to the place? It's not like London as Emmins is only too pleased to remind him, though he'll never know what Jenner really misses.

The nightmare after effects came later. He could take the ribald remarks, the petty jealousy of those unable to believe he'd cracked a case so amazing it couldn't be really authentic. The facts said otherwise, but to closed and unimaginative minds mere facts rarely presented a problem. More difficult was coping with the inner reminders, constantly wondering if he'd missed an alternative dimension to an investigation, not knowing the boundaries between truth and falsehood. He'd always felt it was much more than any other policeman would understand, but how to say that without appearing arrogant? Calverton would know. He'd been there, he'd seen it, but sergeant Calverton had been reassigned to another team. Jenner had asked for him back, but it was not to be. Perhaps they felt it better to split them up. Separated, they were weaker, no focus for irrational explanation.

They must have breathed a huge, collective sigh of relief when in a moment of desperate weakness, he'd put in for a transfer. Jenner had immediately regretted his foolhardiness. He'd tried to withdraw, but the bureaucratic wheels had already moved with uncharacteristic speed. It was too late. It would be better for him, everybody understood the pressures he'd been under, the change would open up all sorts of new possibilities, etcetera, etcetera, etcetera. Now he's here, a hundred miles from his origins, a million from his old life.

A knock at the door, a woman enters.

"Morning sir, Jennifer Heathcott, your new sergeant."

Shaken out of his dull thoughts and taken off guard, Jenner looks up and speaks sharply.

"But you're a..."

"...a woman?"

"A local, sergeant, you're a local. Absolutely essential for this investigation. I on the other hand, as I'm sure you've already gathered, am not from these parts. "

"No, sir."

"We have two DCs, Tye and Duggan. You know them?"

"Yes."

"I hope they're reliable."

"They're both good."

He looks at her intently, his eyes uttering the unspoken question 'are you any good, sergeant?' She hopes her equally intent stare is sufficient answer.

"We've been assigned to a cold case. Bernard Weston, 34, insurance executive, mysteriously disappeared three years ago. He was a part time local historian. Know anything about local history?"

She shifts uneasily and replies hesitantly.

"Yes, it's also an interest of mine."

He looks blankly. God, she thinks, should have kept quiet. He'll think I'm a bloody anorak, not an appropriate diversion for a police officer.

"Good, could be useful. Weston was unmarried and lived alone. He had no known financial, work or emotional issues, no obvious explanation for his disappearance. All possible places or people he might go to proved negative. He had a girlfriend, a mother, a sister and a close friend. He made no contact before leaving, none of them heard from him and couldn't explain why he went away. They were all interviewed together with certain other people with whom he had a mutual interest. I'll come to that in a moment. At the time, the only suspicious aspect about his disappearance was the discovery of an anonymous letter in his flat. It was postmarked a few days before he disappeared and simply said 'Give it up.'"

He pushes across a plastic wallet containing the scrawled note.

"There were no prints, nothing to trace the sender. Now, Weston had been involved in a local campaign concerning a closed canal, called the 'Cross Cut.' you know it?"

"North west of the city near Brinckley."

"Quite, know anything about it?"

"It's quite hilly round there and much of the canal is in a tunnel. About two miles long. It was originally opened to link the upper end of a much older canal to a newer one, built lower down the valley. The two canals both connected with Nottingham and the Trent and ran parallel with each other, a string of hills between. The newer canal cut the time for transporting the coal by at least a day, but some of the mines at the top end of the valley were only connected to the older, longer route. The Cross Cut enabled them to take their coal, part way along the old route and then switch to the newer, shorter one. When the railways came the coal could be moved even quicker. The two longer canals carried on for other traffic, but the Cross Cut became redundant and was closed. The mines closed twenty years ago and much of the area was opened as a country park. The disused Cross Cut runs right through the centre of the new park. Many people thought it could provide a badly needed amenity, so there was a campaign to reopen it."

"Very good, sergeant, you're quite an expert."

Jennifer blushes slightly. Among some of her colleagues, her historical knowledge has been the subject of ridicule rather than congratulation.

"But it seems not everyone agreed. What do you know about that?"

"It was amazing how such a straightforward thing could stir up so much antagonism. There were objections on financial grounds, the cost of cleaning up and renovating the canal was expensive, but the main opposition was environmental."

"Environmental? Wasn't the idea to improve the environment?"

"Not everyone saw it the same way. A counter campaign was launched to *oppose* the reopening. Said it was an eyesore, best left for nature to complete covering up."

"Quite, which explains why other people were questioned. Bernard Weston was a leading light in the group to reopen the canal, but surprisingly his close friend Matthew Usworth was in the other camp, opposing it. Usworth was interviewed at the time as were two others. Martin Sarwell was an opponent, while Sylvia Darrington – Cressley sided with Weston."

Jennifer starts at the mention of Sylvia's name.

"You know this woman?"

"Her family owns the 'Ambro' food company. She's very wealthy, has a big place just north of Brinckley, Elvington House. As a matter of fact, I was there at the weekend. She held what she called an '1840s day.' Some people were in costume."

Jenner looks a little bemused. She's unsure whether he approves how she spends her leisure time.

"Know anything more about her?" he says.

Jennifer is relieved, yet hesitates, only continuing after receiving another raised eyebrow.

"As well as her business interests, she's the leader of a movement called 'Moral Power.'"

"Never heard of it, but I'm not interested in politics."

"It's not political, at least not in the conventional sense. It's a sort of moral regeneration crusade, getting back to old values, that sort of thing."

"Telling people how to behave, eh?"

"Something like that."

"Sounds like politics to me."

Jennifer Heathcott seems competent. She may also be very observant. He must not give himself away. Get a grip, Jenner. Forget the past.

"We'll re-interview all five, splitting them between us with the DCs. Here's a list and their last known contact addresses."

Ella Weston is off duty and is the first to arrive. She's anxious to 'get it over with.' Jennifer assumes this is a natural nervousness about the interview, but Ella's fears go much deeper. She'd gone to Elvington House at the weekend, hoping to merge with other people, determined to lose her thoughts if not herself amidst the furniture and pictures, chandeliers and curtains, memories and reminders. What it must be to spend a day devoid of the spectres of the night, everything seen without the intruding vestiges of lingering dreams. A whole twenty four hours without that creeping encroachment forever threatening.

She'd stopped on the terrace, grabbed the balustrade and nervously scanned the crowds in the garden. Many people were crowded onto the lawn, the few patches of green, hemmed in by resplendent picnickers and constantly overrun by excited children. The day was a success. The old house, basking in the afternoon brightness, stood radiantly against the cloudless tranquil sky, jutting its red brown starkness sharply into the expansive blue. Yet Ella knew the peaceful aura was transitory. When the dark clouds reappeared and the sun waned, a different, colder, closer, sinister atmosphere enclosed. Unquietly sleep the spirits of the past and the past is not for pretending. It's real. She gripped the balustrade tighter as the images of the night imposed, blotting out the trees and the wall at the end of the gardens. Then she'd disappeared into the procession winding its way into the house.

Now she's at the police station and must concentrate, saying "I'll do anything to find out who's responsible."

"Responsible for what?" Jennifer asks.

Ella shakes her head nervously.

"For whatever has happened to Bernard."

"What do you believe has happened?"

She puckers her lips and slightly shrugs her shoulders.

"Dunno, but it's not of his choosing."

"You believe he was forcibly taken away, abducted?"

She nods.

"Was there anyone who might have had a grudge against him, someone he crossed at work for instance?"

"I was asked all this three years ago, nothing's changed. He had people he didn't get on with, don't we all, but nobody who'd want to...you know...do him harm."

"What about his personal life?"

"I don't know why you're dragging all this up again."

"We're reviewing the case."

"He had no personal problems so far as I know. He'd been seeing Denise for some time. They seemed okay, but how can anyone outside a relationship really know what's going on inside it?"

"What about his involvement with the canal, didn't he disagree with his friend, Matthew Usworth?"

"You'll have to ask Matt about that."

So she does, but he's no more forthcoming.

"Can't friends have a genuine disagreement, yet still remain friends?" he says aggressively.

"Depends what they disagree about."

"Whether the damned canal stays open or not is hardly important enough to fall out over, is it?"

"You tell me."

"Wasn't important to me."

"And him?"

He shrugs.

"You worked together in the insurance company?"

"Yes."

"Outside work you shared an interest in the canal."

"Not really, it was Bernard's pet project."

"Why were you so opposed to it reopening?"

"I didn't like the area being turned into a bloody theme park."

"Isn't that a bit over the top, it's only an old canal? Or is there more to it?"

"It's what it might lead to. You can't always control these things. Bernard got wrapped up in all that canal stuff."

"You're not into the past?"

He hesitates.

"Not like Bernard. The past's the past, all this resurrecting relics and dressing them up, false reconstructions like..."

"...a theme park."

"Then to ally himself to that Darrington – Cressley woman."

"You don't approve of her?"

"Bloody plutocrat. Her ancestors scarred the landscape in the first place."

"I didn't know her family were involved in mining?"

He turns away, stares at the wall and then turns back aggressively.

"You're so well informed, why are you bothering to ask me? You know what I mean. It's her *type* that did all the damage."

"So it was because of her involvement that you opposed the canal campaign?"

"Of course not, you're twisting my words!"

"So you wouldn't have gone to her 1840s open day at Elvingotn House over the weekend?"

Another hesitation.

"No."

But it's lie. He'd heard about the 'period day' and the fancy dress gimmick. The prospect of lining the coffers of Sylvia Darrington-Cressley, however indirectly, held him back. He'd never understood Bernard allying himself with her. Ersatz Victoriana had never figured in his priorities. Big houses are not really his scene and he tended to agree with his late grandmother.

'Years ago they did all they could to keep us out, now they want our money to get us in!'

Anyone in 1840s attire could get in for half price and the idea of 'dressing up' as part of her novelty day was even less alluring. The saving hadn't attracted him. He could have saved even more by not going at all. So an afternoon at the grandiloquent pile of the Darrington-Cressleys had not initially excited him, but the seductive spell of those times, even in the bosom of the enemy, was bewitching and he'd been unable to resist.

Despite his discomfiture at 'snatching crumbs from the lady of the manor's table,' he'd not been disappointed. Juxtaposed elements – hamburger stalls and period costume, modern kids' games in the authentic surrounds of the house – incongruously added to the believable and intriguing merge of past and present. The delicately fused atmosphere wove its irresistible trail through the rooms and hedgerows, magnetically beguiling in a timeless yet also strangely time heavy presence.

He exchanged a few politely stilted words with Denise, an unavoidable interchange for appearances only. Though after so much time even that wears thin. What can they have in common now? Only Bernard brought them together and without him there's nothing. The sun beat down relentlessly in the cloudless sky and he'd walked for too long. He stopped to rest on one of the benches on the terrace, leaned back and surveyed the house, high and wide in its ageing splendour. Then he turned to the people. They seemed to hover in immobile transfixion. There was a distinct other worldness to their gait, immured, unable to bestir themselves at a normal pace, the costumes reinforcing the artificial elegance of a bygone age. He knew their lack of movement was an illusion, yet he was tempted to sink even deeper into the enticing fissure of forgetfulness where awareness of place and time shimmers, indistinct and precarious. He had to resist as the man exposed on a freezing Winter night must resist tiredness induced death from the cold. It was ridiculous. It was the place sucking him into the false, fantastic foolishness of the day. Then they moved away properly and the dangerous moment passed.

He noticed two particular people, like himself both in costume. They were at the edge of the lawn, talking excitedly, but it was no amicable conversation. The body language told all. Standing too far apart for friendliness, their arm gestures threatening rather than inviting. He recognised Ella, Bernard's sister. He wasn't sure of the man, but believed he'd seen him before. As he turned away from Ella and looked towards the house, Matt recognised him. Martin Sarwell. They met once, years ago when he came to see Bernard. What was he doing talking to Bernard's sister? In fact, what was he doing here at all? He didn't look like one of the day-outers, but neither did Matt. Maybe he too is irresistibly drawn to the 1840s? Ella turned from him abruptly and headed for the steps. Martin watched her briefly and then he too walked away, across the lawn towards the refreshment tent. Then Matt saw Sylvia approaching and not wishing to see her, got up and retreated into the house.

At the police station Sylvia Darrington – Cressley also remembers the weekend. The idea had been long forming, but something more pressing had always got in the way. There'd always been a reason *not* to do it. Sylvia even set aside dates, but always *something* had turned up. No longer. The event had been well planned and advertised for weeks. Catering, stewarding, ticketing, accommodation, all meticulously arranged and synchronised. Nothing had been left to chance. She'd been up very early, prowling the grounds, making last minute checks and badgering the staff. When she'd called on the front gate stewards for the fifth time their politely obsequious smiles started to wither.

With no one queuing when the gates were opened at eleven, she stepped into the main road, striding over to the far side, scrutinising both directions, willing cars to stop and passing coaches to disgorge their passengers. She stared at a lone hiker with undisguised contempt when he made no attempt to veer from the path, marching on solidly, lowering his head to avoid her gaze and pretending she wasn't there. It was twenty minutes before the first visitors arrived and for an hour it was only a trickle. She remained at the entrance box, hovering irritably in case anyone changed their mind and retreated back to the road, before strolling impatiently around the almost empty car park like a hungry tigress, thwarted from its prey. Just as she wondered whether this really had been such a good idea the numbers increased.

By one o'clock the gardens were quite crowded. Weekend aficionados displayed their limited horticultural knowledge, jostling with the ambling innocence of less pretentious souls. An engrossed stream meandered steadily through the house, the less adventurous examining the furniture with a distantly glazed ignorance, the more daring ogling the more lascivious pictures. The craft fair in the main hall was more successful. The dressmaking stands were particularly popular. Yet there were many bored eyes and needing their stomachs, if not their brains, appropriately stimulated, many gratefully tumbled into the marquee for refreshments.

Sylvia suddenly realised something was missing. She'd hoped half price entry to visitors in authentic 1840s dress would encourage attendance, but never assumed they would be in the majority so she'd arranged for a band of suitably attired volunteers to mingle with the punters. None of these helpers had arrived and without them the impact of the costumes on display was seriously weakened. Panicking inside, but outwardly quiescent, she slipped into the study to make frantic phone calls. Most were on their way. Then she got a message from the gate. A few visitors had arrived in costume. Things were looking up.

The sun came out. The car park filled up. By two o'clock the house and grounds were bustling with subdued, but vital energy. She inspected all locations again and then went upstairs. She could have changed earlier, but was reluctant to appear too conspicuous. Now, with the first helpers arriving and some visitors suitably dressed she regained her confidence. The day will be successful after all. This is the event to put Elvington House firmly on the tourist map. A period open day, well remembered.

After putting on her dress she adjusted her bonnet in front of the mirror, fiddling with it for some moments, tipping it slightly from side to side, anxious to make the right impression. It went well with the dress. She stared at her image, her familiar features framed in the unfamiliar outlines of her ancestors. It could be a picture, not herself at all, a quaint reminder of a lost time, like a snapshot in an album, a sudden incision cut from life, flashed and caught forever in an artificial frame. But it is her, not the past. Only the clothes, the misleading outward appearance, are different. Or do clothes reflect the person within? Do people change as their clothes change? Does all change or nothing change? She shook her head. It's only an illusion, a harmless novelty to publicise the house. Yet the 1840s are not dead, they only sleep. She turned away from the mirror. Today was not the time for reawakening.

She went downstairs, her dress rustling entrancingly on the stairs. She stopped on the landing and looked down into the middle corridor before continuing. It was empty. Keen to move on to the main rooms she didn't linger. Yet, with its fine wainscoting and heavy, but elegant early Victorian banisters, more than anywhere else in the house it exuded the spirit of the age. She could hear the muffled, excited voices from the craft fair. Vigorous and confident, they could be the assembled coterie of a weekend party from long ago. A couple walked in from the main hall. The woman looked up, forcing Sylvia from her reverie. Their eyes met. The woman smiled. Sylvia hesitated, unsure and then smiled back. They moved on. The corridor was empty again and Sylvia continued down, lifting the rope barrier at the bottom of the stairs. Now she could no longer pretend to be in the nineteenth century, yet the close awareness of the past endured as she passed into the public part of the house.

Slightly self conscious, she moved quickly through the rooms, though there were now more people in nineteenth century clothes. Not all the women had done their homework properly, their dresses belonging to later decades, but the overall effect of the long skirts accentuated the atmosphere. It was stronger still in the gardens, where many took advantage of discounted entry and the array of high hats and bobbing bonnets unmistakably revitalised a distant era. Gone were modern dull and repetitive colours. Dresses of many hues swished gracefully and the men's jackets and trousers in yellows and reds were redolent of the past.

Emphasising the event as an 1840s day successfully promoted the house, but it also generated this crisp, potent crucible of another time. Savour it well, Sylvia told herself, soon enough it will be gone. She sat at a vacant bench on the terrace. Some children scuttled past, laughing and shouting to the adults on what they'd seen. It must have been like this in those other 'open' days her grandmother used to talk about when the villagers, colliers' families and hosts of mill workers came to enjoy a day in the spreading magnificence of the home of their employers and betters. It was always popular and very enjoyable. The family loved it. A day when other troubles and conflicts were forgotten, a trucial nomansland of respite from the gathering storms of Edwardian England.

Many gathered on the lawn, the generations mingling and relaxing. Sylvia hadn't expected so many. She saw Matt Usworth moving away as she approached. He was well turned out in a smart, but plain jacket and trousers, felt hat and boots. Plain, but dignified, he could have been one of those mill workers she'd seen in old illustrations.

People always need a place to go on a bright, warm Sunday, but she'd not thought Elvington House would be their first choice. Perhaps it was the sheer space and lack of restriction

16

that attracted the children. Most parents made the most of the temporary peace while their offspring careered around harmlessly, though the more prudent opened up their picnic bags or went off for supplies to prepare for the inevitable demands for food and drink when the children exhausted themselves. The older folk watched contentedly. Some were very old. Old enough perhaps to remember those other open days, not just learning about them second hand. Would their recollections agree or diverge from those of her grandmother? Sylvia considered going down and talking to some of the older people, but then reconsidered. They might not know what she meant and even if they did, could she cope with a different account of those days? Better to leave memories undisturbed, even if inaccurate than deal with uncomfortable realities. Besides, the uncompromising aura of the 1840s had always fascinated her more than the ambivalent precipice of the 1900s. Yet the day was their day and her day, a prospect of a particular past.

A young woman arrives at the police station behind her. She catches only a brief glimpse, but is instantly reminded of the weekend costumes she'd observed with mixed admiration and disdain. Not all were clumsy concoctions. Some showed careful attention to detail. She looks back. No one is there, but the image of someone she'd seen sweeping across the lawn in an awesome outfit persists.

She glides into the interview room, oozing an urbane unctuousness. It irritates Jennifer.

"Naturally I'll do all I can to clear up this dreadful business, though I fear, as they say, the trail is cold."

She tosses back her large shoulder scarf, which has fallen across her front. She's dressed in a light tan, elegantly cut suit, though surprisingly for such an otherwise ostentatious woman, she wears little jewellery, only a signet ring and a cameo brooch on her lapel. Jennifer quickly goes over the previous interview. This established Sylvia was hundreds of miles away at the time of Bernard's disappearance, only learning of it when she tried to contact him to arrange a function to coincide with the canal's official reopening.

"Even now I find it difficult to believe he's gone. So full of energy and enthusiasm, it was so out of character to simply disappear. It had absolutely nothing to do with our work on the Cross Cut. Everything was going so smoothly, despite the absurd opposition, which I'm glad to say was unsuccessful and has long since faded away. No, whatever led to him to leave the area, it must have been some personal crisis."

"Personal crisis?"

"I surmise, I have no knowledge, you understand."

"You talk about him leaving the area as if he might be safely found somewhere else?"

Sylvia twists her hands and smirks in a gesture of innocence.

"Who knows."

"If he was safe somewhere, wouldn't he have got in touch?"

The smirk widens.

"Not if he doesn't wish his whereabouts to be known to certain individuals."

The phrase lingers, an unspoken, pregnant intelligence, Sylvia's wide eyed gaze emanating innocence, yet paradoxically inviting Jennifer to accept an inner deeper meaning. Jennifer doesn't pursue it, meeting Sylvia's stare with an equal innocuousness.

"Your work on the canal is part of your wider involvement in heritage issues?"

"I'm not sure what you mean."

Jennifer reminds her of the weekend activities. Sylvia brushes this aside with a wave of her hand.

"Merely a promotional exercise for the house. One has to stimulate the public's attention if it's to be promoted as an attraction."

"I wouldn't have thought you needed to open up the house to visitors."

"If you are vulgarly implying I don't need the money, then allow me to remind you some of us regard it as our duty to share our cultural inheritance as widely as possible."

"Very commendable, I'm sure. I was merely alluding to your wider financial and other interests."

"I have a living to earn like everyone else."

"*Earn* is hardly the appropriate word. You inherited the family business, I believe?"

Sylvia makes no response other than a slight twitch to her head. Jennifer continues.

"It's a long established business."

"Not really, twenty years or so."

"As Ambro *Foods* maybe, but as Ambro *Clothing and Textiles* it's much older."

The twitch to the side of the head gets more pronounced. Sylvia is irritated.

"We moved out of clothing, sold our interests."

"Your firm was originally in a very traditional local industry, lace and as such goes back many, many years. Then..."

"What has this got to do with Bernard Weston?"

"He was not involved in your company?"

"No."

"What about your other great interest, 'Moral Power,' was he involved in that?"

"Not in the slightest. My only contact with Bernard was through the canal."

She leans back, with an irritated, self satisfied finality. Having dealt with all of this wretched woman's irrelevant questions she's ready to leave. Jennifer studies her notes and meets Sylvia's crusty gaze with a laden smile.

"Your 'Moral Power' organisation, into food in a big way, isn't it?"

"How do you mean?"

"Healthy living means healthy eating, that sort of thing."

"You make my campaign sound nothing more than a glorified slimming programme. I can assure you it's much more than that."

"I'm sure it is, but I'm right food plays a significant part in your material?"

"Healthy eating is clearly essential to an upright lifestyle, but we are concerned with regeneration of the mind and spirit as much as the body."

"Naturally, but promoting certain types of food is very... *convenient* ...to your commercial interests."

"It would be more accurate to describe myself as someone who adopts a *responsible* approach. In any case, I still don't see the relevance of..."

"Bernard Weston never took an interest in these matters? He never questioned the tie up between your moral crusade and your business interests?"

"No."

"He never challenged your moral high ground?"

"No."

"You never found the position he adopted...difficult?"

"No I did not and I resent your implication that our relationship was tinged in some way by a reprehensible disagreement based on some sort of conflict of interest on my part. You haven't a scrap of evidence on which to base these disgraceful insinuations!"

The young woman Sylvia passed is Denise Deverall, Bernard's girlfriend. She's pert, almost breezy, but Jenner detects a defensive nervousness beneath the outward show of confidence. He's surprised she works in a furniture distribution depot. There's nothing in her manner to indicate the mundane world of sales ledgers and administration. Despite any artificial pretence, she has an aspect of something brighter, more exciting. Jenner struggles with the thought as she goes over the well worn ground of her relationship with Bernard and her movements at the time of his disappearance. Then it comes to him. *Elegance.* There's an air of elegance about this woman. What could she have had in common with Bernard Weston?

"Was there any tension between you?" he says, almost without interest.

Her denial is predictable.

"No minor problem that he may have exaggerated, some incident that may have worried him?"

Nothing.

"No one who might have meant him any harm?"

The slightest of hesitations, a quick, furtive glance that could mean almost anything, but there was no one. She's sure? She's sure.

"And nothing that was worrying him, something connected with his work perhaps?"

Nothing.

After Denise leaves Martin Sarwell arrives for his interview. Jenner lets Sandra Tye ask a few preliminary questions, essentially retracing the familiar territory of Martin's movements at the time of the disappearance, while he studies the man carefully. His replies are precise and succinct, matching her questions just sufficiently to avoid any suggestion of holding back or evasion. His eyes hold her with the same measured tenacity, only occasionally darting over to Jenner, to reassure himself he's not missed any unspoken communication. He betrays no emotion, not even the irritation shown by the others, yet the cultured, measured demeanour and very politeness unnerves Jenner and he has to intervene.

"Did the conflict between you and Bernard Weston become intolerable?"

Martin turns his head slightly, but is otherwise unchanged except for a slight readjustment of his clasped fingers, propped on his elbows.

"There was no conflict," he says, with the slight hint of a forced smile, "I was not the only one to oppose the opening of the Cross Cut. He was..."

"That's not what I meant. I understand Bernard Weston accused your laboratory of experimenting on animals. Letters were exchanged in the local press."

Martin laughs, but it's plaintive, artificial.

"All a misunderstanding. We never experimented on animals. Mr. Weston eventually understood the position and accepted it."

The clipped, exact words with their implied criticism of any challenge convey detachment and finality. If it was good enough for Bernard Weston it should be enough for Derek Jenner. Enough said, there's no need for further discussion.

"Quite. You had no contact with him through your other interests?"

Martin loses his flimsy composure.

"What other interests?"

"Over the years you've contributed quite a few articles on the early history of the local railways."

Martin is slightly relieved.

"Anorak stuff to you, chief inspector."

"And therefore all the more interesting, Mr. Sarwell."

"But not to Bernard Weston, so far as I know."

The usual questions reveal the same predictably unhelpful answers. Martin knows of no one who wished Bernard any harm nor has he any explanation for his disappearance. As Jenner accompanies him out Martin is visibly relieved though this reduces when he's reminded he may need to be seen again. Jenner returns to his office where Jennifer is waiting. They exchange information on their respective interviews. Jenner asks about Ella and Matt.

"Both very defensive," she says.

"What about Sylvia Darrington – Cressley, what did you make of her?"

"She isn't in it for the money. My guess is her historical interests may be the real reason behind the house opening, but she's not keen to talk about the past."

"Her own or generally?"

"Both. It's not just the house. She shared with Bernard Weston an interest in the canal. There's a connection there too."

"Oh yes, the *Cross Cut*. Interesting reply by Matthew Usworth about the canal. He said the canal *stays* open rather than *re*opens?"

Jennifer checks her notes.

"Yes, that's what he said. Does it matter?"

"Saying something is staying open implies it was never closed in the first place, but we know it was and for a very long time."

"Figure of speech."

"Not if..."

"Yes, sir?"

Jenner looks at her sharply, cursing himself for almost being too open.

"Nothing, sergeant. Is there anything else?"

"One thing sir. Are you into old coins by chance?"

"No, why?"

She drops a large bronze coin onto the table.

"All the interviews were held in the same room. Afterwards, this coin was found on the floor. It was definitely not there yesterday and must have been dropped by someone today."

Jenner picks it up. It's an old style, pre metric large penny, but is smooth and bright. On one side is the sharp impression of a young woman, the youthful Queen Victoria while the other side is clearly stamped '1840.'

"One of them must be into old coins," she says.

Jenner turns it carefully through his fingers.

"Maybe, but it looks so new, as if it was issued only yesterday."

- 2 -

Ettie Rodway awaits the arrival of her last visitor of the day. She's late and Ettie is getting impatient. Ordinarily she wouldn't agree to see anyone at such short notice, but the woman had been in great distress. Ettie tried to put her off, but she suddenly said she'd be around in half an hour and then hung up. Ettie resents this kind of moral blackmail, but the distress in the voice made her feel responsible and she fears the consequences of not meeting her. That was an hour ago. Ettie has already put on her coat and hat twice, only to take them off again. Her long black coat is slung over the chair and her large black hat is perched on the table, reminders she should have left by now.

After the great case, involving the police, when her house had been the target of attack, she'd needed a distance, even if was really only psychological, between her professional base and her home. Then, with similar incidents as today's, she'd resolved to no longer see people at her house at all. At least, not until she could trust them. So she'd taken this rented room above the bank, which she shares with a part time accountant and a counsellor. They each have their own locked filing cabinets, though Etttie keeps very little in hers. Nowadays she's often away, but if not she attends here two days a week. It's really a little artificial. Outside office hours, the phone calls automatically transfer to the house and, as her confidence has gradually returned she's arranged to see more people there.

An hour and a quarter. Hat and coat beckon. Five more minutes and she'll definitely leave. It's probably some trivial matter about a recently deceased relative. Ettie moved on from such things long ago. The street outside is almost deserted. The time for work almost over, the fading light ushers in the time for play. A taxi stops at the corner. A young woman gets out and walks deliberately along the opposite side glancing at the shops, though she's more interested in their numbers than the contents of their windows. She stops and looks directly across towards Ettie's office. She crosses the street. Ettie gets up and reaches the front door just as the bell rings. The young woman is flustered, bedraggled and desperately apologetic for her lateness. She also needs reassurance she's arrived at the right place.

"You really are Ettie Rodway? I read your pamphlet and it seems to answer so many of my questions."

She continues to babble as they go upstairs.

"Things have reached a pitch and I need the help of someone like yourself. I'm sorry to approach you with so little notice and for keeping you waiting. I am most grateful...I feel anything you say must be of value...when all else is falling apart it's important to find someone who finds these things... well, a little simpler to understand."

Ettie says little, other than confirming who she is. Once upstairs she seats Ella down and makes coffee to defuse her distress and the charged atmosphere. Ella prattles again, though now quieter and more slowly. Ettie pushes the coffee at her, willing her to drink, which will at least stem the flow of her talk. Then, waiting just long enough for her to swallow the last dregs, Ettie intervenes.

"How exactly can I help you, Miss Weston?"

Ella swallows hard, hoping to down not only the residual coffee, but also any remaining inhibitions. She begins with a repeat of her admiration for Ettie and her 'work.'

"I know you're not an ordinary medium."

"I dislike that term," Ettie says stiffly.

"Yes, I suppose time link consultant is more appropriate."

"More accurate too."

"I read in one article that after twenty five years, you decided to specialise in cases which were unusual and opened up opportunities to explore real...links...with the past. I hope I won't disappoint."

Ettie nods, hoping the silence will calm and encourage. Ella stares at Ettie. Helplessly she searches for a sign to show Ettie already knows, already understands, thereby making it unnecessary for Ella to explain at all. Ettie's eyes are reassuring, but not all knowledgeable. After some hesitation in which some of her nervous excitement subsides, Ella continues.

"I've had a recurring dream since I was small. I've never gone more than three months since I was five years old without it returning. The same woman sits in a chair by a fire and turns when she sees me. It's in the past. I'm not sure how long ago, at least a hundred years, maybe much more. I can tell by her clothes and the room. As I've got older I've remembered more and more of the room. I don't always wake straight away, but if not, I always remember the dream in the morning. Remember, remember... these days I remember every detail. She turns to me as if to speak. Sometimes her mouth moves as if she's forming words, but I can never make them out. It's so frustrating."

"Are you frightened?"

"No."

"Not even as a child?"

"No."

"So you're not apprehensive about expecting the dream? You feel no dread about its possible approach when you've not dreamt it for a while?"

"Not dread, in fact nothing at all beforehand, but afterwards always frustration at what I cannot understand. Even as a little girl I felt angry with the woman because I wanted her to speak to me clearly. That frustration has got stronger and stronger and also..."

"Yes?"

"Guilt. I'm filled up with guilt. Guilt because I don't understand her when I know I should. Guilt I've not tried hard enough to understand and just lately a newer, different guilt that's even worse."

Ella stops. Ettie waits expectantly. Ella searches her face again for signs, willing Ettie to understand, scouring for intimations that all her questions can be fully and miraculously answered. It does not, cannot come. She must continue, but to Ettie's disappointment switches tack slightly.

"This woman...she's changed as I've changed."

"How so?"

"She's aged with me. As I've grown older, so has she. Now she's a woman in her thirties, like me. Before she was younger as I was younger."

"When you were a little girl, was she a little girl?"

"Yes."

"I see."

Ella picks up the positive depth in Ettie's voice.

"You know what it means, don't you?"

"Tell me about this other guilt you've been feeling more recently. How is it different?"

She stares now more widely and Ettie wonders if she'll go back to the significance of the dream, but then her eyes narrow and she answers with a concentrated, almost wild intensity.

"It's her guilt! It's *her* guilt I feel. All around and within me I feel it. It's so strong and so desperate, but I don't know what it is. I don't understand. Why won't she say? Why won't she tell me!"

She breaks down, nearly crying and burying her head in her hands. Ettie waits, as yet unsure, but convinced Ella has more to tell. Gradually she composes herself and apologises. Ettie tells her to go on when she's ready.

"Tell me what you want to know about the dream," Ella says.

"Is this woman known to you?"

"It's not I know her...exactly...but I feel...it sounds ridiculous, but...it's as if this dream that I always remember so well is a memory itself. I know it can't be because it's so old, but I read somewhere that sometimes people keep alive a memory through generations...a generated dream?"

"A genetic dream."

"So is that it? How does it work?"

"A genetic dream is a memory from an ancestor, a mother, grandmother for instance passed on through a dream. Such things have been recorded. "

"It's not from my mother or grandmother. Why does she age as I age?"

"It could be part of the process of sympathetic communication."

"So that's it, a genetic dream?"

"It could be," Ettie says guardedly, "but has there been something recently that's given it more significance?"

Ella hoped she might not need to mention Bernard, but now tells of his disappearance and his involvement with the Cross Cut. She's surprisingly calm, almost matter of fact, her voice only wavering as she gets to the new police investigation and being questioned. Ettie slightly raises an eyebrow at the mention of Jenner's name.

"You know him?" Ella says, alarmed.

"We've come across each other," Ettie says, and then adds to distance herself, "it's a few years now. Has the chief inspector any idea what may have happened to your brother?"

"If he has, he's not told me, but then there are things I've not told him. Nothing the police would consider important," Ella says contemptuously.

"Like what?"

"I've started having another dream of the past. A large, grim building with lots of people, but most of them are just sitting around or moving slowly in the yard. I've looked it up. I think it's a workhouse."

"Does this have a connection with anyone you know?"

"No one I know of."

"But what do you feel?"

Ella hesitates before replying.

"It's the past, isn't it? It's all connected with the past and that's why I came to see you. I have this…this heavy weight on me, which grows and grows…something is going to happen. I had to come to you. Who else can I turn to."

Ella's eyes blaze. Ettie is unsure of her, though she has a distinct and gathering sense that by or through Ella a contact has been made which can't be ignored. The disappearance of her brother is both disturbing and intriguing. Jenner's involvement is an added, interesting coincidence. Ella seems afraid of him and Ettie hopes her own connection hasn't upset her. Ettie's also unsure whether Ella is ready for her next question, but if progress is to be made, it must be asked.

"What about you? What do you feel has happened to your brother?"

"That's what I was hoping you could tell me, Miss Rodway."

"But you must have some idea, some feeling?"

"Will you help me or not?"

She thrusts her hands against the sides of the chair and sits up rigidly as if about to stand up. Ettie knows the ice they skate on is getting perilously thin, but she must insist.

"I will help you if I can, but first I'd prefer you to answer my question."

The fire returns to the eyes and for a moment Ettie believes she may have fallen through the ice. Partly resigned and partly irritated, Ella sighs.

"I keep thinking of the things he said before he disappeared. At the time, who knows...we hear such things and shrug them off or don't listen properly. Only afterwards, when it's too late, we go over them again and again, wishing we'd said something at the time, asked more questions...ah well, it's too late now. It was as if he'd found out something, you know, like as children we tease our friends with secrets, 'I know something you don't know, tell me, shan't, okay then."

"Did he say what he'd discovered?"

"No, but he implied it was someone he knew. Either they'd told him or he'd found out and they weren't happy he knew. I think it gave him a feeling of power, something he could hold over them...something important enough for them to...God, how foolish he was!"

"He must have given some hint...."

"No, nothing, I've already told you!"

Ella stands up and points her finger down at Ettie.

"You're not going to help me at all."

"I've already said..."

"No, you're like the police. That damned inspector. Questions, questions, questions, but nobody gives me any answers!"

She goes to the door and runs down the corridor to the stairs. Ettie goes after her, but Ella is already through the front door. By the time Ettie reaches the entrance the street is deserted. Ella has disappeared.

Sylvia Darrington – Cressley insists Jenner comes to Elvington House in his own best interests.

"I'm sure you'd love to get away from that beastly station and the noise and pollution of the city for our clean air."

Jenner's impression of an ex-mining area doesn't exactly accord with Sylvia's pastoral concoction, but he's keen to get away to the country again and he takes the motorway, approaching Elvington House from the north. The entrance appears suddenly as he rounds a bend in the road. He stops the car at the end of the drive, winding down the window to take in some of Sylvia's 'clean air.' Away from the road the house seems smaller. Beyond the wall and away from its protective shield of hedges and trees it's less imposing. Someone is on the terrace and looks towards him. He eases the car back into gear and glides slowly up to the house. The high windows, the decorated balustrade, the heavy chimneys, the gabled roofs of the two wings, all concentrate the grandeur as the sun catches the glass, briefly blinding him, until it disappears behind the imposing façade of the entrance porch.

Sylvia emerges from the corner of the terrace. It was she who was watching him.

"Were you admiring the house, chief inspector?"

"Quite so, madam."

She takes him on a guided tour of the exterior and seems calmer, less stressed than when she'd visited the station. Dressed in a smart russet suit with matching shoes she radiates confidence, leading him around as a lady of the manor of the old days might deign once a year to instruct the villagers in a matronly and stately peregrination. Secure in familiar surroundings, he wonders. He follows dutifully, absorbed in his own thoughts and determined the interview will not become too informal.

"Victorian building?" he says perfunctorily.

"A little earlier, chief inspector. The first part of the house dates from 1805 and was steadily added to."

She's fascinated by the work of her ancestors and passionately reels off the dates of construction of the various wings and abutments. Jenner seems rapt attention, but he concentrates on her rather than what she says. At last, the tour finished, she shows him into the library and orders tea.

"I love this room, such a haven of peace and tranquillity."

It's light and surprisingly airy against the beige walls and brown bookcases. The electric lighting is modern, but there are also what appear to be replica gas light fittings in each corner. She notices him looking at them.

"They're authentic," she says, "the original gas lighting is still in place in about half the house."

They sit in opposite armchairs, either side of the French windows, which are open onto the terrace and the lawn beyond. The chairs are not close, though of the same height, perhaps reflecting her grudging acceptance of him as a social equal, but one still requiring a discreet distance. She settles down with an imperious smile, which he reciprocates with a cool, slightly upward twitch of his upper lip, his eyes remaining incisively concentrated. Perhaps to hide her nervousness and delay the start of the real conversation, she launches into a description of the house's interior, a colourful cocktail of dates and furnishing details, amply laced with anecdotes about her ancestors. The decade between 1835 and 1845 figures prominently.

"A period of particular activity?" he says absently.

She jerks, surprised he's been listening more attentively than she thought.

"To some extent. There was little building work, though a number of rooms were extensively redecorated and re-furnished."

"Quite, but nevertheless a period of particular interest for you?"

There's a slight intake of breath, a brief hesitation before replying and the inner realisation of being politely ambushed.

"No more than others. There was further work at the north end of the house. What we call the Amber room with its fine sunflower paper was decorated between 1852 and 1855."

"Quite. Tell me about your organisation."

"The firm? As you may know, we were originally..."

"No, not your business, your...campaign...what's it called?"

"Moral Power. I've already explained to your sergeant that my business interests and Moral Power's efforts in relation to food..."

"Quite so, I've heard all about that. I was referring to your broader moral concerns."

"If you feel it's strictly relevant to your investigations," she rejoins sharply.

"Allow me to be the judge of that, Mrs. Darrington – Cressley."

Their eyes lock in a transfixed gaze of mutual antagonism. His apparent awe as she talked so effusively about the house and its contents hasn't deflected his attention. She's not sure whether to challenge or acquiesce, but then a maid enters with a message and Sylvia's eyes suddenly sparkle.

"Chief inspector, a most important telephone call from my general manager. Would you excuse me, I'll take it in the lounge and won't be long. Sarah will look after you."

She glides out before Jenner can object, shutting the door resolutely behind her. The maid retrieves the tea cups.

"More tea, sir?"

"No thank you. I wonder, Sarah is it, if I might have a word?"

"Me, sir?" she says nervously, turning to the closed door, either to receive some unspoken guidance or else satisfy herself Sylvia really has left the room. She puts her tray on the table and he motions her into the other chair. She sits on its edge, anxious not to intrude her presence unnecessarily.

"You've worked here long?"

"Five years."

"You must have seen a lot of visitors in that time?"

She nods with another furtive glance at the door.

"You remember Bernard Weston?"

Another nod.

"Was he a frequent visitor?"

She shrugs indecisively.

"Now and again."

"Do you know why he came to visit, Mrs. Darrington – Cressley?"

Another expression of innocent ignorance.

"The canal, I suppose."

"No other reason, nothing else they talked about?"

"I wouldn't know."

Is this loyalty to her employer or genuine ignorance? Either way, he'll get no further.

"Are the other staff in the house?"

"Most of them."

"I might like to see them all later."

The prospect of having to alert the others brings panic to her face.

"Thank you, Sarah," he says with a smile, "you've been most helpful."

As she scuttles out the door, Sylvia can be heard from the other room, concluding her telephone conversation.

"Business can never wait," she says on her return, "Now, where were we?"

"Moral Power, you were telling me it's more than about food."

"Was I really, I thought we'd dealt with that?"

He concentrates his suspicious gaze again and she finally succumbs.

"I've always believed the health crisis facing western nations cannot be wholly resolved by changes in eating patterns, important as that is. It's part of a wider moral breakdown. I'm sure as a policeman you'll be only too well aware how the structural pillars holding together the fabric of our society have been constantly undermined by a continuous and accelerating loss of purpose and responsibility."

It sounds like a convenient off the shelf declaration. He

doesn't respond. His views on the pillars of society are not for sharing with her.

"Well," she says after a short pause for his non intervention, "that is my position."

"And apart from everybody eating less, how do you propose to bring about this transformation?"

She glares. His expression is immovable.

"By returning to the traditional values that made our country great."

Now it's his turn to wait for further elucidation, but it doesn't come.

"Quite," he says at last, "and your husband shares these... enthusiasms?"

She moves slightly uneasily.

"My husband and I live apart. We've done so for a number of years. By mutual agreement we've reached an... accommodation. He relinquished any interest in the business. We have no need to communicate."

His further lack of response increases her uneasiness.

"Naturally opponents of my campaign have sought to capitalise on this, arguing that our living apart is..."

"...neither one thing nor the other?"

"...is inconsistent with the objective, in the words of the tabloid press, of 'clean living.'"

"There's been some adverse publicity?"

"Nothing serious, the usual ineffectual slurs directed by the base minded at any attempt to tackle serious and fundamental issues."

"Indeed."

"None of this has anything to do with Bernard Weston," she says with some acerbity.

"You never talked to him about these matters?"

"It was not relevant to our discussions about the canal."

"Quite."

"I'll give you some of our literature before you go, chief inspector. You may find it of interest."

"I'm sure I will."

She goes to one of the cabinets, pulls out a drawer and hands him a bundle of papers. He takes them without comment.

"I hope our discussion has been of value," she says, impatient for the interview to terminate.

To her intense relief he moves with her, but pauses at the door.

"I wish to see all your staff. Are they in the house?"

"Most of them, but I don't see..."

"Essential and routine. Any one of them may have seen or heard of Mr. Weston, anything we may previously have overlooked. There's a staff room, I presume?"

He marches across the hall in the direction of the kitchen. Suddenly aware this is after all *her* house, she catches up, moves ahead and leads him towards the main entrance, but turns to find him hovering outside the open door of one of the rooms. She walks back.

"Please go in," she says.

It's a large drawing room, sparsely furnished and thereby better showing off the many portrait paintings hung on the walls.

"The Darrington – Cressleys," she says, "they're all here."

Jenner wanders around the room, ending up at the other side of the door from where he commenced.

"Including yourself," he says, reaching the last picture.

"Done a few years ago, not a bad likeness."

"Nor to the others," he says, waving to the other portraits, "Are you a Darrington or a Cressley?"

"Both. The Cressleys were the mill owners. My great, great grandmother Charlotte, married a Darrington, she insisted on retaining her maiden name, so we've been Darrington – Cressleys ever since. I'm the first female to lead the family since. I kept the name for business purposes. I was only known as Sylvia Dandridge privately. Since my husband left I've reverted back for all purposes."

The clipped confidence returns as she whisks him around the room, happily providing brief pithy descriptions of her ancestors. He lingers at the door.

"You don't have any other collections?" he says pointedly.

"Collections, of what?"

"Old coins for instance? You haven't mislaid one?"

"I don't collect old coins."

"Then you have no knowledge of an 1840 penny?"

"No. Should I?"

"It doesn't matter. Now, the staff."

His reminder revives her nervousness. Jenner's earlier talk with Sarah has brought them together, gathered around the kitchen table. Sylvia's surprised and apprehensive. Reluctantly she leaves him at the door. There are two men and four women including Sarah. They are all long serving and all except one, a gardener, can remember Bernard Weston, but none of them provide any further information. One other has a day off, but should be back tomorrow. When Jenner emerges, Sylvia is perched on a sideboard a few paces outside the kitchen door, her ear having previously been closely pressed up to it. She moves away quickly as Sarah sees him out. He wonders how open any of the staff can be in the house even if they do know more of the real relationship between Sylvia and Bernard Weston.

The afternoon is fraught. Matthew Usworth's pleading as ill conceived as Sylvia.

"I wouldn't want to put you out, traipsing around the city. It'll be easier for me to call in at your convenience."

Convenience doesn't enter into it. At least, not Jenner's, but he's acclimatising to other people's prickliness. The interview makes no progress other than confirming Jenner's suspicion that he's hiding much more than he's revealing. He tries to probe the real motives behind Matt's researches.

"Tell me about Chartism, Mr. Usworth, you're not a professional academic, are you?"

Matt takes this as a criticism, which is not Jenner's intention.

"What you might call semi – professional," he says, "Anyway, amateurs have made great breakthroughs in the past!"

"Quite so. Are there opportunities for significant new material in your field?"

"Of course."

"Tell me about it."

"I wouldn't have thought a policeman would be interested in

a nineteenth century radical, even revolutionary organisation. Unless of course it's the role of the police themselves in the 1840s, they were quite new then, you know."

"Maybe I'm no more a typical policeman than you're a typical insurance executive."

Matt smirks back. Jenner remains impassive.

"Chartism was the first wholly working class political organisation in the world. Many of the earlier studies show the usual difficulties of middle class historians dealing effectively with working class organisations. Like the novelists, they treated them with sympathetic condescension, the plebs had legitimate grievances, but were misguided. They're also very sketchy on this area's leadership."

"And your efforts will correct this unfortunate bias?"

"I've tried to identify the local leaders and analyse their working methods. It's not easy. The records are scanty and the local press reports sometimes concentrate on sensational rather than helpful detail. Some of the leaders are briefly mentioned only to abruptly disappear."

"Did your friend, Bernard Weston share this interest?"

Matt puckers his lips and grimaces.

"Bernard had a general interest in the Victorian period, but he was more into institutions, delving into prisons and hospitals and workhouses, that sort of thing. He didn't share my...."

"Obsession?"

"Because I don't play golf or drink myself silly every Saturday night, it doesn't mean I'm obsessed!"

"Quite right," Jenner says, trying to suppress a yawn, "Very laudable on both counts."

"Obviously it's not a riveting subject for everyone. In any case, this has nothing to do..."

"Refresh my school history, Mr. Usworth. When exactly did all this take place?"

"I've been concerned with the second petition of 1842."

"So it failed, the petition I mean, didn't get the vote, did they?"

"That's not the point!"

"No, but all this research, it's all about poking around

where everybody else has been before, isn't it?"

"Not quite everybody."

"Even so, it's like grubbing in the bottom of dustbins, ferreting through the bits and pieces left around by others."

Matt opens his mouth, ready to make an appropriate response, but then reconsiders, leans back and shakes his head.

"I'm not going to indulge in a pointless exchange of insults."

"Gave up the ghost after that, I suppose," Jenner continues, apparently impervious to his feelings, "getting the vote, I mean?"

"Is that all?"

"Yes, except for one last thing. With your interest in this period, I wonder if you have some relevant artefacts?"

"Everything I have has come to me legitimately. I've nothing stolen."

"Quite so, I'm sure. You've no knowledge of a remarkably well preserved 1840 penny?"

"If I did, I would probably have sold it long ago."

So ends a generally unsatisfactory afternoon. Jenner watches Matt leave the station, slightly troubled by the interchange. Not because of Matt's pained sense of unjustified attack or that he's gone too far. Maybe he didn't go far enough and further pricking of Matt's self satisfied balloon might have yielded more. Now Jenner is left with the vague feeling of missing something important in what he said.

Jennifer has left a note with the expert's report on the 1840 penny.

"...it is therefore genuine...to be in such good condition after a hundred and sixty years must mean there has been some form of preservation. It could have been kept in a drawer for instance, and has only been in circulation, either very recently or at some other time, over a very short period, two to three years at most."

Martin Sarwell, Ella Weston and Janice Weston all deny any knowledge of the coin. Forensics find no prints.

After further paperwork and checking some background information with the collator, he goes home. It's a short journey. He's not yet had time to find permanent accommodation and is renting a small flat in a large Victorian house near the city centre. It's reasonably comfortable and fairly quiet. He's seen little of his neighbours and heard even less, which suits him perfectly. He's made no efforts to look around for an alternative, not even bothering to scout possible areas where he might wish to live. He blames it on lack of time, but really he's reluctant to admit he needs to put down roots away from London. For the time being it doesn't matter. He can stay put. He's not very hungry, but makes a sandwich to avoid doing it later. He flicks through the CDs. He'll need something to match his mood. Something soft, but stirring, a subtle stimulation. He chooses Scriabin's Second Symphony and lets the music slither over him. If it works as it usually does it'll permeate and solidify his thoughts, but only after an initial period of hazy contemplation. It doesn't disappoint. Gradually, after the unwinding has fully taken effect, the day's events slide into order and he can reflect properly.

Martin Sarwell and Matthew Usworth bug him, making him itchy. He ought to see them again, but can think of no useful line to follow up. He should also return to Elvington House first thing in the morning and catch the staff away from Sylvia. Only when he goes to bed does he realise the significance of the interview with Matt, but that will wait.

In the early morning he rings a startled DC Duggan.

"I need to see Mrs. Darrington – Cressley again. She'll be pretty anti, but I have to get a feel for the place."

Reluctant to reveal the real reason for his visit, he's also keen not to be seen.

"Drop me off round the corner and come back later."

After the mystified Duggan drives away, Jenner walks down the hill to the house. It won't be easy, but he has to see the staff without Sylvia's knowledge. He walks slowly up the drive, keeping to the grass to hide his footfalls, but avoiding the temptation to creep between the bushes. He glances up at the house. He sees no one, but hesitates at the front door. Should he ring the bell? He glances around again. No one. He turns and quietly walks around to the back, expecting to be immediately accosted by an irate Sylvia. The path he follows ends abruptly at a high wooden gate set in a brick wall, covered in aged ivy. The place seems oddly quiet. He's distinctly uneasy. This is ridiculous, Jenner. You're a police officer conducting your enquiries. The feeling persists, as if he's momentarily lost touch with the normal physical world and is marooned in some eerie tangential existence. He opens the gate and is plunged into a maze of overgrown hedge lined paths. It might be wiser to ring the front door bell after all, announce his presence and demand to see the staff. He walks aimlessly for some moments, hoping to emerge into the rear grounds or better still get close to the kitchen door. Then he turns into what he hopes is a final corner in the seemingly endless line of hedges.

"Can I help you?"

A tall, angular man in his mid forties, who must have been lurking behind the hedge silently listening to his approach, now stands in the path, his leering eyes full of suspicion and cold aggression.

"Who might you be?" Jenner says, stepping back.

"I might ask you the same question."

The voice is deep and sonorous with a strong local accent, more rounded than that of the city.

"Detective chief inspector Jenner. Who are you?"

"Jonathon Cardington, though my mates call me Jon. Suppose you want the 'ouse?"

"Not necessarily. What do you do here?"

"'Andyman. Di'n't you ringt'bell."

"Nobody answered. You could be who I'm looking for. Did you have a day off yesterday?"

"Ar."

"I appear to have lost my way. Can we get out of here?"

Jon leads Jenner through many turnings of the hedge lined paths at the far end of the lawn, some distance from the house. Out in the open, Jenner feels suddenly exposed and an inexplicable sense of imminent threat returns. Like a poacher caught in the gamekeeper's torchlight he looks round anxiously for any cover, not demurring when Jon moves towards a wooden shed, camouflaged by the intricate weavings of a hundred year old climbing rose tree.

"Share it wit' gardener," he says, kicking the door shut behind Jenner.

There are only two windows, both facing away from the house. The rosy coverlet keeps it shaded. Jenner's eyes gradually adjust to the darkness.

"Want owt to drink?" Jon says, pointing to the cups and a large flask by the door.

"Not till we've spoken," Jenner says.

Jon sinks into a rickety wicker chair at the back and motions Jenner to another beside it.

"Been here long?" Jenner says.

"Ten year or more, but beats wokkin darnt' pit, which killed my fayther."

"But the pits round here, they've been closed..."

"Ar, twenty year or more. I went to work up Selby way, but then after the old man died, mother were on 'er own, so I came back. Wa'n't sorry to be out on' it. Took this temporary, been here ever since, so can't be that bad, can it?"

"How do you find Mrs. Darrington – Cressley?"

"Ow's all reyt. Bit stuck up, speaks like she's got red 'ot tattie in 'er marth, but she's fair wi' me, got no complaints."

"In your line of work I don't suppose you see many visitors?

"No, keeps mysen out 'road usually."

"So you've never seen Bernard Weston."

"'Im as went missing? Seen 'im a couple o'times wi'er int'garden."

"Do you know why he came?"

"Summat to do wit' cut."

"You didn't hear anything?"

"No, too far away, though sometimes their voices were raised like they were arguing, but I dun't know wa'rabout. Last time I saw 'im, 'e come a bit early like. Don't think she wor in and 'e left very quick. Wa'n't very pleased, bit gruff wi' me at'gate. "

Jon pours tea while Jenner carefully goes through the dates of Bernard's visits. Keeping himself 'out'n road' means Jon has kept his eyes and ears open, remembering the dates accurately and clearly. They are all in the period just before Bernard's disappearance. The last is the latest anyone saw Bernard and when Sylvia is known to have been out of the area. After leaving Elvington House he was never seen again.

Jon directs Jenner back towards the house. He doesn't relish Sylvia finding out he's interviewed one of her staff without making his presence known, though he doubts Jon Cardington, with his philosophy of 'ow knows what ow needs to know,' will give him away. As he reaches the path near the kitchen door he wonders whether it's possible to get away unseen.

"Are you lost, sir?"

Sarah calls from the kitchen. Jenner smiles with embarrassment.

"Mrs. Darrington – Cressley is on the terrace, I'll take you."

Jenner follows, still unsure exactly what he'll say. Sarah is calmer than yesterday, confident now her own contribution to the investigation seems to be over. Sylvia is at a table, liberally spread with the relics of a large breakfast. She's dressed in a smart black suit and sits very erect, almost stiff. As Sarah announces him she looks across quizzically, as if seeing him for the first time. Jenner puts it down to him returning so soon. His words to Duggan come back and he expects an adverse reaction. She half turns, hesitating over his title.

"Please sit down...chief inspector. How can I help you? Can I offer you refreshment?"

Scanning the breakfast things as Sarah clears them away, he declines.

"I would particularly recommend the mushrooms and tomatoes ...chief inspector and it's a long time to luncheon."

Her composed politeness surprises him. She's more placid, apparently unconcerned by his possible enquiries and now engages in her own line of questioning.

"Have you been a police officer very long?"

"Long enough, madam," he replies crustily.

Ordinarily he wouldn't countenance such a blatant

attempt to deflect his attention, but he's unsure if that's what she intends. Oddly and guiltily, he senses his response is inadequate, almost inappropriate. He feels compelled to reply to her fixed gaze as if caught in the rules of a bygone age, in which he's inexperienced and inept. Unsure what to say, yet desperate to say something, he feebly refers again to her moral campaign. She replies immediately.

"Moral Power is the reinforcement of the individual contributions to the righteous forces in society taking into account the accumulated national cultural heritage."

She smiles courteously as if to counteract her pomposity. The statement seems strangely familiar. It could be taken from one of the papers she handed him the previous day. He's sure her moralistic activities are not wholly altruistic, but there seems little point in probing them now. He wants to get away, but sees no obvious means of escape. Then, she saves him.

"You came over by the east extension," she says, "A particular feature of the house. It was constructed in less than three months in 1841, providing much needed work for local hands. At the time some said the building was unsound, built so fast in that hot Summer. They said it would fall down, but it was well constructed and we were able to go on with the refurbishment of the entire east of the house. Joseph Adderley, the architect went on to do even greater things."

"Was he involved in the amber room?"

"The amber room?"

"You mentioned the amber room yesterday."

"I did...yes...er, no as I said he went on...elsewhere."

The placid smile returns. She hunches herself up in the chair, anxious not to appear to be slouching. Upright and correct, she's attentive without appearing superior, smiling again, with no sign of the previous day's nervous arrogance. Jenner assumes she wants to present herself in a better light. The resulting good manners seem reminiscent of that golden age, which she tries to emulate with her moral campaign. She asks him again about his work. This time he's more forthcoming, even giving a resume of his experience up to leaving London.

"A great power for the good," she says, "the police force and of course, it all began in London."

"We try not to be too conceited in the capital," he laughs, "in any case, I'm a provincial now."

She continues in this vein, Jenner uncharacteristically participating in further low level, good humoured banter. Now she makes no allusions to her time being wasted. Normally he'd resist the small talk, but he's charmed, enticed out a policeman's automatic defensiveness, as if pulled into another more sedate time. Expectations and codes are slower, rules are different and *his* time doesn't feel wasted either. Then, as if suddenly shaking himself from a midday doze, full of half dreams and disconnected thoughts, he's anxious to be away. Quickly, he mentions his other engagements and abruptly terminates the meeting. She sees him to the front door and stands with the same respectful uprightness. Even though she's scrupulously correct, with no hint of condescension, he hesitates to go as if not yet properly dismissed from her presence.

He returns to the station as the main elements of the conversation dribble through his mind, disjointed and unrelated like incidents of a dream from that after lunch nap. While the interview with Jon Cardington is clear, that with Sylvia is lost in a fog of scrappily remembered images. He's taken notes, but wonders if it had been better to have had Duggan with him. He remembers more details as he reaches the outer suburbs of the city and back in the office can pull his mind into normal police gear, but the very process of having to do so disturbs him.

Various threads emerge, but they're not easily tied together and he must brief his officers for the next stage of the investigation. He calls in Jennifer and starts to make a list.

"Any thoughts yet, sergeant?"

"I'm not sure any of them are coming clean about their real relationships with Bernard Weston, not even the sister and girlfriend, so I wouldn't trust any of them, but ...well it's only a gut feeling at this stage..."

"What do your gut feelings tell you?"

"Martin Sarwell and Matthew Usworth are fobbing it off, but there was definite needle between each of them and

Bernard Weston. If only we could find something specific."

"There's the conflict over animal experiments. Sarwell is playing it down, but maybe it was a serious issue at the time. These things can get out of hand, could have seriously threatened his business."

"Perhaps Bernard discovered that, despite all the denials, something really was going on and…"

"They may no longer need to experiment on animals with the important research completed. So he takes the moral high ground and pleads innocence? See what you can find out about the work he was really conducting three years ago."

"What about Matthew Usworth, is there anything we need to follow up there?"

Jenner cups his hands together, grimaces and then leans back, briefly closing his eyes in grim thought.

"The close friend who wasn't really so close. If we knew the significance of what he's *not* saying, we might get somewhere. There were some pointers, which I'll come to later. What about the others? Mrs. Darrington – Cressley for instance?"

"Her alibi checks out," Jennifer says with some disappointment, "She was at a prestigious conference in Scotland during the whole period that Bernard disappeared. Umpteen people can vouch for her."

"Which fits with what the handyman told me this morning. Bernard came to see her after she'd left. Wasn't very chuffed apparently. Anyway it all seems to let her off."

"Unless Bernard followed her up there."

"Any evidence of that?"

"No record of Bernard visiting her, but she could have been involved."

Jenner remembers the morning's meeting with some discomfort, but remains doubtful.

"It would have been difficult," he says, "She's mysterious and holding something back. Even if she wasn't involved, she may know who was. We need to concentrate on exactly where Bernard went at the time. It's damned difficult without a bloody body! Of course, if they find him in Scotland it will be a different matter, but as with Usworth there's no obvious motive."

"She and Bernard were on the same side over the canal," she says grudgingly.

"Which doesn't explain why the handyman said he'd heard them arguing."

"Which she'll deny I suppose?"

Jenner doesn't doubt Jon Cardington's recollection and it fits with his own gut feeling. The root of all these relationships lies in the past. Any of the connections may have sinister implications. That means the case is shaping up like that previous one and he may need help. He daren't voice his concerns to Emmins, but what about Jennifer? He dismisses it.

He asks Jennifer to bring in the others. While she's out he checks his address book. Get to the bottom of these stray ends. Tying up one of them may solve the mystery. He has the number. He may not be able to put it off much longer. His fingers hover over the dial. Then Jennifer returns.

"Ella Weston's disappeared, sir. She's not at home and she failed to turn up for her shift at the hospital. We've checked all known contacts and no one knows where she is. Her mother's quite frantic."

"Son and daughter the same, eh?" Jenner drones gloomily.

"There's something else. A neighbour says Ella had a visitor yesterday and she heard raised voices. Martin Sarwell answers the description of the visitor."

"Anyone seen him?"

"Yes. He denied going round there at first, but Sandra persisted and he admitted it. Says he'd heard Ella was dragging up the old story about his lab experimenting on animals. He went round to confront her. She denied it."

"What does he know about her disappearance?"

"Nothing. He says she was fine when he left and he's not seen her since."

Jenner grunts dubiously. Then the officers complete their reports and sit expectantly. Jenner summarises the state of the enquiries without drawing any firm conclusions. He keeps saying 'early days.' Jennifer's heard this enough times to know it probably means he's formed tentative ideas, which he's not yet ready to share. Yet she cannot know the weightier matter hanging oppressively on his mind, against all his experience, but driven by deep immovable instinct.

"Before we finish, there are a number of issues I would like explored. There's something for each of you. They may not seem relevant, indeed you may feel they are utterly unrelated to our enquiries, but by now you'll have realised this is no ordinary enquiry. If we're to crack the mystery of Bernard Weston's disappearance – and that's not something I hold out more than an evens chance at this stage – then we won't succeed by ordinary means. Therefore, we'll have to proceed by *extra*ordinary methods."

He pauses for questions or comments. There are none.

"All these matters are central to each of the principal players. First you, John. Find all you can about the Midland Counties Railway particularly when it was formed and what happened to it."

John Duggan looks up from his scribbling, looking distinctly perplexed. Jenner moves on.

"Sandra, I want you to find out when anaesthetics were first used for surgical operations."

Sandra waits expectantly for Jenner to say more, but he turns to Jennifer.

"Ever heard of the Chartists?"

"Vaguely, from school."

"Quite. I want you to be a lot less vague and find out all you can by tomorrow."

"Anything in particular?"

"Yes, what our friend Usworth seemed to know nothing about – after 1842 – but don't neglect the rest. The other area I shall be checking on myself and we can bring it all together tomorrow. Right, that's it."

They file out silently, exchanging bewildered glances. Jenner watches them go. Hopefully, tomorrow they might not think him totally deranged. If they do, he'll know how they feel. He's been there himself, but if his deep senses are to be trusted these issues must be explored. If he's wrong it'll further damage his reputation, at best for eccentricity, at worst for foolhardiness.

He checks the number and dials again. After various clicks and clutters indicating being transferred, he gets an ansafone. He doesn't leave a message. Perhaps it's for the best. Some past acquaintances are better left where they belong, with past cases in the bottom of file drawers and in the deep recesses of the memory. Yet if you don't learn from the past maybe you really do have to re-live it. This is a past case and a *cold* case. Maybe the only effective way to heat it up is to use irregular methods, allowing the past to detect unsolvable mysteries?

The telephone rings.

"Jenner."

"Chief inspector Derek Jenner?"

"Yes."

"It's Ettie Rodway, chief inspector, you may remember..."

"Miss Rodway, I've just been trying to ring you."

"Really? It wouldn't be about your investigations into the disappearance of Bernard Weston?"

"Yes, but how did you know?"

Ettie could not ignore Ella's anguished outpouring. She was potentially unstable and Ettie had to follow her. As she drove up that morning her brother's involvement with the canal kept returning to her mind. She'd set out with suspicions, curiosity, hopes, misgivings and soon after arriving at her hotel made for the Cross Cut. She was totally unfamiliar with the back lanes yet found it easily, as if something unseen directed her. Once there, the attraction strengthened. Just as she'd been drawn to the canal itself, she was also drawn to its upper end and the tunnel. She walked along the grassy bank and peered into the deep, silent, still waters. Even without any definite appearances or messages, she was sure of the nearness of other forces. Her impressions were imprecise and just beyond normal sensitivities, but she could feel their presence, as yet beyond sight and sound but not beyond influence. As yet she knew little, yet it was as if she knew *of* everything. Things not yet known, but of which she didn't doubt their discovery.

After he's filled in the background to the case Jenner says, "So you know where she is?"

"I'm afraid not. She ran out on me."

"Curious."

"She may have panicked. I said you and I knew each other. She may not have felt able to trust me."

"Did she tell you much?" Jenner says.

"Not nearly enough, but I'm sure she's returned to the area. She may not be far away."

"Is it something that will interest you?"

"Oh yes, but I have a warning. I sense the involvement of something or someone from the past and its already interfering in the present."

- 3 -

Jenner leaves the city for the east. Glanford Drive is an unlikely place for an old discovery. It's part of a modern pocket estate in the outer suburbs, devoid of shops, pubs, any sense of community and to Jenner's eyes, life itself. The functional, grassless front gardens, with their identical block paved drives remind him of his grandmother's quarry tiled back yard. Neat terraced houses with their identical doors and windows supplanted by these neat, modern, soulless identikit replacements. His grandmother's house isn't there anymore, but it lasted a hundred and twenty years. He wonders where will this lot be in a hundred years.

Denise opens the door before he can ring the bell, almost propelling him into the house as she glances up and down the street, anxious to see if he's been seen by any of her neighbours.

"You're early," she says, banging the door shut, "I said ten."

He looks at his watch. It's nine thirty.

"Quite, Miss Deverall, but I cannot brook delay in my investigations."

She glares, unsure whether he's serious and then, twitching the edge of the curtains, re-scans the street nervously.

"You have a problem with this time?" he says suspiciously.

"No, no, of course not," she says, quickly readjusting the curtains.

The inside of the house seems oddly contrasted with its exterior. Outside, it merges imperceptibly with all the others. All white UPVC windows, dark oak stained front doors, low angled orange tiled roofs, wrought iron gates, coach light guarded entrances, the very epitome of modernity and upwardly mobile trendiness. Inside, despite its contemporary furnishing and fittings, it seems older. As he walks around the room, this feeling of 'oldness' grows. The wallpaper and colour scheme are fashionable, but the composition doesn't synchronise with the external décor. It's the same with the furniture. Individual pieces are up to date, modish even, yet the placing, such as chairs along the walls and in corners is irregular and misplaced, emphasising the old fashioned feel to the room. The walls are crammed with pictures, asymmetrical to the modern fittings. It's almost like stepping back into a Victorian parlour, enhanced by the wall lights, which could almost be gas lamps. Jenner examines the pictures. They are all of women in nineteenth century costume. Then he notices the large dolls. There are at least a dozen, on tables, shelves, some in glass cases and all immaculately dressed in the same period.

"A particular interest of yours, is it?" he says, fingering the delicate and detailed stitching on the miniature dresses.

She comes over as he picks up a doll adorned in an elaborate, flamboyant pink dress and large bonnet.

"I imagine this is authentic for the time," he says.

"Naturally," she says, taking it from him, "French, 1842."

He picks up another.

"And this?"

"English, 1839."

He moves on, picking up a third.

"And this?"

"French again, about 1840."

He moves around the room, examining the dolls in turn before peering at the pictures. He asks questions of each, to which she answers fully. The whole room pervades a past age, an 1840s time box within a modern brick box. Yet it's no

51

museum, whatever is here is alive, immediate. The dolls are very lifelike, their eyes staring back at Jenner with vibrant brightness, while the dresses also seem oddly *new*. Some of the dolls are dressed for the outside complete with bonnets and gloves. For some minutes he's totally transfixed, expecting the inanimate figures to spring into life, tie up their bonnets, rustle past the chairs and slide along the floor, a hundred and sixty years of taffeta and lace sweeping across the room.

"Fascinating," he says at last, "It must have involved a lot of research."

"I've always had an interest."

"You make the dolls yourself?"

"Yes."

"Mr. Weston, was he interested in them?"

She hesitates as if the name is unfamiliar to her.

"Yes...yes, I suppose so," she says at last, without conviction.

She stands protectively close to the doll nearest him, trying to anticipate what might be his next move, ready to defend her dolls against alien intrusion or desecration. She's dressed in a modern suit, but her posture, erect, formal, rigid seems of another time. Almost a cuckoo in her yuppie nest, her modern dress somehow not 'fitting' her. Watching her exacerbates Jenner's detachment, of being in another time. He turns back to the doll to try and recover some anchorage.

"No crinolines at that time?"

She looks at him blankly and doesn't respond.

"Crinoline," he repeats, "None of your dresses have crinolines."

The word seems to hold no meaning with her and her face remains vacuous. As he stares into her limpid eyes, that sensation of intruding on another age returns. Then her eyes refocus. Whatever time or place had momentarily held her attention it passes, replaced by a sudden irritation, which she can no longer hold back.

"Chief inspector, I didn't ask you round here to discuss costume and I'm sure it's not at the top of your list of priorities. Besides, if your investigations cannot be delayed..."

"Quite so, Miss Deverell! I was merely admiring your fine

work. However, you're right, we mustn't be distracted. Now, what is this discovery of yours?"

She goes to an elegant cupboard at the far side of the room. Richly carved at its side with ornate legs and a layer of ancient varnish, only partly renewed, it's the one piece of furniture that might comfortably fit in that former epoch. She pulls the door resolutely as it sticks to the lower frame and takes out an old book, before pushing the door shut again with equal force. It's a large ledger type book, well bound with a stout cover. She opens it up to reveal yellowed, close completed handwriting and pushes it across to Jenner. He opens it at the first page. 'Shearwell Valley Chartist Association Membership and Minute Book 1842' is written in bold capitals. He skims over the next pages, recording meetings with dates throughout the year. Towards the end is a record of membership with names, addresses and dates of subscriptions. He studies it for some minutes and then pushes it back.

"Very interesting, Miss Deverall, but I don't quite see..."

She pushes the book back, irritably.

"Third page of the membership list, about half way down."

He looks down the names until he finds one familiar.

"Samuel Usworth. Any relation to Matthew Usworth?"

"Of course, it's hardly a common name even round here."

"No doubt you'll tell me the significance of this?"

She sits back with folded arms.

"Chartist membership lists are rare enough, but particularly so for 1842."

"Why so?"

"1842 was the year of the Plug Riots. To protect themselves from retaliation by the authorities, many membership lists were destroyed. In the wrong hands, they could be disastrous, not just for the ringleaders, but hundreds, maybe even thousands of people."

Jenner picks up the book again. He flicks over the pages, feels the binding and fingers the smooth cover.

"It's in very good condition. There's hardly any wear."

"Books were made to last in those days."

"Even so," he persists, putting it back on the table, "It's as if it could almost be in use today."

He looks up at her. She stiffens slightly and then smiles, slightly embarrassed.

"Where did you get this?" he says, his eyes remaining intently on hers.

She looks away, but his steeliness forces her to return his gaze.

"Family heirloom," she says at last.

"Indeed, the Shearwell Valley is what, fifteen, twenty miles from here?"

"My family originated from Brinckley."

"You said an heirloom?"

"I found it in the attic of my aunt's house in Brinckley after she died."

"She died recently?"

"About two months ago."

Jenner's raised eyebrows alert her to his disapproval.

"With everything else going on it slipped my mind," she says.

"But now you think it important?"

"It was only when I looked through the list and saw the name Sam Usworth. It must be more than a coincidence. There has to be a connection with Matt. I thought you ought to know."

Jenner looks at her quizzically. She continues.

"According to Matt's researches, Nottingham may have been a much more active and important Chartist centre in 1842 than had been previously recorded. He never mentioned anyone by name, but he referred to a 'lost leader' who mysteriously disappeared at the time."

"And you believe this Sam Usworth is that lost leader?"

"I never took what he said very seriously before, but when I saw the name I wondered if he'd meant his ancestor, Sam Usworth."

"You believe they are related?"

"They must be, such an unusual name."

"What do you know about these Plug riots?"

"The second Chartist petition was in 1842, but it was also

a year of strikes mainly in the north and the west midlands."

"Why were they striking?"

"You'll have to ask Matt."

"You seem well informed."

She hesitates and then smiles to hide her discomfort.

"I picked up things from Bernard."

"Quite. Did either Matt or Bernard know about your discovery?"

"I didn't know myself then, so Bernard couldn't have known and I've not told Matt, but don't you see, how much he already knows? All this work on the local area, the lost leader and now this book, showing just how much activity there was with one of his ancestors directly involved."

"Quite, and your point is?"

"That he knows much more than he's divulging."

His curiosity has been aroused, but not quite as she believes. The Chartist book is interesting, but he's suspicious of her motives especially her delay in bringing it to his attention. Why is she so determined to undermine Matt? What does she imply he's done? He picks up the book.

"I shall study it with interest, Miss Deverall."

"You need to take it away?"

"I need to determine its significance to my enquiries."

She's disappointed with this ambiguous reply and says tartly, "I'm sure it will be of great value."

"You're in a good position to tell me more about Bernard Weston," he says, "just how friendly was he with Matthew Usworth?"

"Friendly enough," she says, as if not wanting to acknowledge more than a superficial relationship between them, "they had certain interests in common."

Just what has been her relationship with Matt, he wonders, closer perhaps than she wants to admit, but what is it now?

"What were those interests?"

"Local issues, the environment that sort of thing."

"Yet they were not in agreement about the reopening of the canal?"

"I wouldn't put it as strongly as that, they didn't really disagree..."

"In fact, Bernard's views on the canal placed him very close to Sylvia Darrington-Cressley?"

Too slow to realise where Jenner is leading, mention of Sylvia catches her off guard and flummoxed, she's unsure what to say.

"What, no...that's not the point..."

"It's very much the point. Wouldn't you say they were very close?"

She bursts out laughing, raucous and loud, but Jenner detects its forced, artificial, hiding her discomfiture.

"Bernard in a relationship with that freak! You have to be joking!"

"I didn't say a relationship."

"I should hope not, the idea's preposterous."

"You mentioned it, Miss Deverall, I merely said..."

"I said no such thing. Good God, he couldn't have seen anything in that woman. What the hell has she that could have interested Bernard?"

"Quite so."

Jenner is silent, but she's determined to plough the furrow again.

"You've probably got the idea from Matt. It's all in his imagination. He lives so much in the past, he can't really relate to the present."

Jenner smiles indulgently. She looks at him quizzically. Maybe he didn't get the idea from Matt at all. He smiles again. She looks at him with disdain. Suggesting the unbelievable, he remains expressionless, watching and considering, which only unnerves her more. He picks up the book again.

"I should like to see where you found this book, if that's possible?"

Again the look of surprised exasperation.

"Is that really necessary?"

"It would assist my enquiries."

With undisguised irritation, she puts on her coat.

"It's quite a long way."

"I'll drive," he says, "subject to your directions."

The journey is longer than he anticipates, along endless roads and junctions through the eastern and northern suburbs of the city until they reach a link road to the motorway, where they take the road west into the Shearwell valley.

"You originally lived close to your aunt?" he says.

"The next street."

"So you were brought up near Elvington House. Perhaps you were curious about the place when you were young? It must have been ... instructive to attend Sylvia's party."

"Reminiscent rather than instructive."

"How so?"

"Oh, at first I was as overawed as everyone else when I first got to the house. I was just as carried away by the atmosphere of the place, but before long it started to pall on me."

Jenner glances across, detecting her insidious jealousy of Sylvia. Is it just inverted snobbery, or something more?

"You said it was reminiscent?"

"I felt I'd seen Sylvia before, but I couldn't have done. I'd never been there with Bernard or Matt. Then I realised it wasn't her, but the place. They'd had some kind of open day when I was a young girl. You know how it is, the Darrington-Cressleys disporting themselves to the local peasantry."

He doesn't know, but takes her word for it.

"We'd all gone up to the 'big 'ouse.' I was about ten. My mother thought it would be a nice day out. In fact, we had a pleasant time. I enjoyed wandering around the rooms. I loved the room with the paintings. So when I saw Sylvia, it was the house, not her I remembered."

They reach Brinckley. A medium sized town, identical to dozens of others except for the permeating smell of malt from its large brewery, all red brick in the centre and 1930's ribbon development at the edges, interspersed with more modern estates. Parallel to a disused railway line, they enter an area of packed Victorian terrace houses and stop outside number 17Addison Street, a substantial house on three storeys with large bay windows on the ground and first floors. Once the front door is shut behind them, an undisturbed silence is omnipresent, the house seemingly insulated from humanity and all else outside.

"I've not had time yet to clear the house out," Denise says, "Except the attic."

A large hat stand, at least a hundred years old guards the dark entrance hall. Halfway along, a brown woollen curtain is stretched across, hiding the steps down into the kitchen. Everything is brown, brown furniture, brown carpet, brown wallpaper, brown lino, brown door, brown staircase. Unchanged for an age, as if it's been closed up for years rather than a few weeks.

"We'll go up," Denise says, leading the way up the stairs.

There's some light on the first landing, streaked sunrays piercing through the heavily netted curtains. Up here the walls are overlaid with pictures and photographs. Without comment, Denise sweeps past the anonymous and unfamiliar 'views' and fierce portraits. Perhaps they're unknown to her or unworthy of mention or simply beyond Jenner's appreciation. All the doors are closed. Despite being slightly less dim, this floor seems older, reflecting a move from the Edwardian to the late Victorian age. Below is the early twentieth century, here is definitely the nineteenth. The stairs above seem steeper, the banister closer. Halfway up the second floor the pictures and photographs finish, beyond only stark, yellowed wallpaper and a dimmer second floor. At the top of the stairs, even the residually faint sounds from the street are lost. Here the silence of the past rules in a world without cars or aeroplanes and Jenner's rigorously logical mind unsuccessfully tries to dismiss the unmistakable feeling of walking into the past. Now, they're well back, maybe a hundred and fifty years.

It's very dark on this second landing, with only a dim light from a small skylight. Denise waits for him to turn the corner, hovering between the light and dark, exuding the aura of a past age. He can see her face clearly, but the rest of her, enclosed in shadow, enhances the sense of a different time. Her dress could be longer, down to her ankles, the bodice frilled, the sleeves long. He blinks as his eyes adjust and sees her more clearly.

"These last steps are very narrow," she says, turning to a small doorway at the rear.

This leads to a steep set of stairs. It's even darker, with only a faint light from above. At the top, they emerge into the attic, partly floored, the partial light emerging from between the slates and a tiny skylight set high in the roof. It's clear for an arm's length around the staircase, the rest of the space cluttered with boxes, bags and suitcases.

"I found it in one of these boxes," she says, standing up in the scant confine. Being a little taller, Jenner stands with his head slightly bowed, his feet balanced precipitously at the edge of the drop they've just ascended.

"A lot to search through," he says suspiciously, "Yet the rest of the house seems virtually untouched. Did you know about the book?"

"Of course not. I found it by accident."

He sniffs the stale air.

"I was looking for something else," she adds defensively.

He pokes at the boxes and bags.

"If the book was an heirloom, it would be known in the family?"

"I meant it's *now* an heirloom. My aunt never mentioned it. She might not even have known about it."

"Why do you say that?"

"Because I found it at the bottom of a very old box."

"You still have it."

She crouches down and pulls out a wooden box. It's crammed with old books, none of them less than eighty years old. The box itself is old, possibly as old as the Chartist book. It has a stout iron handle, the lid decoratively carved and with large brass hinges.

"Did you have a key?" he says, crouching down and examining the lock.

"No, the lock doesn't work."

"Why do you suppose your aunt had the membership record?"

"I have no idea. Why is it so important to see where it was discovered?"

He turns from the box. She's stood up again. Her tone is impatient and slightly belligerent. She now stands between him and the stairs and he feels a momentary flush of fear. It passes.

"Places are as important as things," he says and then adds, "as are times."

As he gradually descends from the attic, time ascends in the opposite direction, reversing the regression he felt coming up. Yet even at the front door, the sense of the past doesn't entirely leave him. She walks quickly ahead, anxious to be away. By the time he's caught up she's making a phone call and asks to be dropped off at a friend's house nearby. She'll get home later.

"You still have my book, chief inspector?"

"Quite so. I shall examine it with care."

"As you wish."

He's relieved to return to the city alone. Driving away, he impulsively turns right at the main road, away from Nottingham. He'll use the time to further explore the country. Even though the generation gone coal mines have been replaced by trading estates and houses, the spoil heaps levelled and grassed, he passes through a man made, man destroyed country. At the next town, Creston, he takes the Mansfield road and all changes. Gone are the endless succession of houses, strung along the road from the city. Fields, trees, open country at last. He comes to a small reservoir, lined on one side by a deep wood, while on the other the road gently curves around its edge and then ascends a hill, to disappear at its summit. As he turns the corner Elvington House comes into view. Perched on its ridge, its two front wings jutting arrogantly southwards, it commands a clear view of the country. He pictures the proud mill owners standing at their windows, surveying the land, so much of which was their own. The road twists by the entrance and from the top of the hill the scene changes abruptly. Beyond the reservoir where the first woods of the ancient forest begin, is it really undeveloped, unexploited untouched, unspoilt? Or is it his wishful imagination yearning to keep it fresh, clean, virginal, an invisible boundary striding across the landscape, separating the old and the new, the natural and the artificial, the ever changing from the changeless, the repository of wisdom from the age of ignorance. Leaving behind the last of the old mining villages, the country rolls gently towards the motorway where the serried ranks of pine trees stretch along each side of the road. Turning back towards the city, his thoughts return to Denise.

Looking at the dolls and pictures, he'd felt removed in time. The modernity of her house exterior contrasting with the interior's penetrating *oldness*. Yet, as at her aunt's house, it emanated from her, not the building. He'd had to remind himself she's of the present, not a figure in one of her pictures or one of her dolls. Not of the past. He found her behaviour disconcerting and erratic. Why the concern at his early arrival? Didn't she want the neighbours to see him? She'd wanted him to know about the old Chartist membership book, but gave no plausible explanation for delaying the information and was reluctant to show him where she'd discovered it. Why does she want to subvert Matthew Usworth? Something he knows about her? Then there was her prickliness about Bernard and Sylvia. Was she jealous of any influence Sylvia had over him? Maybe she had reason to be scornful? Had Bernard and Sylvia cooled, but not enough to re-warm the old flames between him and Denise? How ruthless is she? Could she have killed Bernard?

He reaches no conclusions. Before he sees Ettie he must check at the station to follow up the progress of previous enquiries. Sergeant Heathcott has not yet returned, but the two DCs, John Duggan and Sandra Tye are about. He calls Sandra in first.

"I want you to check on the crinoline."

"Sir?"

"The crinoline, constable, very important to the investigation."

"Yes sir."

"The crinoline, that thing under skirts that made them bigger, they..."

"I know what a crinoline is."

"Quite, but when did it come in? Find out when it was first introduced into this country. It's very important."

She stands open mouthed.

"Well go on, get on with it, shouldn't take long and you can tell me that other stuff at the same time."

"Yes sir."

"And send Duggan in."

John Duggan enters.

"Got it?" Jenner says gruffly.

"Yes, sir. The Midland Counties Railway was built in the 1830s, reached Nottingham in 1839. The station was originally..."

"Quite, but what happened to it?"

"Happened? Well, it's still there, you can get a train...."

"What became of the railway, names, dates, remember?"

John shuffles with his papers.

"I think this is it. The Midland Counties Railway ceased in 1844."

"Ceased, you just said it was still there?"

"Well, in 1844 the Midland Counties was amalgamated with the North Midland and the Birmingham and Derby Junction to form the Midland Railway."

"Important was it, this Midland Railway, well known?"

"Yes. At the time it was the largest railway in the world and remained the third largest in the country up to 1923."

"So, someone who knows about railways would be aware of it *after* 1844?"

"Without a doubt. You see in 1876..."

"Quite so. Excellent work, John."

Sergeant Heathcott returns. She sits down, but unlike John has only a few notes.

"I'm hoping you've become an expert on Chartism, sergeant."

"Don't know about that sir. It's an enormous subject, but the people at the university were very helpful. There's so much material, I needed help to get to the bottom of it."

"Hope your mind didn't get addled spending time with such people," he says gruffly, "Any conclusions?"

"There were three Chartist petitions for the vote, with their activities concentrated in 1839, 1842 and 1848."

Jenner is suddenly more interested.

"*Three* periods? This last one in 1848, not very important, I suppose?"

"Depends what you mean. The first in 1839 was the most violent, the one in 1842 probably involved the largest number of people in direct action, strikes and so on."

"Plenty of work for the poor old coppers," he says cynically.

"But their 1848 public demonstration on Kennington Common in London was probably the largest ever. Their original plan had been to march to the Houses of Parliament, but they called it off because of the large numbers of soldiers the authorities had mustered."

"No small affair then in 1848?"

"Far from it."

"Tell me about these strikes in 1842. Was this area involved?"

"Yes, but the main recorded centres were Staffordshire, Lancashire and Yorkshire. That's not to say there weren't strikes and demonstrations here. Nottingham was usually in the forefront of trouble."

"I can well imagine, but not recorded as a major centre?"

She scans her notes.

"Not as much as the others, at least not in national terms."

"So any work on the activity in 1842 specifically in this area would have to be based on newly discovered material?"

"I suppose so."

"No supposing, sergeant, we have to be sure. Go back to your university contacts and get an authoritative view."

'University' and 'authoritative' are pronounced with slight, but unmistakable contempt. Jennifer hangs her head in disappointment, but Jenner is pleased.

"Excellent work though," he says excitedly, suddenly jumping up, "Three periods, eh, and the last in 1848."

Jennifer is puzzled.

"This research, what does..."

"All in good time," he waves her aside as he approaches the door, seeing Sandra Tye returning, "In the meantime I want you to follow Matthew Usworth, everywhere he goes, everyone he sees."

As Sandra enters he's positively buoyant.

"Got a date, then?"

"Yes sir, the crinoline was introduced from France in 1854."

"Definitely not before?"

"Definitely not."

He sits back down, cautiously satisfied.

"What about the anaesthetics? What have you found?"

"Various anaesthetics were tried in the 1840s."

"But when exactly?"

"Laughing gas in 1844, ether in 1846 and chloroform in 1847."

"Excellent work!"

On the way home Jenner's euphoria subsides. Excellent work by the team, but it substantiates his fears. Fears he dare not express to them. He'd contemplated at least sharing his thoughts with sergeant Heathcott, but had brushed her aside. She's a good officer. He ought to be more confident, but he's not. As yet he can only divulge his misgivings to Ettie. Even now his rational logical mind refuses to accept what his guts are telling him. Not again, he tells himself, it can't be happening again. But, deep down he knows it is.

He stops at traffic lights and rummages thorough the CDs in the glove box. Music will make him think. It might even do more and allow him to work it out. It's worth a try. Nothing too strident, he needs something to ease the lateral mind. Nothing too brassy, he's not feeling celebratory and anything too raucous will only jar his nerves. He selects Borodin's Second symphony. No, those dischords at the beginning won't help. Liadov, 'The Enchanted Lake.' Yes, quiet, deep, extrasensory almost. He puts it on. The traffic moves off.

Can there be another explanation? Has he missed something utterly mundane? Something he can share with colleagues without incurring their silent contempt. He mulls over everything, looking for an alternative explanation that might lead to a resolution. Nothing. Only reinforcing the inconsistencies and deepening the lack of conclusion. At home he sets down the position for each of them. What they say, what they know, what they appear not to know. Everything remains inconclusive. Then Ettie arrives.

Their previous conversation had not allowed for expansion. Now she asks how he's settling into the area. He asks about her recent projects. All very interesting. His mind wanders. This is shadow boxing. It's time to talk about the real fight. It's Ettie who switches to more important matters.

"Have you explained to your new colleagues how we came to meet "

"No," he grunts.

"Aren't they curious? Your new sergeant seems very sharp."

"Too damned sharp at times. I told her you'd helped me in the past with some profiling of potential suspects."

"But I'm not a psychologist."

"I never said you were."

"She's bound to find out."

"I also said you knew about canals, which could be useful to the investigation."

She laughs.

"I don't know the first thing about canals!"

"I know, but having a resident canal expert fitted with the other information I've got them to follow up. The way we're going it might even be the next line of enquiry."

She laughs again.

"None of this sounds like the chief inspector I've known!"

"A lot's changed since then," he says, remaining grim faced and serious, "Have you reached any tentative conclusions?"

"You mentioning canals may not be so inappropriate. What I don't know I may have to find out."

"You've *felt* something?"

She hesitates.

"Don't worry, I won't deprecate whatever you say, not anymore."

"It's too early to be sure, but I'm attracted to that short canal."

"They call it the 'Cross Cut.' It's aroused more controversy per inch than any other length of water in the country. What have you felt?"

"It's not much use to a policeman, a vague sense of contact that I can't explain. I'm afraid you've heard this before."

"Quite, which is why I have to take it seriously."

"I need more time there and also talk to someone about the area, I thought Matt Usworth might be the best person. "

She senses his misgiving.

"Something wrong?"

"I've asked Jennifer to tail him."

"In that case..."

"No, I'll warn her you'll be approaching him. It might even be better, the two of you working together almost. Besides, it may coincide with my investigations. I told you I had doubts about them all".

"You said they were not what they seemed."

He sighs deeply, even now reluctant to accept the full implication of his suspicions.

"Initially I didn't include Denise Deverall, but after today I'm forced to include her as well. Five of them in the frame."

He explains his meeting with Denise, her 'discovery' and views on Matt.

"Still keen to talk to him?" he says.

"Even more so, though I'm not so concerned as you by what you regard as her odd behaviour."

"You've got to see it in context," he says, "She's not alone."

"Not alone in what?"

"I suspected three of them had connections with the past, concentrated on the 1840s. Now I know that's the case with a fourth and maybe a fifth."

"You seem pretty sure?"

"Let's begin with Matthew Usworth, the self professed expert on the Chartists. He talked a lot about the local area, but never mentioned anything after 1842."

"So?"

"Quite. What's important about that? Not knowing anything about the Chartists I thought maybe nothing happened after that date, but I was wrong. I set Jennifer to find out. There was major activity later in 1848, but he never mentioned it. Furthermore, the disturbances in 1842 were not concentrated in this area, at least not as far as the recognised records are concerned. Yet Usworth professes knowledge of *this* area in *that* year that doesn't necessarily tally with the extant documents."

"You're not suggesting....?"

"I'm not *suggesting* anything yet, but let's just suppose he

has no knowledge of events after 1842 because..."

"...to him they've not yet taken place?"

Her words resonate against all his instincts of rationality, but he nods solemnly.

"That's a huge jump?" she says, "in itself it doesn't mean..."

"And then we have his unrivalled local knowledge of the time, including previously unrecorded events in Nottingham. Now, a membership book is found by Denise Deverall, which includes a local leader, Samuel Usworth. Matthew talked about a 'lost local leader,' but never mentioned a name."

"You think he knew about Samuel, who was his ancestor or even...?"

"Let's not speculate just yet. It'll be interesting to gauge his reaction. Perhaps you might do that."

"This assumes the book is genuine. It could be a clever forgery by Denise."

"I've sent it away for analysis. I think she may know more about the book than she's letting on. How did her aunt happen to have it? Is there an ancestor involved with the local Chartists? There are other things about Miss Deverall. This fascination with clothes and fashion is very interesting. She's very knowledgeable, or so she appears, but she seemed not to know about the crinoline. So, what do we find? The crinoline doesn't arrive in England until 1854."

"So someone in 1842 wouldn't have heard of it."

"You're getting the picture, Ettie."

"But even so..."

"Okay, let's move on. Martin Sarwell, research chemist and railway buff. Knew all about the local line, the Midland Counties Railway. So Duggan digs into the history. The Midland Counties amalgamates with two other lines to form the Midland Railway in 1844. The Midland was a very big railway. Not to mention it implies..."

"He wasn't around in 1844."

"Pattern starting to emerge, but there's more. Ella Weston has more than a passing interest in medical history. Knows all about hospitals and surgery in the early nineteenth century, except..."

"Nothing beyond 1842?"

"I didn't take much notice at first, anymore than I did with the others. All that blood and gore, a strange interest, but everybody to their own taste. Then I realised. She never mentioned anaesthetics. So, that was Tye's research. Anaesthetics were introduced between 1844 and 1847."

"And the fifth, Sylvia Darrington-Cressley, does she fit the pattern?"

"Yes and no. I want to talk to her again. She's the most convincing of them all, but she's not consistent. With her background she should know all about the estate and the knitting industry."

"And her knowledge is very good up to around…1842?"

"Yes, but she talked about changes to the house in the 1850s. She also mentioned an architect, Joseph Adderely and said he went on to greater things. I checked on him myself and there is a record of work elsewhere in the 1850s."

"So she's not like the rest?"

Jenner grimaces. He's still doubtful.

"She might just be cleverer. Any facts she's mentioned after 1842 could be easily found. I don't think I've managed to catch her off guard like the others, she's been better prepared."

"Or perhaps she just forgot to mention them before."

"You're not convinced?"

"You're making a lot of assumptions. There could be perfectly sensible explanations for each of them."

"Which leaves a lot of coincidence."

"Not necessarily and even if you're right, where does it take you? That they're all from the past? Okay, you've linked *five* of them. I just don't believe they're *all* from 1842 and have mysteriously turned up together."

"Okay, it sounds fantastic, but I can't rule anything out. They're all a nest of vipers!"

She leaves him dejected. Of all people, he didn't expect Ettie to be sceptical. The irony is not lost on him. His investigations could involve the potentially sinister 160 year transplantation of five people while she points out the inherent absurdity of his conclusions and his inability to take them forward. If he shares this with his colleagues at best they'll regard him as a crank, at worst a dangerous nutter! Get a grip, Jenner. You're losing touch with thirty years experience, walking away from rationality and embracing the uncertainty of touchy-feely conjecture. Tomorrow, after thoroughly sleeping on it, he must embark on new lines of enquiry solely based on solid, reliable police work.

Ettie is also concerned. Used to Jenner's cold, dogged delving, she can't easily dismiss his deductions. Nor can she ignore her own growing awareness of undisclosed forces and the area's possible receptivity to them. Past experience has taught her not to ignore such feelings. She'll start probing the next day with some background from the very man Jenner suspects, Matthew Usworth.

He's defensive on the phone and prefers to meet on 'neutral' ground at Ettie's hotel. She takes off her long coat and large hat as he sits down, though he continues to glance warily at her hat, as if it holds some latent, hidden power. Nervously, he unnecessarily stirs his teacup and fiddles with the sugar bowl. She offers him something stronger, but wisely he declines, needing to keep a clear head. She talks about the reopening of the canal, asks about his and others' involvement and how the campaign progressed, then moves on to those who opposed it. He makes no mention of either Sylvia or Bernard and even after she does, replies with scant comments, implying they were of no importance. She knows this is false and wonders whether he knows she knows.

He's uncomfortable answering questions. His whole manner is stilted and grudging, reminding her of a politician forced to conduct an interview as a damage limitation exercise, awkward and apprehensive, fearing each question will open up unanticipated and unwelcome avenues. Gradually, she steers the conversation more broadly towards the area and its past.

"I suppose its been difficult since the mines closed?"

"Not necessarily," he replies, guardedly.

"I only thought..."

"There's an older heritage in textiles."

As she'd hoped, despite his nervousness and suspicion, he can't help plunging into his own subject.

"Ours is a radical story. In 1817 we even had a *revolution*. Failed rebellion more like, but we still call it a revolution and all from a little village in Derbyshire. Impoverished handloom weavers started out from Pentrich to march on Nottingham. They failed, but it's a stirring tale. We now know government agents deliberately stirred up the men and propelled them into a trap, but it doesn't alter the dignity of their struggle."

His voice wavers with emotion as if he's describing events of the previous week rather than two hundred years ago and then pauses with embarrassment, conscious she may not share his passion.

"You've made quite a study of it?" she says.

He shrugs.

"In a modest way."

"Just those times?"

"No, later too."

He goes on to narrate the local grim struggles through the 1820s and up to around 1836, but seems reluctant to proceed beyond it into the period Jenner specifically mentioned. Is he holding back?

"What about the Chartists, don't you have a particular interest in them?"

"That's a long way from canals," he says with pointed wariness.

"General interest," she says vaguely, unsure how to reply.

He laughs.

"Or you have a well developed fascination for the past, Miss Rodway, but then, that would be natural in someone with your skills."

She looks innocently baffled, but he's not fooled.

"Your reputation precedes you. I know your real line of work and it isn't canals."

"I ask out of genuine interest. I always thought the Chartists were well meaning, but ineffectual, trying to get the vote way before their time."

He smiles with a mixture of satisfaction and uncertainty, but her mixture of flattery and apparent naivety is successful.

"Petitions drawn up by the innocent working class, boldly,

but foolishly trying to get their commanding betters to drop a few crumbs from the table of power."

"I wouldn't put it quite like that."

"They were no fools and it was much, much more than drawing up the Charter, important as that was."

His animation returns as he excitedly sets forth all the details in a thrilling, graphic flow. The careful, chary jumpiness goes and he sweeps across his historical canvas with all the panache and intricacy of an old master.

"It wasn't just about the petitions to Parliament. It was the first truly working class movement in the world, representing our real heritage and stuffed full of magnificent heroes and heroines. It was a broad movement, embracing every aspect of peoples' experience, a whole way of life."

"And at times a fairly dangerous one?"

"To the authorities it was a real threat to their exalted position."

Relishing the opportunity he enthusiastically tells of the rising in 1839 and then the strikes and riots of 1842.

"You're very knowledgeable," she says artlessly.

"I do my best. There's a wealth of material, but much more we need to know. I've been working on the period immediately after the plug riots in 1842."

"Were they successful?"

"Here and there, for a time, but in some areas they were not strong enough. Inevitably, solidarity started to break down as money got scarcer, strike pay ran out, workers drifted back, so the authorities took their revenge. Trumped up charges, packed juries, spreading panic and lies, the usual miserable litany of canting repression."

Again that retrospective passion, forceful, almost pleading returns. He turns to her, lowering his voice and edging closer, ready to impart some special, delicate morsel.

"Many escaped in advance of the suppression, getting away before jail or transportation. Some turn up elsewhere, others simply disappear, but I've discovered a local leader, previously lost to history."

"Was he important?"

He considers this for a moment before replying.

"I believe so. There's so much material, but the documents are tantalisingly vague about aspects of 1842 in the Nottingham area. He may have been as important as the more famous national leaders."

She copies his approach, lowering her voice and getting closer.

"Does he have a name, this lost leader?"

He draws back, wiping his hand across his mouth as he reflects.

"It would only be speculation, I haven't found the essential records."

"So a contemporary record of membership would be very valuable?"

She watches closely for his reaction, but his look is neutral. He nods silently.

"I understand such a record, a membership book, has been found," she says, "It's dated 1842 and refers to the Shearwell Valley."

The neutral, indeterminate expression remains.

"You're not aware of it?"

He shakes his head. If he needs to conceal he's safer with gestures, rather than words, his voice may reveal his true feelings.

"Quite a discovery, wouldn't you say?" she says.

At first unable or unwilling to speak, at last he splutters, "Yes, it certainly would be."

Yet he doesn't ask for the why and the wherefore and the crucial *who* and *when*. Ettie goes on.

"An interesting coincidence. One of the members listed is a certain Samuel Usworth. An ancestor, perhaps?"

A widening of his eyes, but otherwise no reaction.

"It was found by a friend of yours, Denise Deverall."

"An acquaintance," he says dismissively.

"You've not come across your namesake in your enquiries?"

"Where is this book now?" he says trenchantly, ignoring her question.

He makes no response when told it's in Jenner's hands. Ettie tries another tack.

"How might such a document have survived?"

He cogitates, though she wonders exactly which question is receiving his attention.

"It would have been dangerous during the repression to keep such a record. It's one of the problems we have in assessing the extent of membership. Women sometimes kept documents. It may have been deliberately passed on, a younger girl perhaps, someone reliable and discreet, not easily suspected."

"And then passed down the family over the years?"

He shrugs with apparent uninterest.

"Denise had no idea of its existence until her aunt died recently."

Matt is more concerned with the future of the book, asking how long Jenner will keep it. Ettie's unsure.

"You're obviously well acquainted with the police," he says.

She doesn't immediately reply.

"You've worked with chief inspector Jenner before?"

Now it's Ettie' turn to hesitate.

"He called you in?" he says aggressively.

"I came without any prompting from the police."

He glares doubtfully. Slowly the conversation winds back onto less contentious subjects until he gets excited again with his encyclopaedic knowledge of the area's history and geography. Ettie listens politely until, having learnt as much as she can and sure he'll say nothing more incriminating, dons her hat, thanks him for his 'valuable assistance' and leaves. He watches her diminishing black coated figure wondering whether he's said too much or too little, either way inciting suspicion.

Armed now with some valuable facts and Matt's directions, Ettie starts her investigation of the district, heading west into the hilly country always known by the valley of the muddy stream, the Shearwell. She's reminded of Matt's words as she wanders haphazardly across the country. The small towns and large villages, laced together in the exploitation of coal have an older heritage, where textile manufacturing was first mechanised and destitute weavers broke up machines in their desperate struggle to hang on to a reducing livelihood. Yet now, with grim factories and pitheads gone, nature's relentless reconquest has almost returned much of the land to a pre industrial past. She explores the area between Elvington House and Brinckley, taking the minor roads at the far side of the reservoir and finally entering the wide expansive land to the east. In these few square miles there's a unique openness, where for a hundred years no mine or factory has intruded on the neat fields, low stone walls, trimmed hedgerows and sparse farm labourers' houses. A small enclave within an urbanised realm, a terrestrial lung, infusing the heart of industry with the oxygen of the living world.

She stops at Sleavnall church. Seen from afar, the grey tower pierces the horizon with a forbiddingly audacious visibility, but from the ground at its base, it's a protective guardian. Standing on its windswept hill, alone except for its adjacent headstones, the marks of Man obscured behind the hills, she could be in another world where the Industrial Revolution has never been known. Threaded through the middle of this natural embroidery is the only significant man made incursion, the *Crosscut* canal. Well named as it severs the countryside in a neat, but unobtrusive line. Its commercial heyday long passed, its banks camouflaged by two hundred years of growth, it penetrates the land innocuously.

Built to link the two north-south canals, it had to be gouged through the hills, but most of it was hidden within the tunnel. Closed and concealed in its subterranean depths and covered at each end by a vegetative shroud, the liquid link was lost. Not just between the two canals, but as a conduit that breached the boundary between man made and natural worlds, the forest to the east and the pits to the west. Nature held sway, allowing no permanent wounding to the landscape and binding its entrances with an impenetrable latticework. Burrowing under the main road, it crossed yet another boundary, that which linked the prosperity of Elvington House to the north with the hardships of Brinckley and the other towns to the south. Sleeping and almost forgotten, it was reopened to a different, changed world, merged, but distinct.

Now Ettie is drawn by its unseen magnetism and searches it out along the narrow byways. There's a heaviness in the air, as if its very silence predicates some obscured, but actual presence. She walks along the bank near the western end of the tunnel, its grassy overhang now slashed back to reveal the stone arch. The light is dimming, but she can see into the cavernous depths within, the water sparkling in the reflected glow of the fast fading sunlight. She reaches the towpath, but moves carefully as it's slippery after the recent rain. A missed step could send her suddenly into the canal's suspect murkiness.

The towpath, though narrower continues inside the tunnel and is wide enough for her to creep along the wall. She doesn't relish such a walk. Apart from the immediate danger of slithering into the water, the little light only lasts a short distance before the darkness pervades, transforming the canal's glistening surface and walls into a total blackness. Yet she's drawn. Could it be the seductive peace of the country or the tranquillity of the evening, mesmerising her senses, dulling her usual carefulness? Or could it be something else, a receptivity, a triggering of calls from afar? Could it be Matt and his reluctance to discuss the Chartist book or Samuel Usworth, afraid these past strands will fuse into a hypnotic mix?

The water...that enduring liquid ribbon, penetrating deep into the far distance...attracts. Yet it's not just a conduit of distance, it's also of time. Something not easily denied. Dreadfully absorbed, she must go in, she must satisfy her blind curiosity and investigate the source of this mystifying sensation. She moves into the tunnel, the last glinting rays of the sun reflected in the water, dazzling and bewitching her. All reasoned experience tells her to be cautious. Trust those other, older, deeper instincts that kick in at moments of danger, resist the temporary enticement, repel these pressures. Get back!

She turns as the final exhausted shaft of the sun flickers and dies, robbing the water of its enchanted gleam, swiftly plunging it into a leaden gloaming, streaked only with variant shades of grey in the quickly extinguishing light, driven away by the encroaching darkness. The alluring, yet uncertain attractions of the light are replaced with an ambivalent mystery in which each shadow portends unknown dangers. She walks more quickly, slipping occasionally and only narrowly avoiding the edge, but goes on, only looking back when she reaches a clump of trees some distance from the tunnel entrance.

She leans against one of the trees, oddly breathless, even though she's walked only a short distance. She stares back at the tunnel though by now it's difficult to make out anything but its gaping blackness. Though she cannot see it, except as an after image in her mind, the towpath within entices. Then she hears a sound behind her, between a rustle and a slither, something sliding along the bushes and snagging the branches of the trees. She turns, but with only the faintest residue of twilight remaining, sees nothing. Then again, closer now and firmer. Footsteps, muted but distinct. She peers into the darkness, screwing her eyes to capture the last dim light, but is confused by the trembling shadows. The footsteps, muffled yet delicate, get nearer. She steps behind the trees, crouching in the grass, away from the towpath. The footsteps stop. The silence, punctuated only by distant lapping of water at the canal bank and the soft movement of the night air, is oppressive. It's uncomfortable beneath the trees. The footsteps resume, slowly, deliberately with a confident adroitness that's uncannily familiar A figure, furtive, slow and watchful appears. The slight silhouette and the lightness of the step mean it must be a woman.

In the darkness, Ettie feels conspicuous, instinctively believing the interloper sees her clearly. She aches to move, slightly deeper between the trees, but the noise will sound a warning in this eerie quiet. The woman stops on the towpath, very close to Ettie and looks around her. She holds her attention in Ettie's direction. As Ettie wonders if she's been seen, the sense of familiarity returns. Then the woman turns away. Cramped and uncomfortable, Ettie eases her weight from one foot to the other, but in the process catches a bramble in her shoe. Pulled from the bush, it tears loudly and Ettie recoils from the clawing, flying twig. She stands instinctively, presenting with her large hat and long coat, an imposing, even threatening figure. The woman steps back, almost losing her balance. It's then Ettie recognises her.

"What are you doing here, sergeant Heathcott?"

"It might ask you the same question, Miss Rodway."

"I've stayed a little too long," Ettie says, "it's getting late."

Jennifer, now fully recovered, comes closer.

"Did you find out much from Matt Usworth?"

Ettie summarises the outcome of her earlier meeting.

"He's a good source for local knowledge. That's why I came out here, to get a better understanding of the country."

"Have you been far?"

Ettie gives an account of her travels. Jennifer nods knowingly. They talk about the canal, though Ettie careful avoids any reference to her impressions at the tunnel mouth.

"The chief inspector said you'd be following him," she says.

As if suddenly reminded of her mission, Jennifer takes Ettie's arm and steers her towards the trees.

"I was, but after he parked his car up on the ridge, I lost him. He was walking in the direction of the canal. When I detected some movement up here, I thought it was him."

"So you heard me?" Ettie says, disappointed she's been so easily discovered.

"Sensed rather than saw or heard," Jennifer whispers, "copper's hunch."

Whatever it is, Ettie is reassured. Having someone close by with sensitive feelings might be advantageous.

"Will you get into trouble with the chief inspector for losing Matt?"

"*Quite* probably," Jennifer titters.

"Have you learnt anything from watching him?"

"Not really. After he saw you he visited a few people, all pretty routine, though he spent a lot of time in this area. He's been to the canal several times, as if he was waiting for somebody, but he..."

Ettie suddenly grabs her arm.

"I heard it," Jennifer whispers back, pulling them both into the trees.

They crouch down, Ettie now even more uncomfortable, squeezed into less space than earlier. They can see nothing, but hear someone tramping along the towpath towards them and the tunnel. A heavy plodding, clearly a man. Elbowing Ettie slightly, Jennifer pulls a torch from her pocket. He gets nearer. Instinctively they crouch lower though there's not even a sliver of light to give them away. Hemmed beside Jennifer between the trees, Ettie gets cramp and hopes they won't be here too long. They must keep silent. He's so close now they can hear his breathing. He passes them and walks on towards the tunnel.

"It's him," Jennifer whispers when she's sure he's out of earshot.

With Jennifer on the outside, Ettie can see nothing. The footsteps stop. He must be at the tunnel entrance. Jennifer eases forward and raises herself up to the towpath. Ettie joins her. There's a crescent of moon, but obscured by the heavy clouds. Even so, with their eyes now adjusted, they can vaguely make out the edge of the canal. Then, for a micro moment some cloud is wafted by and a fragment of moonlight pierces the gloom to reveal Matt Usworth, standing at the tunnel entrance. He hovers, looking in all directions, but mainly into the tunnel itself. Stealthily Ettie and Jennifer make their way towards him. As they get closer, he turns towards the tunnel. Unsure whether he's heard them, Jennifer slows down.

"What's he doing?" she says to Ettie, "it's pitch black in there."

Getting closer they hear nothing from inside, no echoing footfalls amplified in the yawning enclosure, no receding movement deep in the hillside. They reach the entrance and stand together, still and listening. Nothing.

"Shine your torch," Ettie says.

In the confined space the torch illuminates a wide arc across the full width of the semicircular brick lined tunnel. The brown, white stained, slithery roof drips with condensation, the water droplets glinting in the torch's beam. Jennifer points the light down the receding space and tapering finger of water. The confined towpath narrows, the encircled roof diminishes, the canal's glistening fades and the water dribbles from the roof, but they see and hear nothing else. No footsteps, no splash, no linking figure, no one slipping into the canal. They stop and look back to the tunnel entrance. Nothing. No one. Matthew Usworth has gone.

- 4 -

John Duggan had tried to contact Ella Weston with some follow up questions. There was no answer at her house and her neighbours reported not seeing her for several days. Her apparent disappearance irritates and concerns Jenner. Inevitably upsetting his schedule, it deflects the ordered routine of his investigations, but cannot be ignored. She must be located if only to explain why she needed to take off so suddenly.

"None of these people are normal," he mutters grumpily.

Jennifer tries to talk to him about the other disappearance, but he doesn't want to know about Matt.

"We'll deal with him when we've found her," he says and then leaves.

Jennifer makes the obvious enquiries about Matt, but gets nowhere. Ettie arrives shortly afterwards, looking for Jenner.

"Maybe Matt and Ella have gone off together?" Jennifer wonders, but Ettie is doubtful.

"Wherever he's gone, he's alone."

"You're very sure."

"You saw he was alone."

"Yes, but he could have met her later."

Ettie shakes her head.

"How could he meet anyone? We were at one end of the tunnel and..."

"....I sent Sandra to the other end. He couldn't have got away before we arrived. We've walked through the tunnel since. Even at a brisk run, difficult on a slippery path in the dark, she was there at least ten minutes earlier than he could have got out."

Ettie raises an eyebrow, but says nothing. In her face Jennifer senses a story, but not one she can read. All night and most of the morning the intriguing implications have troubled her. She wanted to talk to Jenner about it, but his late arrival, crotchety mood and rapid departure made it impossible. How will she describe what she'd seen and face his scorn? She looks to Ettie. Was it as unnerving and surprising to her as it was to Jennifer or is it a reminiscence, threatening, but somehow reassuring? Is it a retrieved memory, confirming an explanation she'd rather not accept? She seems relieved, but is it relief loaded with impending danger and what is the inexplicable link between her and the practical, no nonsense chief inspector?

"Have you been here before, Ettie?"

Ettie hesitates.

"I don't mean visiting round here."

"I know what you mean."

"There's no trace of him. Where has he gone? And how?"

"He will return."

Ettie scans and scours Jennifer's face. How far can she can trust her? She doesn't want to embarrass Jenner. Jennifer returns these inquisitorial glances with mild alarm.

"Whatever happened that night wasn't normal."

Ettie wants to share her concerns and even formulates the first few words in her mind, but caution supervenes and she remains silent, her roving eyes still searching inconclusively.

"You're absolutely sure he couldn't have got away from the canal without being seen? Being so recently reopened, perhaps he found another entrance or passage that's not generally known?"

Jennifer senses Ettie's deliberate diversion.

"I'll look into it."

With no indication of Jenner's likely return, Ettie says she'll go back to her hotel.

"We must talk again," Jennifer says at the station entrance.

As Ettie opens the door, the desk clerk calls her.

"Miss Rodway, I didn't know you were in the building. Martin Sarwell's been on the phone for you. He seemed quite agitated."

Jennifer looks baffled, but Ettie doesn't respond to the unvoiced question. She leaves quickly, but reflecting on their guarded conversation, feels guilty at not talking more openly. She hopes there might still be a rational explanation for Matt's disappearance. If there is, better for her not to engage in what might later seem rash if not absurd speculation. She's sure he'll turn up within a day or two at the most. Only then will she know if her fears are well founded.

At the hotel there's another message from Martin Sarwell.

"He's been twice while you were out," the receptionist says, "now he's back again and waiting in the lounge."

Martin sits nervously near the window, constantly clasping and unclasping his hands. In his old sports coat, battered cords, rugged inelegant shoes, clean but non ironed shirt, open neck and no tie he exudes the eccentricity of the solitary scientist. He sees Ettie as soon as she enters the room and stands immediately, self consciously easing his weight from one leg to the other. Still unsure what to with his hands, he puts them in his pockets only to retrieve them quickly and then waft them casually, his fingers spread out like the claws of some predatory, but timid bird.

"I'm sorry to descend on you suddenly," he prattles as she approaches, "I'll try not to interfere too much with your day. I'll be as brief as possible, I know you must be extremely busy."

"Please sit down, Mr. Sarwell," Ettie says, sitting opposite him.

She orders tea and asks how she can help.

"There's no one else I can turn to," he says, his eyes darting from wall to ceiling, to floor, back to the walls, on to the coffee table and again to the ceiling, "its in your professional capacity I wish to speak to you."

This confirms Ettie's worst fears. When people address her with such formal precision it usually means they expect her to wave a magic wand.

"I made a few enquiries and your name cropped up."

"Why did you try to contact me at the police station?"

"A bold guess. The hotel said you'd left very suddenly for Nottingham. I wondered if there might be a connection with chief inspector Jenner."

"There needn't have been," she says, not wanting to admit anything too readily, "You're certainly imaginative."

The tea arrives and she busies herself with the cups. Martin, intent on what troubles him, unburdens himself as a man, having carried a heavily laden sack a vast distance, tips it out on reaching his destination.

"Even to you this may sound strange, even ridiculous," he begins, glancing furtively for signs of disapproval.

"I'm not easily shocked."

He breathes in forcefully as if about to plunge into the sea for a long underwater swim.

"I've always had a logical mind, not easily swayed by the sensational or fantastic, yet lately for a scientist my thoughts have been concentrated on things I would once have dismissed. I never used to think a great deal about the past. What's done is done, no point fretting over what can't be changed. The past was a book out of print, impossible to open again. Not any more. For some months now, such platitudes have given me no comfort. Far from rejecting what's gone before, it seems it's with me all the time."

"The past in general or your own in particular?"

The question seems irrelevant and he rounds on her quite aggressively.

"Oh, my own of course!"

"Is this concentration located around any special event?"

His flow interrupted, he has to give this some thought before replying.

"Not exactly," he says at last, "at least I don't think so. You see my preoccupation is with an idea rather than an actual event though it doesn't rule it out."

He interprets her knitted brows as bewilderment.

"I'm sorry, I'll come to the point. Do you believe that things in the past can repeat themselves?"

"In certain circumstances. Do you mean exactly as they were before?"

"It sounds ludicrous, but I've become obsessed with the idea I may be reliving something in the past."

"But you don't know what it is?"

"That's the hard part. It seems almost everything is being repeated! I sit in the lab or at home, I drive from work, suddenly I get this overwhelming feeling I'm doing something I've done before."

"We all feel that at some time."

"Yes, yes," he snaps impatiently, "but I'm feeling it almost all the time. This is going to sound really weird, but it's as if I've lived before, long ago."

He pauses, looks across, expecting contempt and disbelief, but Ettie is nodding slightly.

"Can you be precise as to how long ago?"

"I can't recall an exact incident, but I get an image of a man in a long coat, tight fitting trousers at his ankles and boots with a tallish hat. I've studied books on clothing. Pictures of the early nineteenth century remind me of him."

"How early?"

"Regency, before 1820."

"Do you sense anything about this man, what he may have said or done?"

"Only that he's about my own age."

"Leading you to believe he's yourself?"

He's reluctant to agree, fearing the words will condemn him as a laughable oddball. She might even consider him dangerously deranged.

"It's a separate feeling," he says, "but I suppose he could be me."

"Have you told anyone else of this?"

"No."

"I understand your need to confide in me, but how can I help you?"

He's still not comfortable with her and shrugs helplessly.

"I have this sense that events parallel each other in the past and the present."

"In what way?"

"Dispossession. I have an affinity with someone in the past. If he was dispossessed then so will I."

Ettie waits and watches, but his pause is prolonged as if he searches for an explanation.

"What did he lose? Who took it away?" she says.

He shrugs once more.

"Is there anything in your own experience that could provide the link with these events in the past?"

He shrugs again, but this time more by reluctance than ignorance.

"Anything you've lost?" she repeats.

"Not lost exactly," he says quietly, almost guiltily, "but something taken away, it did slow me down."

He stops again, but under Ettie's concentrated gaze timorously continues.

"I was working on drug research. Nothing very startling or exciting, but this rumour started circulating that we'd been experimenting on animals. Absolute rubbish, but as the journalists say the story had legs and it started running and running. We kept denying it, but if anything that just made it worse. Damned fool agitators got involved. We were burgled. They found nothing incriminating, but much of my research material was stolen. It's put me back years."

"You've no idea who was responsible?"

He looks away.

"You have suspicions?"

He turns back. His expression is cold and determined.

"Bernard Weston was making a lot of fuss at the time."

"You believe he stole your papers?"

"I believe that man is capable of anything."

"You speak of him in the present tense."

"Oh yes, he's still around. Him and that sister of his."

"Ella? You know her?"

He leans forward, curling his fingers and twisting his hands together.

"We are acquainted. She justifies everything her brother said or did and resents anyone even remotely challenging him."

Ettie assumes 'anyone' is Martin and detects in the acerbic tone a hint of disappointment, even rejection.

"You must treat anything that woman says with extreme caution."

He leaves this vague indictment loosely suspended as an undefined, yet proximate menace. She waits, but either he cannot or will not elucidate further. Conscious perhaps of her growing irritation or his own inadequacy in fully justifying his grave anxieties, he gets up.

"I know it's much to understand. You may need time to give it your full consideration, but any guidance you can give me would be most appreciated."

She accompanies him back to reception. Just before leaving, he turns and says quietly, "Please get back to me soon. I have this fancy that something ...something devastating is about to happen. "

She watches him walk resolutely to his car as if she's already given him the explanation, the reassurance, the absolution he desperately craves. Yet she's only listened and he's given her so little to use. She's unimpressed with his intense pleading except for one thing. Whatever or whoever troubles him, there's a connection to Bernard Weston's sister.

Ella watches the deteriorating weather from the window. Having turned to incessant heavy rain the earlier light drizzle, has gradually drenched the ground. Deep pools are forming in the yard and on the grass. At first unable to escape, the water has at last found an outlet in the stone wall and seeps down the steep path, trickling over the steps towards the lane below. She needed to be alone. Shut off in the hills is welcome, at least for a while. Yet she'd felt a conspicuous stranger in such an isolated place and needed to go out. Her intention had been to tramp across the fields to the hilltop and walk down the other side to the village, but the miserable greyness made her return back up the hill. Unsure what she'd say to strangers, she'd not been disappointed at seeing no one.

Now comes the reaction. The fire in the living room has warmed her body, but not her spirits. Lucy and Gregg won't be back until the day after tomorrow. The place is all hers. She's as free as the mountain birds, as untroubled as the hillside fox, untethered, detached, unconfined. Yet she doesn't feel free. Had she not craved these few days in the Peak? A chance to rediscover essentials, inaccessible in this solitary cocoon, away from pressurised interference and desperate, frustrated imaginings. But the howling, quiet remoteness constantly intrudes, the sun and the sky screaming with unabated intensity, from which there's no escape.

Lucy and Gregg are old friends. Friends she's neglected over the years, but still they support her. Friends like them should be cherished. They've lived out here on the edge of the small village, high in the hills for ten years. No doors or windows in the house are ever locked.

"Aren't you afraid?" she'd said to Lucy.

"Of what?" was her reply, "Anyone coming here uninvited will have had to trudge three miles over the hills. By the time they arrive they'll be so knackered they're not going to do me any harm!"

This is only the second time she's visited them. They've come to her many times, always ready to take her out of herself, or more accurately take her out of her latest self imposed burden. She'd shied from the great outdoors, the spacious claustrophobia of open fields, limitless stone walls and enclosing, unavoidable hills. There'd always been this paradoxical lack of *space,* every corner bringing yet another stretch of rising ground. But now she can escape and welcomes the insulation and lack of contact.

Can it be really possible to remain undetected only thirty miles from a major city? How long before escape from unwelcome introspection becomes a prison of unwanted broodings? Why do the unrequested thoughts intrude when others won't come? At least in the house she can fool her mind with the mundane regularities of ordinary living, the eating, the drinking, the tidying, the cleaning. Outside, the mind is frighteningly unpredictable in those wretched fields, imposing skies and confining hills, its anarchic independence mercilessly teasing and playing.

Mid afternoon and the rain pounds the window, the wind wuthers ominously and the grey skies turn a sullen black.

With no more distracting chores, she slumps into a chair by the fire and closes her eyes, hoping her mind will settle more innocently. She waits patiently, yearning to recapture even a fleeting remembrance of that long, close recollected past, but her mind swings frustratingly between a futile blankness and empty, jerking visions. She opens her eyes and stares out. The Derbyshire landscape glares back uncomfortably.

She closes her eyes again, this time conjuring enough to fix some definite pictures. She sees the snaking turnpike road, hidden under the human coverlet of the bustling, vibrant masses, tramping towards the old mill. Shawled women and capped men, brown cloth and orange sky, grey pebbled road and blue tinged stone, excited, dominant voices devouring all other sounds in the valley, noisily questioning the established order and shattering the peace of the afternoon. Then they're gone, to reappear in the seething flakes of humanity, cramped and collided, muttering and mooching, hovering and hectoring together in the grim bricked clasp of the workhouse. Seared into their faces, dingy corridors and dismal staircases, bare dormitories and custodial yards, murmured resentments and insurgent criticism, unspoken bitterness and indestructible outrage, reinforcing the sad stories clattering down the decades and demanding a hearing she cannot satisfy.

She opens her eyes once more, staring defiantly at the hills and the sky and the rain, willing them not to engulf her before she can seize again that distant age and snatch her ancestral heritage. Surely in this jumbling litter of far flung impressions she can snatch her own connection with the past? It has to be there.

She gets up and wanders the house, irritated and disheartened, anxious not to give up too quickly before any chance of making contact is destroyed by her own anger. Despite this she punches the staircase wall in frustration before sitting on the landing and swearing at the distant horizon. It's their fault. Out there, beyond the gate and the twisting lane, over the hill and into the mass of people. They're all to blame. If only they would leave her alone. Why must they invade her here? She never harmed them, why do they have to interfere now?

She retreats to the bedroom and lies down. How she hates this wallpaper, tiny, minuscule shapes incessantly recurring. Has Lucy no taste? She examines the pattern, dark shadows around a staring, brightly coloured orb. They are staring eyes, watching, waiting for their opportunity to call up the others to ensnare and trap her. She must get out! She gets up from the bed and makes for the door, but stops as she reaches it. This is foolish! It's not these eyes that ensnare her, but the others, those she's escaped from, they are the ones that interfere.

Martin Sarwell's interference is particularly galling. What gave him the right to poke into her family's background? Her suspicions should have been aroused when he wanted to know her mother's maiden name. His eyes had lit up at the mention of Traynor. His preoccupation with the past frightens her. What if he threatens her with more than just irritating and debilitating talk? What if he has other powers and can contact Lizzie? That would be more than an annoyance. She must try again to establish the link.

She closes her eyes, but can't relax. Even though the images of the people on the road and the workhouse don't reappear, any hope of connecting to Lizzie recedes. Another name comes into her mind. Why was Martin so concerned with Foxley? Ella had never heard anyone by that name, but he kept demanding to know if there'd ever been 'any relation between the two families.' She'd no idea what he was talking about.

She goes back downstairs. The rain has eased slightly, but the sky is even blacker. A menacing calm before a devastating storm, perhaps. She busies herself in the kitchen, but yet another name intrudes. Chief Inspector Jenner, with his understated, but persistent suspicion, is an impertinently smiling insect, incessantly boring and burrowing, undermining her confidence and upsetting her delicate mental balance. Just as she feels secure, having rebutted his latest enquiries, he could appear again, uninvited, unexpected, unabashed, uncontrollable, wanting more clarification, greater 'precision,' forever poking and prodding, never satisfied. Even now he could be lurking behind the kitchen cabinet, ready to emerge fully armed, with incisive queries to pierce and dissect, strip out and lay bare in that infuriatingly restrained tone of innocent surprise. She turns nervously from the window, almost expecting his face to stare back from the corner. She looks across the yard to the field beyond. A dank, sheathing mist hangs over the grass, blurring the hills and the road in a saturated shroud, obscuring the path and the walls. It starts raining again and the running rivulets on the window further blear the scene. All is shifting, intermingling greyness.

It's difficult to see anything through the hazy shapes except a trembling, brown and growing concentration. She panics and rushes to the window, frantically smoothing away the condensation to get a clearer view. Peering through the smeared glass she blinks to increase her vision and then steps back in alarm. Someone is walking up the path to the front door!

Matthew Usworth's place is a converted ground floor flat in an Edwardian terrace house in an anonymous street to the west side of the Castle.

"Some of this area was very exclusive about a hundred years ago," Jennifer says, "big houses of rich city traders and the like."

"This bit was never exclusive," Jenner says doubtfully, sniffing disapprovingly as they pass the lines of terraced streets.

He remains sulkily silent for the rest of the journey. Ella's disappearance has unsettled his already questionable equilibrium, all obvious avenues of enquiry having drawn frustrating blanks. Recovering from what he now regards as his unnecessarily fanciful suppositions to Ettie, he'd listened sceptically to both her and Jennifer's account of two nights ago. He preferred to concentrate on finding Ella, but Jennifer wouldn't be put off and had spent most of the last two days trying to find Matt. She now has information he may have returned home. With no progress on Ella, Jenner has reluctantly and wearily agreed to switch his attention. They turn into Matt's street.

"The area's a bit mixed now," she says, anticipating his

further deprecation, "it's close to the university."

"Looks like a bloody student area," he says contemptuously.

He hunches up his coat as they get out of the car and peers suspiciously up and down the street. Jennifer is already at the front door. Jenner ambles across as Matt answers the door. Jennifer introduces herself as Jenner appears behind her. Matt leads them into the flat. In the narrow passageway they have to squeeze past shelves crammed with books and papers before reaching the main room, also littered with boxes and files.

"Ever thought of tidying up?" Jenner remarks curtly.

"I'm a bit short of room for storage," Matt says, clearing a small space on the floor by the chairs.

Jennifer and Jenner sit while Matt continues to stand, hoping their stay will be a short one.

"I suppose this is more about Bernard Weston," he says, "I've already told you about him."

"Quite so," Jenner says with steely chariness, "but not with sufficient breadth and detail. You can start by telling us where you've been for the last two days."

Matt hesitates, trying to assess how much Jenner already knows.

"You've not been here," Jennifer says, anticipating any feeble diversion.

"I've been...with a friend."

"Does this friend have a name?" Jenner says.

Even with rapid thinking time, there's a slight hesitation, enough for them to know.

"E...Edward...Edward Compton."

"You have an address for this Edward Compton?" Jenner says dubiously.

Matt scribbles on a piece of paper and hands it to him. Jenner passes it to Jennifer.

"What were you doing at the Cross Cut near Sleavnell two nights ago?"

"Cross Cut?" Matt repeats as if mentioning a place he'd never heard of, "I wasn't..."

"I saw you," Jennifer says emphatically.

"Is it a crime to take a walk beside the canal?"

"Not a crime, but needing some explanation when you enter a canal tunnel and never come out again." Jenner says.

"Easy to explain. The canal's been reopened, remember, I walked through to the other end."

"In the dark?"

"I had a torch."

"We saw no light," Jennifer says, "it was pitch black."

"You couldn't have been looking properly. I was probably halfway through the tunnel by then."

"But we got there..."

"So, you don't deny you were at the canal that night," Jenner intervenes.

Jennifer shuffles her feet in irritation. She's keen to challenge Matt's disappearance, but is restrained by Jenner's stern glance. Noticing this, Matt relaxes a little and smirks. He moves to the door, ready to usher them out, but Jenner remains seated.

"Why were you at the canal?"

"I like the country."

"At night?"

"Sometimes."

"Then you went to stay with this...Edward Compton?"

"Yes."

"How long had you known Bernard Weston?"

"A few years."

Jenner waves his hands in a circular motion and sighing, invites a more specific response.

"Four, five years."

"What brought you together?"

"We shared an interest in the history of the area."

"But you were...the more experienced?"

"If you say so."

"Regularly walk along the canal do you?"

Matt avoids an immediate reply, unwilling to agree too quickly and wondering where the line of questioning is leading.

"I wouldn't say regular exactly."

"But it's familiar, you know it well?"

"I'm not sure what you mean?"

"Quite straight forward. You know it well enough to find your way from one end of the canal tunnel to the other."

"Well, I..."

"So you've been there before, along the canal, into the tunnel?"

Matt hesitates, shrugging slightly.

"Maybe you've been seen...before," Jennifer says.

"Okay, okay, I've been to the canal."

"It's a very valuable amenity for the community, isn't it?" Jenner says, "But you and your friend Weston disagreed about the canal, didn't you?"

Matt grunts almost inaudible assent.

"He actively supported the campaign to reopen the canal... and the tunnel, yet you opposed it. Why was he so much in favour of its opening, yet you weren't?"

"I told you before."

"So you did. You don't like theme parks."

Matt sucks his teeth and then reacts angrily.

"There's something you ought to know about Bernard Weston. I was a loyal friend to that man and defended him many times against his detractors, but he had a mischievous streak and wasn't always loyal in return. I think he saw the canal as an opportunity to make trouble. It wasn't the first time he'd stirred up the local pot. "

"Stirred the local pot?" Jenner repeats the remark with deliberate emphasis.

"You know the sort of thing, correspondence running for several weeks in the local rag, Bernard would weigh in with a provocative letter, winding everybody up and then disappear."

"Disappear?"

"Metaphorically."

"Quite. Interesting turn of phrase."

Jenner's studied concentration lingers on Matt, who looks away after a few moments.

"Is that all?" he says, not bothering to turn back.

"Not quite. One of the things you and Bernard Weston shared was an interest in the Chartists, I believe?"

Surprised by this observation, Matt scrutinises Jenner

before replying, but the chief inspector's features remain irritatingly inscrutable.

"Particularly in this area?" he adds.

"Yes."

"Something you didn't disagree about?"

"No."

"Very interesting period. You can probably clear up a little mystery for me. Why were the riots in 1842 called 'Plug' riots?"

Matt is nonplussed, bewildered by this sudden change of direction with an odd question for a policeman. Jenner reads his discomposure in his expression.

"I'm genuinely interested."

Matt is still unsure. Should he take Jenner at his word or is this is part of a contrived interrogative trap? He coughs in a vibrato of contempt and fear.

"They pulled the plugs out of the boilers in the factories and so stopped the work. The name stuck."

"Yes, quite fascinating, but most of the activity was further north and west, Yorkshire, Staffordshire, Lancashire, so there's little to study round here. In fact, it wouldn't be too cynical to say you were wasting your time with..."

"Wasting my time? Certainly not! Historians have grossly understated the east midlands activities in 1842. Recent work has shown the untold story. The lives of the local leaders are gradually emerging..."

"So you know about these people?"

Matt gets excited.

"Yes, as I said we now know..."

"So the information has been suppressed?"

Matt laughs at Jenner's suspicion.

"Of course not! This isn't one of your investigations..."

"Quite."

"...we've only scratched the surface of our researches, but I can't do it all alone. For months I've been trying to get everybody to concentrate on important matters. For instance, what became of those local leaders after 1842? I've tracked most down, but one is proving difficult to find in the records. It's as if he's disappeared and..."

"That word again?"

"Figure of speech."

"This 'lost leader' wouldn't be called Sam Usworth by any chance?"

Matt's exuberance is abruptly halted. Feeling dangerously exposed, he hesitates, wondering how much Jenner knows, any response frozen in his mind and jammed in his throat.

"Usworth?" he splutters, "Could be, it's a common name round here."

"Not that common," Jennifer says.

"Could be a relative," Jenner says.

Matt recovers slightly and smiles indulgently.

"You have the better of me. If I knew the name, I'd know what happened to him, wouldn't I?"

"Quite."

Matt's glance at Jenner, brimful of false relief, is returned with that veneer of empty urbane neutrality, beneath which utter disbelief lurks. They leave. Jenner asks to be dropped off at the station. Jennifer tries to reopen the issue of Matt's peculiar disappearance at the canal. Jenner brushes her aside.

"Look into that Edward Compton quickly, sergeant, though I'm sure he'll already be on the phone to his mate, concocting some suitable story."

"You don't believe him, sir?"

"I don't believe he doesn't know about Sam Usworth, whoever he was. More important, he didn't give me an answer about the canal reopening. What were his real reasons for opposing it? Nothing to do with the countryside, that's for sure any more than he was taking an innocent evening stroll that night you and Ettie saw him. Slippery bloody eel."

Jenner's phone rings.

"Change of plan," he says after a brief conversation, "We can't go back to the station straight away."

Ella cringes on the kitchen floor, leaning against the refrigerator, staring through the window and listening fearfully as someone walks to the back door. Maybe it will go away if she closes her eyes, but the coldness of the refrigerator door ominously sharpens her senses. The air seems warmer, tastes sweeter and smells curiously older, staler. Later, she'll be unsure whether she opened her eyes again or it was only an image in her mind, but she'll remember the vision clearly.

The room is dark, lit only by a flickering single candle in the corner, casting long, jerky shadows. A woman in her forties, dressed plainly but well, sits by a small fire, staring disconsolately into the yellow flames, dully concentrating on the wispy smoke and the occasional spurting blue gas from the coals. The fire glints in her large, heavy eyes, her features accentuated and radiated in the dancing light. Sitting in the darkest corner, Ella can feel the cold, uneven contours of the wall on her back. Lizzie's intense stare is unnerving, while her pointing finger and shaking head could be gestures of both reproval and regret, levelled at some other person standing above and behind Ella. She speaks, but the crackling fire at first obscures and then, as she turns to face the flames again, extinguishes the words. She pulls her shawl tighter around her shoulders, though it's not really cold and then turns again to Ella. Should she go across, sit at Lizzie's feet where together by the fire they can share their distress? The heat may thaw her disturbed thoughts and unfetter her tongue. As Ella watches the hunched form with her spidery shadow prancing across the far wall, she senses an impending, imperative message, but which of them must speak first? Is it something Lizzie has to say or something Ella must demand to know? Lizzie turns again, earnestly and questioningly scanning Ella's face. Does she seek reassurance to speak freely or wait expectantly for Ella's approach? Ella pulls up her feet and presses her palms to the floor, ready to get up, but Lizzie's eyes are again fixed above and beyond. If they're not alone and someone waits Ella has to be sure. She half turns towards the wall.

Suddenly it's light again, the air crisp and cool and she can hear the rain splattering against the window. The vision is gone. She's in the kitchen, leaning against the refrigerator, half turned to the wall and the window. Someone rattles the door.

Ettie returns to the police station, to be told Jenner has gone out again.

"He won't be long," Jennifer says cryptically, refusing to be drawn.

"Have you had any further thoughts about the other night?" Ettie says.

Jennifer cannot avoid being direct. She faces Ettie squarely.

"I'm still not sure why you're here," she says, "The boss says you're a special adviser. When I asked him what speciality he muttered something about the canal, but wouldn't say more."

"You have your suspicions. In a sense he was right. I have an interest in the canal. "

"Will you tell me exactly?"

"Let's both put our cards on the table. I'll tell you why I'm here if you'll be absolutely honest about what we saw at the canal."

"I can't explain how Matt got away. He says he walked through to the other end of the canal."

"Impossible without us seeing him. Didn't you put that to him?"

Jennifer feels the cut of role reversal. She's unused to being on the receiving end of sceptical probing.

"He denied we were so close. The boss questioned him about his movements since that night so I didn't get a chance to follow it up."

Ettie nods. She knows. Once Jenner gets the bit of a particular line of enquiry between his teeth, it's very difficult to extract it.

"There seems no logical explanation," Jennifer concludes.

"So you're forced to consider the illogical?"

"Okay, I've been honest. Now it's your turn. What are you really doing here?"

The door is thrust open and Jenner marches across the room.

"Ah, Ettie, I'm glad you're here, you can help me with this wretched Weston woman."

"Ella?"

"Tip off was correct," he says, turning to Jennifer, "out in the Peak in some God forsaken cottage. Hardly said a word all the way back. When she did speak, couldn't make any sense of it. Won't go home, keeps gibbering on about 'he'll be there,' but won't say who *he* is. So I brought her here. She'll have to be questioned, but she wants to speak to you. Could you have a word with her?"

Before she can reply he bellows 'Tye!' and the DC runs in obediently to be gruffly told to take Ettie to the interview room.

"You might be able to get her to open up," he says more softly to Ettie, "I've no reason to hold her, but she's acted very strangely. See if you can find out why she ran away."

"I'll do what I can," Ettie says, exchanging a charged glance with Jennifer, expressing the shared frustration of their unfinished conversation.

As soon as the door closes, Jennifer turns to Jenner.

"Sir, you never told me how Miss Rodway is assisting the investigation?"

He moves over to the window, peers down into the car park and drums his fingers on the sill. Jennifer persists.

"Sir, about Miss Rodway...?"

"Yes, yes, I heard you, sergeant. As I said to you before, Ettie, Miss Rodway, is a special adviser."

"But what sort of special adviser?"

He turns back to the window and rubs the pane nervously with his thumb.

"Well, it's...it's...the canal."

"Sir, with all due respect, we don't need a special adviser about canals."

He turns back aggressively.

"We need one about this bloody canal, this damned Cross Cut! You said yourself Matthew Usworth went in and out of that canal the other night in a way you can't explain."

He stops abruptly. Angrily aware he's precisely revealed the concern he's been trying to conceal, he clumsily tries to retrieve the situation.

"What I meant was, you failed to observe..."

"You meant I couldn't explain how he got out of the canal tunnel and neither can you."

He hesitates, momentarily panics and then recovers just enough to bounce back angrily.

"What I meant was you couldn't have followed up every possibility. Someone with unrivalled local knowledge should know the detailed layout of the tunnel and what you didn't know you should have found out. "

"Find out what exactly?"

"Whether there's an alternative way of escape, sergeant. That's what we need to investigate. It's the only explanation. Somehow he got out of that tunnel by another exit."

"So the explanation of Matt's mysterious disappearance has nothing to do with our specialist adviser?"

Ella is slumped at the corner of the table in the interview room. As Ettie enters, she looks up anxiously and then relaxes slightly. Ettie sits opposite. Ella says nothing at first, studying Ettie's face with a wily intensity until, apparently satisfied she hunches forward.

"I believe I can trust you. Will you give me your word that whatever I say will go no further, that you'll not tell the police."

"That depends on what you say. I can't give a categorical assurance."

"Why not?"

"If you tell me something involving you in a crime, it would be my duty..."

"So you're not independent of the police?"

"I won't be a party to a crime."

Ella leans back, apparently disappointed and studies Ettie again, this time more incisively critical.

"So I cannot speak to you in confidence?"

"I explained..."

"That policeman, I don't want him to make a fool of me."

"Chief inspector Jenner's bark is considerably worse than his bite. I won't divulge anything without your permission if it has no obvious connection with police work."

Ella leans forward again, to some extent reassured.

"I told you about the dream, didn't I?"

She seems unsure. Ettie reminds her what she said before she fled.

"I got scared, you know I..."

"It's okay, please go on."

"It keeps coming, the woman sitting in a dark room by an open fire. At one time, perhaps every three or four months, then it got to be every month, then about once a fortnight, now...it's almost every night. She talks to me, but I can never work out what she's saying. You said it was...what do you call it, a genetic dream? It's real scary. Now, she's quite old. Why is she getting older, what does it mean?"

"It could be connected to you reliving someone else's life. As you get older she gets older."

Ella shudders.

"It's not my mother, nor anyone else I know, except...I know her name. Don't ask me how, I just do. Her name is Lizzie."

"Do you know anyone of that name?"

"No. There's more. Now I'm getting it during the day. I just close my eyes and there she is. I'm not dreaming. It's as if she's here now."

"Have you told anyone else about this?"

"No. There's no one to tell anymore."

"Do you know Martin Sarwell?"

"Yes, I know him. God, I wouldn't tell *him*."

"You said there's no one to tell anymore, what did you mean? Is there someone you would like to tell?"

Ella shakes her head in denial rather than ignorance. Ettie waits. She won't press her about Martin, though she's now sure of the connection.

"Only Bernard," Ella says quietly, "We were very close. So close we sometimes shared the same thoughts. We used to play mind games as kids."

"Mind games?"

"Communicating our thoughts to each other, telepathy. We were good at it. We could even do it at a distance. Just fun really, nothing serious, but it stayed with us as we got older. I wouldn't see him for weeks and he'd say something he'd thought about the week before and I'd say yes I had the same thought!"

"You must miss him."

The inner conflict plays across Ella's face. She looks away briefly, but it's not Ettie she seeks to avoid and soon returns her attention. Her eyes lock onto Ettie with concentrated fervour, but the force behind them is cold and distant.

"He's dead," she says quietly, deliberately, emphatically, "I've not admitted it before, but I know. Bernard has not just disappeared, he's dead."

"How are you so sure?"

"As I said, we exchanged thoughts. At least we did, but not anymore. Not since he went away. When he was reading up on history I'd know what were his latest interests. He had a thing about old workhouses, you know Oliver Twist and all that. I'd see the workhouse in my mind. I still do, but it's not from him. Now I feel nothing from him. I hear nothing in my head. That's how I know. He's dead."

Gradually Ella's gaze softens and comes back, closer to Ettie, but the searing pain remains. Ettie can feel her torment even if as yet she doesn't understand. She puts forward her hand to take Ella's, hoping that meagre contact might lessen the agony, but the door opens suddenly.

"Are you ready to return home now, Miss Weston?" Jenner asks as he enters with Jennifer.

Ella draws back and shakes her head. Jenner and Jennifer sit down beside Ettie.

"In which case, can you tell us why you went away so suddenly?"

Recovering some composure, Ella looks at him sulkily.

"Does it matter? I just needed to be away?"

"Quite so. Before you stayed with your friends, I suppose you weren't in contact with Matthew Usworth?"

Ella is indignant.

"Why would I want to have anything to do with him?"

"You know him well?"

"He was a...he was known to my brother."

"Weren't they friends?"

"At one time, but Matt couldn't be trusted."

"There was a conflict between them? Was that because of the canal?"

"There were many things, but Matt's treachery over the canal brought things to a head."

"How was that?"

"Bernard and Matt worked together on environmental issues such as the old mine workings...then with the reopening of the canal..."

"Yes, quite, but why do you believe your brother was betrayed?"

"Because Matt changed sides and started campaigning *against* the reopening of the canal when he knew Bernard was so enthusiastic. He went and worked on the opposition plans, taking away information to give to the other side."

"Quite and you felt the same way about Usworth?"

The slightest hesitation, a quick furtive glance towards Ettie is followed by a just audible 'yes.'

A knock at the door and Sandra Tye beckons Jenner out to the corridor.

"Sir, a body's been found."

- 5 -

The presence has come suddenly, powerfully, unmistakably. An immediate, total heaviness, beyond normality it follows tenaciously. Moving around will not shake it off. It holds the mind and grips the body. There is no escape. Its receiver sits, part afraid, part excited, wholly expectant. Closing the eyes only increases the power, enabling ideas to form and write in the empty space of the mind. At first all is formless, fleeting, frustratingly flighty, but gradually out of the misty emptiness a picture emerges and scraps of meaning materialise. Are these only the receiver's mental doodles, an overworked imagination scribbling on an expectant mind or a picture of the future? Better not to read too much. Yet if these incoherent images warn of future threats then the receiver must carve words from indistinct feelings and pass them on.

It had been a pleasant enough evening. Convivial, if superficial conversation with what are called friends, who may even be reliable acquaintances. In these times, best not to expect too much, best not to judge too harshly. Maude Wentworth is a good hearted soul even though she flutters like a bird and whimpers like a baby. Gerald Kenworth, pedantic and stiff, but shrewd and honest, a reliable friend to seek advice. Mr. and Mrs. Everley, quaint and talkative, provide agreeable distraction for a few hours, holding back the cares of the real world with the futile defence of a paper stuffed door. All acceptable and comfortable, decorative and conventional, with reassuring uprightness they bolster long held opinions. Charlotte needs such support, but she's glad they've gone.

She sits alone, watching the flickering shadows from the lamp on the far wall. The curtains are not drawn. She prefers to leave the windows unshrouded, occasionally turning down the lamp and peering in the half glow to the gloomy terrace and the wide garden. The heavy rain has abated though there remains the constant dripping from the trees and the eaves of the house. She watches and listens. When the clouds clear, there's just enough moonlight to pick out the trees and bushes beyond the pond. She's not afraid. She knows every inch of the grounds and isn't fooled by dim shapes and fleeting silhouettes. She'll know if anyone is really there. Who would dare? She's always ready. Edwin and Thomas keep a watch. One of them will be in the grounds tonight. Besides, anyone managing to get through will have to contend with her and everyone knows her reputation. She's not her father's daughter for nothing. Too long alone has taught her a resolution and defiance not usual in other ladies of the area.

There are few she can rely on when real danger threatens. Talk is cheap. Action costs more. Even her own family is stronger on talk than thought. Great Aunt Emily is the best, but she's too old. Frequently Charlotte finds the old more reliable than the young. Maybe even the dead are more stalwart than the living. Now her father has gone, the future of the Cressleys relies on her.

So many times before she's churned over the same dolorous thoughts in a morose dialogue with herself late into the night. Her family, successful enough by the standards of those who observe it from outside, has been beset with difficulties for many years. Though still a proud name in the trade, the knitting industry itself is not what it once was. Sometimes she believes it began when her grandfather Edward died in 1811. That fateful year, maybe marking the permanent change in the family's fortunes. They'd weathered the Luddite storms. Unlike so many of their fellow employers they were not cowed by the revolutionary fervour that gripped the area and refused to be intimidated by the machine breakers. Yet much had died with the old man.

Born on the same night he died, she'd never known him, but for as long as she could remember had always identified with him. Even now, thirty years after his death, he's more real to her than most of the living. On nights like this, her affinity with the dead seems particularly strong while the inadequacies of the living are uncomfortably evident. Even as a small girl, she'd stare up at his portrait and feel she alone could properly carry on his work. Only she could effectively inherit. Not just the house and the factories, but more importantly, his unique energy and determination. His deep penetrating eyes returned her gaze with equal force, directing and imploring her to pick up his mantle. She'd affirmed then to be true to him and that resolve had never weakened.

The women of the family were weak and trivial, but the men were worse. To the small girl and young woman, they were irresolute and feeble, unreliable to their friends and pliable with their enemies. Her father James, despite his verbal aggression, physical energy and affectionate nature, lacked grandfather Edward's business acumen and that essential fortitude to carry them through the turbulent conditions of the 1830s. Just as trade seemed to be picking up and they enjoyed some mild prosperity, down turns and depressions quickly followed. These constant, unpredictable changes bewildered and unsettled him, while his dealings with the men swung between rigid, but ephemeral obstinacy to withering equivocation. He died five years ago, perhaps worn out by the unequal struggle between the pressures of the business and his own limitations.

Her brother Jonathon should now be the head of the family, but he holds that position only in name. In reality he lost such pretensions when Charlotte, succumbing in an unguarded moment to her mother's pressures, had married Charles. It had been a mistake. He was utterly unsuitable other than ensuring the continuation of the line, which had been secured by the birth of Timothy. Then, having completed his duty, Charles had died leaving Charlotte a widow at 24. Charlotte had insisted on retaining her maiden name, passing on Darrington – Cressley to her son. The boy is now seven and the image of his father. This and her greater interest in business affairs, has failed to cast Charlotte in the role of doting mother. So Charlotte, sure she's done more than duty demands in such matters, ignores her mother's constant prattling about 'finding the right man' as a successor to Charles. Charlotte knows there'll be time enough for that later, if at all. Finding a suitable man to ensure the continuation of the line wasn't difficult, but finding a man capable of holding his own with Charlotte, let alone leading the family, will be another matter.

Despite his infuriating bombast Jonathon doesn't lack courage, but he has to be stiffened up for a fight. He has the bravado, but lacks the brains. After father's death it was all as much beyond him as mother, so Charlotte had taken charge. Within months the business had been invigorated and she'd quickly established her reputation, hard and implacable with the men, ruthlessly efficient with other manufacturers. The novelty of a young woman running the firm naturally attracted suitors. Despite her mother's protests all these had been suitably rebuffed.

Now there's only grandfather Edward's young sister Emily to mouth the tenets of the family and adhere unwaveringly to the values of her brother. In her, Charlotte senses a fellow spirit, albeit one without power or influence, but she still feels alone. The rest of the family is either ineffectual or has effectively deserted itself. Alone, she must analyse the problems. Alone, she must take the decisions. Alone, she must plan the action. Alone, she must cope with friends and enemies even when it's sometimes difficult to distinguish between them. It might be different if the family itself was larger, but she has no uncle or aunt to turn to. Past conflicts, she only half understands, having deprived her of the mature counsel available to others. Yet, from what she knows, maybe that's a blessing. Her father's elder brother and younger sister in their different ways, deserted the family, one by inconveniently dying, the other by running away.

Uncle Arthur was apparently even less interested in the

business than her father and by all accounts led a dissolute life leading to his early death in 1811, only a few months before the old man. Aunt Anne had already gone by then to marry the penniless Thomas Stacey, who'd been trying to set up his own mill on the strength of his dubious inventions. If he'd been successful, which he was not, he could have been a serious business rival. Grandfather Edward had never approved of the match, but Anne had gone ahead and married without his consent. There was no happy end to the romance. Both Anne and Thomas had died young in a tragic accident. These were the bare facts Charlotte knew. Her father had refused to say any more, though after his death Charlotte discovered they had a child, her cousin Cecily, brought up by Thomas's sister. She could find out nothing further, though it was rumoured they'd moved away. Charlotte was ambivalent towards the aunt she'd never known. She must have been spirited to defy convention, but she couldn't be forgiven for going against grandfather Edward.

"Still up, Charlotte? I sometimes wonder if you ever sleep."

Lost in her own desolate thoughts, she'd not noticed Jonathon enter the room. Glass in hand, he ambles over to the window and stares languidly into the grounds before turning to her.

"What do you hope to see out there?"

"If you stand there, whatever it is will also be watching you!" she says, looking away from the window for the first time.

He starts back in alarm, moving behind her chair and staring quiveringly into the garden. She laughs.

"He will have seen you first," he says.

"No, no, not from here. Besides, there's no one there."

"How can you be so sure?"

"Because I know what to look for without being seen."

"Really, Charlotte, have you nothing better to do? Don't we have men to watch the grounds?"

"Of course we do and they'll be better about their duties knowing they'll have to answer to me in the morning!"

He steps from behind her and sits in another chair,

slightly to her side, carefully positioned not to be seen from the window.

"Do you think all these precautions are really necessary?" he says peevishly, "Men out all night, what are they watching and waiting for?"

"For those that would do us harm."

"Yes, of course, but the disturbances have been over for months. Aren't you exaggerating the dangers, why I've heard..."

"What you've heard, like what you fail to see is of no consequence. What *I know* is more important. All may seem quiet, but not all the ringleaders have been caught. We still live in troubled times, Jonathon, a little prudence is something you would do well to cultivate."

"What I care to cultivate is my business. A man should not be spoken to in this way by his sister."

"No indeed, a *man* shouldn't!"

He bristles as his exasperation rises.

"These are not matters for..."

He stops suddenly as she turns sharply.

"Not matters for a woman?"

Unable to sustain any force in his anger, he turns slightly towards the window to avoid her furious glare.

"I was merely..."

"You may be right, these may not be matters for a woman, but if there's no one else, a woman has no choice."

He looks back, half intent on rebuking her, but quickly loses his resolve, shrugs and gets up again to stride to the door, where he addresses his remarks to the bookcase rather than meet her steely eyes.

"I'll not live on the edge of my chair, chasing phantom shadows and listening for every mouse squeak as if it's a host of hands intent on coming up to the house and murdering us all."

"Just as you ignored all those reports from the north of men drilling in the open like soldiers?" she snaps, refusing to turn to him as she continues to face the window.

"Yes, but what with, Charlotte, what with? Sticks, just sticks!"

As he now faces the door, they have their backs to each other. He opens the door.

"Not all," she mutters, "there were more serious elements than the half hearted fools with their drums and banners."

"But that's all over now, why it's nearly three months since…"

"It's not over," she says quietly.

"Even so, I will not have my routine disrupted."

She half turns to speak, but he's already through the door and closes it forcefully with a final, "Goodnight, Charlotte. We will talk again in the morning."

He steps along the corridor quickly, expecting her to suddenly fly out and remonstrate further, but the door remains closed and he hears no more. The hall clock strikes the half hour of two as he passes. Upstairs in his room he sits on the edge of his bed, struggling to pull off his boots as he mumbles to himself about the 'ill conceived fears of women,' which does nothing to quell his temper or more effectively eject his boots. Charlotte's feistiness irritates him, but he's more irritated with himself for failing to deal with her. Afterwards, when he deliberates on their interchanges, he always deduces what he should have said and concocts potent put downs to her perky interjections, but it's always too late, such conversational post mortems only depressing him still further. Next time, (there's always a next time) she won't get the better of him, he'll assert himself and put his sister (naturally with gentleness and discretion) where she belongs, which she'll accept with appropriate grace and good humour. As he thinks on, sleep eluding him, he knows full well Charlotte is unlikely to be ever put in her place, with or without the little grace or good humour she rarely demonstrates. Sometimes he dreams of the perfect man, endowed with a unique blend of charm and strength who might triumphantly whisk her away. But then, for all his faults, Jonathon usually lives in the real world and knows if such a man exists he's unlikely to come calling. Mother is right to worry. Damn it, other men don't have this problem finding a suitable husband for their widowed sisters! One day she might find someone herself, but it would then be on her terms.

The same unresolved issues churn around his mind until he eventually succumbs to his tiredness, but his sleep is fitful. He wakes just after five and after an hour gets up. Downstairs, he's glad to find Charlotte has gone to bed at last. He mooches around for a time, loping from room to room, unable to settle. Then, seeing the first very faint streaks of light sneaking through the trapdoor of the horizon, he decides to go out. A good tramp towards Brinckley in the fresh air will do him good. Besides, all this talk of trouble and danger has to be emphatically scorned. Leaders of the community cannot be seen to be intimidated. He goes back to his room, pulls on his boots and gets his long coat. He leaves by the back corridor. In the kitchen, the maid is stoking up the fire for the day. Thomas, one of the gardeners is sitting at the table, resting from his night patrol with a mug of tea in his hand. One of the dogs, a buff mongrel with a good deal of Alsatian lies near the door. Seeing Jonathon, it moves to approach him, but Thomas calls it back and stands up smartly.

"Morning, sir. Arta going out?"

"Yes. Have you finished your patrol?"

"Edwin's relieved me. Been on my feet for five hour," Thomas says guiltily.

"Yes, alright, I'll see him on my way."

Anxious to be of service, Thomas moves towards him.

"Dus't want me to come wi'thee? I could bring Jason," he says, nodding to the dog, whose tail wafts slowly at the mention of his name.

"I prefer to be alone. Finish your tea, man," Jonathon waves him back and then, momentarily remembering Charlotte's warning "Is there a problem?"

"Depends how far thou's going."

"Far enough. Have you seen something?"

"No, sir, seen nowt, but I've 'eard."

"Heard what?"

"News from Nottingham. There's talk as t'one o't Chartist leaders is still ont' run."

Jonathon sighs. Has Charlotte's paranoia infected these otherwise sensible men?

"That's all over," he says irritably.

"Maybe," Thomas says doubtfully, "But they're looking for 'im nar. Somebody thou's probably 'eard on afore."

"Who's that?"

"Sam Usworth."

"So, he's back, is he?" Jonathon says nonchalantly as he steps out.

The air is fresh and cool. He skirts the edge of the garden and takes the south path, making for the rear gate, which should be locked. The sun flickers above the top ledge of the wall and the glimmering light pierces a clear sky. The day should be bright, even warm, not to be spoiled by over worrying about unreal troubles and smoking room gossip. Edwin is by the wall and stubs out his pipe as he sees Jonathon approaching.

"Seen anything?" Jonathon says.

"No sir, very quiet."

Jonathon grunts in satisfaction. He must tell Charlotte how unnecessary all this is. They walk together along to the gate, which is stoutly locked. Jonathon steps through and then briskly down the slope, over the road and into the fields. He sees no one as he goes up Warren Hill. By the time he reaches the top, streaky sunlight cuts a fiery swathe across the sky. Twin church beacons top the other hills. To his left, Sleavnell church, lone and beckoning to the surrounding emptiness, while to his right, Creston church, struggles to lever itself above the red bricked clutter of terraces, recently erected by the coal company. Nearer, below the town is the new colliery, the headstock wheels winding the cables for the early shift.

He sees the straggle of miners on the lower road, snap tins and lamps slung from their belts and swaying as they tramp. Even from here he can faintly hear their clattering boots on the road. They snake towards the gate, a winding, reluctant army on its way to wage war with coal, rock, dust, water and gas. Local miners were unaffected by the strikes, though they were out in other areas. Jonathon muses whether agitators like Sam Usworth tried to stir them up. He looks away, this time staring ahead into the broad valley towards Brinckley. He walks purposefully down the other side of the hill, intent on completing a long circular walk before breakfast. At the bottom, he walks along the bank of the stream until he reaches a set of stones where he can get across. From there, it's steady and unhindered through open fields. In twenty minutes or so he'll get to the canal, the Cross Cut.

On the far side of Creston hill, just before the Derbyshire road reaches the narrow bridge over the Shearwell river, a row of three small cottages stand at the end of a stony track. Only the last is inhabited, the other two deserted months ago for new coal company buildings on the hill. The residents were happy to go. The hundred year old cottages with their rotten wooden casements and holed roofs are forlorn and diminutive, dwarfed by the overhanging trees on either side. Ivy has covered their walls, hiding the cracks and splits. There have been no significant repairs for several years.

The third cottage is in slightly better condition than the others. Lizzie Traynor has lived here for over thirty years, staying on alone after first her parents and then her husband died. Her children have gone, but until now she's never considered leaving. Remoteness has never bothered her, but everything is fast changing. There's more traffic on the main road and talk of the railway coming from Nottingham, linking to the line between Derby and Sheffield. Yet, just as the world might be getting closer to Glean Cottages, she feels more isolated. The track seems longer, the hedge thicker, the trees higher and in the night they bring a threatening, forbidding menace, but her foreboding is unconnected to these things. They hold no more terror than they have this past thirty years. Even the departure of her neighbours causes no immediate concern. Weeks after they'd left and knowing she was alone, she'd not feared the wind whining through the trees nor the rain chattering in the roof, untroubled by the quietness of the lane in the emptiness of the night. Her disquiet is an inner, self generated kind and all the more frightening for that.

Now she packs. It won't take long, but it must be done carefully. Her worldly possessions have always been few, but are no less important. She lingers over small trinkets and cooking utensils. All have memories, inconsequential connections, which she alone knows. Such chance associations infuse them with added significance and worth, power even. Power over her, if no one else. Yet maybe others too, for what relates them so strongly to her may also act as a force in others. Pondering on this, she titters to herself as she fingers a saucepan. Then, picking up a string of beads, hers since she was a child, the notion seems less comical. Chattels, not valuable in themselves, may have worth beyond the greatest treasures when bonded to those unseen, unheard, untouchable things of the spirit. As such, their power might be limitless. She shudders. Might there not be a reverse power? She sits as she's sat innumerable times before, staring blankly at the wall, wishing what lies beyond it could unburden the mental weight that's lain on her so long. She knows that beyond the wall are the trees and the hedges and the fields and the grass, that there's no one, but it does not stop her staring. Maybe, one day, someone might hear her unspoken cry.

Her bag is full, yet not complete. She looks around the now empty room, searching vainly for what she's already searched everywhere. She doesn't know where she'll go. Her daughter up the hill in the new buildings, her other daughter in Brinckley or perhaps further to her son in Nottingham? All would welcome her. She's unsure of her destination, but sure she must go. It's not the isolation, the loss of neighbours, the nearness of people or the distance from them. It's the *guilt*. There, it's said, if only to herself. She'll not repeat it. Not today. Using those words, even in the silent loudness of the mind, is enough in a day and may even inflate its latent power. Reverse power. Now the power of what can't be found. The letter, undated, un-addressed, unsent, so long ago written and then put aside should have been destroyed. But it wasn't and she can't find it. Wandering in the wasteland of her home, her futile final forage is really a search through the wasteland of her memory. She must leave, hoping the rats and beetles long since destroyed it. If only it was as easy to erase the memory of her involvement. She hurries through the rest of her packing, anxious to finish before the memories crowd and cascade out of control. After so long, those memories should recede, diminishing gradually to nothing. They should, but they don't. The haunting from the past goes on.

He cannot stay in the house. It's only a matter of time before they find him. If he stays, he'll bring danger to the family. He's probably safe for a few days. The authorities are not *that* efficient, but he'll leave tomorrow. They'll argue and try to dissuade him, but he must be resolute for their sakes as well as his. They'll say the roads are watched and he'd be better taking his chances hiding out, but even if no one comes searching, he can't live like a caged animal. Besides, he'll not be a burden on others. They have precious little for themselves. Already there are others to be cared for, families of those leaders who have been less fortunate, arrested and imprisoned. The people will have to bear this additional burden for their Chartist comrades. Against the prospect of starving children, Sam's needs are small. He'll not indirectly deliver them into the workhouse. He knows that more than most. Any risk is worth taking to avoid *that*. He'll leave the city by night. Not only under the cover of darkness, but also led by Chartist guides through the intricate warren of narrow streets, close courts and back alleys. Fifty three thousand subsisting people are crammed tightly in these filthy hovels, but the compressed, labyrinthine concentration provides a cloaking maze for escape. Then he'll have to make his way along dangerous roads, but he'd rather be taken in the open, free for a time and able to put up some resistance than be dragged like a cringing wastrel from a rathole.

He eases over to the small window and peers into the gloom of the dismal court. There's hardly any light even though it's midday and the sun is high. Most of the tiny room's little space is taken up by the stocking frame. Grimly forlorn, it stands idle with no work. All the family is out, scraping whatever living they can in the streets of the city. The trade depression in hosiery hardens and the mass unemployment of the stocking weavers continues. It's little better in the lace mills where thousands have been thrown out of work. Even in the good times they'd existed on bread, potatoes and treacle.

Chartism in Nottingham grows in the fertile soil of hunger, anger and disillusionment.

He hears voices. They come from the back wall and the house at the rear. Hemmed by three sides, the slightest sound pierces the thin walls. The family must have returned. The parents from whatever ill paid casual work they can find and the children from foraging in the detritus of the pavements. Maybe there will be a scant meal tonight. Maybe there will not. Guilt envelopes him. It must be tonight. He must not stay into another day.

High hopes and high dreams, shattered in the bitter memory of the Mapperley Hills. Scarce three months, yet those August days now seem so long off, it could be an age as far away as the workhouse. He'd almost missed it. He'd been busy in the north for two years, working himself almost to exhaustion for the cause, lecturing and organising, stimulating the latent strength of the working people whenever he could. Then the strikes began, sweeping across Lancashire and Yorkshire, an accelerating tide of incessant energy, its insistent waves bubbling through every workshop and factory. He'd seen thousands on the march, challenging the employers with a strident confidence, bolstered and invigorated in the knowledge of the rightness of their demands. He'd been with the massed hosts, shrugging aside the threats of the magistrates, watched the Stockport workhouse stormed and, as he crossed into Yorkshire, heard of the police station demolished in Newton. How many times had he heard the Riot Act read and ignored? The crowd had pelted the soldiers with stones in Preston, but when they refused to disperse, four of them were shot and killed. Sights and sounds he'll never forget, memories of valour and despair to haunt him to his last days. He'd stood as the thousands of Halifax women, many of them barefoot and swelled by their comrades from Todmorden and Bradford, sang the union hymn, then attacked when they wouldn't go home. The earth itself seemed to rise and judder with a mounting angry revolt as every area rose up to convert the strikes into a political stand for the Charter. For only the power of the vote could curb hunger and disillusion and change their conditions.

Just as now he must leave, then he had to return. In the midst of all the turbulence it seemed oddly disloyal not to be in Nottingham. He arrived in his native city just as the strikes began. It was over a year since he'd seen the place. The last time had been for the few stirring days in the Parliamentary by-election of 1841. Three hundred Chartist electors marching to the polls together to avoid the charge of bribery. Then the meetings in the Market Square, the Whig candidate surrounded by his hired protectors, local butchers, but always known as the 'lambs of Nottingham.' Fergus O'Connor, the great Chartist leader addressed the crowd while the lambs attempted to disrupt him. How foolish! Fergus called forth 'those with fustian jackets, blistered hands and unshorn chins' and led them into the fray. Sam piled in with the rest, setting about the 'lambs' with gusto! What a joyous scrap, what energised clamour!

Yet how long is a year? A gulf as wide as reversed fortune, a breach as deep as broken expectations, a grasp as far as the snatched away hand from the promised land, a rupture quick and sure as the snapped final link in the chain of freedom. Gone. But now it was 1842 and it was going to be *the* year. This time it was really going to happen. No more futile dead end talk of *moral* force, waiting for the momentum of the serried masses to somehow tumble down the monolith of the rulers by sheer appearance. Now all hands would be *forced*. The vote was the flour to the bread of freedom. The unrepresented multitude would grab their birthright, knead that flour with the yeast of power and raise their brothers and sisters to prosperity and deliverance.

All was feverish activity when he returned on Friday, August 19. The crowd in the market square already resolved to stop work until the Charter was enshrined in law. When the magistrates forbade another meeting the strikers marched through the city. With his experience in the north, he left the main march and toured the factories, calling out the twisthands from the lace mills before making contact with his old friends in the city. From then it was hectic and bustling tumult. He scarcely had time to sleep and every waking hour was filled with meetings, discussions and organising. The next day, Saturday he joined those visiting the factories in Radford and from there they tried to get the colliers out in the west. Troops were called out and in the clash, Sam just managed to avoid being arrested. Hundreds were taken to the barracks, though they got out later. There was trouble on Sunday at Arnold, just north of the city. Soldiers were out again, trying to disperse the crowd. On Monday, Sam joined all the men released from the barracks along with hundreds of others and marched up the Mansfield road to join the immense crowd in Arnold. That night at the meeting Sam was officially recorded as a member of the local association, but everybody was getting nervous. Somebody suggested the record and minute books should be spirited away into the safer hands of one of the young girls. In troubled times membership lists could be dangerous if too easily discovered. Sam felt a momentary shudder even though he agreed. Was it a prescience of things to come? Might it have turned out differently? Had they properly considered their next steps?

Tuesday came, the 23rd, all their work now culminating in the great meeting on Mapperley Hills. Thousands gathered. At first the atmosphere was relaxed, airy, almost casual. At any other time it might have been a *real* holiday rather than one *forced* by circumstances. It was a bright, sultry day, an enclosing peace, captured by the gentle warmth of the breeze, the calm protectiveness of the trees and the warbling reassurance of the birds, set against the sparklingly frocked and bonneted women in the broad openness. There were some speeches, rousing, stirring, improving just like an ordinary meeting. But this was no ordinary meeting. His old friend and local leader, Arthur Acklam reminded them of recent events. The long cruel Winter, the poor harvest, lack of work, the damnable indignities of the new Poor Law and the construction of the hated new workhouse, the many petty impositions and barriers to earning a decent livelihood, the wretchedness of the squalid housing; all welled and inflated in the hearts and spirits of the throng. A murmuring fury rippled through the crowd.

The soldiers arrived, holding back at first, then ordering the crowd to disperse. The murmur became a chattering, angry remonstrance. They'd done nothing wrong. Poor, starving, defenceless people, sitting for their hard won, pitiful meals, ensconced only to the sky and the earth, threatening no one. They were two miles from the city. Why should they disperse? The colonel commanding the dragoons wouldn't relent and ordered the soldiers and police to arrest a large number.

"Blue vampires," some shouted at the police.

"Scientific cut throats," others shouted to the soldiers, "Hired assassins!"

"The unboiled blue," Sam shouted at the police, "When the day of boiling comes, woe to the unboiled!"

Four hundred men were rounded up, many handcuffed, others roped together. Held back by the drawn swords, the crowd, screamed and shouted. At their head was Sam, hooting and cursing vehemently, but he was pulled apart by others.

"Don't let them take you," a large man said, as he hustled Sam back, "They've taken enough, you'm got more to do yet."

The crowd followed the march of the men back to the city. Sam followed, but was kept well away from the front by his new comrades.

"Thou's'll need protecting," said one as he was gently jostled along.

"We"ll hide thee," said another.

In the oppressing confusion and constant jostling Sam lost his view of the arrested men, but he could hear their tramping feet through the continuous grumbling, vituperative interventions of the crowd. The soldiers were hissed incessantly and persistently stoned as they escorted their prisoners. As they trudged through the outer villages, people streamed out in greater numbers, houses, pubs and shops disgorging a swelling company that collected like a snowball running down a hill, all howling in a rising crescendo of rage. Sam was carried along with the others in the grim cavalcade of noise, dust and anger, his ears battered in the cacophony of protest, his eyes screened within the defensive shield of his protectors. Only later did he learn that in the confused rush to arrest so many, one pregnant woman had gone into premature labour, with other stories of the soldiers' brutality trickling out in the following weeks.

Surging through the narrow streets, Sam wondered what dire fate awaited them all. Impatiently tetchy, the mass stopped outside the jail, singing resolutely, calling encouragingly to the men and menacingly to the authorities. Eventually, individually and in groups the men were dragged before the magistrates. Slivered rumours from other parts seeped though the crowd. There'd been arrests in Staffordshire. Some men had been imprisoned on dubious charges and fabricated evidence. In the heady atmosphere, no news bred bad news and spread with the lightning unpredictability of a virulent plague. Noisy gangs congregated at corners, bandying disparate information in futile and depressing discussion. They said some men were sought. Names were exchanged. Some were known, national figures with impressive reputations. At the mention of others, there were only blank faces and quizzical looks. One name persisted. A local man, active in the disturbance three years before and in the election a year ago. He'd been away, seen it all, now he was back in town and the authorities were eager to find him. Samuel Usworth, you remember Sam the shoemaker?

Some men were released and returned to their families. The ominous mood unwound as more and more of them were released, after coming before the magistrates. Against promises of good behaviour and on their own recognizances of five pounds they were discharged. A victory of sorts, perhaps? No, an inconclusive farce. Some said the rulers had still won, but they were glad their companions were out.

The mammoth snowball now started to flake away. In pairs and then small groups, then larger, greater detachments started drifting apart. Sam had heard the talk and so had the men around him, whisking him away quickly before he became conspicuous in the crowd's scattered remnants. So ended the 'Battle of Mapperley Hills.' The strikes were over, the second Chartist petition rejected. The unemployed and the destitute would still shamble along the mean streets, the sullen people forced to collect for another day and support those caught in the vicious net of the authorities' repression. Many imprisoned, some even transported, others escaped, never to be seen again, but some were still sought and on the run. One of these is Sam Usworth.

He snorts derisively to himself across the puny room. Where were their so called allies, the stout and valiant 'shopocracy' at Mapperley Hills? The class lines had been drawn sharply and it would be many years before they would be blurred. Fergus O'Connor had been right. They had to maintain control of their own organisations and not trust the middle classes. Empty talk of standing together was unimpressive. But sneeringly lambasting petty businessmen gives little satisfaction in the aftermath of failed revolt. Failure to mobilise and sustain the national strike is not their fault.

Cooped up too long in the acrid atmosphere of his self imposed imprisonment has poisoned his mind. Time to leave this tinder box city, its spark now dampened by defeat and disillusion. Yet running like a wounded fox, where will he be safe? Inflicting himself on other well meaning souls in other towns and villages, widening and deepening their danger and distress? Whatever he does he must lessen the impact on others. He's been on the move most of his life. This will be no different. Looking down at the dark, dismal court, the afternoon sun now glimmering timidly to cast a narrow sliver of light on the stones, he could even consider this miserable place as home. Yet home is a place he has never known. Even at the beginning it was something denied.

He calls Nottingham his native city, but that's not strictly true. He'd know it from his earliest days, lived here in his youth, learnt his trade and here made all those first flushing mistakes turning from a boy to a man, but he was born outside its old walls. Scarce ten miles east in that open, green tract of the Trent valley, far away from the stormy turmoil of the Regency city. Yet where he was born could have been anywhere, for their oppressors seek to copy its desolate uniformity across the whole of England. This small room, its meanness a constant reminder of their poverty, yet its emptiness is only material, the people fill it with their souls. Not like *that* place. There the emptiness was total. There was no soul.

Destitute and desperate, abandoned by those who should have cared for her, his mother had turned in her hour of need to the only place she knew she wouldn't be turned away. Even then she'd hesitated, but as her time approached, could delay no longer and entered the new 'workhouse.' It was the year of the troubles, 1811. Threatened with drastic cuts to their incomes by the new machines, the men called 'Luddites' had fought back, smashing the machines of those employers who wouldn't heed their protests. Maybe it was a fitting augury for the new baby's future. At the time his mother's pressing need was simply to survive. It was a hard, purposeless and above all *plain* early life. Plain walls, plain yard, plain stairs, plain food, plain bed. Theirs was a dull, colourless existence. Survival had been achieved at the expense of freshness. No fresh fields, no fresh air except the dull yard, no fresh faces except those few unfortunates who found their way out of foul necessity, no fresh conversation. How he longed for that. His mind yearned for the stimulation of fellow creatures whose imagination was not constrained by the damning incarceration of those confining red brick walls.

Yet he was educated. Uninspiringly honed with the religious obsession of their guardians, but educated. Their poor teacher, hardly better housed and fed on the same monotonous fare, she seemed as imprisoned as her charges. But she tried and within the circumscribed institutional monotony succeeded. Sam emerged with the basics of reading and writing. The keys to the doors of knowledge had been given, only needing him to unlock them. He wouldn't flinch for he burned with the passion of improvement and the fires of injustice. Alone, unmarried and abandoned, with no relatives to protect her, the misery and shame could have engulfed his mother, but she recovered her strength and passed it on to her son before she died. He must not forget his origins. He must remember his dead father. One day, one better day, he might face those that had rejected them. So Sam had burned for that better day, though as yet he knew not how to bring it about.

First though he had to be equipped for the important business of work. Like all the other boys, he had to be given a trade. A suitable master must be found, willing to take on an apprentice so he was no longer a burden on the parish. So young Sam, scarce fourteen, was apprenticed to Josiah Gurney, at his shoemaking shop next to Butterworth, the chemist in the old medieval heart of Nottingham, which was later called the Lace Market.

Gurney was a gruff, taciturn man, but he treated Sam reasonably well and taught him the trade conscientiously. It was a life of long hours and spare, though adequate board. He slept under the bench in the shop though he took his meals with Gurney and his wife in the back scullery. Seven long arduous years, but at the end of them he was a journeyman shoemaker, well skilled in the craft. Freed at last from his indentures, Sam could have stayed in town, but trade was depressed. Gurney could only offer him a little work on a poor wage and even this he wouldn't commit beyond a couple of months. With his mother dead and no other ties to hold him, Sam decided to move on. It was not just the depression. Things were probably as bad everywhere else. He was filled with the enthusiasm and adventurous spirit of youth. He thanked his employer politely and took to the road, though unsure which way to go. Outside the old city wall he tossed a coin. Tails. He went north. After ten miles he began to realise just how big the world was!

The escape through the narrow alleys is uneventful. He lingers at the top of Drury Hill, remembering how he'd stopped there all those years ago and contemplated heading south before the toss of the coin sent him in the opposite direction. How might his life have turned had he simply stepped unthinkingly down the hill and continued out of the city to the south? What different fortunes or misfortunes would have befallen him? He might never have been involved in Chartism or maybe all roads lead in the same direction? Lower wages in the south might have driven him closer to the movement even earlier. Who knows, perhaps a third course, unrelated to anything he knows, erupting unexpectedly out of the vast convoluted levels of the London world?

The others call him and all thoughts of might have beens and unlived imaginary lives are lost. Now is the most dangerous time. From here the safety of the streets cannot be guaranteed. If they meet the watch, there could be difficult questions. Who is out at this hour on innocent business? Maybe many in the wild, raucous city, but few like him, alone, sober, packed for a journey. They must take another course, one he has heard of many times, but never used, sometimes even doubting its existence beyond tap room tales. Down into the red flecked underbelly of the city they go, into a gloom, even darker than the night, where those with the knowledge can pick their way to an uncertain safety. Twenty, thirty minutes, it seems longer he follows in the heavy, oppressive blackness, stumbling against the rock and slipping on the wet stones. So far it seems they travel through the caves, the way lit only by the dingy, flickering flame of a single lamp until at last they emerge far to the west on the Derby road. Anxious for themselves and unable to help any further, they leave him here. He's not troubled, thankful they've taken such risks.

Even in these straggling outskirts he must be careful. There are always those, too suspicious or too treacherous, willing for gain or villainy to help the authorities. Even in the darkness of this dangerous half land, neither town nor country, he feels exposed. There are fewer houses and not yet the dubious cover of hedges and trees. He'll feel safer in the open road where an enemy might either be seen from afar or avoided in the undergrowth.

He passes the last house. He's not overly considered which way to go. His friends in the city gave no advice. They said with gloomy confidence, that for him, all directions are as dangerous. Thinking only of going back from where he came he takes the Alfreton road to the north west. Seeing no one and equally sure he's unseen, he makes good progress, covering two, maybe three miles. Just before the outlined houses of a small village, he stops and looks around. Instead of offering hope and security the houses seem threatening and perilous. Uncertain, but convinced he can't go on, he moves to the side of the road, only to miss his footing and slither into the ditch. Trying to keep his balance and also keep hold of his bag, he stumbles further, letting go the bag, which then falls on his head, pushing him down into the mud. He curses loudly and is about to climb out when he hears the distant, low rumble of a cart. Judging by its creaking axles it's heavily laden and making towards Nottingham, perhaps for the early market. He stays down as it nears, emerging only when he's sure it's passed. If it had been going the other way, he could have chanced to hitch a ride. Too risky, too many questions to answer, but why not a journeyman shoemaker on the tramp? Clambering out of the ditch, he brushes himself down as it starts to rain.

Hoping he can find shelter in the fields, he crosses to a track with a broad hedge between him and the village. In the distance is a clump of tall trees. Underneath them is a relatively dry bank of grass, where he settles down to sit out the rain, pulling ferns and branches around in case of chance visitors. He ought to sleep and recover his strength, but he's anxious and his mind is too unsettled. It's not the first time he's spent the night under a hedge.

Through most of the thirties he'd stayed in the north. It was a time of sudden, short lived hope and sometimes desperate despair. Often work was difficult to find and he'd learnt to save in the fleeting good times to keep going in the more frequent bad times. Those that didn't or couldn't save might be faced with starvation or the workhouse. For Sam anything was better than that. Even the cold Pennine road in the deep midwinter snows. Then came the accursed *Act* of 1834 and the compulsory imposition of workhouses. How would he have reacted if he'd gone south? The demoralised southern workers, still reeling from the vicious repression after the failed agricultural revolts in 1830 could only put up a weak resistance. It would be different in the north. A short upturn in trade delayed its impact, but when the inevitable downturn came and thousands were thrown on short time or no work at all, the authorities tried to apply the full rigour of the new legislation. No more outdoor relief meant the workmen had the stark choice between the workhouse and destitution. With the next upturn in trade they could obtain work and look after their families and therefore only needed temporary help, but the *Act* didn't allow for that. Unlike their southern counterparts, the northern workers were still unbowed and relatively confident. They would fight!

Incensed by the blatant injustice, Sam joined the agitation against the Act as he travelled widely across Lancashire, Yorkshire and Staffordshire, looking for work. The wandering life suited his mood and his growing radicalisation. The new onslaught, applied in its indiscriminate ferocity to all working people echoed like a distant church bell on a Sunday morning with his own past, his own origins, his own flickering fires of discontent, now fanned by a fierce wind of anger and retaliation. The fight against the workhouses was not wholly lost. Although eventually, they would be introduced, it was very patchy with long delays. While the long war of attrition went on, there were numerous local victories, the conflict ensuring Sam could never be tempted to forget or forgive the pain of his past. However secretly, quietly or slowly, the fire must now burn with a constant, unquenchable flame. Inevitably, his interests widened and he was pulled inexorably towards Chartism. Surely if working people obtained the vote they could change the laws and the way the system worked so harshly against them. If Parliament was reformed they could get rid of the workhouses, provide protection against the constant swings in trade and end the long hours in the factories. They would begin by stopping the weariness of the young children, labouring endlessly and dangerously in the dust and noise. Education not exploitation. Sam's words rang across the counties as he spent more and more time organising, agitating and speaking, always, always speaking.

Chartism was taking over his life, but he didn't object. He gladly gave his time to the clubs, reading rooms, schools, tea parties and meetings. The movement grew and grew, leading to the first great petition presented to Parliament in 1839. Everything was reaching a crescendo of activity. Everywhere the spirit of the people moved in a tremendous tide of boundless energy that seemed unstoppable. The limitless breadth of Chartism, its myriad pursuits, affecting every aspect of their lives engulfed him with a conviction of victory, denying any doubt. Failure was impossible. With so many signatures, the sheer force of the people must break down all barriers and convince even their greatest opponents of the truth of their cause and the inevitability of their demands.

Success would be soon, immediate. A new wonderful world is dawning!

Of course, there were those who argued otherwise. The ruling classes would not willingly give away their power. They controlled the soldiers and would not hesitate to use them just as they had in the past. But it really *is* different this time. Even so, despite his abounding enthusiasm and unwavering faith in their triumph, Sam helped to store weapons, though in his heart he knew primitive staves, forks, sickles, axes and knives would be no match for well armed, professional soldiers. They had few guns, fewer modern ones, even fewer that worked properly. Never mind, are not revolutions primarily made with words and they had plenty of them. There were plenty of people too. We are many, he would frequently say to the spellbound crowds, they will cower in the face of our fortitude and determination.

Then he was asked to go south. Experienced speakers were needed in the east midlands. It would be his first time back in Nottingham since the old days. The new railway meant he could get there much quicker than on the tramp, but he'd alighted before Derby to speak at meetings in other towns. All these went well, people as confident as in the north. He met local Chartist and trades union leaders, picking up on the politics and the local characters, learning of those to be trusted and those to be treated with caution. Certain names cropped up, again and again, including the Cressleys. Jonathon and Charlotte were pointed out as they rode by one day and they saw him at one of the gatherings, but now wasn't the time to be overly absorbed with past scars. He made his way to Nottingham with hope in the future, filled with the joyous ebullience of the previous weeks. He was not to know their petition, the great Charter would be peremptorily rejected in London, nor of the revolt in Newport and the defeat of those putting their faith in physical force. In the months to come he was not to know how he would have to watch his words in the presence of strangers, choose his companions carefully and spend much time working to protect and free those less fortunate than himself, caught up in the aftermath of that defeat. He was not to know any of these things as he came towards Nottingham.

Now, three years later, back in the same area, inevitably his thoughts drift back to those events and to the curious, sinister incident he witnessed on the way. Should he have done something? What could he have done without risking himself? Who would have believed him? The authorities would be bound to impute his involvement, conveniently indicting him on a charge he'd find great difficulty refuting. He had no choice. In the aftermath of their defeats, he had to put aside what he'd seen. Yet it continued to trouble him and he conscientiously kept up a rigorous perusal of the Nottingham press for several months, but oddly heard nothing more.

It's surprisingly dry under the trees and he manages a couple of hours sleep in the early morning. When he wakes there's already a dim light and the rain has finally cleared. He stretches out and then hunches up the bank to peer across towards the village. Soft smoke from chimneys, a dog barking, hens clucking, the grating movement of farm implements, a village coming alive. Best not to go that way. He gets back to the track and, keeping close to the hedge, trudges along the fields, away from the village, hoping he'll not meet some early rising labourers. With the glimmering, creeping sunlight to his right he knows he's heading north. After a half hour he loses the shield of the hedge and walks across a wide valley with low hills to his left and right. He knows the small town on the receding horizon, slowly disappearing behind him, is Brinckley. Dimly in the distance he sees the tower of a church on the hills to his left. He remembers. Creston. So Elvington House is only over the next hill. He's reluctant to return the way he came from the north west through the Derbyshire towns. To the east there are fewer towns and it'll be closer to the north road into Yorkshire.

The land levels out except for a slight bank where a low, straight hedge severs his path across the valley. The *Cross Cut*. As the sun's rays pierce further from the eastern sky, they gradually pick up the waters of the canal, reflected in a searing sliver like a streak of glass slicing through the fields. For a few moments he watches transfixed, as the light, held as a single linear barrier from hill to hill, ripples across the surface. He walks on. He'll follow the canal until it reaches the eastern hills and the woods, through which he can move quickly with good cover. He reaches the bank. Exaggerated in the light, the canal is narrower than he'd expected. He walks along the path. There's a bridge ahead, next to a small lock, where the canal rises some two meters in its gradual ascent to the hill. He crosses over. It may be the last place to get onto the northern side for some distance. He nears the entrance to the canal tunnel. A low, dark cloud passes across the sun and the widening light abruptly closes as if some celestial shopkeeper has suddenly closed the box lid of the earth, leaving only narrow cracks to seep twinkling light to the ground. Reacting instinctively to his sharply enclosing vision, he slows his pace as the expanding radiance is gone and a baleful, forbidding gloom casts a pervasive, hanging murk. Brief, but indistinct shadows, not there a moment ago, project threateningly and make him look around intensely. The canal and the tunnel, no longer stretching innocently forward are now lost in a vague, lurking haziness, from which hidden dangers could attack without warning.

As his eyes adjust, much of the shady menace recedes, but one shadow on the path persists as the cloud passes. The sun's rays penetrate the pallid atmosphere and in the growing light the shadow becomes a dark, but distinct figure. His foot dislodges some gravel on the path and the sound resonates ominously. The figure turns. A man, young, tallish, with an upright, familiar gait approaches. They are close enough now to see each other clearly.

"Usworth!"

The call is a sharp, cutting bark, spouting fury, challenge, ridicule, though unknown to Sam, also fear and alarm. The man comes on, unabashed or unable, despite his trepidation, not to hold back what he feels is expected of him. Class solidarity and family pride demand it. So also with Sam.

"You're a wanted man, I should hand you over now!"

"You'll have to take me first, Cressley."

Jonathon is surprised.

"You know me?"

"Aye, I've seen you. Every garden has its share of slugs!"

"And you're one known throughout the county. You'll not get far."

Jonathon moves closer. Sam drops his bag. They stand at the path's edge, leering at each other with undisguised disgust. Jonathon, his back to the tunnel and the sun, is a couple of years younger than Sam, but otherwise similar in height and build,

"However far I get, I'll have been here first and dealt with you."

Doctor Charles Foxley puts down his pen for the last time. It's finished. There were many times when he doubted he would reach this day. Many times the spirit faltered, many times the determination to include everything had been weak. Many times he'd opened the book only to close it again after hours of inactivity. So long it's taken, yet now as he scans the few pages he sees it could have been written in a day, nay a morning, but it's not the writing that's taken the time. The sheer physical effort of putting ink to paper has not been the challenge. The real trial has been the thinking and the remembering, above all the remembering. Yet he persisted. Over the months the book has lain in his drawer, a resurgent reminder each time it was opened of a task he had to finish, however painful the process.

He closes the book, a slim delicate volume with handsome binding, a pretty, dainty perspective of delights, inviting like a child's toy. Yet no trivial treatise to while away a rainy afternoon. A toy in which no child would find pleasure. A handsome covering, like a gilded pleasure box, but a false friend, belying its grim interior. A gritty, aching labour, not of love, but of necessity. Necessary to purge. The purging of guilt by truth. The truth which should have been exposed long, long ago. Yet even now he lacks the courage to do it well, but better it's done badly than not at all. He's persisted. It's finished. He'll take it with him and later decide what use is to be made of it. Reconciling the truth to oneself is the first stage, explaining it to others requires another brand of courage he's not yet able to summon up.

He looks across the room. His bag is packed. He's made his arrangements. The practice will be covered in his absence. A longish holiday he's told his friends and housekeeper. They may have believed him, but he's sure she has not. In any case he's delayed retirement. A *longish* holiday may well turn out even longer. Running away usually solves nothing. Didn't he run away when he left the old practice in Brinckley and moved to Nottingham? Will he find the peace he craves in some far flung, pleasant place? It's eluded him here. Peace isn't in any particular place, but in the mind and he carries that with him.

He glances at the clock. He shouldn't delay. He picks up the memoir and slips it into the bag, but seems unable to get up from the chair. He stares around the room, taking in every detail without perception, his concentration drifting disconsolately. His eyes alight on the bag once more. He can see the bulge in the side wherein lies the book. It mocks him. Take me out and read me to the world. He looks away. Can he sit in some distant hotel room, always aware of its power to shame him? Should he give up this venture, cancel his travel plans and set about completing the undertaking, releasing himself utterly from this omnipresent burden?

He shudders. Why does he torture himself? He's done his duty in writing it down, but there would have been no need if he'd not allowed these things to come about. He gets up. Nothing to be gained rewriting the past. It's unchangeable. A life lived is a life recorded. It cannot be written away. No, but it can be unwritten. Perhaps he should have left the past where it belongs. Gone, finished, not rooted up and laid out like some dead plant unearthed to rot in the sun. But it's not laid out. It lies beneath, hidden within that dainty binding. Waiting. Some day to rise up and destroy all those involved in its interment.

He must leave before his housekeeper returns. She'll expect him to have gone and will want to know why he tarries. More importantly, he should be away before his visitor returns. A visitor who asked too many questions and received inadequate answers. Given time to think over those answers, that visitor may realise the inconsistencies of his replies and seek clarification. Next time he may not be able to fend off such questions. Next time he may say something that embarrasses. Next time he may even tell the truth.

He hovers at the door, putting down the bag as he looks around the room for what may be the last time. He'll go the station. He's always been a man of the past, but this is 1842. The Midland Counties Railway has been open three years, yet this will be his first time on a train. He contemplates the journey with mixed feelings of apprehension and excitement. With a change at Rugby, he could be in London before the end of the day. He tries to quell his nervousness. It may be crowded even in second class. Should he travel first class? If he doesn't control himself he'll leave his bag on the train for the book to be discovered by a stranger. Then his secrets will be exposed without explanation. Serious enough to be found by a stranger of the present, but what if it's not found at all and is lost in the deep recesses of a railway carriage to be unearthed in the distant future? In the future someone may know, already knows. Somewhere on the way he must hide the book before he reaches the station. He opens the door, picks up the bag and is gone.

Since he left the canal, Sam has been running continuously for a half hour, the fast spurts broken up as now by a more leisurely pace to recover his strength. He's seen no one, but takes no chances. Running is instinctive. It fills the yawning gap, the fear of inaction. He must do something and running meets that need with an immediate burning of energy that might otherwise be fruitlessly wasted worrying for hours over a few desperate minutes. Nothing to be gained by endless repetition, but even as he runs, the parallels with three years before are too close to be ignored. No one will believe him. The same anguished drone taps incessantly in his mind, a relentless reminder, reverberating from his heavily thudding feet. But he runs for more than emotional escape and political expediency. Though sure he's not been observed, the open country that broadens out from the end of the canal tunnel is too vulnerable. He crosses the Nottingham road and avoids the pits and the few houses. The stabbing pain in his side intensifies, but he must go on. He must reach the woods. The south western extremity of that vast forest that once shielded Robin Hood, may yet cover his retreat. The ground rises sharply. Beyond, he can see the close clustered trees, not far now, less than fifty meters of flat, open ground from the top of the rise. He slips on the smooth grass at its edge and slithers back.

Then he hears them. Footsteps. He hunches forward and carefully peers through the grass towards the trees. Three men, one armed. Gamekeepers perhaps. They stand at the edge of the woods, looking in his direction. He lowers his head still further, his chin sinking into the earth. He can't see them, but detects no movement either through his ears or through the ground. They stare into the valley, but don't see him. The man with the gun says something to the others. They turn and walk back into the woods. After a few moments, Sam inclines his head towards the trees. They've gone, but the danger hasn't passed. The darkly latticed wood no longer offers defence and escape. Suddenly it's charged with concealed peril and mantled insecurity, peopled with suspicious guardians who know every branch and twig. He looks back, down the slope, through the fields, over the road, and across the valley to the canal. There's no alternative. He must go back.

Carefully, constantly stopping to check he's not followed or observed, he careers back down the bank, dragging himself along the field to the road. Exhausted from earlier exertions, he can't run fast without the pain in his side becoming unbearable. He crouches at the roadside, glad of the rest as he scans both directions. With no sign of anyone and firmly clutching his side, he runs across quickly to slide towards the cover of some bushes at the edge of a field. Still no one. He can't run anymore or his side will split open. From here, it's a relatively short walk to the canal where it turns at the top end of the tunnel. If he can get there without being seen, he might be able to rest up for the day.

It's a long, painful, dragging walk down to the canal. Every few steps he turns nervously, surveying up the hill and down the valley. It's eerily quiet, unnaturally empty. He reaches the canal bank and looks back. No sign of a barge, but one must come along some time. What then? Is this no safer than in the trees? He stops at the tunnel entrance, looks round again and then, as his eyes adjust to the darkness peers into the cavernous, receding hole. He steps in, his footfalls echoing and re-echoing. It's cool and damp, the walls laced with a film of condensation, the bricks seemingly oozing a constant moisture like some subterranean animal seeping an ominous sweat. He can see no light. Either the tunnel turns or it's too far to the other end. His eyes jump around haphazardly. All is narrowing, pressing down, receding. The narrowing brick lined bore with its closing arched roof receding into an unknown, unseeable end. What if it recedes to nothing, an inverted, ever blackening cone that finally closes, crunching to a tiny point? What if the path abruptly stops as the wall jumps in to bar his way?

He looks back. Walls don't jump, but still he panics. He's shut in. He can't go forward and can't go back. He's entered a trap as an animal is caught in a poacher's snare. He walks on, but more slowly, his hand sliding along the bricks, uncertainly staggering forward, into the cold, doubtful comfort of what lies within against the certain danger of what lies outside. If only he can find safety until nightfall and then perhaps... the wall is suddenly gone from his fingertips and his hand clutches the emptiness. He stops. He steps forward and puts out his hands, feeling the wall again.

Then he steps back and again feels the wall, but between there's nothing. He stands and turns round to catch what little light there is from the entrance. A small inlet is set into the wall, just wide enough for a man to step in. It's less than a meter wide though a little deeper and higher, big enough for him to squeeze in and sink down to the floor, where he sits, hunched in relative comfort. It's as good a hiding place as he'll find and with luck even if a barge or someone comes by, he'll remain unseen. He falls asleep, but his last waking thought is of the last few hours. His mistake was to believe he could safely travel by day. Only at night does he stand any chance. Soon he must make his way again.

All on the move now, all desperate, all firmly resolved their lives must quickly and irrevocably change, but only one can and must seek aid from elsewhere. The presence is the future and the future is the presence. Yet time itself is no friend, for it allows only a brief, concentrated opening. The future has sent messages before. Now the future must receive as you have received from the future. The contact is fleeting, but the power is strong. The link is discernible. The opportunity is here. Do not hesitate and do not over indulge the mind. Let the feeling flow, leave the heart to disclose unhindered. The future is listening and will understand. Speak!

- 6 -

Jenner sits at the edge of Nottingham's slab square in glum mood. He's been out all morning and needs to return to the station to catch up on events, but he's not yet ready. He watches people meandering around the wide, open space and then glances up to the looming edifice of the Council House. In the opposite corner of the square a small crowd is gathering around a lone figure who stands on one of the stone seats, preparing to address them. Jenner could go over, it might while away a few amusing minutes. He used to listen to all the eccentrics at Hyde Park, but gave up when he felt the place was being monopolised by a narrow range of speakers without the old loonies and fascinating extremists. Maybe they were like old soldiers. They just faded away.

It might be different here. Perhaps some rational debate still lives on. No doubt laced with prejudice, but still lively and mildly informative. If only he could be sure. Information of any kind, but based on incontrovertible *facts* would be welcome. Better than hosts of guesses, conjectures and bold, but flimsy assertions, nothing conclusive.

At least the discovery of the body has stiffened up Jenner's resolve. The Bernard Weston enquiry had begun to pall. Despite Emmins' insistence on its importance, Jenner's own gut feelings that something more sinister lay behind his disappearance and Ettie's growing concerns, they seemed to be putting a lot of effort into what was only a missing person enquiry. Matthew Usworth could have made more trouble, accusing him of harassment, not to mention Ella Weston being pursued unnecessarily, while Sylvia Darrington – Cressley...but now such doubts can be cast aside.

The body was discovered out of town, in open hilly ground. It's already been identified as Martin Sarwell. Meanwhile, the search for Bernard Weston will have an added impetus while he must transfer resources to the new enquiry. He's convinced the two cases are connected. Now he'll have to reconsider the disparate strands surrounding the first investigation while undertaking the second.

The group around the speaker is now quite large. Plenty of people have been tempted away from their sandwiches and the pigeons to listen. It might have been interesting after all, but too late now. With a last, lingering look across the square he walks away and up the hill.

Back in the station, Jennifer Heathcott waits for him.

"We've solved part of the mystery, sir."

With his mind still in slab square, he stares vacantly, as yet only dimly aware of other matters.

"Remember he was found by somebody walking their dog in the fields?"

Some semblance of understanding jabs his consciousness. He drops with weary resignation into the chair.

"The dog was scrabbling around in a gully and then disappeared. The man followed and heard the dog in the undergrowth. It kept barking, but wouldn't come out. He had to break through and found the entrance to the disused mine. Ten meters in he found the body. We couldn't understand how Sarwell had got there without breaking through in the same way."

"Not unless he'd come up from inside the mine, which is pretty fantastic. Even then how could the murderer get away?"

"Exactly, but I think we've got the answer. I spoke to a mining engineer I know and asked him about these adits."

"Adits?"

"Small drift mines. There were hundreds of them in the

old days and many are completely unrecorded. They tried to locate and survey the whole area twenty five years ago, some sort of job creation initiative. They ran out of government grant and had to give up with the job only part completed. The Brinckley area was never surveyed."

"So there are hundreds of disused mineshafts all over the place?"

"Most have either collapsed or been filled in by later development. Those that are left..."

"Would only be known to those with very good local knowledge."

"There's more. Sometimes these adits had vertical shafts added later or they were dug close to old shafts. So that gave me an idea. What if there's also a disused shaft connecting with the adit. I extended our search this morning, further up the hill. We've found an opening, recently disturbed. The engineer's there now, but it looks likely Martin Sarwell fell into the drift mine below."

"Good work, sergeant! You see the value of local knowledge and contacts. Any news from the PM?"

"Not yet."

"Did he fall or was he pushed? We need to know if he was dead before the he went into the mine. Chase it up."

Jennifer relaxes, gratified by this sudden commendation. Jenner remains in thought.

"He was found around five o'clock. Do we have anything else to pin down the time of death?"

"We've located someone who was with him in the afternoon, name of Alan Banning. They're old friends, share an interest in exploring disused railway lines. He and Martin Sarwell had located the site of an old branch line near Brinckley. They'd reached a new housing development and apparently Martin wandered off, saying he thought he knew where they could pick up the line of the old track on the other side."

"Why didn't this Banning go with him?"

"He wanted to go in a different direction. They agreed to explore separately for a half hour and meet up about half a mile away near the brewery. Martin Sarwell didn't turn up. Banning waited around and then retraced the route he assumed Sarwell would have taken. With no sign of him, he gave up and went home. Tried to ring him and got no answer. He's only just heard. He last saw him about two thirty."

"So he died between two thirty when Banning last saw him and five when the body was found."

He muses thoughtfully.

"Local knowledge, which all our suspects have. What do we know about their movements?"

"They've all got alibis," she says, "All with friends at the crucial time."

"Very convenient. Even Ella Weston?"

"Her friends in Derbyshire thought she was delicate. Came over to see her and didn't leave until the following morning."

"Damn! It has to be one of them. Check out those alibis again. And don't forget that post mortem."

Could it have been a genuine accident, Jenner wonders Obsessed with finding the old railway track and probably anxious to outsmart his companion, Sarwell strays from the path. Not looking around properly, he runs headlong through the fields, recklessly careering through the densely overgrown remains at the head of the mineshaft, crashing to his death in the adit below. Tragic and unforeseen, but not necessarily sinister. Such things happen in the most regulated situations, let alone when zealous, single minded individuals take off after a quarrel. Yet this man knew the area well, an expert on the local topography. Even in the heat of the moment, fired up to prove his point, surely he wouldn't lose his way? Unless he'd been watched and then attacked when he left his friend. Maybe it's an opportunistic killing. Out on his own, unseen, unheard, he's taken unawares and then conveniently thrown down the mineshaft to make it look like an accident?

He's not convinced. There's too much coincidence. He'll have to await the post mortem to reveal the real cause of death. In the meantime, he must trust his gut feeling and further investigate Martin Sarwell's background to see if there's anything indicating why anyone would want to put him out of the way.

Jennifer leaves, slightly disappointed. There's a meeting tonight she would like to have attended. She'd mentioned it to Ettie who approached her old friend Phil at the university for advice.

"Not my period," he'd said, "but there's been a flurry of interest lately. A local amateur has been causing a stir, digging up all sorts of intriguing material."

Ettie attends the meeting billed as 'The Chartists in the Shearwell Valley.' The speaker is Matthew Usworth. She sits at the back of the room, trying to be as inconspicuous as possible. She's even taken Phil's advice and left her distinctive black hat at the hotel. She'd not said why she was so interested in the 1840s. Vague generalisations wouldn't fool him, but he'd know she would have her reasons for secrecy. Matt is a good speaker, lacing his presentation with gossipy anecdotes and concentrating on the personalities as well as the broad issues. Both appeal to his listeners.

"....Finally, I would like to explore the local Chartist activities that took place in the Autumn of 1842, after the disturbances in August had quietened down and the authorities, having regained their nerve, started to take reprisals...."

He quickens his pace, his voice rising to a higher pitch as he reaches the main thrust of his talk. In the room's absolute silence, his audience is spellbound as he passionately sets out the destiny of the movement's local leaders in the wake of the turbulent events of Summer 1842. Ettie makes a careful note of every name he mentions. Some return to obscurity and are heard no more. Some, after a spirited defence, fail to be convicted, leading a life of less spectacular agitation. Some are less lucky. Tried and imprisoned, their families have to be sustained by the meagre resources of their comrades.

"...yet the fate of some others are unknown to us. The lost ones who simply disappear from history as a candle flame is snuffed out at the end of the day, for a short time leaving only a snaking sliver of smoke to tantalisingly indicate they ever existed at all."

He pauses and sweeps his eyes dramatically across the room. Ettie bows her head. Then he takes questions. They're mostly confined to the detail of his talk, though a couple seek amplification of his sources. He successfully bats these away with a mixture of over talking through the material again or switching to another subject. One man persists. At first Matt seems disconcerted, but then, almost as if he's all along been waiting for just such a theatrical opportunity, he slides some sheets from within his notes and holds what appears to be a newspaper in front of him.

"Here is the origin of much of this information. Neglected by others, it contains almost all we need to know about those crucial few months. The 'East Midland Working Peoples' Examiner' of October 1842, an obscure Chartist newspaper sets out the trials of the Autumn."

A great gasp of awe followed by further questions, concentrating on the origins of the paper and those behind it. Matt answers these points with relish, but one question interrupts his flow.

"A valuable document, were there any later editions?"

Matt hesitates and then responds with a stilted, jerky reply.

"I believe the paper closed down early in 1843, so I've been unable to trace subsequent events."

The moment passes. No one challenges him. Ettie remembers Jenner's theory. No information following the 1842 watershed and the most important gap in his presentation remains unquestioned. Matt has given no names for his 'lost ones,' the mysteriously disappeared leaders. Who were they? How is it he knows so much others do not? The newspaper lies on the table. A few people examine it. Perhaps it will give a clue. She must get to the front and scrutinise it without him seeing her. Revelling in his newly found adulation, albeit really only a medium sized fish in a very small pond, Matt holds court in the corner of the room. Wholly surrounded he cannot see the table, which is now almost totally neglected. Seizing her chance, Ettie strides forward to examine the newspaper

It's much smaller than she expects, only a four page sheet, but crammed with information on meetings, articles not just on extending the vote, but on many other social and religious issues, together with poems, advice on household matters and economic questions. Conscious she holds a hundred and sixty years of history she fingers the paper carefully. The style of the type and the close columned layout seems unmistakably nineteenth century, but something is missing or at least unexpected. Ettie, usually so sensitive to the aura of old things, doesn't *feel* its age. Then she realises. The paper lacks that crackling, folded, faded essence. It seems fresh and firm, like an old man in the flesh of a young one. There's an unbelievable newness about the paper. After all this time the distinctness of the print is unreal. She examines her fingers, almost expecting to detect ink as sometimes occurs with modern newspapers. There's none, but the unmistakable sense of agelessness persists. It's as if she holds a tactile photograph, an object frozen in time just as the dead stare back in old snaps with the vibrancy of their own age. There's nothing dead about the newspaper. In one of those brief moments, minute in real time, but immensely long in feeling, Ettie is as held as she in turn holds the newspaper. The sights and sounds of the room fade and fuzzily recede and another, older yet oddly contemporary reality subsumes the present. She sees and hears nothing, but in a silent, indistinct presence knows she's gripped in the newly printed period of the paper.

It passes. The people and the room return to her consciousness. By the clock on the wall only a few seconds have passed, yet it seems much longer. She still holds the paper. Its inexplicable newness defying explanation, yet she believes its age is measured in days rather than decades. She replaces it on the table, looking down as a beachcomber may stare incredulously at an ancient object washed up by the sea as if it's been cast aside only minutes before.

The meeting is breaking up. Others are coming towards the table. She ought to challenge Matt. She could catch him and query the paper. But query what? Its authenticity is not the issue. If anything, it's *too* authentic, lacking the wear and tear of the years. Unsure what to do she goes outside and waits at a discreet distance. People file out and saunter away. How will she approach him? 'Prove this paper really is a hundred and sixty years old or allow it to be forensically examined!' If her suspicions are correct he'll prevaricate and probably hide the evidence. If she's wrong she'll make a fool of herself. Matt comes out and walks in her direction. He sees her. No time now to escape. She stands and waits for him to reach her.

"Your find is very impressive, Matt," she says, "do you have any other examples of contemporary material?"

He looks at her carefully, perhaps assessing how far she can be trusted.

"I'm surprised you're that interested, Miss Rodway. It's not really your period, is it?"

"I don't have a period. The past is always fascinating."

He doesn't respond, moving his jaw slightly as if trying to dislodge a particularly troublesome piece of meat lodged in his teeth.

"I always believe you have to go back to the original sources," she continues, "so often new and sometimes startling interpretations arise simply by carefully reanalysing things, as you've so clearly shown. I suppose you had to scour many documents in various locations?"

His eyes shift nervously from her face, seeking unsuccessful consolation elsewhere, darting jerkily until settling on her again.

"Yes indeed," he says, "I really do have to go. It was nice seeing you again, Miss Rodway."

Before she can pull back the conversation, he turns swiftly and almost runs to his car. Now Ettie is sure. Things not said, sometimes reveal more than those that are.

Surrounded by tall hawthorn hedges, the large detached Victorian house stands in a half acre of grounds, at the edge of the village. It might once have been the vicarage and exudes a faint remoteness, loyal only to something higher and better. The pond, greenhouse and thickly overgrown flowerbeds seem as old as the house itself.

Duggan waits at the front door, having rung the bell three times. Jenner is irritated and prowls impatiently on the gravel path, peering across to the garden and the drive as if his quarry might suddenly appear from behind the bushes. Just as he's about to go to the rear of the house the door opens. Holding his spectacles in his hand Alan Banning has obviously been disturbed and looks irritably as Duggan introduces them.

"I suppose this is about poor Martin Sarwell?"

Banning leads them, without turning or even acknowledging their presence, into a room at the back of the house, crammed with books. There's a large desk, untidily littered with papers.

"Not some sort of academic are you, sir?" Jenner says, disapprovingly glancing at the bookshelves.

"No, no," Banning says, "Just an amateur. I'm an engineer."

He sits in his swivel chair, his long floppy cardigan trailing almost to his knees. He replaces his glasses and ruffles through some of the papers. Uninvited, Jenner sits in the armchair opposite the desk. Taking out his notebook, Duggan settles into the hard chair by the door.

"Hence the interest in railways?" Jenner says.

"Sort of, though I'm also into aircraft."

"Quite. Just some routine questions. We'd like to know more about Mr. Sarwell."

"Which means you don't believe his death was accidental?"

"We're keeping an open mind at this stage. You were friends for some time, I believe?"

"Yes. We were both members of the same orienteering group."

"Both railway historians?"

"Not really. Martin had an interest in the history, but our surveys of old lines really developed out of orienteering. In many ways it was an excuse to get out and ramble."

"But the other day you disagreed and separated."

"Ridiculous looking back on it now. We were trying to find the original trackline of the Midland railway branch line through Brinckley. I said we'd inadvertently found the Great Northern railway branch, which ran parallel to it. Anyway, he took off. I knew he was wrong because..."

"Quite. You'd known him a long time. Wasn't married, was he?"

"Had been. They separated years ago."

"Anyone else since?"

Ruminating on this, Banning glances down to his papers. Perhaps these wretched policemen won't take too long and leave him in peace. Help them as much as possible and they might go away quicker.

"No one at the moment."

"And in the past?"

"He was seeing someone a few years ago, a little younger, but it didn't last. She was pretty upset when Martin ended it. I think the relationship was getting in the way of his other interests."

He says this dismissively. Jenner notices the room's bare, austere masculinity. This is a house without a woman's touch.

"Did she have a name?"

"She was the sister of that chap that went missing... Weston. That's it, Ella Weston."

"More than a passing fling was it?"

"It was for a time," Banning shrugs, adding as an afterthought, "But it wouldn't have worked, thoroughly incompatible you see."

"Quite. Just how upset was Ella Weston?"

Banning squirms and stares tetchily, but is unable to deflect Jenner's concentrated gaze.

"If you must know she was a damned nuisance, forever ringing him up in the middle of the night. He complained of her for weeks. I told him to be firm, it would be better in the long run. Once he did he heard no more of her."

"She resented her rejection, then?"

"Good God, you're not suggesting she had something do with his death?"

"I'm not suggesting anything; yet. Now, were there any other problems in his life?"

Banning hesitates again, only to receive a further piercing glare from Jenner.

"Martin was a research chemist and he part owned the business. He felt very strongly about one of his ventures, but couldn't get sufficient capital to back it. He had to put it in a

144

lot of his own money. The snag with research is it can take a long time before there's a return. Consequently..."

"He was in financial difficulties?"

"In a way, yes."

"Which particular way?"

Finally irritated beyond further endurance at this interference with his ordered routine, Banning erupts.

"Look, chief inspector, I was not privy to the finer details of Martin's business affairs!"

"Quite so, sir. Name?"

"I beg your pardon?"

"You can give me the name of someone who would have been privy to that information?"

Banning's cold scrutiny of Jenner is answered by a broad, whimsical, enquiring smile. Banning feebly glances down at his papers and shakes his head.

"You could try Richard Baslow, his accountant."

They find the accountant at Sarwell's laboratory. He's also the part time company secretary and sits in his office, troubled and subdued, surrounded by files, piles of unanswered correspondence and harassing staff. He's composed about being interviewed by the police. Perhaps they are a welcome respite from his other worries. Relieved, he cajoles the staff out of the office and, sweeping his hand through the mounds of paper, clears a space on the table. Several files drop unceremoniously to the floor. He eyes them fleetingly, kicking the nearest under the table. For a moment at least he'll be free of them. Compared with the straight jacketed tyranny of printed paper, what threats can the police pose?

"There were some problems with the firm, but this last year Martin hadn't told me everything. I'm just discovering how serious things had become. I can't rule out some form of liquidation. But then, much of the losses will be borne out of his own money, which now means only his estate will suffer. I don't know who inherits, but they won't get much. I'm seeing his solicitor this afternoon."

"Any particular reason for the losses?" Jenner says.

"He'd been working on a new idea. The project was increasingly dominating the work of the whole place. He was banking on a major breakthrough to prise him out of the financial impasse, but of course the scheme itself needed more and more capital."

"Speculate to accumulate, eh?"

"Unfortunately for Martin there was a lot of speculating and very little accumulating."

"What was this work?"

"Much of it is commercially sensitive, but he was trying to develop a food additive, which paradoxically induced a degree of weight loss."

"Sounds perfect. Did he manage it?"

"It doesn't appear so, though I'm advised that it was well advanced. Now, of course, it'll have to stop. We have to use what resources we have to keep the other bread and butter work going. There'll be nothing to pursue the project. It's a great pity because apparently he was almost at the stage of trials."

"Did he get into debt?"

"Certainly to the bank."

"Anyone else?"

"I'm not sure yet. From the documents it looks like he was approaching everybody he could think of. "

"I would like a list of all those contacts. Anyone that he borrowed from and anyone he approached."

After dropping off Duggan, Jenner collects all the files from the station and goes home. On the way, he wonders about the real Martin Sarwell. A loner except for a few close friends and associates, all of whom speak about him with respect and admiration rather than affection. His loss might even be an irritation. A reflection on his choice of friends and colleagues, but also on the man himself. A brilliant mind, curiously combining narrow interests in the past and a professional project with wide contemporary application. Once inside, Jenner reflects on all the doubts and contradictions, emptyng his mind in the brooding melancholic belly of Tchaikovsky's Pathetique symphony. As always, the music's opening gloom resonates with his mental emptiness, but slowly he recovers and out of nothing *something* usually materialises. Go down to go up. From the depths there can only be ascent. Suitably prepared, he opens the papers. Something will emerge.

Interviews with other associates as well as Banning and Baslow have produced an interesting bundle of pastimes as well as foraging along old railway tracks. He shared with Ella Weston an interest in nineteenth century medicine, in his case particularly in the career of a local doctor named Foxley. At the time of his death, he'd been collecting information for a possible biography. No one knew what had been the special attraction of the physician other than Sarwell describing him as 'a local character.'

There's also their personal connection, which neither of them acknowledged in their interviews. Was the woman scorned sufficiently to commit murder? Now another link has also emerged. As well as the mysterious Doctor Foxley, Sarwell had been looking into another local 'character,' a midwife called Lizzie Traynor. This snippet of information, picked up accidentally by an officer talking to one of Sarwell's staff, had not at first attracted Jenner's attention. Then he remembered Traynor was Ella and Bernard Weston's mother's maiden name. Was Lizzie Traynor an ancestor? Like Usworth, it's not a common name. Usworth, Weston, Sarwell, Traynor. The names reverberate.

Then there are Sarwell's financial problems. Had he borrowed way beyond his means? Had someone got particularly impatient at his failure to pay? Baslow's list of contacts could be very revealing. What about his new drug? Even without proper trials, had it attracted dubious interest he couldn't control? Had his obsessions with the past rebounded? Had he made some sinister discovery leading the past to dangerously interfere with his present?

He flicks through the files once more. His old copper's gut instincts tell him it cannot be an accident. The feeling will return. It always does. He also has a number of telephone messages. Most are routine, except for the last. As the music finishes the doorbell rings.

He lets Ettie in and talks about mundane matters. How is her hotel? Does she have everything she needs? She's slightly amused by this uncharacteristic conversational fussiness. There must be something on his mind. He fidgets and walks around, finally getting her a drink, while he reads that last telephone message. He's unsure what to say. Ettie asks about his enquiries and he crumples the paper into his pocket.

"We're still waiting for the PM, but it looks like an accident," he says blandly, before updating her on the investigation.

"What do you make of Martin Sarwell?" she says.

He's not yet ready to speak honestly and would first prefer to hear Ettie's own speculations.

"There's undoubtedly much more to him than first appeared," he says, tapping the files.

She mentions her strange discussion with Martin, his obsession with the man from the past and how he may be repeating the events of a previous life. He tells of Martin's interest in Doctor Foxley and Lizzie Traynor. She starts at the latter name.

"Something familiar?"

"Perhaps."

"Ettie, I was wondering if you...er...you'd had...you know...."

"...felt anything from the past?"

"I couldn't say anything outside of this room, but..."

"You asked me to help so you must have suspected something from the beginning."

"I know we've very little to go on and I'm unsure where it takes us, but I was wondering, is it possible..."

"That Martin Sarwell and Doctor Foxley are one and the same man?"

He nods silently, afraid to say anymore. Perhaps by not mouthing the words he may lessen their ludicrousness.

"You're not convinced it was an accident?" she says.

"Sergeant Heathcott's enquiries have produced an old shaft which leads into the disused mine. He could have fallen down it. My gut feeling tells me otherwise."

"What's it tell you?"

"That's the problem. I reject the logical explanation, replacing it with the most ridiculous. What if Sarwell discovered something or even brought something from the past which was too sensitive?"

"So sensitive for someone to kill him?"

"He had this premonition of danger, believing a terrible event was imminent. If he was reliving the past...."

"He could hardly be killed twice."

"Okay, he didn't envisage it happening exactly as it did."

"You really believe he's Foxley just because he implied he'd lived before?"

"There's something uncanny about them all. Remember my questions and their answers hitting the barrier of 1842? His railway interests, this interest in the doctor, it's all up to 1842."

"His knowledge of chemistry seems to post date 1842."

"I suppose so," he says, embarrassed.

Had he really said those things? Did he really believe Sarwell and Foxley are the same person? The absurdity of it hammers in his mind. Where's the evidence? Gut feelings don't secure convictions. At best they only lead to more productive lines of enquiry. Where to go from here?

"What's the significance of Lizzie Traynor?" he says, suddenly diverting the subject.

She tells him about her conversations with Ella and the recurring dream of Lizzie.

"Does she believe this Lizzie is her relative?"

"If she does she doesn't say."

"Sarwell could have told her. We have this link between him and the Westons."

"Martin believed Bernard stole his papers. If he felt strongly enough..."

"He could have killed Bernard Weston."

"Then there's the personal relationship with Ella. We know it ended acrimoniously and on her part unhappily, so if she knew he killed Bernard..."

"....she had two reasons to kill him."

She leans back, putting her fingertips over her mouth.

"This link may be much more significant," he continues, "Love, especially if it's spurned can turn to hatred. She may have resented his probing into her family. What if he found something about Lizzie Ella didn't like? Something she preferred to cover up."

"Enough to kill?"

"Quite."

She glances at the files. One at the bottom marked 'Usworth' is undisturbed.

"You've not mentioned Matthew Usworth."

"Slippery eel," he says, "I've put him aside for the moment. I'm not now so interested in his mysterious disappearance from the canal."

"You may change your mind, especially with your concerns over the 1842 threshold."

She tells of the local history meeting and the dramatic presentation of the newspaper.

"He was very reticent when asked about later editions of the paper."

"And you believe there was something, how did you call it, *contemporary* about the newspaper?"

"I'm no expert, but it just didn't seem that old."

"Could be a forgery. If we could get hold of it, we could get it analysed."

"You asked me earlier if I'd *felt* anything from the past. The strongest thing I've felt yet was when I handled that paper. It was uncanny, as if it was transporting me back to that time."

"But if the paper is not that old?"

"It's not a question of how old it is, but whether it has *aged*. Does that change your view of Matt?"

"It might and there's another thing..."

The doorbell rings. Jenner looks at his watch. Eight o'clock. He's not expecting anyone and is surprised when he opens the door on Jennifer Heathcott.

"Sorry to disturb you sir, but I thought you'd want to see the post mortem report without delay."

He takes the report. Initially starting at the back, he scans it quickly and then lays it down.

"Have you read it?" he says.

She nods.

" 'Blow to the head, not consistent with a fall indicates he was dead before being thrown down the mineshaft.' So my gut feeling was right. It's murder and we're no longer working on a cold case."

"Still a cold case, sir or perhaps a newly warmed up one. Message from the chief super. We're to continue investigating the disappearance of Bernard Weston as well as the murder enquiry."

Jenner grunts. The chief superintendent could have rung him at home. He doesn't approve of his sergeant being used to carry messages. He turns to Jennifer.

"We've yet to discover Bernard Weston's body. It could still be a missing person enquiry, but if not...one of this nest of vipers is responsible for Weston's disappearance, his probable murder and the murder of Sarwell. We have to find a more substantial link with one of them."

Ettie is unsure.

"If the same person is responsible, then your thoughts about Ella Weston fall. She'd hardly kill her own brother."

"No obvious motive, but I wouldn't rule it out."

He gets up and paces irritably.

"There has to be a connection, but too many things are missing. Weston's body for example."

"Ella's convinced he's dead," Ettie says.

"Why is she so sure?"

"Because she can no longer feel his presence."

"It could also mean she knows who really killed him. If she was Sarwell's lover she could have been covering it up. Then they split up. Suddenly she's grieving not just for a finished relationship, but also for her dead brother. She decides to take her revenge."

Jennifer and Ettie exchange glances.

"It's neat, sir," Jennifer says, without commitment.

"Too bloody neat," he says, "but at least it avoids even wilder ideas."

"I don't follow," Jennifer says, "What wilder ideas?"

Suddenly aware how dangerously he's been thinking aloud, he turns to Ettie with a look of pleading desperation.

"You were going to tell me why you were no longer considering Matt Usworth?" she says.

Jennifer remains bemused. Jenner grabs the lifeline eagerly.

"The two of you were so adamant about the timing in the

canal that night. I couldn't believe he'd just disappeared into thin air. He must have been able to get out quickly without being observed, which meant there *had* to be another exit. So I did my own research. One of the criticisms levelled against those who wanted the canal reopened was that it would only be partial because it was being rushed. It was claimed there wasn't enough time before the opening date for the whole of the canal to be assessed, cleared and, where necessary repaired. With all the furore that followed this little argument seems to have been forgotten, but it bugged me.'

'Just what was meant by *partial* opening? One of the objectors who'd raised this point was Matt Usworth, but he wouldn't explain what he'd meant. I had to go elsewhere. Old mines, old railways, old canals, we were thrashing around in the detritus of the past. Then I remembered Jennifer and her mining engineer friend. If there were parts of old mines to be discovered, what about other parts to the canal? So I checked the records with the waterways people. I drew a blank at first, but somebody rang back and left a message this afternoon. I've only just read it. Where these canals were tunnelled in mining areas, they sometimes deliberately took advantage of the terrain and opened up underground branches connecting directly with the mine workings. It meant they could transport coal straight from the pit without having to bring it to the surface."

Jennifer is amazed.

"That's incredible, I've never heard of it."

"Quite so, sergeant. It only goes to show that however much local knowledge you have there's always room to learn some more."

Suitably chastened, Jennifer slinks back in her chair, but Jenner doesn't gloat.

"It's a specialist area," he says.

"Did Ettie suggest this?" Jennifer says.

He looks at her blankly.

"As the specialist adviser," she says.

"Oh yes, yes of course. Now, there's a reference to just such an underground branch in the Cross Cut. Apparently it's been disused for two hundred years, but could still have provided an alternative hiding place, possibly even an exit for Usworth."

"Assuming he knew about it and was able to find it," Ettie says.

"That's why we have to question him, but remember it was him that was so sure not all of the canal could be opened up in time."

Ettie closes her hands together decisively.

"Which raises the question of how he could possibly have known about something that had been out of use for so long."

"Quite. Tomorrow we get on to the waterways and get them over with their records to survey the place. We have to find if there's an alternative exit."

"In which case we'll know how he got out of the canal without being seen," Jennifer says and then, pointedly to Ettie, "without having to consider any other explanation."

"Maybe," Ettie says, "maybe not."

"Did you go to the meeting?"

Ettie tells Jennifer about Matt's presentation and the 'old' newspaper. She doesn't mention what she felt as she handled the paper. Jennifer's reaction is muted.

"It doesn't shock you?" Jenner says.

"It might have done if it wasn't for another discovery," she says, "while examining the site of the old mineshaft we came across this."

She places a handbill, slightly larger than A4 size on the table. It's faded and stained, but the main text can still be discerned. 'National Charter Association – Maintain the struggle for complete suffrage – Support the Six Points.'

"It's a Chartist handbill, you see from the date, it's advertising a meeting in 1842."

"That year again," Jenner says, "we need to get it analysed."

"No identifiable prints. It goes to the lab in the morning."

Jenner reads and examines the paper carefully.

"It seems old," he says, "The six points – the vote for all men, equal electoral districts, no property qualification, votes by secret ballot, payment of MPs and annual parliaments.

Voting, eh? If they knew then what we know now, would they have bothered?"

He hands it to Ettie. Jennifer reacts passionately.

"That's unbelievably cynical, sir. These people struggled and suffered for us all those years ago!"

"Quite so, sergeant. You're quite right to correct me."

He turns to Ettie, "Feel anything?"

She returns the handbill to the table and studies it for a few moments.

"I feel what I felt with the newspaper, but your tests will confirm or deny. If it's not authentic it's an unbelievably clever copy."

"Anything else?" he persists.

She shakes her head.

"Does this put Matt Usworth back in the frame?"

"If it's him, he's either incredibly stupid or mind bogglingly arrogant. He knows anything connected with the Chartists must point to him. Where exactly was it found?"

"Under a bush, about fifteen meters from the mineshaft," Jennifer says, "If it's that old, then how..."

"Quite, sergeant. How did a hundred and sixty year old handbill survive so long in the open? It's not possible."

The following morning is not a happy one. As soon as he's held a short meeting with the team, including the all important need to get forensic information on the handbill, Jenner is summoned to the chief superintendent. It's not a meeting he relishes. Since arriving at the East Mercia force he and Charlie Emmins have not enjoyed a positive relationship. Jenner doesn't warm to Emmins' gruff, loud bluntness. He dislikes the lacing of serious discussions with illustrations from his vast fund of stories to amplify his points. Jenner groans inwardly whenever his superior commences with 'I remember a time,' hoping his prodigious memory might suddenly, inexplicably, but permanently fail him. Alas, despite Jenner continually wishing it, Emmins shows no sign of premature senility. His mind, sharp and acerbic, retains its incisive ability to dissect, probe and, when necessary, even wound. For his part, Emmins finds Jenner's pedantic accuracy annoying and detects a thinly concealed disrespect beneath the formal cordiality.

Emmins listens to Jenner's resume of the investigations with growing irritation. Once it's finished he doesn't mince his words.

"Not much bloody progress, is there? We're no further forward on the missing person investigation. Obviously this latest murder is related to Bernard's Weston's disappearance and we're looking for the same person for both. This group of suspects, they're an ill assorted bunch. You're going to have to find the common thread, Jenner and then you've cracked it."

"Quite so, sir, you're absolutely right, but at the moment..."

"Motive, that's the answer. Find that and you're home and dry. Why, I remember a time..."

Jenner switches off, his best plastic smile hiding his swelling anger. He knows what he has to do, why doesn't Emmins let him get on with it!

"Unless of course, you're contemplating lines of enquiry out of sync with normal police work? Unconventional approaches, shall we say?"

The jibe hurts and Jenner responds unthinkingly.

"I rule nothing out in any investigation."

Emmins leans forward menacingly.

"Listen to me, chief inspector. This isn't London. You don't get to run around doing your own thing here. No madcap ideas. You keep strictly within the bounds of bloody common sense, understood?"

"I don't know what you're talking about."

"Yes you bloody well do or do I have to spell it out?"

"Will that be all?"

"Yes, for now."

The handbill hadn't the power of the newspaper. Ettie had no doubt about its age, but it failed to capture the spirit of the past in the same way. She'd felt no transmission to another time. The lab report is due in the morning and Jenner has promised to let her know the results without delay. She considered approaching Matt Usworth, even attempting to borrow the newspaper on some pretext. Would he trust her? She sits in her hotel room concocting plausibly innocuous reasons to take it away, but they become more and more outlandish, unlikely to convince a child let alone a highly suspicious adult.

Eventually, unsettled and impatient, she goes out, driving in the advancing twilight through the surrounding urban perimeter and into the green oasis towards Brinckley. She stops at Sleavnell church, high on the hill, its walls forever whistled by the wind. It's a lonely place, but walking through the churchyard, examining the headstones she gets some respite for her troubled thoughts. Jenner's latest discoveries put Matt back in frame. If Bernard's disappearance and Martin's death are connected, is Matt the common link? The Chartist handbill, found so close to the head of the mineshaft and Martin Sarwell's body points to his involvement. Who else would have access to such a document? Had Martin arranged to meet him and deliberately 'lost' his friend Banning as part of the plan? Did Martin and Matt discuss what each had discovered? Matt and his delving into Chartist activities in the 1840s and Martin's probing into doctor Foxley, Lizzie and the Weston family? Were they drawn together by this common interest in the Westons? Had Martin discovered the same as Bernard Weston?Things go wrong. An argument, a scuffle, Matt doesn't mean to kill Martin and tries to hide the body, dropping the handbill in the process?

Ettie reaches the west end of the church. Here the wind is strongest and she leans against the wall for protection. It's almost dark, but she can still see the sharp outline of the hills and the remains of pit slag heaps. In its twenty year encroachment, nature has enfolded their bulbous intrusion in a green blanket, gradually returning them to the land. Soon, only the curious and the knowledgeable will know there were once pits. Surface buildings, shift changing sirens, humming clank of winding gear and the tramp of miners' boots all long since consigned to a creeping obscurity. The land is longer, deeper and the more powerful past reclaims its own over many centuries.

Darkness, but the twinkling lights of the town across the valley pierce the blackness. What of the people of the land? Does their forceful presence, seared into the very stones and grass by the passion of past struggles live on? In his unearthing of the Chartist wildfire, has Matt unwittingly stoked and strengthened the spirits of his forebears, releasing their latent energy, beckoning the gentle subtlety of the undefeated generations? Or do they remind us not to forget, reinforce our resolve, enticing with the will of the not dead, but only sleeping masses, to carry on the fight? Do they strike out to sway us now? What is the finality they seek in their restless sleep? Is it justice or revenge?

Ettie turns away, returning along the church wall to the south door. Such lightning, potent thoughts frighten her. She can dismiss her imagination, but they are not really expelled. It's only a transient, illusory relief. She knows, she feels. Somebody or something has been getting nearer. There's a presence from the past and though the message is opaque, distorted even, it's been getting stronger and deep down, within, cannot be denied.

The wind chills and she returns to the car, watching the enveloping darkness enclose the churchyard. In the faint moonlight only the needle point of the church tower, set against the scudding thin wisps of low, white cloud, pierce the gloomy horizon. Her thoughts return to Matt. Jenner's researches have revealed a previously lost alternative exit, but it provides no closure. Even if it had been possible for Matt to break through the closed canal spur and escape through old mine workings, how did he know where to look? How long ago was such an exit closed off? Ettie is sure it's well before the 1840s, but Matt's disappearance that night and the apparent impossibility of getting out without being seen raises other possibilities. However and wherever Matt emerged from the tunnel, Jenner's possible explanation is not consistent with what she *felt*. Jennifer was also ambivalent about his canal investigations. Perhaps she'd also been thinking along unconventional lines of enquiry. It may now be time to tell her about her and Jenner's shared background.

She drives back to the hotel. Carved into unnatural slices

by the headlamps, the country has lost its broad, sweeping openness of an hour ago. Now the hedges enclose and inhibit an alien world, from which she longs to escape. Then, rounding a corner she recognises the reservoir, illuminated by a few streetlamps. She ascends the hill to the Mansfield road and the short motorway hop to the hotel. Another corner, fleetingly she glimpses the lights at Elvington House. If she could have seen or heard what was going on she might even have stopped and gone inside.

The old library, at the rear of the house relatively isolated from domestic crises, its thousands of books for long a repository of wisdom, is now the scene of a fierce interchange. Sylvia Darrington-Cressley, her clenched hands resting on the long table, glares venomously at her visitor, who stands idly just inside the door, with one hand gripping a chair at the opposite end. He's wheeled his way into the house with a mixture of guile, flattery and deception, to arrive unannounced in her sanctuary.

"I don't usually see people without an appointment, Usworth," she says, but her abruptness is ineffective.

Matt Usworth doesn't budge and then harangues her mercilessly, dragging up issues she thought long since closed. He's particularly antagonistic on her relationship with Bernard Weston.

"It's none of your damned business!" she rails.

"Unnatural, that's what it was," he shouts.

"Don't allow pathetic jealousy to cloud your already limited judgement."

He laughs raucously, repeating the word 'jealousy' questioningly, almost spitting it out as if it's a persistent fishbone stuck in his mouth.

"We were hardly close," she says, "Bernard supported opening the canal. It's too late to come here now and blame me if you regret your breach with him."

"There was no breach, we were united!"

She waves him aside.

"You're a meddlesome trouble maker, Matt. You always were. It's very juvenile, one day you might grow out of it."

He moves closer, along the table.

"Don't patronise me."

She stands up, her hands still resolutely held on firm fists at the table's edge.

"You come here stirring things up. You're up to something connected with the past, but it won't work."

"I don't know what you're talking about."

"Don't play the innocent. I've figured it out. I know who you are, Matthew Usworth, direct descendant of Samuel Usworth!"

- 7 -

Two more days on the road. Two more days sleeping rough in hedges and fields. Two more days further away from his pursuers. Then a night in a real bed amongst friends. An evening to swap tales of the past and information of the present. A night of respite, but also of reality. Respite from the hard world after failed revolt and the reality of repression. Two days he'd taken to reach Mansfield. Two long, slow, laborious days dodging anyone else on the road, avoiding anywhere that might harbour those looking for him, running away from phantom pursuers. At this rate it will be Christmas before he reaches the heart of Yorkshire.

Even so, he's determined to press on, dodging, avoiding, running. Perhaps this will be his new life, at least for a time, until the blazing fires of repression die down to only smoking embers of suspicion. Then he can move cautiously, but more easily. His friends think otherwise.

"What's thy plans, Sam, where's t'a planning going?"

"North, keep moving north."

Much shaking of heads and firm grimaces.

"Do you have to go north?"

Sam's heart sinks.

"Is there an alternative What choice do I have?"

"Could be the choice between being taken and remaining free."

"What do you advise?"

"There's trouble even in Worksop and Retford, let alone Yorkshire. If thou can go back, at least for a time, it'll be safer."

"I can't go back to Nottingham."

"They're watching everybody further north. There's many already gone south. Best go back, take thy chance."

Taking his chance is what Sam has been desperately trying to avoid. Now he's being advised, with the best of intentions, to open up the lion's mouth and step inside.

That night he doesn't sleep soundly. Despite a good bed, good company and a good meal, the prospect of retracing his steps, however carefully, constantly interrupts his rest, pounding into his mind as he continually reconsiders his options. Go south, but where? Plans are formed and rejected, reformed and amended, only to be rejected again. He'll go further east, pick up the north road and head south to Newark and Grantham, away from the main centres of unrest. But he has no contacts in that direction, no one to turn to in an emergency. The country is unfamiliar. Why worry about that? He's tramped through a dozen unknown counties in normal times without adverse effects. But these are not normal times. He may need to act quickly and decisively. Not knowing the country will mean hesitation, mistakes, vital minutes lost could be disastrous. However unpalatable it may be, going south has to mean going through familiar territory. With this unattractive thought ringing in his mind, he finally gets to sleep.

Early next morning, tired and in low spirits, he starts out, travelling south west rather than the direct southerly road towards Nottingham. His Mansfield friends think it safer. More dodging and avoiding, more listening for distant travellers, more peering into the fuzzy horizon for the first signs of potential enemies. An hour of walking and he's at his most vulnerable, the sun is up and the world is beginning to work. He's lucky. No one seems to go to work along this dismal road. Mid morning he rests behind the hedge. He's getting closer now. Soon, he could be re-entering that other country. Fears of going north replaced by this older, greater fear. How many big halls he'd spoken in over the years, how many big factories with their mighty gates he'd had to pass to rally the people. Big and ugly, dark and daunting, unrelenting in their grimness, yet none of them fill him with the same misgivings as the imminence of coming closer to another big building. Yet he knows of no workhouse along this way and it's the wrong side of Nottingham to that forlorn pile of his childhood.

Yet he cannot shake off his anxiety. Resuming his tramp, he thinks only of big houses and walking back into those fears. Each step brings him closer, but he goes on, tramp, tramp, tramp into a distant, unknown future. He tells himself to keep concentrating on real threats and not give in to unfounded, foolish and unformed imaginings. It works for a time, but with a new, indeterminate pull a vague apprehension returns. He doesn't understand, yet the draw gets stronger. He should resist, but can't. Even if he's pulled against his will, it seems benign. Something, someone watches over him and will look after him.

Ettie has been restless all day. She'd got up ill at ease. Breakfast had been a long and tiresome process. She'd hovered over the toast, continually picking it up and putting it down, playing with her eggs, pushing them around the plate until they were finally uneatable. Then she squashed the tomatoes into an unrecognisable gooey mess. Only coffee, which she'd drunk in Herculean amounts, had been finished.

"Anything more, madam?" the waitress had said sarcastically as she cleared away the detritus

Up in her room, she reads through all her notes and papers, but her concentration continually lapses. She reads a whole page and realises she's not taken it in, having to read it again and even then her understanding is skimpy. She goes down to the hotel's small garden with its long veranda, providing shielding from both the sun and the wind. The sun peeks between the clouds all morning. Its dismal light frequently disappearing altogether as the wind picks up, briefly flicking its chilly fingers along the veranda. Ettie persists for a while, scanning her notes and trying to form some conclusions, but her mind wanders aimlessly, fanning her thoughts into a whirling confusion of trivial and irrelevant images.

Unable to contain her unease or focus her restless energy she gives up on the garden and goes inside. It's midday and she heads for the dining room. In that she finishes it, lunch is more successful than breakfast. She deliberately sits in the far corner by the window, hoping no one will join her. No one does. It may be because other people prefer the centre of the room or wish to be near the bar or because Ettie radiates some rebuffing force. Perhaps her continual staring out the window, examining and re-examining every blade of grass, faded petal and crunched leaf sends a silent message of rejection. Yet no matter how hard she concentrates her mind won't settle. The same waitress clears the table without comment. Ettie goes up and changes. The root of her distress is not from within, but something levering relentlessly from outside. She feels better with her coat and hat on. Before she'd been the gamekeeper without his gun or the poacher without his traps. Now she's ready, prepared, but is she the hunter or the hunted?

"Will you be in for dinner, Miss Rodway?" the receptionist asks.

Ettie turns at the door. With her long back coat hunched over her shoulders and her black hat cocked slightly at an angle, she seems to the young girl a slightly sinister, other worldly figure. Her prolonged stare and magisterial stance only exacerbating the receptionist's discomfort, as if she's said something improper.

"No," Ettie says at last, "I cannot guarantee I shall be back in time."

She drives purposefully, but indeterminately, seeking only the solace of an open road. Yet, with the accuracy of the sleep walker, she's drawn along as resolutely as if each turn and twist has been precisely planned months ahead. At the country park she stops near the entrance and walks towards the canal. The struggle for supremacy between sun and clouds persists. One moment the clouds are ascendant, the suddenly darkened sky enveloping the ground with a pervasive gloom. Then the sun, ever persevering with its rapier flashes finds a chink in the leaden canopy's armour and a piercing glint illuminates the earth, invigorating the greens, browns, reds and yellows in a burst of vigorous, hope filled intensity. This fluctuating fight continues relentlessly, the pendulum of light and darkness endlessly swinging between the two rival forces. For most people it's too much. They gather up their belongings and retreat from the country to the predictable environment of homes, pubs, restaurants and routine conversations around welcoming fires. The sun is supplanted again. Ettie buttons up her coat, but otherwise is as unconcerned by the weather as that which draws her forward. Yet it may be unwise to ignore the messages of the physical world. She must also trust her feelings. Ignoring them can also lead to mistakes.

She reaches the canal, the *Cross Cut*. Does it cut across lives and cross over cuts in time? At the towpath she looks in both directions. There's no one around, but she's not alone. The unseen that draw her here are at their strongest. Momentarily the sun breaks through the heaviness with four piercing shafts of light. Slender, graceful yet immensely strong, they hit the surface of the water, which reflects their brightness with beaming intensity. She cannot look away from this sudden dazzling power, magnetised by the four condensed streaks burning into the water and rippling the air with their brightness. This evanescent moment can't be more than a few seconds, but seems much longer. Time lingers as she's held by the four radiant pinpricks, searing like mighty lances and reflected in sparkling circles of light across the surface of the canal, then bounding against its sides, to send further glaring fingers into the distance.

Then they are gone, the stretched instant of time finally springing back as the cloudy curtain closes once more on the sun. She walks slowly along the canal, the luminous echo still pervading her eyes as she looks across the surface of the water. The four distinct points of light still ignite the water just as the sun's after image is held in the eye minutes after looking away. Now she feels the gathering forces that have been drawing her. Close to the water, their proximate strength intensifies. The four slivers of light, aimed with such exactness must be prescient of deliberate communication, unmistakable signs of four presences.

She feels them. Four distinct messages, desperately trying to make contact, but they speak together in a confused clatter. They have no names, no places. They have not come far if measured in miles...but in time? She opens her mind as she walks, waiting and willing the messages to disentangle so she can understand, but this only increases the clamouring noise in her head. It's as if they all know she's asking them to speak clearly, so all shout the louder to silence each other. It's so difficult to understand as the disparate messages seek to command her attention, but through the cacophony one common feeling transcends. An immense sensation of movement forces through. They are all on the move, but it's not possible to distinguish the pursued from the pursuers.

It's safer to travel by night, but it wearies the soul. Hiding and sleeping out the days in ditches and barns, he'd seen little light. Already Sam is beginning to understand how the miners must feel on the Winter shifts. Rising before dawn and plunging in the rattling cage to be hauled back up the shaft and deposited at the surface after their hot, dark and dusty toil like escaping rats from fire or flood in the depths. Having completed their day's purpose, spewed from the sump of the earth like unwanted effluent, escaping from one blackness to emerge after sunset into another, gulping the cool air like drowning men, surfacing from oblivion to tramp home, exhausted in body and desolate in spirit. No light by day, no light by night, constantly drawn back in the unquenchable thirst for coal.

Forewarned in Mansfield, he'd made no contact in Sutton and, fearful of being seen, had last night skirted around Kirkby. So far, he's been lucky, but knows his luck can't keep up much longer. Eventually, he'll have to break cover, assume a new identity and start earning some money. He tries to convince himself the risks are minimal. After all, tramping shoemakers aren't that rare.

This night he reaches the edge of the detached woodland, part of the old forest. Beside a hedge he hesitates, wondering whether to break through the trees or follow the road west towards Derbyshire. The forest's doubtful covering makes him nervous. At least he has a reason to be on the open road and will see anyone from a good distance. If he keeps close to the verge he can quickly run into the undergrowth. In the woods, if he's found he has no reasonable explanation for being there. But where to hide out during the day? If he stays close to the road he'll encounter other travellers with their dangerous questions. The woods daunt him, packed with concealed perils, but their concentrated symmetry offers greater opportunities to hide. Risks have to be balanced and quickly, for he can't remain long, exposed at the side of the road, while his aching body, drained by the night's slog, cries out for rest. The full moon is high now. While making him more visible to an enemy, it gives the woods a warmer, welcoming aura. The desperate need for rest triumphs.

He slips down the bank and hearing a cart approaching from the west, lunges forward, falling painfully through the hedge, ripping his trousers and snagging his jacket. As he tears himself free, he slips down, grazing his hands on the stones and scratching his face from the overhanging branches. He stays down as the cart gets nearer. Any moment he expects the rumbling to stop, while someone jumps down, followed by ominous footsteps on the road toward him. The rumbling gets louder. He stays down, his head inclined to the side, his eyes incongruously scanning the hedgerow as if he should now be concerned by hedgehogs, rats or fieldmice. The cart proceeds without stopping, its dull rumble, reassuringly softening as it carries away both its load and any potential danger.

He waits patiently for the silence of the night to return, pierced only by the far off hoot of an owl and the rustling of the leaves in the slow whispering breeze through the trees. Only when he's sure he can hear nothing else does he gradually lever himself up, glancing in both directions along the hedge and carefully slinking over to the trees. Within a few steps he feels the enclosing mantle of the woods wrap around him, the trees' interlacing barrier pierced by the glowing moonlight. He trudges on. His feet crunching the twig strewn ground seem to cry stridently, 'He's here, he's here, come and get him!'

He stops and tensely listens. He knows the silence of the woods is illusory. No matter how carefully he moves, again they'll catch his footfalls, throwing them loudly and mockingly in all directions to be avidly picked up by unseen ears and unknowable enemies. Tiredness permeates every sinew as he staggers forward, eager to find the relative safety of some cover to rest and remain unseen for the remainder of the night and into the day. Through the twinkling moon tinged shadows he sees a thick outgrowth of ferns and bushes at the base of three trees, rooted close to each other with twisted roots and entangled branches. They stand like three weird sisters, vainly sprouting in all directions, to rid themselves of the other two, yet in their proximity, eagerly embracing in their entwined strength and defence. He stops again, surveys the ground and sways as a top totters at the end of its spin as he twists around on one leg. After a few seconds of eerie silence, distant calls remind him the woods are never at rest. He's not alone. Birds and badgers, spiders and snails, all are at their work. He kicks the solid vegetation at the base of the trees, hoping only they will hear his dull thuds reverberating into the night. The packed mass of grass, leaves and stalks seems impenetrable, though he can see it's quite hollow within, around the trees' roots. A good hiding place, if only he can get in.

Yet he must rest and he must hide! In his desperation he pulls at the tangled clump, lugging away spindly strands and tearing wildly with handfuls of leaves and root. At first he only succeeds in creating an untidy outer mass, but after some more directed writhing a small hole appears, which he's then able to prise apart sufficiently wide to climb down into the small space. He squeezes down between the undergrowth and the base of the trees. The grass inside is soft and dry. He looks back and is amazed by the smallness of the hole he has just climbed through, but wary of being seen, pulls back the twigs and stalks, weaving them closely with leaves and grass. The hole is soon closed. In this den he can look out in three directions, but will not be easily observed. He can only hope no one comes by with a scent hungry dog.

He makes himself as comfortable as possible. It's cramped, but dry. While he fabricates his shelter it starts to rain. A soft, delicate, almost protective rain, it's too gentle to permeate the hanging tresses of the three trees. Only occasional spots drip noiselessly onto the outside of his hideout. Despite his tiredness, he cannot rest. He scrutinises the view and listens intently, trying to hear beyond the rain and see beyond the immediate trees and bushes, vigilant for any sign of life beyond the normal residents of the woods. The water running down the trunks gathers in small puddles and glistens in the moonlight. It's raining harder now, though he remains snug and dry in his leaf laid nest. Further raindrops splatter into the puddles sending out tiny concentric ripples, only to be supplanted by others. More and more circles of water, an accelerating performance of myriad liquid diagrams, ever beginning, never finishing, always changing. The rain, singing through the trees and the hazy mist rising from the sodden ground, mesmerise as distant thunder accompanies the now expansive downpour. Through the vaporous air the woods take on a shaky opacity and his concentration lapses, only to return as he remembers the time he last sought refuge in the trees, on his tramp out of Nottingham and after the confrontation at the Cross Cut.

"You might impress those foolish hands in Nottingham, Usworth, even scare those employers without backbone, but you won't frighten a Cressley," Jonathon calls, standing away from the canal's edge and blocking Sam's path, "we've never been intimidated by worthless upstarts with big mouths and puny brains!"

"Get out of my way," Sam replies, keen to be on his way in case any prolonged altercation attracts others.

"Just come along quietly with me and you might be given a light sentence."

"On your recommendation, I suppose?"

Jonathon stands back, glancing around him. Sam follows his eyes, anxiously scanning for any confederates.

"I'm surprised you're alone, so early in the morning," Sam taunts, "Makes things more even."

Jonathon turns back to face Sam.

"I need no help to deal with you."

Jonathon adjusts his stand, taking up more of the path, but makes no move forward. Sam thinks quickly. He can't go back. Jonathon would chase him and raise the alarm. He has to get past and make for the country above the canal. If he can get to the woods, there's a chance he can get some territory between him and his pursuers and also make it difficult for them to follow. He's unsure of Jonathon. Is he just a man of strong words or is there more to him? Does he hesitate from strength or weakness? Then Jonathon forces the issue.

"Left to me I'd string up you and all your kind!" he says, though still making no move.

Sam says nothing, wondering if he might step to Jonathon's side and then make a run for the canal tunnel.

"What's the matter, Usworth, you're usually good at making fine speeches to stir up the rabble? Or is it different when you're faced with your betters? Too much to expect when you're confronted with the truth of all your works, just like all thieves and murderers!"

It's sudden and irreversible. The word reverberates in a way Jonathon can never understand.

"There are many kinds of murderers," Sam says quietly.

"Oh yes, you're good at twisting straightforward words into the opposite of what they mean, but you're not peddling your silver tongued lies now. Murder means murder, not a base slander against honest employers going about their lawful business, who should be free from being molested by your kind."

"I only represent honest working men."

"Idle fools who follow your words to carry out the foulest deeds."

Such absurd statements can have dire consequences for many of his comrades. Sam feels the anger bubbling inside him, but tries one final time to contain it.

"You don't know what you're talking about, let me pass."

"Never! The Cressleys never give in."

Sam's had enough. All thoughts of escape, prudence or avoidance are gone.

"The Cresleys!" he shouts, uncaring now whether the whole valley hears his call, "The Cressleys never give in, never admit what they've done and never accept responsibility."

Though not understanding Sam's meaning, this attack on his family is a furious provocation to Jonathon.

"I've more reason than most to condemn the Cressleys," Sam continues, "but I've not allowed my own feelings to interfere with my Chartist work."

"You blame us for your murdering activities!"

Jonathon thrusts forward and raising his arm, aims a blow at Sam's head. Sam steps back, at the same time parrying it away, striking his hand across Jonathon's face. The slap is not hard, but it unbalances him slightly and he staggers a few steps back, steadying himself just before the canal's edge.

"I'm no murderer," Sam says as he stands with clenched fist, his back to the canal bank, glaring at Jonathon, " which is more than can be said for you!"

"Foul mouthed ruffian!" Jonathon shouts.

He leaps across and lams into Sam, who shoves him away. Unable to strike upwards, Jonathon hits him several times in the kidneys. They struggle for some moments, alternately coming together and forcing each other apart, each time exchanging pushes and punches of varying accuracy and effectiveness. They're both severely winded and lurch around, indiscriminately lashing out.

"It's no use pretending. I was there," Sam says as they briefly break apart, "I saw everything, I know what you did. Report me and I'll tell them."

Jonathon catches his breath, replying indignantly between his desperate breathing.

"What...don't know what...you're talking about...threats, lies...more threats and lies...I'll take no more!"

He hurls himself at Sam, battering wildly as he crashes into him. Sam avoids the blows and Jonathon loses his balance again, allowing Sam to land at least one strong thump on his face. Jonathon leans back and returns with a side swipe, knocking Sam back towards the canal. Jonathon follows immediately and they grapple frenziedly, both losing their grip on the slippery edge several times. They wrestle together, unable to land any successful blows, yet unable to force themselves apart, moving around in a weird slow waltz of fury. Several times both of them only manage to keep one foot on the path, the other hovering precariously over the water, before it regains the edge again.

Then Jonathon frees one arm and hammers Sam, violently pushing him nearer the edge. Sam struggles desperately to regain his balance as one leg is suspended over the water while the other sways dangerously closer to the edge. His whole body rocks wildly and he fights to control what seems an inevitable swing into the canal. As his left leg steadies he seizes the air with both hands to pull his other leg clear and inadvertently his right arm catches Jonathon squarely in the side. Jonathon reels back, loses his balance, his body vibrating momentarily and then crashes into the canal, disappearing immediately beneath the surface. Sam rights himself and then waits for Jonathon to reappear. He waits and waits. The water closes around the ripples where Jonathon went down, calms and is still again. Jonathon does not come up.

The ground is still wet from the early morning rain. It may well return tonight. Dark clouds have drifted across the sky all day like professional mourners at an expensive funeral, hovering in the late afternoon as if waiting for payment. Now they gather, fused into a black, threatening monolith. So much water, hanging around like bored youths at a street corner they can't remain immobile much longer. Soon they must disgorge their accumulated liquid ire on the quiescent valley. Ettie has come prepared for all eventualities. A little rain will not deter her. It's quiet now. All the day's visitors, dog walkers and kids have surrendered to the creeping darkness and the ominous heaviness of the sky. She's stopped walking and sits on one of the seats, beside the towpath, close to the tunnel entrance.

Those earlier contacts now seem muffled, like a huddle of noisy children waiting for a teacher to shut up or go away and let them quarrel in peace. Ettie is not their teacher. She must learn from them, though she's glad to be free to think, unconnected, at least temporarily from their divergent, even conflicting messages. Muffled they may be, but they've not gone away. A residual presence remaining as a kind of spectral white noise, cancelling out each others vibrant messages.

Holding her umbrella securely, she looks along the canal and up into the sky. Concentrated water, above her and around her. When the rain comes it will accentuate that power, splattering down onto the canal to puncture and energise its convergent mass. More water, more strength. She's in the right place. Far off, a thunderous grumble reminds her it may not be long before that strength is felt.

She's sure of the time too. Jenner had also been sure, convinced all his suspects had 1840s connections. Their talk left her puzzled. Much of his analysis was based on a great deal of speculation, but his conclusions can't be ignored. Beyond 1842, Matt, Ella, Martin and Denise all had knowledge blocks in subjects they were supposed to be expert. Coincidence, errors of recollection? Emphasis on such flimsily based evidence was out of character. Calling her into the investigation admitted the need to take in extra normal factors. It must have gone against all his gritty feelings and experience. When the explicable can't explain issues, only the inexplicable are left, but has Jenner drawn too much significance from trivial slip ups?

Not entirely convinced when they spoke, her feelings about that year have grown and grown. Yet too much has happened since their last conversation to expect him to follow up everything. Busy investigating Martin Sarwell's murder, he's too immersed in the new enquiry to substantiate any suspicions he may have into the intricacies of Bernard's Weston's disappearance. Perhaps also embarrassed by his too openly expressed airy fairy musings, he's cooled and now avoids the subject. So she's made her own enquiries and the more she's learned, the more convinced she's right about the time.

The canal was closed very suddenly in 1843 amidst local controversy almost as bitter as that surrounding its reopening a hundred and sixty years later. By that time the Crosscut was owned by a larger canal company, which favoured rationalisation to stem falling profits. The official reason was the coming of the railway, making the canal redundant. There was a railway line in 1843, but it was along the next valley. The construction of the line to which the collieries were eventually connected was delayed and was not fully operational until a few years later. In the interim the canal would still have had some justification. Why didn't they wait? There was some disagreement between local landowners and colliery owners, not resolved until the new line made their arguments superfluous. Those keen on closure were either major shareholders, anxious to cut their losses or those able to influence them.

The actual closure was swift and decisive. The tunnel entrances were bricked up without delay, so there must have been a similarly rapid end to the underground spur that connected the canal to the mines, assuming by that time it was still in operation. The survival of any alternative exit to present times is therefore highly unlikely. This sudden activity in 1843 convinces Ettie the disturbances she feels surrounding the canal must have taken place in the year before, 1842, which Jenner regarded as the turning point in the recollections of his suspects. She has no doubts about those disturbances. The presences are too forceful as is their message of movement.

The distant rumbling thunder she'd heard earlier becomes an immediate rolling, heralding the onset of the all day threatened rain. The rolling persists, accompanied by broad panels of sheet lightning that light up the horizon in every direction. Enormous unseen boulders with their long, low continuous boom roll like enormous balls in a universal pin ball machine, obstinately bouncing around the sky, trying to find the right points and hit the heavenly jackpot. Yet the only prize is the accelerating rain, now pummelling her umbrella and running in gushing streams from its edges, dancing on the towpath and wetting her ankles. It's not just the need for shelter that drives her into the western entrance to the tunnel. She's drawn to its heart, an undiscovered banqueting hall, replete with concealed dishes that must be savoured despite all risks of poisoning.

The singing rain sends Sam to sleep just before dawn. His hideout proves more effective than he'd hoped. If anyone ventures through its glade they don't spy him and he remains undisturbed until waking in the late afternoon. He starts suddenly, his eyes filled by the bright sunlight between the cracks in the undergrowth. He shifts slowly, aching now from the hard ground. He squints into the woodland, where a shimmering heat haze obscures his view. As his eyes adjust and he finds a better position to stretch his cramped limbs, he's reassured by the stillness, hearing only the usual woodland sounds, laced by the soft dripping from the leaves.

He sits and listens, charily waiting for the quietness to be broken by the sounds of people, but no one comes. The sun sinks lower and he's tempted to venture out, but despite the discomfort of lying so long in a hard, constricted space, he waits a little longer for the twilight to screen his movements. A long, dark sleeve of cloud shrouds the sun, presaging further rain. His confidence returns and slowly, deliberately, watchfully, he emerges from his covert. He opens up his exit with care and precision, replacing each twig, leaf and fern with the same delicate nicety, anxious not to disclose his past presence by a new and obvious disturbance to the vegetation. An abandoned hideout is almost as dangerous as an inhabited one, betraying recent movement and providing a pursuer with the beginning of a new trail to follow.

Once sure he's alone, he walks quickly, glancing upwards to see if the brooding sky is likely to unleash the threatened rain, but the clouds hold back, content to send a chilling breeze across the ground, quelling the animals and birds into an edgy silence. The western sun, obscured into an overcast dullness and frequently blotted out altogether, gives no guidance or direction. He could easily lose himself, tramping through a wide disorientated circle. Yet he feels no sense of being adrift. There's no melding of the trees into a bewildering throng and individually they seem to guard, not confuse his way. He's sure he'd know if the same ones reappeared. Soon he'll emerge from the wooded skirt into open country, but for now he's enclosed in its dense veil, neither protective nor menacing. The trees, stout, impassive, neutral wooden mirrors reflect his thoughts without accusation or challenge. Yet in their bouncing back and forth those mirrors force him to remember and relive three years before.

It was a day not like today. Travelling north, away from the main road, he was close to the city, but the country beckoned and he soon left the houses and all traces of people behind.

Walking between two low sandstone hills, warmly glistening in the late sultry Summer, his other cares were set aside. The fields, the trees, even the grass and the insects, intent on their own priorities untroubled by the pathetic conflicts of human beings, made him feel small. The late afternoon sun was still hot and he felt its uncomfortable radiance through his shirt. Temporarily unconcerned by recent events, his mind emptied as the natural world offered a short, distilled interlude of peace. Communing only with his immediate surroundings, he wound down into such a mellow, untroubled tranquillity, that even mundane concentration lapsed and his foot lodged in a rabbit hole!

He turned painfully to rub his aching ankle. Not badly injured, but slightly shocked, he took advantage of his sprawling position to lie back in the warmth for a few moments. He watched the clouds, scudding cheekily towards the sun and felt a light, cool breeze above his head. The flitting clouds, like unruly urchins tripping around an old man in the street, reached the sun and covered it with their downy billows. The breeze picked up and he shivered slightly. The sky dulled, he heard footsteps through the ground. Someone approached. One, two people. They were after him. How could he run with the damned ankle? They got nearer, then stopped. At first he froze and then lifted up on one elbow to spy through the grass. He saw two figures at the far side of the field. The heat of the day, the overlaid sun, the distance and his own incapacity making him see through an apparent dim, glimmering haze. He squinted for a better view, lifting up on his other elbow, though ready to drop down immediately if they should look towards him.

Two men, around the same height, were arguing. As one turned he stared across towards Sam, who ducked instinctively, scraping both elbows as he dropped down. Yet in that moment, the gawking face was familiar. He knew it. He'd seen it before. As he crouched fearfully, hoping he'd not been seen, he seared his memory to recall it. Then he remembered. He heaved up a little, just enough to peek slightly. They'd stopped arguing. One man had moved forward and looked into the distance, away from Sam and with his back to the other man. He seemed engrossed, gaping into the depression between the hills. He waved an arm, perhaps to amplify something he was saying. The other approached from behind and held something in his hand. It was small. Now Sam knew. He lifted himself a little further, losing all fear of being seen. He watched, immobile and horrified. The scene, played out lethargically yet, losing none of its drama by its slowness, was awfully predictable. The unbelievably languid pace should have given him time to intervene. If he too was a player surely he could jump up, cry out and warn, but the slowness was total and got slower. Sam too was caught in the lumbering vice and could do nothing to avert the unavoidable tragedy. He could only watch, frightened, frustrated, frenzied.

The hand was raised. As it came down the man turned, but he was too late and too delayed. Like Sam he conformed to his part in the play. Sam had to watch and he...the blow was struck. Even at that distance, Sam heard the deep, dull thud. It could have been a large stone, well lobbed into a deep river, hitting the surface squarely and sinking to the bottom, quickly, smoothly, without a ripple. The man fell.

In the long, empty moment that followed there was no question of intervention or exclamation or even escape. There was only stillness and an absorbing, enveloping, bitter emptiness. A moment as long, if not longer than that awful, staggering immobility that petrified Sam into his desperate, yet engaged inactivity. Now that face turned again, but Sam held it and they stared towards each other in another instant that seemed without a time described boundary. The features, hazy and shimmering were unmistakable. It had to be Jonathon. The moment, perhaps really only less than a second, passed and Sam was released. As normal time sprung him from the trap, he was slung back to the real world, all his troubles returning to pound with tremendous and uncontrollable energy. The figure turned away. He'd not seen Sam, spying through the grass from his lowly perch. Helplessness pervaded Sam and now he could only think of flight.

Ettie hovers just inside the tunnel entrance for a few moments, watching the rain. It hammers the ground, leaping up to pirouette briefly before dropping down into the constantly forming pools and rivulets, running inexorably over the edge in myriad tiny waterfalls, before slipping beneath the canal's watery blanket. The concentrated ballet with its constant thrumming accompaniment grips her briefly, but cannot hold her long, for the real business must lie within. With her folded umbrella in one hand and the torch in the other, she ventures along the wall. Within only a few steps the sound of the rain dulls, replaced by the silent stealing dampness of the walls.

Warily, she walks further until all vestiges of the storm are lost except for vague splintered relics of brightness from the lightning. She continues and then stops. Only the dull echo of her breathing or the occasional soft slurp of the water at the edge disturbs the quiet. Yet all is not quiet in her mind. Three of the presences remain muted, but the whispering of the fourth, no longer cloaked in the babbling of the others and invigorated by the water acting as a conduit of time, chatters on.

Way, way back, along the tunnel and across the valley, she hears the long distance thunder, reduced to a fraction of its former impact. Out and away, a celestial domestic drama draws to its end as a heavenly housewife shakes her rugs and grandfather emits a resurgent smoker's cough across the sky. A faraway, smothered reminder of the world beyond the whirling, time confounded canal.

"La...la...laz..."

A voice, indistinct, but insistent tries to break through. A woman.

"Lu...le...luz..."

Ettie concentrates, but the chattering is not clear.

"Speak, speak," she whispers.

"Li...li...liz..."

It fades.

"Speak, damn you, speak!" Ettie shouts in her frustration.

The voice dies down, though Ettie still hears its muted insistent whispering. She must not give up. Someone is desperate to communicate and she must remain vigilant to receive the message. She walks on, away from the storm and into the darkness, stopping intermittently to listen in case her elusive communicator breaks through.

They are after him, just as they were after him three years ago. Sure he'd not been seen, but desperate not to be around when the body was found, he'd run in wild, unthinking panic, away from the field, away from discovery and away from questions. If he'd stayed would they have believed him? If he'd reported Jonathon then, would there have been no Jonathon three days ago? Would he now have no reason to run again? His life would have been so different, but not better. *They* would not have believed him. *They* would have believed Jonathon. He would have sworn he saw Sam wield the fatal blow. Roles reversed, one word against the other. No doubt who would be believed. *They* would have swung him high. Three days ago there would have been Jonathon, but there would be no Sam.

Now he's back, three years after witnessing Jonathon destroying another and three days after he destroyed Jonathon. Then he'd escaped. Three years ago he'd avoided the big houses, especially the territory of Jonathon, Elvington House. Now, after three days, he's returned, slinking sadly, stupidly into that territory, having exhausted himself in a wide, futile circle of pointless and dangerous wandering. The trees, high, shielding and protective are gone, long left behind in his aimless, unintended ramble towards this, the last place he would wish to be. Yet, though pursued, he's also drawn. He looks up at the rising moon, hoisted now by invisible, yet strong threads into the night sky. No unseen boot kicks it upward. No hostile host hurls it heavenward like an unwelcome guest flung into the street. He too feels no thrusting hand, shoving him recklessly into a nebulous future. He does not want to be here, yet cannot help himself.

Yet was the blow fatal? No newspaper reported the murder. Who then was the mysterious stranger and what was he doing with Jonathon in such a lonely place? No report could mean no one missing, no murder, no need to run away, but how could Sam know that at the time?

The rain comes on again just as he reaches the canal. Water above and water below. He feels enclosed, the solid meat within a watery sandwich, confined as if the water were as firm as a wall, dammed and secured within its liquefied ramparts. Yet the fluid film, enfolding in its totality doesn't threaten, but directs and channels as a conduit in which all sense of the present is lost. The *Cross Cut*. Well named, for it connects times as well as places, but *whose* times and for what purpose? He reaches the edge of the eastern end of the tunnel and just inside pauses to tip his hat and splatter the collected rainwater onto the path. Inside, he shakes it vigorously and then walks on into the dimness.

The further he paces deeper into the tunnel, the stronger he senses progression not only into the constricted space, but also in time itself. Suddenly, stabbingly, he's fearful as if not really in this place at all, but somewhere else, imagining or even looking from outside as through a window on some unreal, compacted, unconnected scene. Alarmed, he turns to make sure he really is in the same place. The tunnel entrance, though further, fainter and now just a narrowing gap of light, is still there.

He goes on, only slightly reassured. The sparse light is almost gone. Yet, intrepid or reckless, he continues, his hands stretching to the wall and his feet prodding and nudging the path with mechanical, undisputed confidence. As he loses all sense of place, so he loses any sense of time passing. Just as he may have travelled a few meters or a few miles, he may also have been here a minute, a day, a month.

His hand abruptly grasps the air. The wall is gone. In the darkness, he can see nothing and gropes into the emptiness, thinking he may as before have found another small inlet, but after several steps he stops, having still not found the comforting moistness of brick and mortar. This nothingness frightens him and the confidence of walking in the darkness evaporates. He stops and listens. The gentle lapping of the water exacerbates his fear. He could stumble at the next step and be unable to find the edge to get out. Even if he finds it, what if it's so slippery he slithers back, flounders in the blackness and unable to raise himself submerges with the same finality as Jonathon? A grim, rough equality perhaps.

He waits, listening. The water is at his left. He edges to the right, slinking nervously, cautiously, desperately. His feet creep in micro steps, which seem as giant, dangerous strides in the emptiness, the tiniest distances magnified into dread expansive chasms. Then his head touches something solid. He shivers in his ignorance, his mind instantly filled with gruesome images of horrific perils. Gingerly he stretches his hand. Cold, wet, slithery, he recoils, then puts out a brave finger. Skating his fingertip along the surface, he slowly picks out the hard, yet slimy texture. He puts out his hand again, stretching his palm onto the cold surface. Wall. Relieved, he walks on. He's turned a right angle. There's still a path and the sound of the water doesn't recede. This must therefore be a spur of the main canal, an underground connection heading north.

He stops. He must have covered some twenty meters and wonders how far this extension goes. It's very quiet, the sound of his breathing and the low swish of the water, both expanding in the tunnel's hollowness. The rain, the moon, the trees could be a thousand miles away. Then he hears a distant thudding, slight, subdued, heavy, not the booming, rolling, deliberative reverberation of thunder, but sharper, repetitive, almost rhythmic. He listens again. The sound increases, the thudding intensifies, now coupled with a piercing metallic scrape, accompanied by a muffled, continuous sigh like a huge subterranean beast breathing heavily in its sleep.

It must be the mine. Nothing else, deep within the earth can expand and transmit such sounds. But how? An underground connection, a quick cheap passage to get the coal through the hill and away. He'd heard of such things, but never knew there was one here. How often is it used? Can he expect a coal barge to sidle by? The noise from the mine gets louder as if the miners in their vigour have turned on the canal itself and now advance towards him. Louder, louder until it seems a pick will burst upon him, striking him down in a shower of coal and stone, ramming him into the canal or trampling him down as they move on relentlessly. Hammer, thud, strike, scrape, ploughing ever further, deeper, then again, hammer, thud, strike, scrape...he puts his hands over his ears and staggers against the wall, his legs buckling under the pressure. He sinks down the wall until he crouches with his head almost buried in his knees.

There he remains. Prone and vulnerable, eyes tight shut, waiting hopelessly for the onslaught. The jingled, jangled row rushes onward, ready to engulf and overwhelm him. Hammering, thudding, striking, scraping...lapping, slurping, swishing. Water! He can hear the water! All the other cracking, crumbling, crashing diminish and then subside rapidly. He opens his eyes and lowers his hands from his ears. Leaning one hand against the wall, he lifts himself up again, the quiet once more only interrupted by the water and his breathing.

He stands, shivering slightly, suddenly overcome by the chill of the tunnel. Straining his ears to catch the slightest sound, he hears nothing more. Now, no prospect of blackened miners bursting over him, their silence as complete as had been the insistent blows of their imminent appearance. The proximity of the mine brought the miners, incessantly wrenching aside the narrow and confined tunnel, extracting forces that threatened to cleave it open with their hewing and hacking. They'd pulled at him just as the water had pulled him. Now, all has gone and he senses a new danger though he hears and sees nothing. What was faced with opening may now be threatened with closure.

The walls and the roof of the tunnel implode and descend. Only the water reassures. A slither of light from the main tunnel and reflected on the surface pierces the darkness. He turns as the new fear grips him. They are closing! He will be crushed as they contract around him! Only the water and the light offer any escape. He can see the water gently rippling back towards the main tunnel and the light. That is the way.

It's his only escape. He walks faster. Then in the dimness and the slipperiness he starts to run, following the directing and pulling water, towards the light, away from that which closes. He has to escape! He has to get through!

Ettie has been walking quickly for several minutes, driven on further into the tunnel. She'd not checked the torch batteries before starting out and its light had suddenly dimmed after she'd gone twenty meters. She must now be some two hundred meters from the western entrance. Yet there remains a pale splinter of light, dully sparkling on the surface of the water, its bleak, tapering glow enough to prevent her from losing her way and slipping into the canal or bumping into the wall. Even so, it seems oddly persistent. Any natural light should have faded out long before. She looks back to detect its source, but sees only the light, dim, but relentlessly propelled along the shaft of the tunnel. Common sense and prudence dictate a careful retreat and return to the hotel, but other powerful instincts impel her to go on. Understanding is not always enough. Avoiding what cannot be explained makes no progress. Deeper, intuitive senses tell her to ignore the perils.

Still she feels four distinct presences and the further she enters the tunnel the nearer those feelings become. Four entities from the past, but only one voice. La or Lu or Li or whatever she's called remains the only one to speak or at least make some sort of utterance. If it's speech, so far it lacks words, but Ettie persists, believing the message will eventually become clear. Yet she knows the others are also here. On the periphery, their silence, except for sporadic incoherent interventions, remind her they remain and will not easily give way to 'L.' All are on the move, but from where and to how far?

"Li...I say...Li...listen...important."

Ettie stops, waiting, hoping. The voice is definite and loud, but most of the words remain indistinct. They will come, if she's patient. Then, just as she's confident of a breakthrough the babble begins again and the fierce cacophony of all four blast her mind.

"Got to get away…cannot tolerate this…got to take action… guilty … run …will tell…someday…get them…get away."

Four separate voices assail her mind, none of them making any sense. Convinced that 'L' is the best contact, she tries to pick out her sound, but it's lost in the muddled prattle!

Throughout it all Ettie keeps walking, resolutely, deliberately, without doubting her unknown destination, guided by the diminishing, but never extinguished strange light. All the time her left hand skirts the wall and she starts as the brickwork suddenly indents. She stops. Immediately the voices are gone. She examines the indented wall, which is about ten centimeters further from the canal's edge. This continues for about the same distance as the canal's width. It must be a bricked up section and the path too is of a different texture as if it's been built at a later date. She remembers Jenner's own investigations and the underground branch of the canal, which connected with one of the mines. This could be the original junction, long ago closed and sealed off.

As she reaches the end of the construction, where the wall resumes its original shape, a sudden coldness passes over her and that pervading pulling power, which has sustained her on this weird perilous walk is gone. No longer pulled, she feels an immense surge of energy, coming as if from that bricked over entrance like the rush of air, propelled forward in advance of an underground train as it enters a station. Yet there's no movement of air or of any other physical force, but the impact is overwhelming and immediate. Instinctively, she turns away and looks back the way she's come. The light, her uncanny guide is gone! The tunnel is plunged into impenetrable blackness. She stands motionless and petrified, afraid to move forward and afraid to move back, but she must turn and face that closed off entrance. She sees nothing, hears nothing, but feels the terror of someone about to be closed up forever. Closed, bricked up, desperate to escape! Now she knows something beyond that sudden outpouring of energy transcends the wall. Someone is coming through!

- 8 -

The past should be ended, secured, ceased. Its performance has finished, the theatre closed, the players departed, the play forgotten. But it won't lie down. It keeps standing up, dragging out dead players and making them recite their old lines. The first time threatening, now returning with menace.

They've almost reached the last item on the agenda. Sometimes these meetings of the 'Moral Power' Trust can seem interminable and Sylvia hasn't been concentrating properly for the last fifteen minutes. She'd wanted to curtail discussion on the last item – a new publicity initiative – but James Bannerman, an important and generous benefactor wanted to peruse the proposals in detail and she didn't want to upset him. Her mind has been wandering more than usually today. It could be the heat, the soporific effect of the good lunch or the droning monotone of the treasurer's delivery of his report, but it was really none of these things. David Underwood, her young assistant, scribbling avidly at her side, had noticed, several times politely nudging her when she'd missed some indeterminate discussion needing the chairman's intervention. Each time, he'd woken her from a persistent reverie. Such prodding is usually unnecessary. She's an expeditious chairman, moving business forward with a ruthless efficiency. Today, her skills seem to have been deposited outside on the ante room table with the empty coffee cups and wine glasses.

"We still need to pursue the dietary aspect of our campaign."

David nudges Sylvia. The discussion has been proceeding for several minutes and he suspects she's not been paying attention. Her concentration revives, her eyes focusing on the speaker instead of drifting vacuously to the opposite wall. His reminder is timely.

"I recall the meeting before last, chairman, when you undertook to pursue this matter yourself? Are you yet in a position to report?"

Sylvia hesitates. Last meeting but one? She wracks her brains, but her memory fails her.

"Remind me again," she says with a smile of liquid insincerity.

Dryly he intones, displaying his remarkable memory for the unnecessary detail of the empty discussion of that previous meeting. It gives her time to think. Meeting before last, was that the meeting that...? God, can't remember! Then, nervously realising the old connection no longer applies, whatever she *may* have said at that meeting, her mind races for an appropriately bland answer, which won't appear evasive.

"I've been awaiting responses from several sources," she says with a broad, empty smile, "you're right to raise it, I need to follow them up."

"Indeed, I would like to propose that by the next meeting..."

"I'm sorry to interrupt, chairman, but the next item is very important and we'll shortly be running out of time."

"Thank you, David," she says, casting him a grateful glance.

Twenty minutes later the meeting ends. A few people linger, fortunately not including the member with the particular interest in dietary issues. David confirms various actions arising, but makes no mention of the penultimate item.

"I noted your prompt intervention, " she says.

"I hope you didn't mind, I only thought..."

"It was much appreciated, you have nothing to apologise for..."

She turns as if about to say more, but then breaks off. He takes it as a favourable sign to be bolder, but begins cautiously.

"Mrs. Darrington – Cressley, please don't take this as a criticism (her eyes, curiously incisive, arrest him, but are unthreatening) just lately I've noticed you've not been..."

"...properly conducting the meetings!"

"No! No, certainly not. I would never say anything like that!"

"But I might," she says with a depressed sigh, "What *would* you say?"

He breathes deeply and sonorously before replying, perhaps reconsidering the wisdom of his boldness as she fastens her piercing eyes on him again.

"You've seemed self absorbed at times, as if something was on your mind. I may be wrong, of course, perhaps I shouldn't make such assumptions."

He shuffles his papers nervously, ready to collect them up and leave.

"It's alright," she says reassuringly, "Assuming you're right, what do you propose I should do?"

Familiar with her usual acerbity, the question could be a put down rejoinder, but her tone lacks sarcasm and seems genuine. Nevertheless he hesitates, but the rapier eyes demand an answer and not doing so may be more hazardous than giving the wrong one.

"A holiday perhaps?" he says tentatively.

She grunts wordlessly. He returns to the important business of gathering up his papers.

"The problem with holidays," she says as he reaches the door, "is leaving other people in charge."

He smiles politely and then leaves, having probably exhausted his ration of forward speaking for some time.

She returns home quickly, giving little further thought to David's suggestion. He means well, but it's utterly impractical. As for her waning concentration at meetings, that's something she'll have to rectify quickly. Better to act on David's observation than wait for others to come to the same conclusion. For now, she pushes out all thought of Matt Usworth, though she knows she must soon confront both him and what he represents. He'd stormed out immediately after her accusation. Silence is guilt. He could be dangerous.

Sarah greets her at the door even though Sylvia has driven slowly up the drive and parked the car quietly. She must have been watching for her. Sarah takes her coat and then steps back, approvingly.

"I must say madam, I do admire that trouser suit, it's very fetching."

Sylvia eyes her doubtfully.

"If you don't mind me saying so," Sarah adds quickly.

Sylvia looks at herself in the long hall mirror. The stylish brown outfit does suit her well. She brushes some hairs from her shoulder. But it's not new and she always wears it to Trust meetings. Sarah has seen it many times. Why does she choose to compliment her now?

"Something you need to tell me, Sarah?"

Sarah steps back slightly, concentrating her eyes nervously over Sylvia's shoulder.

"You have a visitor, madam."

Sarah has shown Jenner into the library and given him some tea. He sits with his legs crossed at his ankles, but otherwise upright and rigid, as if wanting be in a suitably appropriate position if anyone comes in. It's not his posture, but his eyes that show the disdain for his surroundings. He rises as Sylvia enters.

"Back again, chief inspector, you must be developing an interest in country houses," she says sarcastically.

"Quite so, madam," he says gruffly, ignoring her remark.

He resumes his seat by the desk as she sits down, forced to take the chair by the window. He might even have planned it this way, taking her chair in her favourite room, her inner sanctum. He might even have insisted on coming in here.

"Making any progress with your investigation?" she says pointedly, her eyes staring accusingly.

"My enquiries have now widened as you may know."

"You're surely not suggesting this latest unfortunate business with Martin Sarwell is in any way connected with the disappearance of Bernard Weston?"

"Quite so, madam. I'm not *suggesting* anything. I keep an open mind."

"Well, as for Martin Sarwell, I hardly knew the man. The only time..."

"I've not come to talk about Martin Sarwell, though you obviously feel the need to mention him."

"I merely meant..." she splutters.

"Perhaps we could come back to him later. For the moment, I'd like to go back to your relationship with Bernard Weston."

"Relationship? What are you implying?"

He smiles.

"I imply nothing. I'd just like you to tell me more about the basis of your...association."

"We've been over all this before. As I said then..."

"Quite, but I don't think you were being entirely...*fulsome* in your answers."

"I've told you all about our links with respect to the canal."

"But what about your personal relationship with Bernard Weston?"

The hesitation is momentary, the intake of breath almost inaudible and she responds quickly and vehemently, but it's enough to confirm Jenner's suspicions.

"I had no *personal* relationship with Bernard Weston!"

"Oh I think you did," he says firmly.

Their eyes engage in a lock, which would be worthy of champion wrestlers.

"In fact, I have information indicating that..."

Jenner's telephone rings.

"Yes, it is...this morning ...where is this ...I see...yes...no... I'll be there immediately."

He puts the phone away.

"I'm afraid I must go," he says, "we will have to resume this conversation later. Something has come up which I must attend to without delay."

He leaves. Sylvia remains silent, profoundly angry, but also relieved.

Is it 'L'? Is 'L' Ella Weston's Lizzie? Or in these last few moments is it one of the other three flinging itself forward, rushing through and elbowing her aside? With its passing comes the darkness, leaving her perilously alone and unprotected. Ettie hadn't realised the mysterious light had been part of that opening, part of the process of connection and once completed, disappearing to leave her stranded. With its extinction comes the closing, which means not only her being cut off from the light, but the impossibility of whatever has passed through from easily returning

The first moments of blackness are filled with indeterminate, unfathomable noise with no obvious character or origin. A discordant, jangled intensity without respite or break between its ceaseless din. A bright, brilliant commotion, whitening out the darkness as a dying candle displaces the shadowy gloom of a room. Then it's gone, as rapidly replaced by a yawning awesome silence as the speed of its appearance. She stands as still as the stillness surrounding her, petrified into fearful immobility, unable to penetrate the absolute blackness. The sounds held within the echoing walls and immersed in the water return, slowly, painfully, misleadingly by size and distance.

She waits and wonders, gradually feeling her eyes adjust to the darkness, hoping all her other senses might miraculously compensate for the sudden and absolute blindness. In the confusion of the onrush of energy and the deafening roar of its escape, she swirls around and loses all sense of wall and canal. Left, right, forward, back, she could be in the centre of a whirlpool for all they mean. She no longer has the umbrella, dropped into the canal in the confusion. She listens desperately for the slightest indicator, fearful the presence might return to again swing her around senselessly. By some slight waft of the enclosed air, the stagnant water, slowly, chillingly, agonisingly releases a faint, short slurp. In confined spaces such scant sounds can bounce around and confuse the ear. Unsure, she listens again for another signal.

The seconds pass excruciatingly, the wearying delay turning them into hours. Then, again, a longer, louder splatter. Now she's sure and puts out her arm in the opposite direction to locate the wall. Nothing. Empty, cool, a frightening void. She must be very close to the canal's edge. She scrapes one foot a tiny amount and then, hoping she's not misread the signs that will send her plunging into the water, moves the other with even greater trepidation. Firm ground, if the slithery, deceptive fluidity of the path can be called hard. She feels the small indentations in the stone with her feet and tentatively puts out her hand again. She touches the wall and sighs deeply with relief.

Now knowing where to walk to avoid falling into the canal, the only other issue remaining is which way to go. She waits again, straining her eyes to catch any snatch of light that might guide her towards the entrance. Nothing; but in the intervening minutes since first she twisted and twirled in the wake of the escaping force, her dual senses of smell and touch have heeded her anguished hope and sent a pointer. From behind she feels the gentlest, shortest, wisp of air and with it the slightest tang of freshly rain soaked grass. She creeps round to face it, anxious not to lose her vantage by the side of the wall and then, with care heavy steps budges jerkily forward. A few wary paces and another subtle waft of crisp, damp air reassures her. Keeping a cautious hand on the wall, she goes on, with firmer, longer strides.

Edgily she gets back along the path until narrowly, dimly some light returns and with faltering steps gradually emerges towards the moonlit open country night. Expelled like some latter-day Jonah from a brick encased whale, she gets nearer to the tunnel mouth. It should mean release, but she feels a closing, not of a door or the narrowing of a track, but a final, unalterable closure without prospect of return. All her physical senses tell her it isn't so, but all her extra psychical ones tell her the walls and roof are imploding. Whatever allowed that presence to come through is no longer open and the process of closing has been completed.

In her stumbling retreat she gradually pierces the tunnel's impenetrable blackness, but her mind is consumed by an absorbing oppression. No real demons can ever rival those of the imagination and in her panicky retreat and helplessness Ettie's mind constructs fierce and harrowing ones. The old gods, so long neglected, resurrect their horrors and conjoin with modern mechanised terrors to create new and irresistible nightmares. Winged monsters peck and pinch her from behind while huge ogres bar her way with their enormous gaping mouths set to consume her in seconds. If she trips and falls, tiny, squawking, millions of reptilian creatures lay ready to consume her.

Yet the most horrid of these animal constructions can't compare with the human fiends she imagines. All the enemies she'd made in the past, all those misguided people who'd not understood the intricate subtleties of time and foolishly tried to bend it to their will, unite now in a malignant conspiracy to hammer and grind her down. They whisper virulently from the waters below, shout vociferously from the walls at her side and drone viciously from the roof, all to drown her in an incessant flow of vengeful words and venomous phrases. The condensed water seems to flow from the roof in foul drips as if they spit their foulness on her.

She arrives at the hotel in the early hours, utterly exhausted, filled with foreboding, fuelling a continuous stream of dire thoughts that make sleep impossible. The more she tells herself rest is the best cure for anxiety, the more it eludes her. All the perturbations line up like a reverential line of loyal servants, insistent on performing their duties even after they've been dismissed. They refuse to be sent away, waiting patiently for their turn. After delivering their unwelcome messages, they return to the back of the stoic line, shuffling forward again to continue the harrowing performance, the recurrent and disturbing images marching on towards dawn. Only the rising of the sun, with the inconclusive verdicts of the morning can end it.

She feels like the negligent prison guard falling down on his duties, allowing an important, perhaps dangerous prisoner to escape. No amount of encouragement by his colleagues and reassurance from his superiors will ever take away the humiliation and self directed anger. How could she have missed the signs? She's been used and the shame will take some time to heal. Instinctively following her intuitions she'd blundered blindly into the tunnel without recognising the contrary impressions telling her, that like the water of the canal, she too could be the conduit, the unwitting channel through which an unknowable force might travel unchallenged. She should have known how ill equipped she was in that short, sharp instant to resist, adjust or reshape the restless, desperate energy sweeping through the opening that connected with the past.

As the images persist throughout the night, she gets up, paces around, makes tea and sits by the window, staring over the moonlit hotel car park and the rolling land beyond. The canal, with its submerged encased secrets, is in that country yet seems so far away. Having served its purpose it may no longer be a danger, but she's unsure how she'll react when the fallout from the trauma of getting back has been finally subsumed. In the coldness of the morning she must give it more rational consideration.

She'd felt at least one, possibly more of the four presences, but they are no longer detached in expansive time. The uncanny drawn out closeness is gone. Now she knows he, she, they are near, no longer separated by a tenuous void. The 1840s relation is definite. While her feelings are disjointed, confused, she's convinced of that connection. All her previous sensations and discussions with Jenner return – Ella's 'Lizzie', Sam Usworth and the mysterious Dr. Foxley, the abiding interest of the unfortunate Martin Sarwell, and a fourth, all from that same timeframe of the 1840s. Whatever else she may *not* know, of that she's sure. No time to lose, she skips breakfast and heads into town to see Jenner at the police station.

The city traffic is heavy, but its congealed metallic mass keeps moving and she crosses the river without incident at the usual bottlenecks. The journey is just long enough for her to run over in her mind what she'll say. He'll hide his concern for her welfare, say she should 'coordinate activities' with him, grumble because she's gone off at night on her own and remind her of the 'nest of vipers' surrounding the case. He'll want to know how she interprets her foreboding. Who *exactly* has come through and, more importantly, with *whom* does it relate in the present time? How can she be specific? His policeman's mind will get frustrated with any vagueness. Yet he won't dismiss anything out of hand. Whatever the consequences, good or ill, for his career, their shared experiences preclude that.

She parks across the road, having checked the yellow line gives her half an hour, hovering at the kerb, watching the traffic for an opening. Maybe it would be better to go back to the hotel or return to the canal? Drive around town? Anything to stimulate her thoughts and perceptions, formulate some rational explanation, put forward a working hypothesis to satisfy the enquiring mind of the professional investigator, get in touch with clearer vibrations. No point going in with vague feelings. Better to get it all sorted out in her mind first. The road clears. She hesitates, but delay may be a mistake. Better share what she has than leave emotions bottled up only to crack or explode disastrously later. Anyway, two minds are always better than one. Her mind's made up. She crosses over.

"Chief inspector Jenner?" the receptionist says, glancing down at something on the desk, "is out."

"Will he be long?" Ettie says.

The receptionist turns to an officer behind her.

"Hard to say," he says, "serious incident, could be some time."

Jenner drives west through the northern suburbs. He's unsure, but knows there's a direct route if he takes the correct exit from the large roundabout where the main road meets the motorway. Four thirty and heavy traffic. The swirling four lane circulation always confuses him and several times he takes the wrong road, heading into one of the bypassed villages or joining the long procession of hospital visitors. Anxious not to make a wrong turn and avoid those coming off or onto the motorway, he makes a third complete navigation of the roundabout, bobbing under the motorway six times, before finally deciding which road to take. Three times a third of a mile. A whole wasted mile of time and fuel. These concrete and tarmac scrapings scar the landscape and here's me adding to the wholesale desecration. He passes a new industrial estate, developed on the site of an old colliery. There's no sign of its former use. Maybe a good thing, he wonders, but skirting the faceless factory units, he isn't so sure. It's close to the city centre. How far did the coal workings reach? Jennifer said there was another mine even closer to the town, jammed between the old cigarette factory and closed lace mills. Who knows what lies beneath? He reaches another, smaller roundabout and briefly hesitates. He has to find a level crossing. It might have been better if they'd sent someone. No, he won't be beaten. He takes the road downhill, turns a sharp corner and to his relief sees the level crossing ahead. Soon be there.

Maybe now he can make some headway and progress on Bernard Weston, though in which direction? It's unlikely to unravel any of the complicated tangles surrounding Martin Sarwell. His relationship with Ella Weston has to be bottomed out. Alan Banning's surmises aren't enough. Then there's the accountant's list of people he approached for money. Sylvia Darrington- Cressley is hardly surprising. At least she must have some to tap into, but Denise Deverall? There's a surprise. Ella and Denise. The two names reverberate. Definitely further enquiries.

He turns north and after a mile takes the left fork away from the Mansfield road, passing the 'road closed ahead' sign before entering Best Hill. It's a mixed area of old Edwardian houses, some of them in poor condition, others refurbished and quite smart. Further on, there are old commercial properties, some occupied, some boarded up. He slows down as the road rises steeply. On his left an area of levelled ground where buildings have been demolished, the plots fenced off awaiting development. On his right another cleared area, also fenced off though contractors' mobile offices and parked excavators indicate work has already commenced. Beyond these on both sides steep streets of neat terraced houses rise up the hills. The empty, cleared land lies in a small rising plateau between these two heights. The road levels off. Hailed down by a uniformed officer, standing beside a number of police vehicles, he shows his card.

"Best to park here, sir, there's no room further up. I'll take you through."

They cross the road and enter a large building site, the whole area closed off by a cordon of uniformed officers as a crime scene. Construction activity has stopped. Most of the ground has been cleared with some trench excavation for a new building. The remaining demolition of an older building, mounds of rubble and twisted steel, can be seen at the rear of the site. Much of this has been loaded onto lorries for taking away, which now stand idle within the cordon. They pass a number of contractor's excavating vehicles. Workmen and drivers stand around, some of them being interviewed. Further on a red tape is stretched around a smaller area, guarded by further officers. Within this area Jennifer and John Duggan are looking down into something he cannot see. As he ducks under the tape to join them Jennifer points into a shallow hole about three meters by two meters and about a meter deep. Halfway down the excavation there's a clear line between the characteristic red sandstone and brown topsoil. In its bottom and at the centre of the hole, lies a skeleton being carefully cleaned by two white clad scenes of crime officers. Jenner and the other two look down impassively for some moments.

"How was it found?" he says at last, without stirring his eyes from the ground.

"They've been clearing the site for a new development," Jennifer says, "diggers have been gradually lowering the level for weeks. One of the JCB drivers stopped for his tea break and noticed something hard at the edge of the shovel, which fortunately was still embedded in the ground. If he'd not stopped when he did, the whole skeleton might have been smashed up in the next few minutes. He poked about a bit and realised it was a bone, actually part of his leg..."

"His?"

"Male, about five feet eight."

"Same height as Bernard Weston."

"Whoever he is, he's been well dug down," Duggan says.

"Well dug down?" Jenner repeats.

"It's going to be prestige office development," Jennifer says, "They need to get deeper into the bedrock for more secure foundations, but the site manager says it shouldn't haven't taken so long. The ground had to be deeply excavated and they kept going through what he calls soft soil and rubble."

"So somebody's gone to a lot of trouble," Duggan says.

Still staring at the skeleton Jenner says to the men in the hole, "How soon before you can get it cleaned up?"

"Couple of hours, sir," one says, turning upwards, "Doc's been out, but said he can't say anything till we get it to the lab."

"Quite," Jenner grunts and turns to Jennifer, "Sandstone's the bedrock round here, isn't it?"

"Most of the city's built on it," she says.

"But why have they had to dig down so far to get to it?"

"Don't know."

"Have another word with that site manager. We need his plans, including depths of excavation for the foundations. What was here before, was it waste ground?"

"No, there was a derelict building, one of those horrible 1960s blocks."

"I think they came down so far to level off the ground for the new building," Duggan says, "you know for a car park and so on."

"What you *think* isn't enough," Jenner says, as he turns away from the hole and surveys the whole site, "Find out who has precise plans of the old building. What was located immediately above where the skeleton was found? Was it within or outside the building and if it was within, what use was made of the rooms. Who had access to them? Was it a council block?"

"Yes, they sold it as part of some overall regeneration scheme."

John intervenes.

"The Best Hill area was cleared in the sixties. It was one of those new housing schemes, you know all concrete and open balconies."

"Yes, I remember, we had them everywhere. Bloody awful places where you could never find your way out and the lifts never worked. Ready made to be run down and then they became perfect breeding grounds for crime."

"There may not have been any lifts here. I think some of these blocks were only a few floors and..."

"Quite so, constable, you *think*, we need to *know*. Know who owned the site and the building and whether any of our potential suspects in the Bernard Weston investigation had any connection with it."

"We can't be sure yet this is Bernard Weston," Jennifer says.

"No, sergeant," Jenner sighs, "we can't, which means our enquiries will have to be oblique at this stage. We don't refer directly to this discovery."

"It'll get out, sir, all these people, the press..."

"Yes, I know, but we don't link it directly to our investigations into Bernard Weston's disappearance, so no point hanging about here any longer. Let me know when the pathologist has a report. I'll deal with Sylvia Darrington – Cressley, if you and the others concentrate on Matthew Usworth, Denise Deverall and Ella Weston."

"You still feel the sister is a suspect?" Jennifer says sceptically.

Jenner looks from her to the officers in the hole and then back to her.

"Wouldn't rule any of them out yet," he says, before turning away and walking back towards his car. Then he stops and calls back to Jennifer.

"Check out all previous uses of this ground, I want to know every previous owner."

"How far back?" Jennifer says.

"Domesday Book if you have to."

The following morning Jenner returns to Elvington House. Despite the possible breakthrough with the skeleton, he needs to reopen his unfinished discussion with Sylvia without delay, but he's reluctant to approach her. David Underwood, her young personal assistant has not been interviewed. It might be better to follow up any association with the Best Hill site with him first. He could be an invaluable source of information. People close to power not only bask in the reflected glory of their superiors, they take pride demonstrating how much *they* know. Of course, he may be ultra loyal and not susceptible to the wiles of an experienced detective, but with care he might be tempted to divulge something without realising its significance. If Jenner can establish an association between Sylvia and that particular piece of real estate on the north side of the city, then...

The Moral Power Trust office stands at the corner of one of the Georgian streets near the Castle, a plain brass nameplate the only distinguishing feature from the surrounding solicitors and accountants. A national organisation locating its headquarters in a provincial city seems odd. It could indicate its relative weakness or Sylvia's reluctance to stray too far from home on a regular basis. The headed notepaper includes a London address, but from the postcode Jenner surmises an accommodation address only. The reception is surprisingly small, but well appointed with comfortable chairs, tasteful decoration and one wall devoted to 'Moral Power' posters. Jenner's avoids them. There's no one at the desk and he rings the bell. A middle aged, smartly dressed woman appears and smiles broadly.

"Good day to you, sir, how can I be of assistance?"

The unctuously treacly greeting momentarily unsettles Jenner. He feels suddenly part of a training video. He shows his card as he announces his name. The beaming smile recedes slightly.

"I wish to speak to David Underwood."

The smile disappears completely, transforming into a stiff scowl. Obviously this is not an organisation that likes policemen.

"He's not here."

"Where can I find him?"

She hesitates. He senses her wondering whether to be obstructive, but his incisive gaze rules out prevarication.

"He's assisting Mrs. Darrington – Cressley with the Victorian event out at Elvington House," she says, regaining some of her composure and warming to her subject, adding pointedly, "It's a major fundraising opportunity for the Trust, very exclusive."

"Quite. There now, is he?"

"Oh yes, will you be going immediately?"

He says nothing, the steely eyes responding with wearied contempt.

"It's not easy to find, I could give you..."

"I know where it is."

She may call the house and alert David or even worse Sylvia, but it can't be helped. He'd hoped to get some advantage from an element of surprise, which is probably now lost. Better to have gone straight to the house, but he wanted to avoid an immediate confrontation with Sylvia. She never mentioned this 'Victorian event' the other day, but if it's so exclusive, it's not a matter for discussion with a policeman. *Victorian event*, all the way the phrase teasingly recurs. Deep down he knows *which* Victorian period.

He arrives at the house. The whole place exudes Sylvia's influence and he imagines her prowling the grounds in readiness for his return. A number of other cars are parked at the front door. Whatever the event is, not just David are engaged in preparations. David is likely to be inside, engaged in some administrative function, but Jenner's anxious to avoid Sylvia, so the front door is not an option. He parks at the bottom of the drive, not wanting to draw attention to himself and approaches carefully. Even if he creeps around the side, Sarah or another member of the staff will probably show him to her. Instinctively his legs slow until his feet almost slither along the gravel like some disabled family retainer creeping obsequiously to an appointment with the lady of the manor. Then he sees a familiar face.

Above the hedge to the right of the house, Jon Cardington stares across, part puzzled, part resigned as if Jenner's behaviour mystifies, but also confirms all his lifelong prejudices. Jenner picks up his feet and marches over quickly. Not keen to talk Jon turns away and strides down the path. Jenner skips along beside the hedge, calling when sure he's out of earshot of the house. He catches up with Jon, who feigns surprise at his presence.

"Oh, thou's back art'a? 'Ast'a sorted it out then?"

"We are continuing our enquiries."

Jon stares long and hard, eventually letting out a cool, low whistle.

"Could mean thou knows who done it, but canna prove it!"

"There's a lot going on here today?"

"Ar, 'er's got some junket on for 'er moralising, thou knows, getting money out'n them 'as too much and dunna know what to do wi'it."

"So you're all helping?"

"Ar, them 'as got nowt else to do. I'm keeping out o' bloody way. Which means, if thou's got no more questions, I'll gerron afore somebody gi's me a job."

He glances across to the house and turns to go. Jenner also looks towards the house and then steps in front of Jon.

"I'm looking for David Underwood, do you know him?"

"Ar, I know, young feller from 'er office."

"You've come across him?"

Jon shakes his head.

"Ow 'as nowt to do wi' me," he says approvingly, adding, "Seems all reyt, bit serious abart things that dun't matter, but that's up to 'im."

"Is he here?"

"In't 'ouse."

Jenner groans. Jon reads his mind and says with a wry smile, "If thou goes round side o'ouse you'll see 'im int'big drawing room, doors open."

Jon points and then gives more precise directions around various alleyways and hidden corners.

"Mrs. Darrington – Cressley, is she..."

Jon reads his mind again.

"Ow's at top end o' grounds, supervising."

The last word is emitted as a long, derisive whine and a knowing wink. Jenner thanks him and following his instructions finds the open door of the large drawing room. Inside a young man sits studying papers at a desk in the corner. It's the room containing the portraits of Sylvia's ancestors. Jenner enters from the path and shows his warrant card.

"Name's Jenner, I'm a police officer."

"Detective chief inspector," David reads the card, "You'll be wanting Mrs. Darrington – Cressley?"

"You are David Underwood?"

"Yes."

"Then it's you I want to talk to. You've been long with the Moral Power Trust?"

"About three years."

"As Mrs. Darrington – Cressley's personal assistant?"

"Yes."

"And in that position, you're conversant with the Trust's business and financial affairs?"

"Yes, what's this about?"

Jenner mentions the general enquiry into Bernard Weston's disappearance, but nothing more.

"I never met him," David says.

"He never came to the offices of the Trust?"

"No."

"Has the Trust ever had any interest, directly or indirectly in the Best Hill area of the city?"

"I don't think so."

"I'm particularly interested in Fenman Street, Eversleigh Street and Jarvis Road."

David shakes his head.

"What about Mrs. Darrington – Cressley herself, has she ever had any interest in property in that area, perhaps through her clothing company?"

"Certainly not through the company, I would know about that."

"What about a private investment, do you assist with her private financial affairs?"

"Occasionally. I'm not aware of any involvement. If you could tell me what this is about ...?"

"I'm afraid I can't do that at this stage."

David suddenly stands up and declaims forcefully, "Whatever it is you're investigating, I'm absolutely certain Mrs. Darrington – Cressley has had nothing to do with anything unsavoury involving property."

"Quite. Your loyalty does you credit. Please carry on, you

must be very busy preparing for this…event, what's the theme again?"

David resumes his seat, loosens up and, as the consummate administrator explains the detailed arrangements with gusto. As he talks, Jenner ambles around the room, studying the pictures on the walls.

"So there'll be a specific emphasis on the 1840s?" he says, "No earlier and no later?"

"Very much so, Mrs. Darrington – Cressley was most insistent on the particular period. Everything must be genuine. You've probably noticed the old gas lighting fitments have never been removed from most of the house. New mantles have been installed, the whole system checked over by an engineer and reconnected to the supply. In the evening the electric lighting will be turned off and the gas turned on. You see what I mean by accuracy. It will be as if you really have returned to the 1840s."

For an instant Jenner suddenly feels uncomfortable and looks towards the open door as if a chill breeze has just blown in from the garden. It passes.

"It's wonderful to see someone going to so much trouble," he says, "Fascinated by the past isn't she?"

David agrees, explaining further details and delighting in the imaginative arrangements to authenticate the event. Jenner only half listens as he peruses the pictures. He stops at a break in the line of portraits. He's sure one of the pictures has been removed.

"Looking for something, chief inspector?"

He turns quickly. Sylvia stands at the door to the corridor.

"If you've finished talking to David, maybe I can assist you?"

"Yes, quite," Jenner mumbles, turning again to the gap on the wall.

"Then, we ought to leave him, he has a lot of work to do."

With intense relief David reburies himself in his papers. Jenner dutifully follows Sylvia as she strides along the corridor, quickening his step to match her brisk clipping on the wooden floor. Despite his instinctive defences, he feels like the naughty schoolboy approaching the headmistress's study with anxious trepidation. She marches into the library, her ultimate sanctuary and sits in her favourite chair, which she pulls slightly away from the desk. She folds her arms and crosses her legs while motioning him to the chair by the window, reversed positions from their last encounter. She asks why he wants to see David, her eyebrows lifting when he mentions Best Hill. It could be surprise or concern or both, but her denial of any connection to the area is immediate and unhesitating. Why didn't he come to her first? No one knew precisely where she was and he'd found David. He ignores the disbelief in her eyes and mentions the forthcoming 'event.' She latches onto it enthusiastically, relieved not to be talking about other things, but her respite is short lived. Recovering from his sense of scholastic transgression, Jenner returns to Bernard Weston.

"He knew about your relationship with Martin Sarwell, didn't he?"

She fingers her chin nervously for a second as her confident, almost arrogant composure evaporates. Then, conscious of him watching, she puts her hands together and smiles nervously

"I've already told you, chief inspector, I hardly knew the man."

"This is a murder investigation, Mrs. Darrington – Cressley, it would be better for you to be frank with me now, rather than later after I've found..."

"I hardly knew the man. How many times do I...?"

The voice is harsh and demanding, but the legs are no longer crossed, the hands fidget at the side and the shoulders are hunched slightly.

"Once is enough if it's the truth," he says.

She says nothing, swaying slightly as if recovering balance after a sudden surge of emotional energy. She looks at him with tightly drawn lips and a forceful, angry stare, hoping that might hammer home her sincerity and stop his questioning. After a few moments she looks away, unable to decipher his inscrutability. He gets up and moves to the door. She rises too, relieved he might have finally given up.

"Interesting event," he says, "It should go well."

"I hope so."

He opens the door.

"I noticed the picture in the drawing room."

"The picture?"

"The one that's missing. Which of your ancestors is it?"

"Oh, yes, the portrait of Charlotte, my great, great grandmother. It's gone to be re-framed."

"Pity she won't be around for your big night."

She flushes slightly and then laughs.

"Not here...yes, I see what you mean. Actually she would probably have preferred not to be here. It was a sad time for her. There was a dreadful accident at the time. Her brother Jonathon drowned in the canal. Charlotte never really recovered and she campaigned to have the canal closed. Too many sad memories."

"Yet you were keen for it to be reopened, family ghosts and all that?"

"What? Oh, yes. I've never really thought about it like that."

"Strange thing, the past, how it can come back to haunt us."

"I never think of it."

He holds the doorknob, hovering at the threshold. She waits, impatiently, irritated by his inability or unwillingness to move.

"Well, if that's all, chief inspector..."

He leaves.

Sandra Tye and John Duggan report back to Jennifer on their discussions with Ella Weston and Matt Usworth. Ella was distant and withdrawn, her vacant eyes struggling to concentrate on the questions while Matt was defensive, countering questions with monosyllabic thrusts. Both appear to have no connection with the Best Hill site. For the moment their denials will have to suffice. Denise Deverall's office says she's working from home. Probably better. Jennifer will arrive unexpected.

As if expecting someone unwelcome to call, Denise sneaks the door very slightly Anxiously looking through the narrow gap, she's reluctant to open it any further and only lets Jennifer over the threshold after the warrant card is poked into her face.

"Surely I've already answered all your questions?" she says grumpily.

She appears to have been working, though not necessarily on her employer's business. The dining room table is littered with designs and papers rather than invoices and ledgers. She gathers these up feverishly.

"Often work from home?" Jennifer says, eyeing her from the door.

"Yes, sometimes."

Denise stuffs the last papers into a box, but not before Jennifer notices them.

"Clothes design part of the job too?"

"We'll go in the other room."

Denise ushers her into the lounge. Remembering Jenner's description Jennifer expects to see the dolls, but there's only one and many of the pictures have also been removed from the walls. Denise must be eager to conceal her interest in Victorian clothing. Jennifer ambles round the real reason for her visit, waywardly talking about anything that takes her fancy, inconspicuously slipping in references to Best Hill. Getting no response, she raises it again.

"Did Bernard have any involvement in the area?"

"Not that I'm aware of. Will you be talking to Ella about this?"

The comment seems sympathetic to Ella. Jennifer probes.

"Did you get on with her?"

"Yes, we were on friendly terms. I know she can appear a bit weird, but she's harmless and really very likeable."

"As a friend you would know about her personal life?"

She shifts uneasily.

"Maybe," she says guardedly.

"Didn't she have a relationship with Martin Sarwell?"

Denise laughs.

"Very short lived. Not really a relationship at all, at least not on his part."

"What about Ella, what did she feel?"

Reluctantly, Denise concedes Ella's stronger feelings, 'at least for a while.'

"She was upset when the relationship ended, angry even?"

"Not enough to kill him!"

Jennifer stares dispassionately and then deliberately scribbles in her notebook, creating a charged silence, crammed with uncompleted significance. Denise obligingly enters the void.

"They were both obsessed with the past, that was all."

"Seems many people were, you yourself..."

"Not like those two!"

Jennifer needs to prod and stir only a little more before Denise eventually admits her strong dislike for Martin.

"He was always grubbing about. Ella particularly disliked his unnatural interest in her family's past."

"What was his reason?"

"Ella never knew and neither do I. He was just like that other one."

"Other one?"

"Matt Usworth."

She rattles on about Matt. It's the same virulent detestation she'd bewailed to Jenner. Jennifer doesn't interrupt. The puffing outburst of bile will soon blow itself out. Yet, either she protests too much or there's a particular reason for such intense dislike. Jennifer wonders whether Jenner's suspicions are right. As Denise finally subsides, Jennifer returns to Bernard with a deliberate, apparently unconnected reference to Sylvia. Predictably, Denise dismisses any link with a contemptuous laugh, but it seems hollow. Jennifer talks about her work. Denise is defensive, though finally admitting her 'work' at home has nothing to do with her employer.

"I know I can make it as a dress designer, but I need the time. Working at home I can polish off all those invoices in a couple of hours and spend the rest of the day on my designs."

"In your employer's time?"

Denise dribbles out some pathetic whinge about the inefficiency of the depot. Jennifer isn't interested in the internal machinations of the place, but it has succeeded in getting Denise flustered. She mentions Bernard and Sylvia again. This time the denials are less forceful, even contrived and lacking any obvious conviction. Eventually, after another of Jennifer's manipulated silences Denise admits she suspected something going on between them. Even now she finds it difficult to believe.

"Just a short time, just a fling," she says uncertainly.

"Did you tackle him about it?"

"I was going to, but then..."

"He disappeared."

Denise nods. Her eyes well up. Then her face hardens.

"Anyway, that worm Matt Usworth also had suspicions. He taunted me, told me Bernard was carrying on with her. I told him it was ridiculous and he didn't really know, but he kept going on about it."

"Has he talked about it since Bernard..."

"No! Well, once he did, but we've not seen much of each other."

Jennifer talks about the one doll and the interest in costume. Denise is relieved, now willing to talk about her design ambitions, enthusiastically expanding on her ideas. Jennifer appears interested. Then, on a whim, she probes the past, but it leads nowhere. Not wanting to waste any element of surprise on the wrong issue, she drops it. Then she strikes.

"That old Chartist minute book, you showed to chief inspector Jenner...fascinating."

Anxiety returns, searing Denise's face as a hot poker might dance uncontrollably on an unprotected arm before falling to the floor. She mumbles a feeble agreement.

"You'd known about it for some time, hadn't you?"

Denise is speechless. She doesn't want to face this unwelcome challenge, her mind still wanders aimlessly around dresses, old and new.

"Minute book?" she murmurs.

"You didn't just find it when your great aunt died, did you?"

Denise nods silently. She'd known about it for years.

"You told chief inspector Jenner no one else knew about it."

"That's what I told him."

"And now you're not so sure?"

"I can't remember. It's just possible I told Bernard, but I didn't show it to him?"

She says his name resignedly, but her voice lacks any hint of finality, her eyes betraying a strange mischievousness as she says, "And I suppose he could have told Matt."

"But you don't know for sure?"

"No."

"So he may or may not have known about Sam Usworth?"

"There's one other thing I didn't tell your chief inspector, something my great aunt told me, which I certainly didn't tell Bernard. The minute book was given to her ancestor for safe keeping, but the minute taker was someone else. My great aunt said there had been a local middle class woman involved with the Chartists. (Matt said there were such people) I only know her name was Cecily. Ever since she told me the name, I've felt oddly close to her. They say you can feel an affinity with someone you've read or heard about, even if you know very little about them. Yet, it's as if you know them and are in touch with them."

She looks at Jennifer, but it's a mysterious faraway look and her eyes seem oddly focused beyond, at an indeterminate distance. Then, as if suddenly losing the momentary other worldly transfixion she blinks, refocuses on Jennifer and shakes her head.

"Don't take any notice, I'm being silly."

But Jennifer does take notice, doesn't think she's silly and wonders about the significance of such things much more than she has before.

Ettie remained at the police station for a couple of hours, before giving up on Jenner and returning to the hotel. Not exactly afraid, but sufficiently wary not to let curiosity overcome caution, she resisted the temptation to go out. It even stopped her going round to Jenner's place. She considered telephoning, but put it off until by the time she was ready it was too late. Filled with the sense of the past encroaching on the present, another disturbed night followed. The past was out there, alive, energised and mysterious. She felt someone close, wandering, searching perhaps, sure yet unsure, sure of the area, yet unsure of its place within it. There was anger, even aggression, but also fear, loneliness, confusion. Yet perhaps not alone, for in some moments in that long, dark night she'd felt another, maybe more.

She skips breakfast and goes back to the police station. It's probably the best place to be. Jenner has to come back at some stage. No one gives any indication of when he's likely to return. After an hour she's ready to leave, but at the front she almost collides with him as he struggles with several box files. Relieving him of some of these, she follows him to the office. Both are anxious to tell the other their findings and feelings. After he's recounted his meeting with Sylvia he asks Ettie for her views, but intervenes before she can respond.

"Something not quite right about that woman, but I can't put my finger on it. She has a cast iron alibi for Bernard Weston's disappearance, but there has to be a link with the past ..."

Ettie is calmer. Leaving his unspoken doubt hanging means he's unlikely to dismiss her own experience in the tunnel and, more importantly, her apprehensions since. He listens patiently until she's gone through it all.

"What do you make of it?" he says.

"I'm not so sure you're right about Sylvia," she says, "The Chartist handbill found with Martin Sarwell and then the document Matt Usworth produced at the meeting..."

"You think it's him?"

"His behaviour is...."

"Quite, but none of them behave exactly...normal. We've not got the report back on the handbill yet. Anyway, even if you're right, I'm still not ruling out Mrs. High and Mighty Darrington – Cressley. Besides, you *felt* there was more than one?"

Ettie's unease returns. He doesn't mean to be critical, but he has the policeman's need for concrete evidence.

"I can only say... what I feel."

He grunts a soft 'hmm' and then taps the box files.

"Well, I'm not ruling Usworth out either. More might be revealed in here, plus what sergeant Heathcott may have turned up. You've not seen her, I suppose?"

He opens one of the boxes and pulls out a bundle of documents, spreading them out carefully across the desk.

"Looks like you're going to be busy," she says limply, retreating to the door.

"Yes," he says, glancing at his watch "could be all night."

"I'll leave you to it."

He continues studying, looking up just before she closes the door.

"I'll ring you at the hotel tomorrow."

It'll be a long, but necessary job, particularly after the discussion with Sylvia. It could take several hours just to sort out the files, having to discard a great deal of chaff before he can begin to examine the wheat. It's lucky such old constabulary records still exist. He's surprised by the sheer quantity of documents. A policeman's lot, at least so far is paperwork was concerned, was no happier then than now. He soon adjusts to the 1840s style of reporting, but frequently frustrated by the superficial and inconclusive standards of investigation. The force was then very new, feeling its way, borrowing from London experience wherever possible and not always successfully grappling with the difficulties of the troubled times. A breakdown of public order and the possibility of revolution then seemed closer than ever before or since. At least that was the view of the ruling authorities, mirrored in the sometimes frightening and frightened reports. Jenner smiles at times, before reflecting on a hundred and sixty years of experience his counterparts could not call on.

Even when he's whittled the mass down to a manageable load, a huge quantity of similar activities leap at him with alarming frequency. The perception was of continuing disturbance and violent incidents, real or implied by circumstances, all making his task more difficult. No doubt the crisis passed and the frenzied volume of reported activity abated, but for that time, 1842, he must wade through them all. So many sightings or rumours of suspicious people, few of them properly followed up. Someone attacked in some isolated place where there are either no witnesses or at least not one willing to be identified. So many unexplained attacks, inevitably blamed on agitators could have been the work of other, more local, personal villains. They remind him of Ettie's concerns about Matt Usworth. If he was to return in some inexplicable way, his obsession with Chartism provides the vital motivation and he could have been responsible for any one of these unexplained murders.

At last he finds what he's looking for. Slightly peremptory report, Jonathon Cressley, local employer, unfortunate accident, found drowned in the Cross Cut canal, out alone, early one morning, but what's this...it *might* not have been an accident. A *possibility* of foul play. At last a more imaginative officer, but it was not followed up. Did he have too many other enquiries or did he conveniently grasp a neat explanation? Jenner puts the papers down. He's uncomfortable with the ambivalent report with a lingering sense all was not as it seemed. A hundred and sixty years is a long time. He'll not resolve it. Even if it is an unsolved crime, there are plenty of others. Anyway, too late now... or is it? Is this the work of Matt Usworth, dangerous fugitive from the present wreaking his twisted vengeance on an unsuspecting past, interfering with history itself? He laughs it off, but the idea won't leave his mind

Ettie's discomfiture hardens as she walks down the stairs to the front door. Inadequacy nags at her, as if an opportunity has been missed, yet she doesn't know how she might have said or done things differently. A feeling of desperate loneliness overwhelms her. She sits down at the reception to gather her thoughts before leaving.

"Hallo, Ettie!"

Jennifer stands over her.

"Chief Inspector Jenner was looking for you," Ettie says.

Eager to tell someone, Jennifer ushers Ettie into a side room, describing her morning with Denise, several times repeating the reference to Cecily.

"Does it mean anything?" Ettie asks.

Jennifer grimaces and shrugs, mystified by the potential implications.

"It could, but I'm not sure how. More than usually this case is a jigsaw puzzle. You know, a thousand pieces. You can't fit them together though you know they have to and you wonder if all the pieces are in the box? Are there whole sections missing or is it just your inability to fit them together? Trouble is, unlike a jigsaw, if some parts of this are missing, you don't know what they are."

"Tell me what's troubling you?"

"It'll sound ridiculous."

"Try me."

"The chief inspector asked me to follow up some new things. I have to say, at the time I wondered...I'm sure he's a good detective, but...."

"You couldn't see the relevance?"

"No, but ever since Denise talked about Cecily, I wonder..."

"What were those things?"

"Everything about the previous uses of the site where the body was discovered, not just the last few years, but way back. He was very particular about any railway line that used to run through the area."

"Shades of Martin Sarwell."

"Yes, but this is a separate enquiry. Anyway, as it happens there was a branch line, closed a hundred years ago when the north-south main line was built. I couldn't see its importance, still can't. Then there was the other thing connected with the past. He wanted me to dig out all I could on Sylvia Darrington – Cressley's ancestors. I got reams of what I thought was useless information. Now, I'm not so sure."

"Something Denise said?"

"Sylvia had a distant relative, a cousin of her great, great grandmother, Cecily Stacey."

"What do you make of it?"

Jennifer shakes her head.

"A possible link between Denise and Sylvia, though over

such a long period of time, what could it mean? Denise's remark about feeling close to Cecily, at one time I would have dismissed it, but not now. Concerns with the past, however far back, keep recurring in this case. I felt it when I was talking to Denise. I tried to talk to her about the dresses and dolls the boss had seen, but why did I feel it was important to probe? I know it sounds crazy, but I'm beginning to wonder just what is the link between Denise and Cecily."

"It's not crazy."

"Then I wonder how it can be important to the investigation? I think the boss puts me through this because of my interest in local history."

"What will you tell him?"

"If I tell him what I've told you he'll think I'm demented. At best I'm allowing my imagination to run away with me."

"I doubt it. He'll be more concerned to know your ideas."

Jennifer groans, putting her head in her hands.

"Don't be afraid to say what you think," Ettie says, "You obviously don't know everything of the chief inspector's background."

Jennifer looks up. Ettie continues.

"We first met when he was investigating the Sarah Layman case."

"I remember it."

"Yes, but you don't know the full events that preceded it."

- 9 -

All is prepared. The staff, dragooned like soldiers have been allotted their roles and deployed with precision. Time left now only for last minute amendments. Yet time, with its persistent irritating unpredictability, has given a little extra of its precious resource, so Sylvia sits in the drawing room surrounded by intricate plans and lists. Many lists, lists for food, lists for drinks, lists for clothes, lists for furniture, lists for staff time, lists for staff locations, lists for suppliers, lists for those who will be here, lists for those who should, but won't. What seemed concluded an hour ago, is now doubtful. What had been bastions of efficiency are now punctuated by potential pitfalls. What *could* go wrong now seems destined *to* go wrong. Possible errors and potential mistakes loom up like hidden rocks in a calm sea, unknown when the voyage was planned, now surfacing from every direction and alerted by the lookout with alarming frequency. The more she reviews the plans the worse her fears become. She goes through the lists, reading more quickly each time and then, panicking she must have missed something, starts all over again. She forgets what she's read and then goes back to check the missing item which was never missing in the first place!

Interviewed in a series of quick fire, stoccato, one sided conversations, staff previously fairly clear of their duties end up more confused, while Sylvia in turn is not reassured. Having exhausted all other lists, not to mention the staff, she turns to the guest list and sends for David, conscripted from his normal duties assisting in the grounds. Still recalling their discussion at the end of the Trust meeting, he enters a little apprehensively, unsure whether he's to be assigned to the removal of algae from the fishpond or some similarly unpleasant task as punishment for commenting on the state of Sylvia's health.

"Don't stand at the door like a waiter," she bellows, "I need your help with this guest list!"

He steps over with relief, her rumbustious tone showing she's in normal spirits and good health. She rattles through the names for him to check against invitations, interspersed with cries of 'oh I invited him myself' or 'I *had* to invite them' or 'I'm not sure why I invited *them*.' As with the other lists, once she's finished she starts again, belting through the names even faster, muttering to herself, while David struggles with his papers, dropping many to the floor and getting them out of order in a vain effort to keep up. As she pauses briefly after the third machine gunning rendition, David checks the names carefully.

"It's very long," he says guardedly.

"It is," she says, "but then it's only a list, they won't all come. We have to allow for the usual crowd of insufferable persons who say they'll come and then at the last moment always have that pressing, unavoidable engagement."

"Even so..." he begins, passing his finger down the sheets.

"Nonsense, David, don't fuss."

"But if all these people come, we won't be able to get them into the house."

"Like I said, they won't all come."

He remains dubious. They exchange looks of 'Trust me I know what I'm doing' and 'I only hope you're right.' To his immense relief, she doesn't read off the names a fourth time. He flicks over the pages again as he replaces them in the correct order.

"East Mercia Constabulary?" he says incredulously.

"God, I'd forgotten them. Oh well, public relations," she says as if further explanation is unnecessary, "They probably won't come. If they do…well as long as it's not that dreadful chief inspector Jenner who's been bothering me lately."

He goes down the list more deliberately, picking out names having no obvious reason for inclusion. She dismisses each one with a curt 'won't come' or 'need their support' or 'wait and see' or 'can't remember that name.' Sometimes she shrugs her shoulders or shakes her head. David remains troubled.

"Are you sure you've only included the people you really want?" he says.

"Too late to remove any now. All the invitations went out, didn't they?" she says, adding before he has time to confirm, "Go down the list again and check them off."

He opens his invitation records and starts a careful re-examination, but has to constantly backtrack and sheaf through other papers as she barks out other names. Jerkily and with much sidetracking, they get through another run through of the names. As she pauses for breath, he returns to the issue.

"You said yourself some people won't come. I've heard there could be a black market in tickets."

"Nonsense, "she explodes, "This isn't a football match!"

"Even so…"

"In any case, this is an 1840s party, everybody needs a costume to get in."

"Yes, as was the recent open day and then…"

"But this isn't the same."

"Isn't it?"

"How will strangers get through?"

"You can't be everywhere at once and with this many people, the staff will only have time to check the tickets, even if they know the people, which they won't."

She reminds him not to get 'alarmist' and then insists on a further check of the invitations. Eventually after two more complete scrutinies of his papers, double checked against her list, she's reluctantly satisfied and lets him return to his duties in the grounds. She seems lost in thought as he moves to the door, but he's only half way over the threshold when her attention switches and she barks details of the outside arrangements, demanding he ensures proper supervision of the grounds staff with precise instructions of their whereabouts and activities. Finally, after assuring on his life he'll carry out her wishes to the letter with unbounded alacrity, she lets him go.

"Whatever happens," he says, closing the door, "The sponsorship and corporate invitations will bring in valuable funds for the Trust."

She nods absently, continuing to stare at the closed door for some minutes after he leaves, forcing her mind back to where she'd left it that morning. With all the detail and organisational worries, she'd almost forgotten the reason for the party. David's use of emotive language (black market indeed!) shows how the breadth of the guest list has unsettled him, but he has a point. Yet, does it matter? All this fine tuning management, to which she's been dedicating so much of her time, is important only on one level. Other levels need equal planning. Unwittingly, he may have made more of a point than he realises. Ostensibly, the party is arranged to raise the profile and financial support for the Trust, but certain gate crashers might also be welcome. Despite what she said she's concerned some people may *not* come. They need to be flushed out and this is the way to do it. They were there at the open day, so why not this time, with or without an invitation? Matthew Usworth will get in. This time he might show himself properly.

Police stations are built to withstand sieges. Fortunately, such precautions are usually unnecessary. Jenner feels under siege, though it has nothing to do either with the architecture of the station or with anyone outside it. His state of siege is purely psychological. Sitting with his back to the window, the late afternoon sun glimmering around the broad shadow he casts across the desk, he scans the files dozens of times, reading, doodling, analysing, but mostly thinking. Thinking forwards and backwards and any innumerable directions laterally, all increasing his bewilderment and frustration. The trouble with lateral thinking is it produces more ends that refuse to be tied up and Jenner's already had his fill of those.

At different times and for different reasons, but always with good intentions, Sandra Tye and John Duggan have tried to gain his attention on various pressing matters. To no effect, nothing being allowed to disrupt his sitting...and thinking. They've been waved away with a cool grunt or a warm 'hmm, yes' or a distracted 'thank you, constable.' Worst of all, they've got the occasional 'quite, so.' Not the 'quite, so' for suspects, meaning 'I don't believe a word of it,' but a withered, wearied 'quite, so,' delivered with an irksome detachment which, for all its demotivation is directed more at himself than them.

So many disparate, antagonistic leads, most of them leading nowhere. His sense of missing something obvious increases each time he goes over the material. Somewhere in the mire of confused and layered facts there has to be a hidden explanation waiting to be uncovered, a gem, a signpost, a description, a statement, an implication, an interpretation so far undetected, but there all along. If only he could find it.

Just as he's at his lowest and before Sandra or Jon can warn her, Jennifer almost bounces into his room with a bundle of routine papers. Hardly looking up, he waves to a small blank space on the desk. She drops them down loudly hoping to attract his attention, which she achieves in the form of an upward glance and a pained expression.

"Must you be so noisy, sergeant?"

Jennifer is not so easily put down.

"Some of these things need to be looked at quickly, sir?"

She smiles cheekily.

"All in good time."

"Which reminds me. Later, when you have more time, don't you think we should go to this party?"

"We?"

She sits down, uninvited. At least his eyes are now on her with some curiosity rather than boring down into the accumulated papers with enough intensity to make a hole in the desk.

"Well, I don't think either of us should go alone."

"Don't you?"

"No, but on the other hand it's an opportunity not to be missed."

"Quite, now what *particular* party are we talking about?"

"This one."

She pushes the invitation card into a pile of papers, much as a bulldozer might clear a path through a mound of rubble. He picks it quickly from her sliding fingers, before they can do more damage. He mutters incoherently as he reads it, until he reaches 'East Mercia Constabulary,' which he pronounces in a clearer, but slightly disdainful tone and then reaches 'Mrs. Sylvia Darrington – Cressley,' which he says more slowly and deliberately.

"It's at Elvington House," Jennifer interjects.

"Yes, I can read," he grunts, adding pointedly, "just like that open day you went to."

"This is different. It was sent to the chief super and he passed it on to us. Probably thought as we were involved in the case..."

He bristles at Emmins being mentioned.

"Being involved in a murder investigation doesn't necessarily involve us attending parties."

"They'll all be there, sir."

"They could all be here at the station, sergeant, if we had enough evidence to charge any of them."

"But if we go we..."

"I totally disapprove, sergeant. In any case, I'm not in the partying mood."

Jennifer gets up and leaves, allowing the door to swing shut, rattling loudly as it closes. Annoyed, he's about to call her back, but she trips quickly through the outer office and is soon down the stairs to the lower floor. He stares for a moment at the invitation, sighs deeply and then returns to the papers. Yet again, his attention lingers on the accumulated building plans of the Best Hill site. Jennifer has done a good job. There are detailed reports on her interviews with the site manager, city architect and any other professionals connected to the development of the site.

He should have known it would be too good to be true, but the evidence is undeniable. The discovery had been the only rock in the shifting sands of confused information. Though the case might still be cold, with the body of a young male of the right size, they could concentrate on real investigations and end the infuriating surmising. They might still have to find the murderer, but it seemed they'd at least found Bernard Weston. The excitement was short lived.

The plans were clear and they'd gone over the ground several times, taking and retaking measurements. All the experts were agreed. Damn them! The location meant it couldn't possibly be him. One wing of the original building had straddled the ground. Even if the measurements weren't accurate there was plenty of room for error. Even several meters out, the body would lie within the boundaries of the building. Bernard Weston was alive three years ago. How could it be him? He would have to have been in the ground *before* the original building had been constructed. That was forty years ago. It couldn't be Weston. Indeed, it didn't appear to be anyone recent.

Jenner's disappointment contrasts with the gratitude of the archaeologists. Apparently the new building could lie within some medieval quarter outside the old city wall. Such a site had never been discovered before. How exciting! For them. With no known forty year old mystery to solve, the skeleton had to be much older and the archaeologists were delighted when it was handed over to them. So far they've found a few odds and ends, but no more skeletons. The contractor was less pleased, especially when his schedule was further delayed when the archaeologists were granted more time to excavate the site. Meanwhile, the search for Bernard Weston has to go on.

The archaeologists' involvement brought back mixed memories. Another case when people had grubbed in the ground, discovering more than they bargained for. He told sergeant Calverton to keep his mouth shut or they'd be written off as bonkers. Calverton said nothing, but somehow someone had picked up enough inconsistencies to draw unreal conclusions. Unreal, yet ironically real. They'd cracked the case, but with what kind of help? He should have known when they took Calverton away from him. Yet maybe it was as much himself and his growing unease rather than any pressure from above or questioning by peers, that made him leave. Now, here it is, happening again.

Last night he'd gone through the same strands and threads, indicating the same frustrating lack of resolution. Endlessly he'd gone over the leads and suspects. The number of suspects never seems to decrease while leads – if that's the right description – are painfully rare. Not leads exactly, more like issues, potentialities that sometimes seem like possibilities, only to be dashed down again. Frustration mounts on frustration. Having sunk down in his depression, ready to ascend, he accepted what he'd been trying to avoid. The case could only be solved if one or more of the suspects had concrete links with the past, which had been exploited to commit one or more crimes. A month ago, he'd reluctantly faced this possibility, clinging to it even when Ettie of all people, was doubtful. Then, aware he'd have to share such a conclusion with his colleagues with the inevitable ridicule, if not worse that might follow, he'd backed off. He's not sure how much longer he can keep Jennifer in the dark. She must question the purpose of some enquiries. She'd not swallowed his reason for consulting Ettie. He'd seen them talking. Ettie will feel she should be told or Jennifer will force it out of her. Perhaps it's time be straight and to hell with the consequences. Then he remembers Emmins. Perhaps not yet.

If the disappearance of Weston and the murder of Martin Sarwell are connected then Sarwell's relationships may be the clue. Despite what she says, his contact with Sylvia was probably connected with his research and she doesn't want that divulged. He had a relationship with Ella Weston which soured, she was upset, angry at his interest in her family... why was he interested in her family? Was it connected to his interest in the mysterious Dr. Foxley? There was bad feeling between him and Bernard Weston, who had some sort of relationship with Sylvia. This caused ill feeling with Denise, who also knew Sarwell and didn't like him. Now we have new information linking Denise and Cecily, a distant relative of Sylvia and, through the Chartist minute book, connected to Matt Usworth and his probable ancestor, Sam Usworth. Round and round, interconnections crossing and re-crossing. Jenner's own researches have revealed Cecily

Stacey was the daughter of Anne Cressley, who ran off and married Thomas Stacey, her father's unsuccessful business rival. Anne was the sister of James, the father of Charlotte and Jonathon, the latter 'accidentally' drowning at the time of the Chartist troubles. The same troubles that involved Sam Usworth, recorded in the minute book, apparently compiled by Cecily. Now another little piece to add to the collection. John Duggan has tracked down a local doctor called Foxley who mysteriously disappeared in 1842. One of the doctor's previous patients was Edward Cressley, the grandfather of Charlotte, Jonathon and Cecily.

All these pointers, however conflicting and in whatever direction, can only lead to the explanation Jenner doesn't want to believe, forcing him down a path he'd rather not tread. Maybe Emmins is right. Maybe he should put the past, his past, behind him and concentrate on the *facts*. But how can he put *his* past behind him when *the* past keeps forcing itself on him? Ignoring the past doesn't make it go away, it just makes it unavoidable and more dangerous. Yet even if he could detect the secrets how would he prove them? For the first time in his life he's seriously questioning his abilities. There'd always been frustrating factors, reducing his efficiency, producing flawed results, but there was always another time when things would be different. Besides, those factors were extraneous, outside himself. Now, there are fewer other times to come and time brings more than experience, it brings growing doubt and waning confidence. It also brings renewed reality. Complex cases are no longer challenges, they're just bloody complex! Perhaps he's not such a good policeman after all.

He pulls himself up sharply, seeking safety and diversion in the papers. He lifts one of Jennifer's reports. Yes, the railway, that could be significant...

"Time to go, sir."

Jennifer is in the doorway, dressed in a long crimson gown elegantly edged with a lace collar and sleeves. He looks at the clock. It's seven thirty. He hadn't realised he'd been musing for so long. It seemed only a few minutes since she'd last been in.

"Go?" he says.

"To the party."

"Is that why you're dressed so...."

"Stylish, yes sir, at least it was in the 1840s. It's not genuine, of course. I hired it from..."

"It's very...interesting, but I thought I made myself clear."

"Ettie Rodway also got a specific invitation from Mrs. Darrington – Cressley."

"Indeed," he says in a distinctly changed tone, "and is... she going?"

"Oh yes! She believes it's very important to be there."

"I see."

"She also thinks we should be there."

"Does she."

"So, sir if we..."

"Sergeant, this is still most irregular..."

"But it gives us a unique opportunity to observe them all and with Ettie there as well..."

"I'm not sure. In any case, I have nothing to wear."

"Oh, I've thought of that. I've found something very appropriate."

Gradually, almost imperceptibly the house has moved from hollow silence punctuated by the occasional laughter and echoing footsteps, through a gentle murmur and chattering rumble to a continuous clamorous hubbub. Within a couple of hours the pervasive emptiness has become a close, embracing fullness. Despite her experience of many similar events, Sylvia's apprehension has burgeoned to almost neurotic trepidation. Constantly she flits between the staff's vantage points, checking, directing, fussing, irritating, pacing the entrances, pausing to stare through windows, ambling through doorways, scanning the drive and paths until it seems the floors and casements themselves might cry out 'Enough! Enough!.'

Her plan demands she supervise the internal staff as well as those at the perimeter. She tries to be in all places at once, spending more time in the moving than the staying. She only subsides when the guests, or those purporting to be, start arriving. The numbers build up. Eventually, more by default than design, she transforms from the peripatetic sergeant major to the genially circulating host, but much of her unease remains. Her speech is stilted, edgy, forcibly chattering as if all confidence has drained from her. Even then she hovers with the staff, nodding to the visitors she knows and introducing herself to those she doesn't. Most of them she recognises. The first trickle becoming a steady stream and then a continuing pressured surge. As David predicted, staff can't cope. They stop double checking the guest list and later abandon more than a cursory examination of invitations. Effective entry control is lost, engulfed by the excited thronging mass. Yet Sylvia is only dimly aware of this and her confidence, at least outwardly, begins to return. Between exchanging conversational snatches with so many people, she scours the crowd, nodding to acquaintances and glancing tensely at so many strangers.

It's a success. Moral Power's coffers will be substantially swelled. The dress code has been universally observed. The specialist dress suppliers for many miles must be emptied of their contents. Everyone is in authentic clothes. Some may even be original judging by their sheen though only an expert could detect the difference from modern copies. Some of the women have interpreted the guidelines too loosely for aficionados, turning up in what are clearly *morning* or *afternoon* dresses, but Sylvia is unconcerned. Period authenticity suffices. Some of the gowns are quite stunning, enlivening the ambience and contrasting with the dark, sombre outfits of many. The men's clothes generally reflect the masculine drabness of the 1840s. Usually no gaudy trousers or brilliant waistcoats, but some have offset the ubiquitous grey and black by appearing in military, naval and other uniforms with splendid trousers, buttons, braid and modish jackets.

Sylvia has made no exceptions in her quest for the genuine flavour of the time. Only the food and drink obtainable then is available tonight. For some this seems an unusually sparser fare, while others revel in what they regard as denser, more sated refreshment. The resplendently displayed dishes in the dining room are of course, those generally enjoyed by at least the upper middle classes. The humbler, meaner diet of the workers has been excluded. People are, after all, supposed to be enjoying themselves.

The entertainments have already begun. Something approaching the musical evenings of a social gathering in a large country house is in full swing in the rear lounge. For those with a more earthy taste beyond discreet parlour songs, the large drawing room at the front has been crammed with chairs facing a small platform at the far end, the nearest approximation to a music hall of the times. The room is packed. Even without the size and robustly garish interiors there's a distinct uninhibited flavour of the original. A blue haze of cigarette and cigar smoke wafts around the ceiling, the raucous vibrancy of the music blaring cheekily above the ribald laughter and exuberant blather of the excited audience. At the rear a constantly changing contingent of drinkers hovers near the door, flitting in and out, deliberating discordantly on both the performers and the onlookers. Unwittingly they replicate the clientele of the bars of the old establishments.

Their guffaws and glass chinking shuffles can just be heard across the corridor where another group in a smaller, but no less packed room listen in delighted concentration to a string quartet sawing out light pieces by Victorian minor composers. Their tuneful delicacy contrasts with the whirling commotion from the drawing room, both sharing a common destiny of extinction, briefly revived for these few vital dazzling hours. The period is authentically captured, one hundred and sixty years rolled back like a thick curtain in a long closed old house to reveal in the daylight the delights of another age. No matter if the drawing back of the curtain is only temporary and the opening of the window through time is only a tiny crack, it could be an actual experience, a real night in 1842. Yet still an illusion, for surely with the delights of another age also come the dangers?

Away from the music, food and drink, the guests thin out though by now almost the whole house echoes their presence. On the ground floor, the hundreds of candles in the crystal chandeliers cast brilliant yellow pools of light, supported by the flickering glows from the gas mantles. Away from the main hall and corridors the gaslight a shimmering twinkle, only the dullest candles brighten the dimness. Upstairs, where fewer guests have ventured, the shadows lengthened in the meagre and obscured light, the banisters mould into sinister shapes on the opposite walls. Corners assume exaggerated proportions, walls and ceilings merge with no definable boundary, tables and chairs grotesquely fabricate into strange and mysterious figures, sporting spindly arms and spiky legs, vases contort into huge opaque structures, drapes deform as mangled silhouettes. Such shivering monstrosities, familiar and unimportant nightly apparitions to our ancestors, frighten us in our pathetically insecure technological cocoons. In this deceptively shady world of half light and half reality, a few human interlopers creep up the stairs to sneak along the galleries and gather insecurely in small knots at corners. Not daring to disturb the uneasy silence, save for the soft hiss of the gas mantles, they speak in muffled whispers, in case they upset the rule of the shadows. Yet in their bygone garb they also add to the baleful gloom. Men's hats and women's ruffled sleeves, caught in the murky obscurity, add their own personal shapelessness to the shadowy atmosphere and watch their own silhouettes with anxious foreboding. After skirting the upper floors to satisfy their brazen curiosities, most return downstairs, leaving only a few sturdier souls.

Sylvia's spirits are rising. The event has achieved much more than she ever dreamt, fund raising having outstripped all projections. Realising they can't be everywhere at once, she's finally given up checking on the staff. Meandering around the guests is more interesting, assessing them from afar or sizing them up at close quarters. With everyone properly dressed and all the props of décor, music, food, drink and lighting in place, a truly 1840s scene has been created, the crush of people doing nothing to dilute the house's charged atmosphere. Why, it really could be 1842! Then she shudders, her gratification tinged with nagging misgivings. Might such authentic visions bring with them the realities of the past? In her euphoria she might see someone unwelcome.

She can't be exactly sure *who* is in the house and now regrets telling David to leave his post at the entrance, which he'd been guarding resolutely for nearly two hours. From her vantage point at the bottom of the stairs, she looks tensely towards the front door. She turns away and then looks back to make sure. Four people, two men and two women. At first she doesn't know them and then in one instant she recognises something dreadfully familiar.

"Chief inspector Jenner! How incredibly...formidable you look."

Jenner is flanked by Jennifer on one side and Sandra Tye and John Duggan on the other. Sandra is dressed in a blue gown similar to Jennifer's, John in a light buff suit with a short, square topped hat, but it's Jenner's outfit that catches Sylvia's eye.

"Is it authentic?" she says.

"An authentic reproduction, "Jennifer says proudly, "made up for a period television series. It had to be correct in every detail."

Sylvia walks around Jenner approvingly as the others stand aside.

"Yes," she says, fingering the lapel, "Very good, I'm very impressed."

She steps back for a thorough exhaustive examination. Jenner stands in embarrassed silence. He feels like the young boy being bought his first suit. Standing impassively in the shop, not knowing what to with his arms and feet, all of which seem to hang or splay awkwardly, while his parents and the tailor pass dubious judgements as much on him as on the garment. Like the boy he's unable to control those around him. Sylvia, the 'tailor,' is menacingly if fleetingly in command of the situation while his colleagues, like the critical parents seem to gawp in concert, friends and foes hardly discernible.

"It's even the correct rank," Jennifer enthuses.

Jenner coughs pointedly.

"It's an inspector's uniform," he says, "not a *chief* inspector."

"Even so, it's really splendid," Sylvia adds.

Recovering some of his aplomb, Jenner detects in her admiration a hint of disquiet. As she scans his clothes, he wonders whether it's they, rather than his appearance that concern her. She takes in every detail, perhaps checking them against something she's seen or *remembered* before.

"You do look distinctly different in uniform," Sylvia says pertly, determined to make the most of his obvious discomfort, adding with relish "it also means we'll be able to know you from a distance in the crowd."

"Quite. Such dress would not be appropriate for my normal duties."

"So tonight you're not on duty?"

"I'm always on duty."

Momentarily her face loses its assertive, provocative abandon and the cheery expression is creased away, but the upward lines are quickly resumed.

"The house seems full," Jenner says, "Are we the last? Has everyone arrived?"

Sylvia hesitates, cursing herself for letting David go with his invaluable guest list.

"Er...yes, I...think so," she says, half turning to escape.

"I believe Ettie Rodway was invited," Jenner says, "is she here?"

"Yes, she's arrived, I saw her, though I don't know where she is now. Actually, chief inspector, you've reminded me that she is one person I particularly want to meet."

She pretends to see a particular guest, excusing herself to get away, calling over one of the staff to look after 'our friends from the watch.' Jenner waves him away with a gruff 'We know the way' and then leads them across the front hall into a small ante room where a large array of assorted hats have been deposited. Jenner and John add theirs to the nearest line. Jenner hovers at the mirror, fiddling with his 1840 police uniform, smoothing the sleeves, adjusting the belt, pulling the jacket and hauling up the trousers only to wiggle them down again so as not to expose any sock above his boots. Eventually, having failed to make himself sufficiently presentable he moves away irritably.

"Remember you're all on duty," he says stiffly as Jennifer

and Sandra arrange their hair in the mirror and John glances longingly to where the drinks are being distributed across the hall.

"I'm still not happy about this," he says to Jennifer as if preparing the ground to blame her later for any mishap.

"I think we should circulate, sir," she says, "see what we can find out."

"Duggan should have been in this...this uniform," he says.

She sighs despondently.

"We went through all that at the station. John couldn't get into either that or the constable's uniform, but it fits you like a dream."

She looks at him admiringly and adjusts the jacket. He pulls away quickly.

"Don't do that, sergeant. It's bad enough as it is."

"Okay, sir, I was only making it look a bit...smarter."

He glares and obstinately pulls the jacket back up.

"At least it *is* the inspector's," she says, "Now, do we circulate?"

He looks in the mirror again, hoping it might yield a different image.

"You take Sandra and I'll take John. We'll meet back here in half an hour, but first I need to find Ettie."

After wandering through the ground floor rooms the hostess at last immerses herself in the atmosphere and enters the party spirit. She sees no new faces and is no longer concerned by those she doesn't recognise. Imbibing the successful potion of an ersatz past she feels at home in her own house, not something she's always felt recently. At the top of the stairs she chats with a pleasant older couple. She doesn't know them, yet something about them remind her... no matter, on such a night it's not surprising the mind might tease. They return downstairs. She watches them carefully, they seem frustratingly familiar, but she can't locate...home of the past, home is the past, the past is the home. Those from the past and those of the present, while those that leap between the two, make a mocking, fluid future. Should she look backward to the past or is the past propelled forward?

Her agonised broodings return. She must flush him out. She prowls the upper galleries, carefully scrutinising everyone. Neutral mannerisms are suddenly nefarious. The raising of an eyebrow, the slackness of a mouth, the scratching of an ear, become expressions of undisclosed foreboding. Harmless snippets of conversation abruptly converted into conspiratorial messages, scraps of trivial observations, tail end pieces, uncompleted beginnings violently grabbed out of context and transformed into suspicious revelations. When obsession blows apart innocence who can be trusted?

She relaxes again. The careful screening at the doors has worked. David's fears are groundless. Matt Usworth is not in the house and she settles into an easy and relaxed interaction with her guests. Now she sees no one she doesn't know. So many interesting costumes and how eager everyone is to talk about them! Such fascinating stories, such wonderful people! Then she's alone again at one of the darker corners where she can observe and not be easily seen. She sits down. The night is still young, but she's already weary. There's been so much to do, so much to plan, to organise, to check...check...has she left anything to chance? Who is that?

At the head of the stairs an older woman in a dull plain dress loiters, staring across with an unnerving absorption. Is that a stain on the bodice? Who would come here in a stained dress? Not someone concerned for the occasion, not someone taking care with her appearance, not an invited respectable person. But uninvited? Someone not in leisure time. Someone working, but not working for her, not one of the staff, someone else? It's one of the staff. It's a wine stain from a drunken guest's wavering hand. She must go over and tell her to change. She gets up, but there's no one there. She looks around, but the woman has gone. No swiftly disappearing black back either in the corridors or on the stairs. No one. No sound. How quiet it is. Then the hum from below, the chatter, the banter, it returns as if the volume on a radio is being gradually turned up.

Now there are people on the stairs, in the corridors, coming from the rooms. Why have they suddenly reappeared? She wants to go to them and shout 'Where have you been?

Why weren't you here when *she* was here?' People pass her, acknowledge her, exchange pleasantries, all is normal there's no cause for alarm. She's being foolish. An unfettered imagination plays tricks, aided by the twinkling light and her mind's ambient closeness to the past.

She remains at the banister, gripping it tightly, struggling to regain her composure. A merry group ascends. She knows them. They talk. Her hand loosens its grip. She's well again. They go off. She looks along the corridor. No one. Then the eerie silence invades again, her ears gradually plugged, all sound from below muffled and indistinct. A man emerges from one of the rooms. She relaxes. He carries something. A hat, a box, no a bag, a small, dark leather bag. Why would he come with a bag? He looks across, anxious, yet also angry. Their eyes meet briefly, then he turns away. As he walks down the corridor, determined, purposeful, not the ambling leisurely stroll of a guest at a party. It's as if he knows his way. As if he's been here before!

She looks away, towards the stairs. The sound from below returns. She looks back. He's gone. Then as she looks at the stairs again, there he is, halfway down, striding resolutely, quickly as if to escape. He pauses at the landing and looks up. A cold, defiant, reproachful, accusing stare that sears into her. She stares back and he turns away, resuming his descent. She watches him as he mingles with the guests, but loses him in the crowd. His steady, upright gait lingers in her mind. That deliberate, correct, solid movement has an occupational air. A professional man, intent on his business and somehow familiar.

Jenner has been the butt of a few jokes and many commendations.

"It's so real, why you could be a real policeman!"

John Duggan suppresses a laugh and hides his smirk whenever Jenner faces him. They've already completed two complete inspections of all the rooms on the ground floor, but have not yet found Ettie. John is tiring and longs to remain in one place if only for a few minutes.

"Keep up, constable," Jenner grumbles, "We might miss one of them."

They go upstairs, where at least there are fewer people to

comment on Jenner's clothes and fan out. Jenner mooches a few steps along each of the corridors. A few guests emerge from the rooms. He eyes them suspiciously. One young woman says he looks 'real weird,' but trips quickly back to the ground floor from his glare. He watches her for a few moments and then rejoins John at the head of the staircase.

"Bit bloody gloomy up here," he says, "plenty of places for people to disappear. Seen anything?"

"No sir."

They look down together in silence.

"Who's that?" Jenner says after a few moments, nudging John's elbow and wagging his outstretched finger, "Bloody gaslight, everything's yellow, those two near the wall."

John's eyes follow Jenner's finger to a gaggle of people crowded in a corner outside the 'music hall.' A man in a plain, drab, but clean woollen jacket. He could be a working man, just returned from a shift in the factory. His face is partly obscured by his square peaked cap, but even in the shadowy corner, it's clearly Matt Usworth. The woman too is conspicuously ordinary, in a black dress and wearing a buff scarf around her head. Such plainness is surprising in one so usually bound up with the finery of both past and present. For it's Denise Deverall. They seem reluctant to come out of the corner and are deep in conversation. Away from the protection of the wall and the dim light, their proletarian clothes would mark them out immediately.

"The way they're dressed," John says, "he could be one of those Chartists, couldn't he?"

"Quite so," Jenner says, "and she could be that woman that helped them."

"Cecily."

"Look how they talk so earnestly and they're not even supposed to like each other."

"Does t'a want owt?"

They turn quickly to see Jon Cardington, with his long boots and heavy jacket, unmistakably attired as a Victorian gamekeeper. He stands erect with his hands plunged deeply in the long pockets. Out of his natural habitat what 'game' could he be protecting tonight and for what sort of poacher does he patrol? He and Jenner exchange lingering examinations of each other's outfits. Jon feels the need to explain first.

"Ow tho't it'd mek a change, me as old style gamekeeper like."

'Ow' was, of course Mrs. Darrington – Cressley.

"Quite, very fetching."

"Ar, could say't same abart yow."

Jenner pulls himself up stiffly, fingering his belt as a slightly authoritarian tick.

"Is it reyt? Is that howt' police looked in them days?"

"I believe so."

"I'm supposed to be mekin sure on everybody's comfortable up 'ere, so canna get thee owt?"

John Duggan moves to make a suggestion, likely to be liquid, but Jenner cuts him off.

"No thank you. Have you been up here all night?"

"Up and down, tha knows, wandrin' ararnd, mekin sure..."

"Quite, quite, but have you seen anything...unusual?"

"Unusual? Well, I dunna think any on this lot's what tha'd call *usual*..."

"No, but what I meant..."

"Course I was outside earlier, supposed to be mekin sure nob'dy gorrin that shouldna."

"And did they?"

"Did they what?"

"Get in when they shouldn't."

"No idea, wa'nt watching door, only t'wall. Strikes me there's a lot 'ere 'er never wanted to be, but that's nowt to do wi'me. I did warra was told. Once inside, different job. If tha says owt, tha gets another job."

"So you saw nobody getting in over the wall?"

"No. Mind, can't say abart doors, people runnin' and flittin' abart all overt' place."

"Quite."

"Tell thee what though, saw a rum looking feller, 'e wa' runnin' across back lawn as I wa' comin' in."

"Where was he going?"

"Went towards back door, but when I got there from

t'ouse, he wa'nt there."

"Have you see him since?"

"No."

"Describe him?"

"Too far away to say, but he was moving pretty quick, as if he was fitter'n any o' this lot."

"Clothes?"

Jon pauses, trying to remember the fleeting figure he'd seen earlier in the grounds.

"He wa' dressed plain, not gor up fancy like. At first I tho't he might've been one o't staff, but I couldna place him an 'e 'ad an 'at."

"What sort of hat?"

"Square wi' a little peek and..."

Jenner pulls Jon gently over to the banister.

"Like him, down there in the corner," he says, pointing.

Jon peers, but all he can see is a hazy throng of clustered people, none of them dressed in the way he's described or with a hat of any kind. Jenner follows Jon's mystified gaze, but Matt Usworth and Denise Deverall are no longer there. Jenner mumbles a meaningless explanation and Jon moves along to further 'mek sure' of the guests, though he's probably more there for their amusement than assistance. Either way, he doesn't care, so long as he keeps his nose clean and thereby avoids 'another job.'

After another cursory perusal of the upper galleries Jenner, followed by an increasingly tiring John Duggan, reluctantly returns to the bustle of the ground floor. Satisfying themselves Matt and Denise are not still lurking in the corner behind hat stands or potted plants, they embark on a further cruise around the rooms, indiscriminately barging and battering into people. Despite the crush most are able to dodge out of the way while others are provoked into comment.

"Do you mind? Probably thinks he's a real copper."

Jenner plunges on, ignoring the aggressive glares and nasty remarks, muttering irritably, "Where the hell are they?"

"Seem to have disappeared, sir." John says.

"Slippery as...come on, constable, we'll track 'em down."

Another spate of bumping and ramming yields nothing other than Jenner suddenly colliding with a woman in a large black hat and a long black elegant gown.

"Ettie!"

"Why, I didn't recognise you in...uniform."

"Where have you been?"

"I've been trying to get you all day! Don't you ever check messages?"

"I've been preoccupied."

"Haven't we all."

"Never mind that now, we need to talk."

He leads her towards the library, but the door is locked. He looks around for another safe vantage point, away from prying eyes and the tumult. Stepping along the corridor he finds a small external door which, surprisingly moves outwards to his touch. It opens onto the end of the terrace. John examines the door.

"The lock's been forced, sir."

"So, someone uninvited preferred not to come through the usual entrances," Jenner says, "could have been the man Jon Cardington saw in the garden, which would explain why he didn't see him later."

"Maybe he was just an opportunist thief. He could be anywhere now."

"Yes anywhere, but in the house."

They can hear the constant hum of the party, but shielded by the blind library wall this end of the terrace is fairly quiet. Ettie sits down on the low wall and looks out onto the garden. It's dimly lit from a lamp on the corner of the house. Jenner joins her while John returns inside to watch on the other side of the door for anyone venturing to their end of the corridor.

"Did the bountiful hostess find you?" he says, "She was asking earlier."

"Not yet," she says, continuing to stare into the garden.

"You were privileged to be invited."

"She probably wants to pick my brains."

"That could be significant in itself."

She doesn't respond.

"Seen anything?"

She turns to him.

"Not so much seen as felt."

She tells of her experiences in the canal and then of the mysterious presences she's sensed since. Several times she pauses for him to tell her to stop wasting his time or ask questions, but he says nothing, sometimes nodding and always waiting patiently until she's ready to begin again. As if detecting her embarrassment he's careful not to send any negative message, which might interrupt her flow. Only after he's sure she's told everything does he move and then only to signal to John inside, who shakes his head to indicate the corridor remains clear.

"What about tonight?" he says.

"They've successfully created a very good impression of the 1840s, " she says obliquely, "All these fabulous costumes, why even you have..."

"Ettie, what have you felt here tonight?"

She glances back at the garden, seeking reassurance in her thoughts as they bounce back from the trees and grass. She turns to him.

"These feelings have never really gone away since the night at the canal, but tonight...tonight they're stronger, closer...God, this house!"

"What about the house?"

"It's absorbed them, taken them into itself, swallowed them in the roof, pushed them into the walls, which now heave with them, extrude them. All these people...such a mass should inhibit such spirits, but...tonight...the music, the chattering, the clothes, the gaslight, the candles, the coming and going...it's too much, it exults them."

She turns away, shaking. Jenner takes her arm, she calms slightly.

"I'm okay," she says, "It's just so...so strong."

"The four you mentioned earlier, you feel the presence of all four?"

"Definitely the one that came through in the canal..."

She hesitates.

"...at least another... maybe two ... it could be all four. You must think me an absolute idiot!"

"Of course not. You said spirits. Is that what you believe they are, *just* spirits?"

"Do you still believe what you said before...that your enquiries may only be resolved by some sort of time transference by a suspect?"

He looks towards the door. John stands on the other side with his back to them.

"He can't hear you," she says reassuringly, touching his arm.

"I never believed this could happen again. I thought it was a one off, an aberration, particular individuals with occult powers you come across once in a lifetime, a set of crazy circumstances you can't explain, a case you solve, but have no real idea why. I tried, but I couldn't really settle afterwards. I kept getting flashbacks, remembering incidents, images..."

"It's alright, such feelings are quite normal."

He stands up, takes a couple of paces and thumps his right fist in the palm of his left hand.

"Normal for you, Ettie, but not for me! Damn it, I'm a detective, I deal in facts, not bloody sensations!"

"You deal in *evidence* and so do I."

"Yes, but...."

"Sit down, you'll attract John's attention."

He rejoins her on the wall. For a few moments they both stare silently into the garden, where gnarled branches and twisted shrubs, fantastically distorted, cast freakish shadows in the unnaturally streaking light from the house.

"Why do you ask me if I think they're only spirits?" she says, "Is it because of the man seen earlier and the forced lock on the door?"

"Maybe, though it could have been Matt Usworth. He wasn't invited and we saw him dressed just as the man in the grounds."

"Where is he now?"

"We've lost him, together with Denise Deverall."

"Have you seen Ella Weston?"

"No."

"She should be found."

John joins them.

"Sir, you said we'd meet Jennifer and Sandra..."

"Yes, yes, in a moment after I've fin..."

Jenner turns to Ettie, but she's gone.

Someone else has also seen Matt and Denise and has also tried to accost them, but with no more success than Jenner. While he scurried down the stairs, frantically trying to keep them in sight, she swept through the human lump congregated in the hall. Like him she'd arrived too late. Now she's gone back upstairs, imbibing more and more punch as she sits holding a makeshift court to anyone who cares to linger, eulogise on her splendid happening and congratulate her on the moral crusade. She enjoys the attention, acknowledging their adulation with a superficial smile and meaningless replies. It's a wholly automatic response, requiring no real involvement. Her peripheral concentration supplies the gist of the words, leaving her mind free to return to its usual fixation.

She'd expected, virtually welcomed Matt's appearance, but she'd not envisaged Denise. He's a dangerous, but calculated player in a desperate game, but she's an unforeseen, unpredictable rogue element. His clothes, a gratuitously insulting swipe, ostentatious in their denial of ostentation, their plainness shouting their crude message across the decades, could be almost anticipated, but hers were unnaturally shocking, irrationally contemptible in their bewildering unpredictability. Hiding in the corner, afraid to show themselves, yet confident enough to appear at all. It couldn't be missed. They *had* to be here. Before her fruitless attempt to ensnare them, she'd watched Matt with a canny, intensive attention. Usworth of the present or Usworth of the past? Then she'd switched scrutiny to Denise and similar, alarming thoughts disturbed her. Was it Denise she saw in those plain clothes, or someone else, also dressed out of natural inclination, out of place, out of class? Are they also from the past just like those other two she'd seen earlier? The other plain dressed woman and the man with his bag.

The adulatory gathering leaves her. She shudders. She looks round anxiously and goes to the stairs, incisively scanning the heady crush below. Dozens and dozens of 1840s people, but no one is real. Suddenly as if a crystal glass shatters, the sham froth of the night overwhelms, a melancholy sinew tightens and she longs for it to end so...

"No! No! No! Ahhhh..............."

The scream, high pitched and piercing continues for a full minute before gradually subsiding, followed by loud stabbing sobs and raucous throaty croaks like those of a mewling, fractious child. As the whole house turns in startled unison towards the terrified eruption a deafening, unbelievable silence follows. Jenner and Jennifer bound up the stairs followed by David. John stands on the landing holding back those from below, while Sandra keeps any upper floor rubbernecks away. However, Sylvia is before her and races round the gallery.

Before any of them, Ettie has reached the beginning of a small staircase leading to the second floor where Ella sits on the bottom stair, holding her haunches, rocking backwards and forwards, her eyes intent on the floor and snivelling. Ettie gently cradles her. Jenner, Jennifer and David arrive. Ettie holds up her opened hand and shakes her head. Ella pauses to look at them and then continues rocking. They hold back. As Sylvia arrives, Jennifer motions her away.

"What did you see?" Ettie says quietly, while slowly and delicately massaging one of Ella's hands.

Ella stops whimpering while her rocking subsides almost to a pronounced nodding.

"Saw her," she says, lifting a finger towards Jenner, "just there, saw her."

"Who? Who did you see?"

"Her, she was saying something, but... I couldn't hear her, always the same... I couldn't hear her. Why, why can I never hear her?"

"Was it Lizzie?"

Ella turns to Ettie. Her nodding stops, then she starts to whimper very quietly before burying her head in Ettie's shoulder.

"It was Lizzie wasn't it?"

She nods her head slowly and then forces herself back before pointing again towards Jenner.

"And him, I saw him!"

"Chief inspector Jenner, you saw…"

"No, no, no, not him, *him!*"

She starts shaking again, this time from side to side, repeating 'him' and putting her hands to her head. Jenner moves to speak, but Ettie pushes her hand forward and shakes her head. Ella suddenly stops shaking and faces Ettie with wide, gaping eyes and a hollow, gripped expression.

"Him, him with the hat, not like the others."

With the thumb and forefinger of both hands, she draws in front of her forehead the shape of a short peak.

"Usworth?" Jenner says.

Ella nods.

"Where did he go?"

Ella points with a wagging finger beyond him and then collapses again into Ettie's shoulder before standing up. She tries to step forward, but stumbles.

"Get her downstairs into a quiet room," Jenner says to Sandra.

"I know a place," David says.

Together they help Ella towards the stairs.

"In the meantime," Jenner says, glancing at Sylvia, "I don't want anybody getting near her."

"I'll see to my guests," Sylvia says curtly, turning to usher everyone away with a brisk "It's all over, let's get on with the party."

Within a few minutes the music restarts and the dynamic din returns as if there's been no interruption. Jenner turns to Jennifer.

"We need to check everybody's whereabouts in the last few minutes, but especially Matt Usworth and Denise Deverall."

Ettie still sits on the stairs.

"You think Ella saw Matt Usworth," she says.

"Don't you?" he says.

Ettie shakes her head.

"I was coming to find her. I'd just seen her when she screamed out."

"Did *you* see anything?"

"No. Before she cried out, I saw her looking as if into a deep pool."

"She was frightened?"

"Not at first. It was a curious, questioning look, but then it changed to a harrowed, haunted expression."

"When she saw Usworth."

"I wasn't near enough to intervene and help her, but close enough to feel a distinct presence."

"So you don't think it was Matt Usworth?"

"I only know what I feel."

"And now?"

Ettie shivers.

"I feel I'm in the canal again. They're all here, all struggling, but one struggles more than the others. If only I knew which one it is!"

"Is it Lizzie, as Ella said?"

Ettie shakes her head.

"I can't be certain."

John returns.

"They can't be found sir. We've turned over the whole house. Matt Usworth and Denise Deverall have disappeared."

"No, no, I know they're here!" Jenner shrieks, " you need to..."

He's interrupted by a commotion from the staircase. Returning up the stairs, David is arguing with a man on the half landing. He's plainly dressed and to Jenner distressingly reminiscent. Voices are raised though the exchange is unclear except for "you can't go there" from David and "get out o' my way" from the other man. The altercation goes on in muted tones as David tries to block the other man advancing further. As they struggle together the three police officers move to the stairs. As they grapple, Jenner tries to get a better view of the other man. The clothes are familiar, but in the pathetic gas lamps' frustrating half light, it's difficult to make out his face.

They're about the same age and build, but the other man, fitter, stronger, nimbler, pushes David aside and leaps up the stairs. John blocks his way. The man pauses, wild, desperate eyes searing at John as he sways slightly on arched feet. Then he springs to the top of the stairs in two great strides and a final vault. John crouches and grabs at his legs, but spurred by the momentum of the jump the man pushes him down.

The man looks round quickly. His best escape will be towards Ettie and the small staircase, but Jenner and Jennifer bar his way. Instead, he turns, clutches the banister and goes towards the opposite end of the gallery. He tries to run, but slows after a few bounds, pulling at his leg as if a recent injury has suddenly returned.

Despite this he quickly reaches the gloomy far end. Jenner goes after him, motioning John to follow along the other side of the stairwell to cut him off. The man stops by one of the corner arches, massages his ankle and looks gravely from side to side, desperate for a way of escape. He gapes in anguished despair at his pursuers and then steps out of the shadow. Jenner is sure now. The man moves towards the banister. He leans over and after staring wretchedly into the gaping stairwell and the throbbing maelstrom below, grabs the banister and lifts one leg. He's going to jump! He wobbles precariously as he lifts his other leg. John races to the corner. The man painfully eases himself upward as he scrambles to get up on the banister. He has both legs up and crouches on the banister, gripping it with his hands and swaying slightly, preparing to jump. As he leans and sways one last perilous time, John dives and grabs his shoulders, pulling him back and rolling him to the floor. Jenner arrives and puts his 1842 boot resolutely on the man's upper arm.

"Get him up."

John hauls him to his feet. Though he makes no move to escape, John holds him securely. Jenner fingers the button on his jacket, polishing it slowly between his thumb and forefinger as he studies the face. Closer now and illuminated by better light from the high chandelier, there's a distinct blue shadow indicating he's not shaved for a couple of days. His eyes are also drawn from lack of sleep. Jenner takes off his hat.

"Usworth, you're under arrest. Tell him his rights, sergeant."

Jennifer does so and then says, "Charge, sir....what's the charge?"

Jenner hesitates before saying, "Assault...assault on Ella Weston. Got anything to say?"

The man's eyes dart uneasily between the three of them, before resting anxiously on Jenner who continues to finger the buttons. The man looks down at these and seems in some awe of the uniform.

"Keep a good hold," Jenner says to John, "We don't want him slipping away again. When we get him down the station we can crack him once and for all."

The man is led down the stairs, through the crowd and out the front door. The sombre exodus causes little stir. Many of the guests even think the whole episode is part of the evening's entertainment and soon return to their revelries. Sylvia watches their departure from the library door with mixed feelings, part relief, part pleasure, part concern. Relieved it's over, pleased Usworth and Jenner, those equally unwelcome thorns seem no longer to be in her side, but left with a residual nagging concern all is not as it seems.

Ettie has watched the striking spectacle without moving from the bottom of the small staircase. Conscious, but detached, her eyes and ears have seen and heard, but her mind has been elsewhere. The brief, inconclusive conversation with Ella got her maddeningly close to the core, but she's been unable to grasp what Ella really felt or saw. Lizzie and another? And others, for Ettie knows there are more, still here, around, within. Watching and waiting as Ettie does, but who do they watch, for whom do they wait? Suddenly becoming aware of the noise and activity below she looks around in bewilderment. Why is this upper floor deserted? Where is everyone? She must talk to Jenner. He's not got it right. But he's gone.

Jenner concentrates on the road, rehearsing how he'll tackle Usworth and mulling over his questioning. Occasionally he looks across at the man. He had to be almost rammed into the car and even now looks out of the window fearfully as if he's never seen the inside of a vehicle before. He says nothing and doesn't look at any of them. Sometimes he shakes slightly as if cold. Jenner isn't fooled. Matt Usworth was desperate to get into the house for something. Had he arranged to meet Denise or was it a chance encounter?

He seems more cooperative at the station, keen to get

out of the car, though he has to be dragged out, apparently unfamiliar with the narrowness of the door. It's a good act, Jenner muses. He's going to play up the whole 1840s charade as a cover, playing dumb and masquerading some sort of memory loss or mental disorder. They'll probably have to go through an irritating initial phase, listening to wild protestations of bafflement. He'll finally realise they're not going to be fooled and it's best to assist the enquiries and cut his losses.

The duty sergeant looks askance at the three of them.

"Fancy dress is it, sir?"

"Quite. Just book him in, sergeant."

The man is agitated in the station, constantly looking around uneasily. He studies the duty sergeant with a magnetised stare, his eyes wandering up and down his uniform incredulously in a way he's not scrutinised the others. His pockets contain little and most of that is very grubby. He has no means of identification. He shuffles along the corridor, his eyes swooping fearfully along the walls. As Jennifer watches him she's also uneasy. Something about the whole situation isn't right. He surveys the interview room nervously, paradoxically only calming slightly when the others sit down. Of course, like him, all three are dressed for the 1840s.

Jenner formally introduces everyone in the room. Addressing the man as Matthew Usworth, he asks him to account for his movements during the evening. Though still apparently perturbed, he's calm enough now to glare at Jenner and shake his head.

"Who is this Usworth?" he says, "I am...Secker...Edwin Secker."

Jenner sighs deeply.

"Quite so and I'm the Tzar of Russia and for the record, where do you live?"

He gives an address in Bradford. Jenner sighs again.

"You're not helping yourself like this."

"Why have you brought me to this place?"

"You know why, for the assault of Ella Weston tonight. Now, I would like to talk..."

"Who is this Ella Weston? I've never heard of her."

Jennifer nudges Jenner.

"Sir, can I have a word?"

They go into the corridor, leaving the man with John and a uniformed constable. The door remains open.

"What is it?" Jenner says irritably, "We can't let up the pressure now. Sooner or later, he'll break."

Jennifer glances back into the room. The man, sitting opposite her, gapes back fearfully, curiously, but also defiantly. She turns back to Jenner.

"Look at him, look at him carefully."

Jenner turns to the man who now stares at him with equal disquiet, but also with a fixed, almost calculated intransigence, that he doesn't recall ever seeing in the face of Matt Usworth.

"Are you sure it's him?" Jennifer whispers.

The man, watching them talking mutely, gets agitated. He knows they're talking about him and their sidelong, furtive glances unnerve him. He pulls back the chair and stands up, pointing menacingly towards Jenner and Jennifer. The two officers rush to restrain him just as he shouts.

"Alright, I admit it. My name is Usworth, but I didn't do it...it was an accident."

Ettie has scoured the whole of the upper floor of the house. Only those few rooms whose doors have been locked throughout the night have eluded her. Guests have drifted back upstairs, an impromptu group elevating some of the musicians to initiate a mini party of first floor revellers. Even in the dimly lit Victorian atmosphere they seem impervious to the many disparate sensations assailing Ettie. Are they messages, dire intents to be heeded, even warnings or declarations of menace from across the decades? She tries to concentrate as she continues her search, but can't disentangle the jumbled words in her head from the jumbled cacophony assaulting her ears. Why can't these people understand the more they engage in this fierce re-enactment of the past the more they encourage the past to interfere with the present? Why don't they stop!

Half an hour ago Sylvia cornered her downstairs and swept her into her 'personal sanctuary' as she called the library. She'd read some of Ettie's articles, always been an admirer and wanted to meet the real woman, explore how she went about her investigations. Was it just a gift or something anyone with appropriate training could develop? How many times before has Ettie fielded such probing? How many other smooth talking pains in the proverbial has she had to endure?

Yet as she smiled politely, dribbling out the standard bland fend-offs, desperately hoping she could soon get away, Ettie had felt something different. It was beyond the usual mining for future dinner party stories, collected as others might collect stamps or old masters, depending on taste and bank balance. This woman had more than a dilettante interest. There was an earnestness, an impatient craving, a yearning to know beyond mundane curiosity, an intensity, a desperation even. What had she experienced, what was she holding back and of what was she afraid? Ettie posed a few ostensibly innocent questions, but they were skilfully kicked aside. Whatever lay deeper, it was not going to be revealed tonight. Sylvia was there to listen, not to tell. It was getting late. Some guests were leaving. Sylvia had to return to her hostess duties and at last Ettie got away. She was with Sylvia about ten minutes, but it seemed much longer. What she felt may have lengthened her sense of time passing. For even in the library, distracted by Sylvia's enquiries, the presences had not abated. Nowhere in the house would she escape them.

Her search of the ground floor, hampered by the crush of people, is no more successful than the upper floor. She should have intervened. She'd allowed herself to become so enmeshed with Ella she'd forgotten about the forces unleashed at the canal. It, they, are on the loose! Yet some kind of distinctness emerges. As her search for Jenner becomes more desperate and her guilty foreboding increases, one presence stands out. She has to warn him. He's tackled one danger, but in so doing he's allowed another to freely roam!

She races from room to room, searching, hoping she'll not be too late, blundering into people, inadvertently becoming part of crazy discourses or being bludgeoned into participating in whatever sudden fanciful delights appeal to the late night drunks, now in the majority. She returns to the first floor, stopping on the half landing to catch a glimpse of a fleeting figure who seems oddly familiar, yet strangely unknown. She reaches the top, but looking around sees no one until Sandra Tye appears from a corner.

"Did you see someone?" she says.

"No, Ettie, there's no one up here, I was just coming down."

Ettie runs along the gallery followed by a mystified Sandra. She finds no one. Then she remembers Jenner.

"The chief inspector, where is he?"

"At the station with that intruder."

"Then I may be too late!"

"So, now you say you are *Samuel*, not Matthew Usworth?"

How many times must Sam repeat himself? Obviously the police are detaining him, but it's not as he imagined it. Convincing them of his innocence seems remoter than ever and he realises he may have left everything too late, but now there's no alternative. He'd used a false name in the hope of being released on some lesser charge, but that had been a mistake. Why do they keep calling him *Matthew*? He still can't understand the odd vehicle they'd used to transport him from the house. He must have been deluding. So many days on the road it's hardly surprising. But then there'd been the other policeman, the one they called the duty sergeant, dressed so differently to the others, in fact not dressed like anyone else he'd ever seen. What does it mean? Is he going mad? He'd been so frightened at the house, they'd misunderstood his behaviour, but what could he have done? It's always best to try to get away. He's never been taken before.

"What were you doing at Elvington House?"

It's the one who seems to be in charge. He speaks so oddly and keeps asking the same questions in different ways. Such persistence, almost as if he really wants to get at the truth rather than just cobble together enough to get him convicted and out of the way. Must be important though, up from

London, surely he's not come all the way up here just after Sam?

"I was hungry. Everybody has to eat."

"Quite, so now you're admitting to burglary?"

"I'm admitting to nothing."

"You were seen creeping through the grounds and it was you that broke the lock on the door, wasn't it?"

If he admits to this, will it go better for him? Serious enough, but better than a murder charge. He may have been hungry, but that wasn't the real reason for going to the house. How can he tell the truth? He'd been *drawn* and foolishly allowed himself to follow. But follow what? Some*one* he knew he had to find at the house. Foolish maybe, resistible, probably not. How can he tell them he doesn't know? He must stall for now.

"I had business at the house, unfinished business."

"You had no invitation."

"Invitation? What are you taking about?"

There's another break while the senior one and the woman confer again. Who is she anyway? Dressed up for some swanky do, what's she doing here? She talks like a policeman. Never heard of such a thing. They'll be back shortly. They never go out for long. Every time they talk it gets worse. Why do they click that thing on the wall before they go out and what's it mean 'the tape?'

If only he'd not felt the need to go upstairs. It wasn't just to get away from the people. He'd managed to mooch around, virtually unnoticed downstairs, merging in between them. Some high class do, though even for the upper classes they talked peculiar. Whatever *it* was, he knew it would only be found upstairs. It seemed the house itself drew him. The house and someone he had to make contact with, but why... why do they keep calling him Matt?

They're coming back. It's not looking good. They've clicked that thing on the wall again. Why do they keep saying what the time is? Nothing to lose now, have to say what I know.

"I've told you I didn't do it."

"Quite, many times, but what is it you didn't do?"

"I didn't kill Jonathon Cressley."

Jenner stares in amazement.

"Jonathon Cressley?" he repeats.

Sam becomes agitated again.

"It was an accident. He fell in. Alright, there was an argument and maybe a bit of pushing and shoving, but it was an accident. He fell into the cut."

Jenner watches him. Is this the guff he's been working up for the last hour while they've been going round the houses getting nowhere? Deflect the questioning by dragging out a hundred and sixty year old crime. Conveniently admit to some incidental involvement, denying any real culpability. That's if he is Matt. But what if he's not?

Jenner's silence perturbs Sam. He waits and watches for a reaction, but the intense eyes and the locked lips give away nothing. Sam's already in deep and slipping fast. He must do something to halt the slide. He can't let them pin Jonathon's death on him.

"Jonathon was an accident, but the other wasn't."

Jenner's blankness is broken.

"Other?"

"I saw it all. Came from behind and killed him."

"You witnessed a murder?"

"Yes."

"Where and when was this?"

- 10 -

Ettie has hardly slept since the party. She had to make contact and after leaving the house, went to the police station. They wouldn't tell her anything, not even whether Jenner was in the building. A wall of ignorant silence had been erected in a few hours. A dangerous wall, built on treacherous sand. She waited for a time, but restlessly uneasy she couldn't settle and left. She'd driven out of the city, unsure where to go, but desperate for the open road. She must have wandered down every minor lane and hedged back road in search of some openness in the black, moonless night.

The dawn is slow and dismal, the sun struggling through the grey clouds. The solar prisoner, ponderously eases a trapdoor of light, painfully piercing the dark dungeon of the night. The sky is hung with long impregnable banks of grey and black cloud save for a narrow slip of white at the horizon, punctured intermittently by the plodding sun. Yet it is light. Morose, depressing, boding no hope for the day, but dragging its weary course, the faint lustre emerges.

Ettie watches the agonised germination of the day from her vantage on the hill at Sleavnell church. She sits on the lone, decrepit bench at the darkly shaded west end, looking across the valley where the wispy, hesitant ribbons of light gradually prise away the darkness to expose again the land's latent mysteries. In this half revealed beginning of the day, half the landmarks stand up in salutation while the other half, still shrouded by the night's lingering pall, cower in their darkness. At first only the electricity pylons, circumscribing the valley in a wide arc, can be made out. In these first few minutes of creeping light only those that know the land intimately see with their minds what their eyes cannot. So it is with the half understanding of the inner senses. Half awake, half known, half connected, half prepared, half asleep, half ignorant, half occluded, half unready. Half in the past and half in the present, sporadically touching them both, but resolutely attached to neither. Half of something, half interpreted by a half woman is surely half of nothing?

She sits until the sun is reasonably ascendant. The world awakes. Cars crawl through every tarmaced fissure. Suddenly she's aware of her mid nineteenth century clothes. Soon, maybe even this solitary sanctum will be invaded. Weary nocturnal travellers pulling in for a short rest or illicit lovers, marking out its robust loneliness for their early tryst. Before being spied by passing gawpers or unwelcome visitors she must return to the hotel. Not wishing to advertise she's been out all night by her distinctive costume, she tries to slip in unseen, but the receptionist hails her.

"Miss Rodway, there's someone waiting for you. I told her we couldn't get an answer from your room, but she insisted on waiting. She's in the lounge."

"Did she give a name?"

"No, but you can't miss her, there's no one else there. The night porter said she was outside the hotel in the early hours."

"I'll just go up and cha..."

"Oh, Ettie, you've come back. I must see you!"

Ella Weston stands or rather hangs at the doorway to the lounge. Her hair is bedraggled, her face drawn, her eyes peeping from within dark ovals, her cheeks sallow. One hand tightly grips the door handle while the other paws the doorjamb as if it might suddenly slip into the floor and unbalance her. She too still wears her dress from the night before though it's crumpled and slightly smeared with dirt at the cuffs. She lifts her hand with apparent pain and much effort from the doorjamb and fiercely thrusting the door with the other, lopes back into the lounge. Ettie is reluctant to leave her. Smiling politely to the awestruck receptionist, she follows.

Ella sits in the far corner away from the window, with her back to the light. Ettie sits opposite, the morning sun glinting in her eyes. At first, Ella continues to gaze forlornly at the floor, only looking up when Ettie speaks.

"You should be at home."

"They took me home, but I couldn't rest. I had to speak to you."

"You saw Lizzie, didn't you Ella, but who else did you see?"

"I should have spoken to you again last night, not let them take me away, but I was so confused."

"And now you're not?"

Ella fumbles in a bag at her feet.

"I've brought you some things."

"What things?"

"*Things!*"

She deposits a large coloured scarf on the coffee table. Various metal objects spill out. They are all old, some a little rusty.

"Part of your collection?" Ettie submits.

Ella nods.

"Sort of, some been in the family a long time."

Ettie gently pokes around the assortment. Knowing Ella's interest, she surmises they are medical or surgical instruments.

"Some of these must be very old?" she suggests

Ella leans back to stare at the pile with mixed pride and anxiety. Just looking at them distresses her. She tries to be detached, but it's too difficult.

"Why have you brought me these?" Ettie says.

"Some of them must be hers, got to be."

"Lizzie?"

Ella nods briskly, mouthing silent 'yer, yer, yer, yer.'

"Spoke to me this time."

"You said, at Elvington…"

"No, no, after, at home. In the house she was there."

"Your dream again?"

"No, no, no, no! Not a dream. Lizzie was there. I saw her. She was in her house 'cept it was in my house. What I mean is, she was there, but she was with..."

"What did she say?"

"Told me what she did. Said she was a midwife. Done it for years. Everybody knew her. They all knew her and she knew all them."

"Where did she live?"

"Round here."

"Creston?"

Ella nods forcefully again.

"Told me to guard her things."

"These things?"

Ella looks down furtively, her eyes flitting across the instruments, assessing whether each one can be truly associated with Lizzie.

"Told me about the doctor too. What was his name, I think she told me, what was it?"

She holds her head in her hands, shaking vigorously. Her hair lollops over her face and she grips the chair so tightly her knuckles turn incandescent white as she desperately tries to remember. Getting alarmed, Ettie leans over, ready to catch her if she falls forward or take her hands to comfort her, but Ella suddenly sits straight up with a satisfied glint.

"Foxley, Doctor Foxley!"

Ella sees the recognition in Ettie's eyes.

"You know him?"

"I've heard of him. Did Lizzie say any more?"

She leans back again, drumming the side of her head with her middle finger.

"There was something else, what was it? Yes! They worked together. Lizzie and Doctor Foxley. I suppose they would, wouldn't they, doctor and midwife and there was something else...yes something they did...that's what she said...something they did...I had to look after the instruments..."

Ettie takes her hands, which are gripping the edge of the table.

"What did they do, Ella? Try to remember what Lizzie said."

Ella shakes her head, mumbles incoherently, looks quickly into the now empty bag and then turns her attention back to the floor.

"Can't get...anymore...too difficult...but both affected... had to get away ...Lizzie had to get away...so did he...Doctor Foxley...had to get away..."

"Why did they have to get away? What were they afraid of?"

Ella looks up, her eyes now wild and fearful. She stands, picks up the bag and starts scooping the instruments into it. Gently, Ettie tries to stop her. Some pieces drop on the floor as she tries to ram the larger ones into the bag. She gets more agitated and then gives up, grabs the bag and runs out of the room. Ettie runs after, but Ella is quick, darting out the front door, throwing the bag into her car and driving away rapidly, scraping the tyres noisily on the gravel. Ettie stands on the hotel steps, watching the car disappearing down the lane with mounting desolation. Yet again, Ella has slipped away leaving her frustrated and angry. Frustrated that once more she's left with the crack of contact, glimmer of part explanation, a toe hold on resolution. Angry for allowing Ella to run out, not knowing where she'd gone wrong and how better she might have handled the situation. She goes back inside, mutters some limp excuse to the bewildered receptionist and goes up to her room to change.

She discards the elegant black dress, tossing it carelessly onto the bed. It lies, untidily folded in a heap. She looks down and rolls it over. Gone now the counterfeit skin of 1842. She takes a shower, allowing the cleansing warm water to blot out her thoughts and allow her mind to switch to purely mechanical processes for a while. The slithering water, as it runs and removes, reinforces her dispensing of the past. Yet the past is not so easily evaded and as she dries herself its long tentacles enfold again, digging and delving incessantly. She dresses quickly. She's been awake all night, but dare not lie down. Not sleep, but those ceaseless, inexorable thoughts will engulf her. In any case she's not tired, but hungry. They'll be serving breakfast now.

She goes back down. The entrance hall is deserted and there's no one at the desk. If there had been people she might have gone directly and unthinkingly to the dining room, but the hotel lobby's bareness makes her pause before hurrying on. She's drawn back into the lounge. Only when she opens the door and enters the empty room does she understand. No one has been in and the crumpled pile lies on the corner coffee table, still partly wrapped in the coloured scarf. She sits down and casually rummages through it. Ettie knows nothing about medical instruments, but their age calls to her as she smoothes their handles and runs them across her palms. It's not just that some are time heavily discoloured and stained or that others are marked and etched by time filled use. As she slips them between her fingers the old steel sends shivering pulses, gradually replacing the coldness with a gathering heat, too quick, too immediate to be from the warmth of her own hands. When such coldly sterile implements transmit such an ardent feverish glow they must be conductors, intense relaying chains, ignited by someone intent on making contact. All those years the dream had come to Ella, but she who sent it had been unable to make herself understood. Now at last she had spoken, jarringly, infrequently, but she had spoken. Poor Ella, her descendant, she has the connection, but lacks the sensitivity to be a true receptor. Can Ettie, a stranger, establish and maintain that contact?

She takes two of the instruments and grips them fiercely, concentrating her whole mind with a single focused intensity. She closes her eyes. Vaguely, waveringly she sees a middle aged woman in a sparsely furnished room with bare walls. The image jars, but she manages to hold it. The woman turns. She speaks, but the words are indistinct. In her mind Ettie sees, but does not hear. Just like Ella. What is it Lizzie is saying? The image blurs. Ettie is losing her. Then, for one keen, sudden second she's sharp and clear. Her lips move again. Ettie grips the instruments harder and harder in an effort to retain the connection. There's no sound, but she speaks so slowly Ettie can read her lips.

"Go...go now."

"Where, where must I go?" Ettie shouts back in her mind.

"Go...go to where we...where...there is..."

The image dissolves. She's gone, but one word remains in Ettie's mind. *Contact.* She opens her eyes. The sun is streaming through the garden window. She loosens her hold and finally lets the instruments go. She sits back. She's tired now as if the disturbed night has suddenly buried her in weariness. Yet, even with its constant pummelling of her own misgivings it's not the night that refuses to let her rest. It's this swathing, clamouring message from the insistent messenger that demands to speak yet cannot be heard.

She gets up and pulls the instruments together into the scarf. In her impatience and alarm, Ella has unwittingly given Ettie the help she needs. The connection is still weak, but it's moved forward and without these tools she would still be terrorised in writhing despair at the canal tunnel. Tools? She thinks of them as tools, but who uses such tools? She picks up what are clearly forceps, not normally for a midwife, but maybe for a doctor. These are not Lizzie's. What was it she said?

"Go to where *we*..."

We? Her and Doctor Foxley? But where, where must she go?

Ettie sits again and holds the scarf, now tied around all the instruments. She closes her eyes. No new image enters, but there is a residual vision of Lizzie. She brings back the room and Lizzie speaking, remembering the words again. Nothing more. She opens her eyes again. *Contact!* That was the word Lizzie had used. Go to where we...*make contact?* It can mean only one thing. She shivers in trembling fear of that dark, dank place where Ettie had felt them all. It had to be Sam that rushed past her, but she felt others. Were two of them Lizzie and Doctor Foxley? She must go back! She shakes now. Back to the canal, back to the Cross Cut tunnel! She pulls her hands together to stop them shaking and then grips the chair as Ella had done. She stops shaking, but shudders at what must be faced. Lizzie has spoken in her desperation and it's the only way to make contact. She must return to the tunnel.

She misses breakfast and hurries to her car. Yet, just before driving off, she looks back. There's no one around, but no sooner has she lost the hotel in the mirror, her misgivings close in. She can't delay going to the canal, yet she's troubled at not working closely enough with Jenner. Will he realise it's not Matt he's arrested? Sam will be confused and frightened. She must warn Jenner how to tackle him. There's also the Weston family history to be followed up. If she can fill in the gaps, perhaps her tenuous contact with Lizzie can be expanded. Driving automatically, she turns into the lane leading to the country park. Nervously she checks the mirror. No one is following. Now her mind is open to residual echoes of Lizzie.

The demanding, imploring expression surges along the road towards her in the form of a massive, imposing face. The lips are parted, ready to speak and though Ettie can make out every feature and line of her image, she only utters soundless, wordless breaths. She nods her head slightly as if not wishing to draw attention to herself or perhaps indicating someone or something is in front and to the side of her. Again, Ettie nervously glances in the mirror. When she looks back to the road the huge Lizzie face is gone. Yet in her mind, the bare room and the bending, turning figure with its insistent if mysterious expression remains.

She enters the country park, but leaves the car some way from the canal. She needs to walk, gather her thoughts and prepare herself. She takes the scarf and its contents from the seat, clutching them in her left hand. The place is deserted. It's still chilly from the night. She turns up her collar. The towpath with its trim hedges and clumps of trees slices the grassland, innocently masking the canal. She stops for a moment at one of the seats, staring into the cold, murky water, the tranquillity undisturbed except for an occasional tiny ripple activated by a water beetle or passing gnat. Hidden beneath the shimmering, peaceful surface, unsuspecting travellers might never know its potent depths, Calm to the eye, but to the sensitive mind and spirit, deeply charged. Is this the catalyst to strengthen the feeble connection with

Lizzie? Is it enough to wait beside the water for Lizzie to break through or must she go into the tunnel to establish the link? Lizzie is the essential contact, but will she also need to make contact with Doctor Foxley or maybe others? Maybe the forceps will provide the connection.

She looks around, but the hedge obscures her view. She stands up to peer nervously across the empty ground to where her single car stands near the entrance. No one. Ella made contact with Lizzie at the house. Sam was at the house. What if the house is the attraction? She must return to Elvington House. But it can't be. It was the party, the unwitting magnetic night, the sparkling brilliant candle pulling the moths out of the dark layers of the past. That was the attraction, but the candle has been extinguished. It no longer burns and the moths must find another, sturdier attachment, one that doesn't flicker in the capricious heat of the moment or is easily snuffed out in the pervasive, exposing dawn.

Her uneasiness grows. It's not just the prospect of returning to the scene of presences breaking their time wrapped bounds. She's alone and the further she penetrates the tunnel, the stronger will be the perils from those lying within and those following from outside. She checks the field again, staring anxiously over the canal towards the hills. No one. Must she do this alone? There's little time. Lizzie may not be patient, but should she wait until making contact with Jenner? That too should not be delayed. They must work together ... working separately splits their strength... especially when there's so little time...time is limited...she must move quickly...go back...go on...go back...

Stop! Her mind made up, she walks towards the tunnel. Not without doubt yet knowing there's no realistic alternative, for she knows it holds more than dank bricks, dark water and damp air. Crossing the threshold feels as if a heavy door, incapable of being reopened closes behind her. Ignoring her misgivings, she trips the first dozen carefree steps with nonchalant confidence, fired with fatalistic courage, temporarily blinded by the flames of ignorance. Suddenly it's darker though she's barely twenty meters from the entrance and the morning light is strong now. She looks back, half expecting to see a dusky figure crouching in the shadows, but no one disturbs the arch of light that's her diminishing window on the outside world, her semicircular last gasp of openness, opportunity to retreat or even escape. She goes on, her steps now heavier, slower, portentous, reverberating in ominous echoes from the walls and roof. She must soon receive the next message, but further inwards may not tell her more, but leave her exposed and unprotected. Best avoided. She stops and listens. Silence except for the water, the soft, misleading lapping beneath and the unceasing dripping from above. She edges forwards, a few, tremulous steps. Then she sees. Then she hears.

Jenner too sleeps little during the night. He leaves the station late in something of a haze, even forgetting he still wears the uniform of an 1840s police inspector. By the time he realises it's too late as he's left his usual clothes in the office. No matter, there are few people about. He stops the car and walks along the river bank, hoping the cool air might clear his thoughts before he goes home, but all it clears is any residual warmth from his tired frame. The crisp, sharp night and the murky river, untempered by a moon, force their chilly dampness into every bone. After an hour, raw in the body and frozen in the mind, he returns thankfully to the car and switches the heater to maximum. Is it the coldness of the night that stings him or his own doubt laden conclusions?

They'd finally conveyed Usworth to a cell, ostensibly to 'let him sleep on it and be more amenable in the morning,' but it was as much an opportunity for Jenner as well as Sam to reconsider his position. Ella's outburst, the pinnacle to the night's heightening tension, led to Jenner's panic and Usworth's arrest for a non existent assault. He asked Jennifer to get a statement from Ella Weston, but holds out little hope she'll cooperate. He'd been sure he'd arrested the reprobate Matthew Usworth, but now…? Ella never said 'Usworth' or anyone else had 'assaulted' her and there's less chance she'll so say now. Ettie said they both dealt in evidence, but what sort of evidence does he ask Jennifer to investigate? She was convinced it wasn't Matt Usworth, but passed no comment on the implications of him being *Samuel* Usworth. She knew he was recorded in the Chartist minute book found by Denise Deverall.

As they parted at the station, she'd said, "Ettie told me about the case in London, sir."

So now she also knows about Jenner's past. Are such things repeating themselves? He'd not responded. How can he explain what he doesn't understand himself? It would mean opening up avenues he'd rather not go down. In the car his body, if not yet his mind, begins to thaw. He turns the heater down slightly. He needs to be alert and doesn't want too much warmth sending him to sleep. If 'Sam' is Matt, why admit to witnessing a murder? Why not prevaricate a little longer? Unless he's afraid of something worse. What could be worse than witnessing murder? Carrying one out. Yet what has he really given away? He's vague about the date – about three years ago – and as for the place – indefinite directions to the north of the city centre. What about a street? No street. An area, a district? In the country, a field. Where was this field? Jenner had spread out a map of the city and circled the whole northern sector. Usworth's glazed eyes had pored over it in utter bemusement.

"All these streets?" he murmured, "Never heard of them. You're fooling me, this isn't Nottingham."

"Yes it is. Are you saying you don't know the place?"

"Course I do, but not this...this counterfeit. I was born here."

"When was that?" Jennifer intervened.

"1811."

It was then Jenner abruptly took a final break.

"Making a monkey out of us."

Her silence irritated him.

"You surely don't believe this, sergeant?"

"No sir...I suppose not."

"*Suppose* not!"

"It's just, I don't think this is Matthew Usworth. He's like him, but it's not him."

They'd gone back, but got no further. Maybe Jennifer had only expressed the same doubts that had been gnawing at himself all night? Maybe the stubbornly steadfast story and the persistent single mindedness of the man had got to him, undermining his own resolve. He stays in the car by the river a long time, hours, grinding the grain of disparate material in the mill of his mind until a useless thin trickle of powdery conclusions are left, inedible, unusable, impractical. Eventually he goes home, but still cannot settle. He lies on the settee and dozes for an hour, continually waking from wild, frightening half dreams, discordant visions, where the logical conclusion of enquiries are overruled by dead suspects, insisting on declaiming their guilt and refusing to lie down.

He's an early arrival at the station. After downing several cups of black, sweet coffee in an effort to clear his head and settle his nerves, he gets out the maps. So far, enquiries have not revealed Matt Usworth's whereabouts. He's not yet ready to grapple with the disturbing prospect of the prisoner downstairs *not* being him, but the murder he alleges he witnessed must be followed up. On the pad is his unbelievable note of Usworth's exact words. When and where the murder had taken place. The when is as absurd as his alleged year of birth, while his broad description of the location is so general it could be many places. North of the city centre, open country, some surrounding hills, but how far north and which hills? There are dozens of possibilities. He makes a list. Even if he accepts the ludicrous date and allowing for open country at that time, there are no appreciable hills. It just doesn't fit. Nevertheless, do they investigate the nearest locations, see if there's any possibility...?

Better go over the statements from last night. They are all routinely obvious. Everybody where he would have predicted they would say they were. No one was near Ella Weston at the time of the incident, except Usworth and Ettie. Where is Ettie? He could use her wise counsels now and not just about her movements the night before. He rings the hotel. She's already gone out. He flicks through other statements and earlier notes, pausing over the interview with Alan Banning. It nags him. He reads it over several times. There's something significant he can't put his finger on and nothing on which to base any follow up. He puts it aside. Sometimes these things return when the mind isn't too engrossed. He turns back to last night's statements and peruses David Underwood's, the only other person relatively close to Ella at the time.

"I needed to inform Mrs. Darrington – Cressley about the drinks stock. I caught sight of her heading towards the stairs, so I followed. When Ella Weston screamed out I was at the bottom of the stairs, so I ran up to render any assistance that might be necessary. The police passed me as I went up."

Jennifer comes in.

"What do you make of David Underwood?" he says.

"Seems very proper and precise."

"Quite, just like his statement."

"Something you're not happy about, sir?"

"Has everybody else been accounted for?"

"Just a few at the house, servants, it's being dealt with this morning."

Jenner nods absently. Then he spreads out the maps and goes over Usworth's description, pointing out relevant places from his list. Jennifer listens, attentive, but also a little bemused.

"What are we looking for? she says.

"Anywhere that might fit his description."

Jennifer is still bemused. He senses her unease.

"Anything you're unsure about, sergeant?"

"No sir, all very...clear."

He strikes a line through the middle of the list, tears off the bottom half and hands it to her with another map.

"Good. I'll take Duggan with these. You organise yourself and look into the others. We'll meet up later. Not too long now, but thorough, you understand?"

She nods. He leaves, barking at John Duggan on the way. She clutches the paper, wondering how much of the exercise is designed to find the alleged murder location or a means of filling Jenner's time while he comes to terms with his prisoner's real identity.

The dimly widening glint, first a speck, then a twinkling signal, an oval of opaque lightness approaches. Then the framed features, growing in size and distinctness and reflected in mirrored clarity in the water emerge from the depths of the tunnel. They fill its cavernous darkness, Lizzie's searching eyes, like two vast beacons dazzling and beckoning. Her wide lips part and she speaks with the strident immensity of clanging cathedral bells, sonorously reverberating over and over themselves across the walls and the water. Ettie struggles to extract the words from the ringing echoes, flung at and around her like an expansive audio discus, bouncing repeatedly through intricate patterns that defy the ears to capture and the brain to interpret. Lizzie's eddying messages flush and flow incoherently. Ettie perseveres, filtering the jangling whirligig until they solidify. Then, as rapidly as she's appeared, a tremendous force erupts from the right hand wall to lever Lizzie aside with ruthless speed in wild jabbering shouts and screams, vocalised spear thrusts accompanied by incandescent light that glaringly kicks its way across the tunnel. Now Lizzie contracts to the humble woman in the plain room, feebly mouthing pathetically voiceless protests. The light turns whiter and with a pervading coldness relentlessly expands into the tunnel's constricting and shrinking narrowness. Ettie shudders. She could soon be trapped!

Lizzie's image fades frighteningly fast and Ettie loses her only friend, her only hope of retreat, of escape! She edges backwards slowly and then turns, first walking and then running from the deafening roar and the overtaking light. Unless she moves very quickly it will immerse her in its pervasive flood. It lasts only a few minutes before she recovers her wits and runs from the tunnel. Driven by terror fuelled panic, slipping and slithering on the wet stones, somehow she reaches the tunnel mouth without falling and then pounds painfully along the towpath, almost vaulting the hedge, sliding down the bank and sprinting across to the car. There she delays only long enough to scan the vacant field before jerking the engine into life and hurtling away.

But she's not totally escaped. As she speeds through the lanes, wildly baying voices hammer her mind, showering sharply sculptured shafts of images, in a vortex of confused and harrowing visions, constantly shifting and shearing over each other. Huge crowds, bent on destruction seethe along narrow streets as a sinewy mass, brandishing sticks and weapons only to be flung aside by a stately ceremonial procession, headed by colourful notables, in turn thrust away by a charge of sword wielding soldiers, clearing aside an ugly mob.

Ettie focuses her concentration on the road ahead, but they come on quicker, clearer, louder than before. From the clothes she knows these images are not from the 1840s, but earlier, twenty, thirty years. Do they come from Ella's disturbed imagination, memories of her ancestors, imprisoned so long in her troubled mind and now thrusting at Ettie in this manic attack? Now comes many men in darkly, ragged clothes on the road. A twisting, shearing, breaking, crashing, louder and louder, drum her ears, fiercer and fiercer. A workshop, crammed with wooden machines and even more men, striking and pulling them apart with vitriolic intensity. Another procession, but without acclamation, an announcement from a large building, the crowd shouting abuse, stamping their feet and shaking their fists. A swirling, shouting mob, surging through the streets, like an immense slithering snake, smashing its way towards some shrouded, secret enemy. Then in the distance she sees intense fire, billowing smoke and more shouting, screaming, defiant people. Jabbed into these flying, unreachable incidents are jerky stabs of unconnected phrases. At first Ettie ignores them along with all the other incidental flotsam assailing her mind, but then they make some sense.

"...get to Foxley...get what he can tell...don't ignore Foxley... where is Foxley...doctor, doctor...it's not yet finished...help me...the big house... awful place...the poor...help them...help me..."

Then they too are swallowed into the spiralling morass of spooked missiles, seemingly unrelated to each other by any clear time or place. Ettie hardens her mind in a final, desperate bid to get rid of the battering torrent, gradually quelling their invasive blows until they're trimmed to a muttering under feel of insignificant sounds and pictures. Are these turbulent apparitions just the crazed outpouring from Ella, rammed up by a despairing Lizzie? Or haphazard impulses, others' past memories, summoned by those presences, jostling and jockeying for Ettie's attention? Whatever they are, she must separate them from the real messages Lizzie may be trying to send. She must be free! Frantically, she summons her last vestige of strength and focuses her mind on other things, anything to escape. Then at last, the divergent sounds and furious images are gone.

At the city boundary she slows down. She's covered the few miles from the country park in a few minutes, taken blind corners much too fast and driven too quickly through the built up area. Luckily, she's not met a lorry or bus coming along the narrow roads. She slows again on reaching the heavier traffic and then stops at traffic lights. She taps the steering wheel nervously, muttering to herself and glancing across at the car in the next lane, wondering if the driver has noticed her distress. A young man hammers the wheel even more forcefully than Ettie, though in tune to the booming beat from the car radio rather than any exploding dread from inside his head. The lights change. He accelerates away without a care. Why should he? She moves in behind, like a goose in a flock, flying in the carved air stream of the leading bird. Perhaps he can chop out a path for her to scuttle through the heart of the city to the police station? He turns off towards the west.

Another set of traffic lights, ten miles now from the Cross Cut. Her tattered, gashed nerves begin to ease and the criss-crossed time jumbled memories abate. She focuses on Lizzie's words before they were so violently cut short, rehearsing what she must say to Jenner. At last she understands about Doctor Foxley, what Martin Sarwell was really after and why he was killed. But first there are other, more immediate issues to be resolved if Jenner is not to prejudice the arrival of Sam Usworth. They must access the workhouse records and get to the truth. She hurries from her car at the police station. A few more minutes will make little difference, but there must be no further delay. Inside it's unbelievably quiet. A man and a woman wait at the reception, but otherwise the building lacks any sense of burning tension or bustling activity. After spending the whole night in a state of swelling agitation and a morning on the precipice of disaster, she can't believe the place is so calm!

One of the visitors is having difficulty understanding the receptionist and starts to argue about some trivial matter. Ettie's desperate urgency shouts in her head. She fidgets irritably at the back of the room, getting more distressed as she waits. At last, the man, clutching a form, which he holds at arm's length as if it might bite him, accepts the receptionist's explanation and leaves. The woman has an appointment with an officer and is quickly ushered inside. At last Ettie reaches the counter, but only to have her hopes dashed. Jenner is out.

Already threadbare from constant thrashing, her shattered nerves now plunge out of control. She steadies herself and then sits, but feels herself falling headlong into a deep, dark well, the grim dank walls rushing past her as she waits for the final fatal crash. She leans back, closes her eyes, her head spins. The sensation of falling continues, though she seems to be slowing. The bottom looms up. She will land and be crushed by the violent force of her own body.

"Are you alright?"

She opens her eyes. She's avoided the crunch. The receptionist leans over the counter, anxiously. Ettie dabs the moisture, which has formed in her eyes.

"Yes, yes, I'm fine, thank you."

The reception phone rings. Ettie closes her eyes, expecting the whirling drop to return with no sense of purchase in her feet, but she feels balanced, her mind as fixed as her body, except for a slight tingling in her feet. She opens her eyes again. The receptionist is still on the phone and doesn't notice her ease up, shakily. Nothing to be gained from waiting. Go home, try later. She shuffles towards the entrance, a reassuring firmness spreading back into her feet. She almost reaches the door when it's thrust aside by a familiar figure.

"Ettie!"Jennifer shouts, grabbing Ettie as she stumbles forward.

"I'm okay," she says, grasping the edge of the counter, "Just a little tired."

"Come inside."

Seated in the office, the colour in Ettie's face gradually returns though she has to gulp down several cups of coffee before her strength is restored. Jennifer sits and watches her carefully.

"Not just lack of sleep," she says at last.

Ettie nods and then laughs it off, saying she'd allowed her imagination to work overtime on her way to the station. Jennifer listens patiently as Ettie describes the weirdly tangled and conflicting images that flooded her mind.

"Can't make sense of them," she says.

"Did you recognise anyone?"

"No."

"What about the place, was it local?"

Ettie thinks carefully, but doesn't know.

"Hard to say, could be, I suppose. Why do you ask?"

"Some of those things sound familiar."

"I couldn't pin down the period, but it was certainly earlier than the 1840s."

"It is. The machine breaking and the way the men are dressed puts it during the Luddite troubles. As a major textile centre, Nottingham was a hotbed."

"When was that?"

"At its height, about 1811."

Jennifer suddenly catches her breath after saying the year, the final syllable almost lost as her voice lifts.

"Anything wrong?" Ettie says.

"No, just something I remembered."

"So it was all about the Luddites."

"Not all. Some of it is definitely later, the 1830s. They were hard times, depressed trade, unemployment. Then there was the agitation surrounding the Reform Bill and the new Poor Law."

"The introduction of workhouses?"

"There'd been workhouses before. In fact, one of the oldest was in Nottinghamshire, but the new law made them compulsory. They were very unpopular and were strongly resisted in all the manufacturing cities."

"Was there a lot of trouble over the Reform Bill?"

"You mentioned a fire. Nottingham Castle was burnt

down during a Reform Bill riot, though the crowd were probably just as intent on attacking the property of the local landowner, the Duke of Newcastle."

"Sounds like Nottingham was a violent place."

"It was. *Turbulent* Nottingham they called it. These visions seem very vivid, as if you were there yourself or reporting from those who were."

Now Ettie sighs quickly, conspicuously. Jennifer understands.

"Someone's memories?"

"Or the memories of more than one. I thought they could be some kind of genetic remembrance, passed on through Ella Weston, but from what I saw and heard before..."

Ettie breaks off.

"Now, you're not sure?" Jennifer says.

Ettie draws back, partly in fear, partly in embarrassment, partly incredulously not wanting to believe her own eyes and ears. Jennifer will not be put off.

"Why aren't you so sure, Ettie? What else have you seen and heard?"

Slowly, hesitantly, often repeating herself as she tries to give coherence to such confused, frightening and mystifying incidents, Ettie tells of her dread filled night and the canal morning's hope and despair. Forced to relive so much in the telling, her hands begin to shake again and her voice trembles. Jennifer takes hold of her hands just as Ettie had taken hold of Ella's. Gradually, the shaking stops though her voice continues to waver until she finishes.

"So, you're sure your main contact is Lizzie Traynor?"

Ettie nods.

"But who are the other people? Are they all from the past?"

"Doctor Foxley certainly."

"Could one of them be Matthew Usworth?"

"If he is, then he's not in the present."

Jennifer is silent and then says, "One thing I'm sure of, the man in the cells is not him."

"Is that what chief inspector Jenner believes?"

"I'm not sure what the boss believes, even if he knows

himself after the interview with the man *called* Usworth."

"Why did you start at the mention of the year 1811?"

Jennifer is silent again.

"It's something he said, didn't he?" Ettie exclaims.

"He said he was born in 1811."

"He has to be treated very carefully."

"You're sure he really is Samuel Usworth?"

"There's no doubt of it. What did he tell you?"

"The boss has had us traipsing all over the countryside looking for a place where there might be...a body... just because he said he'd witnessed a murder. The boss and John Duggan are still out there looking. I've finished my stint."

"Have you found anything?"

Jennifer shrugs.

"How? We don't know what we're supposed to be looking for."

"But if you believe he's not Matt, he could be telling the truth?"

"If he really is Samuel Usworth, then..."

Jennifer stops, her eyes betraying her unspoken thoughts. Baffled and bewildered, she accepts the probability of the incredible, but can't yet give it the credence by uttering the words. Ettie needs to know more.

"Tell me everything Sam said."

Jennifer summarises the interview. Ettie wants to know what questions produced particular responses. She's also interested in the breaks and Jenner's reactions, which Jennifer explains as far as she's able.

When Jennifer gets to the death of Jonathon Cressley, Ettie nods and says "Was that why he was at the house?"

"Not really. It didn't make sense. The boss didn't take any notice."

"But what did he *say?*"

Jennifer studies her notes.

"He said he had business at the house, unfinished business."

"Unfinished business," Ettie says and then, remembering Lizzie's words in the tunnel, "It's not finished yet."

"What do you mean?"

"It fits. I now know what to do, we must…"

"Ettie! Where have you been?"

Jenner is at the door. He comes in, sits down opposite them both and then turns to Jennifer.

"Found anything?"

"No sir, what about you."

He shakes his head and clicks his teeth in disappointment. He turns to Ettie.

"We need to talk."

"Yes," she says, "there's so much…"

"Quite, but first I must check with Tye and Duggan, a few loose ends. I'll see you shortly, don't go away."

Ettie wants to stop him and speak, but she's still not wholly recovered and as she pauses to put her thoughts in order, he gets up and with a bouncy wave is gone.

"How can he be so…blasé, so calm?" Jennifer says, slightly annoyed.

"He's not calm," Ettie says, "Not inside."

"He'll be back."

"I hope so."

Jenner catches the two constables in the corridor and whisks them into his office.

"Anything on Matthew Usworth?" he says to Sandra.

"No sir, gone without a trace."

"You've followed up every possibility?"

"His description and picture have been circulated nationally. Definitely no findings. It looks like he really is the man downstairs."

Jenner grunts doubtfully.

"Shall we get a doctor in to see him?" she says.

"A doctor, what do we want a bloody doctor for?"

"I was thinking of a psychiatrist to examine him, tell us if he's disturbed, thinks he's Sam…"

"He's bloody disturbed alright, but not in a way a damned shrink's going to tell us."

"I was just thinking if he and Sam are, as it were one and the same…"

"It's not what you *think* constable, it's what you know. Now, do we have all the statements from last night?"

She hands a sheaf of papers to him. He skims through them, stopping to study Jon Cardington's.

"Did you take this?" he says to Sandra.

"Yes, I spoke to him this morning. He disappeared last night."

"Disappeared? Didn't we cordon off the place after the incident with Ella Weston?"

"Yes we did, but he must have slipped out before..."

"Quite, slipped out. Where did he go?"

"Says he went home as (she consults her notes) he'd done all his jobs and he didn't want anymore."

"Can it be verified?"

"His wife confirms he came home about that time."

"Strange time to suddenly decide his work's finished and get away. Let's see where he was at the time of the incident."

He reads the relevant part of the statement again.

"I was carrying out my duties downstairs and had just taken a break with other staff in the kitchen...resume my duties...when I was approached in the kitchen corridor by Mrs. Darrington – Cressley, who informed me...and I reported on.... then heard the screaming from upstairs...Mrs. Darrington – Cressley left me...went into the hall...other staff...no one to report to...went home."

"Shall I talk to him again?"

He hands back the statements.

"No, not yet. He's clearly placed on the ground floor at the time, though he may know more than he's letting on. We may need to talk to him later about his sudden departure from the house. Alright, constable, I'll see you later."

Peremptorily dismissed, Sandra leaves. Jenner takes another bundle of statements out of his desk and pushes them across towards John Duggan.

"Somewhere in this lot there has to be some inconspicuous item we've missed that'll shed some well needed light on all this bloody darkness."

John turns them over.

"These are all the original statements, We've been through them a dozen times."

"Quite so and you may need to go through them another

dozen times, but you'll have to keep at it until you get there. I'll help you."

Jenner pulls back a very small proportion of the pile and settles down to study the statements. John looks up. Jenner nods and flicks his hand towards the larger pile. After only a few minutes they are disturbed by Ettie, followed by Jennifer.

"You were going to talk to me," she says.

"Yes I was. I'm sorry, I'll get to you just as soon as I..."

"Jennifer's told me about the interview of Sam Usworth. Do you intend to talk to him again?"

"At some stage today, but first I need to examine..."

"There are a number of things I need to talk to you about, but the first priority is to track down the original records of the East Notts workhouse around 1811."

Jenner sits open mouthed, but before he can speak, Jennifer interrupts.

"Listen to her, sir, When you've heard what Ettie's found I think you'll agree we need to act without delay."

"Is this connected to the death of Jonathon Cressley in 1842?"

"It could be," Ettie says, "you see..."

"Sir, look at this!"

John Duggan shuffles across one of the statements.

"It might fit with what Usworth's been saying."

Jenner stares down where John has ringed a particular section. He looks bewildered.

"It's Alan Banning's statement, the friend of Martin Sarwell."

"Quite, but you'll still have to help me."

"Usworth said he'd witnessed a murder and gave us a description of the location."

"Which we've signally failed to find."

"Which is my point. We've been looking in the wrong places, but we knew it all along. You remember you asked me to look into the early history of the local railways because it was an interest of Sarwell's?"

"Fat lot of good it did us."

"He and Banning were following the track of a particular

line and they had a disagreement about it."

"You're not suggesting we should be looking at that location, near where Sarwell's body was found?"

"Bear with me sir. I gathered a lot of material that we didn't use at the time. Banning said Sarwell was trying to find a line where even the original tunnels and embankments had disappeared. He told Sarwell his interest was of no importance because after the Great Central Railway was built, the old line was closed."

"So?"

"That line was built after 1842 while the Great Central Railway reached Nottingham in 1899, which means it was open sometime after 1842 until around 1899. If we get a map of the old line through the city then we…"

The telephone rings.

"Jenner…yes, we're examining all options now…yes, sir… indeed…but I do need to…yes, of course…quite…right away."

Jenner puts the telephone down with an emphatic "Damn!" and turns to the others.

"I tried to put him off, but the chief superintendent's insistent on an immediate update. I'm afraid all this will have to wait for a while. John, get all that stuff written down so I can understand what you're talking about. I'm sorry, Ettie, I shouldn't be long."

Emmins motions Jenner to a chair, clasps his hands together and leans forward. Jenner sighs inwardly. This isn't going to be easy. Emmins' lips part and curl in a gesture towards a plastic smile, though it's forced and feigned. Jenner responds with an equally bogus facial tick.

"Time for a general talk about your investigations," Emmins begins.

Jenner notices how whenever an investigation seems indeterminate or bogged down it's always *his,* whereas if a successful outcome can be foreseen it becomes *ours.* Jenner gives a broad resume of the enquiries, much of it a rehash of his previous report. Emmins nods absently.

"This suspect you've pulled in, Matthew Usworth, is he our man?"

"It's a little early to say…"

"Too early? You've had him in overnight. Where's it leading? It's time for some results on this investigation. I understand he's come up with some fantastic story that he's not really Matthew Usworth at all, but some other man, some relative or other?"

"Yes quite, that's what he says…"

"Must think we were born yesterday. You've got him on assault, but I assume you really want him for Bernard Weston's murder?"

"That was my original intention."

"Go over him again and get him charged properly."

"We have a number of other lines of enquiry that we…"

There's a knock at the door and after a barked 'Enter' from Emmins the duty sergeant steps into the doorway, lingering as if afraid to proceed further.

"Sorry to disturb you, sir, but I thought you ought to know immediately."

"Know what?"

"There's been a bit of a cock up. The chief inspector's prisoner, Usworth; he's gone."

- 11 -

The town, so unfamiliar yet so tantalisingly reminiscent, peers down at him with disdainful rejection. He feels like a mouse, creeping out its hole, anxious and frightened, unable to find the way back. Everything is so big and so different. No carts or wagons in the streets, only people, but in the distance he hears a low murmuring that means the traffic must be near. He runs from the town only to find there's yet more of it, stretching endlessly on. He staggers into the yard of St. Mary's church, leans against the door and tries to gather together his thoughts. At least he knows this old place, but is he in the past or the future?

Two old women pass by. They glare so venomously he gets up quickly and moves swiftly on down the hill. Another church, St. Peter's, a welcome landmark, but now more scuttling folk, cramming and surging the street so it might suddenly burst from their pressure. The formidable, featureless buildings, erect in their watchful austerity, look down, ever ready to crush him under their concrete feet, an insolent beetle daring to invade their territory. Carried along by the surging river of people, he manages not to sink in the flow and despite his confusion recognises some street names. He heads for Drury Hill, erstwhile bearing for fateful decisions, but can't find it. Circling and wandering with increasing agitation, he retraces his steps in wild panic, but it yields nothing. Drury Hill has gone. It's no more. Panic turns to dismal failure, the loss of the street ripping away part of his life, never to be recovered. He goes, hopefully to find welcome escape from the bewildering danger of the streets.

Everyone looks at him. Even when he turns away, still they stare so bewilderingly. So big, so bright, so full of people, there are no places to hide. He'd hoped by now the frightful hallucinations would have passed. It must be the continuing fatigue of the journey. He can't remember when he last had a proper night's sleep. Mind and body can't continually go on without adequate rest and he's been at fever pitch for months, not helped by the distorted chaos of these last days.

They won't go away, these people, so oddly dressed, rushing around in this enormous palace with its hundreds of enclosed stalls, fabricated in glass. Everywhere glass. And lights. Bright, glaring lights. And colours, so many colours. Loudly they shout, these colours, almost as much as the people as they buzz and breeze along in their endless searching and screeching. Once searched and found, they stagger around, laden with so many parcels, smoothly sealed and wrapped just as the people are glossily draped and loudly sheathed. So bitingly, blaringly, hollowly dressed, it jars and frightens him. And no hats. No one wears a hat. Such perpetual chilling of the head, it must freeze up the mind? Perhaps that's why they icily scurry forth, jostling and bumping, no one acknowledging another, like a herd of blind crashing cattle, each intent on its own concerns, but without direction, unable to seek or give help to each other. What *are* they looking at? Is it *his* clothes? They're not of the best, it's true, but it's more than that. He slinks away, avoiding their hostile, curious stares, furtively slithering between the garish shops, not venturing to enter, afraid he might be swallowed up as a greedy giant ensnares unwitting travellers or worse still spew him out, neatly trussed as an appetising delicacy for the swirling hordes.

Now he regrets entering the 'Shopping Centre.' Rather than submerging unnoticed, the crowds inside threaten him more than the throng outside. He meanders around the shoppers with their fearsome wheeled machines, supposedly for carrying their small children, but projecting like mobile battering rams. Lurching from theses attacks he desperately searches for a way of escape, darting between the frighteningly wide shop entrances without real doors. The mass of people scramble along intersecting aisles, which confuse him and he forgets the way he came in. In his bewilderment all the shops look the same and he wonders if he's been trekking along a wide unending circle from which he'll never escape. He stops at a large hoarding, standing away from the shops. There are vacant seats on either side. He takes one of these and tries to hide by sitting askance, slightly behind the hoarding. The constant movement and noise prevents him from thinking and he has to think!

He had to get away to search, but how can he search when everyone is watching him, following him, chasing him? The searcher has become the searched! He has to find him. It's the only way. If only he could kick these disturbing images from his mind. If only his eyes would stop seeing the frightening people with their strange clothes, intimidating buildings, abundant glass and constant noise! Yet, what if this is not a horrible concoction of his disabled mind, but a monstrous reality? What if it's all *real*! How will he find him then, unless he too is confined in this limitless constriction, without bars and locks, but just as much a prison? So much changed, so much torn away to be reborn with the enormous sweep of a vast unstoppable hand that wipes away the printed page only to instantly reprint it. It's here. It *was* here. He must keep searching.

Then, in the opposite wall, he sees two doors. He keeps watch for several minutes. No one goes in or comes out. The doors remain undisturbed. There's a counter next to them with a notice displaying 'Enquiries,' but no one is there. He waits a little longer. Still no one. It could be a way out. It could lead nowhere. The doors may be locked. It could be a cupboard. He waits for a slight lull in the swirling mass and then steps across. The door gives to his grip. He opens it, steps inside and enters a dark passage, briefly catching sight of another notice. 'Entrance to caves...wait for next tour.' A voice behind him shouts "Stop! Where are you going? Wait!"

He can't go back. The noise outside gets louder. There are other voices now and footsteps. Someone shouts 'He went that way!' He edges further into the passage, quickening his step as his eyes adjust to the gloom. There are dim lights in the distance. He runs towards these as the doors are thrown open behind him. A corner at the end leads to some descending steps. He reaches the corner as his pursuers enter the passage. Loping and leaping down the steps he hears voices ahead of him and more shouting from behind. There's more light at the bottom. He turns into another passage, a little narrower than the one above. The walls have no brick lining, only hard, irregularly shaped sandstone rock. He's in the caves! Ahead is a small knot of about a dozen people. Along one wall there are wooden bunks, various implements and unfamiliar clothing, though unlike that worn by the people. It's drab and seems old. One man is standing slightly apart from the rest of the group. As he speaks they all listen very carefully.

"...caves are very extensive. It would be possible for the entire population of the city to be accommodated in them. In fact they've been inhabited at various times throughout history. During the last war they were used during air raids and here you can see a reconstruction of just such a shelter..."

War, what war? Air raid? How can you be raided by the air? What's he talking about? Some of the people turn as he walks towards them. He stops, but hearing footsteps behind, suddenly runs forward. As he approaches the group the passage gets narrower. He nudges the bunks. The guide stops talking. Those behind reach the bottom of the steps. He moves forward, jostling some of the people. The guide becomes concerned.

"Er...do you mind...you should wait for the next group."

They are coming along the passage. He elbows people aside. One woman cries out. A man protests. A child cries as he inadvertently steps on its foot. The guide takes up his position at the head of the group and stands astride the passage, barring his way. They are close behind. The guide will not move. Abruptly pushed aside, he hits his head on the side of the bunks. Those in pursuit have reached the group and are trying to get through. The people won't stand aside and are roughly jostled a second time. One woman screams. The guide's legs are splayed across the passage. They must not get him. He has to get away. The guide's knees bend as he starts to get up, further barring the way. Everyone is shouting. Another child is crying. So much noise! The dark brown menacing stone oppresses, bearing down and closing in. The men are forcing their way through the group. The guide slithers back down to the ground. He steps over his prone figure and runs further along the passage to another set of steps. He must get away!

There's an unreal calm in the police station. A mood of suppressed anxiety hangs in the air. Officers exchange remarks on every conceivable subject except the one concentrating their minds. Intense, detailed conversations intricately dissect utterly trivial enquiries. Acquaintances ask about family members they neither know nor care about. Administrative chores, usually put off for weeks are suddenly addressed with boundless enthusiasm. Anything to avoid focusing on the embarrassment of recent events. Jennifer joins in this exercise of institutional irrelevance, but hers is tinged with alarm and frustration. Jenner has been gone an hour. She has no idea where he is. Already she's had to fend off questions about his whereabouts, but what she really dreads is a call from Emmins. Ettie sits opposite. In the confusion, she failed to talk to Jenner before he left. Now she wonders whether any warning would have been too late anyway.

"We have to find him," she mutters.

Jennifer doesn't reply. She's not yet fully taken in what's happened, her mind still directed on loss rather than recovery. Humiliated in front of the chief superintendent, Jenner had stormed downstairs with the duty sergeant, collecting Jennifer on the way, demanding an explanation for the 'monumental cock up!' At the desk near the cells he held a brief, vitriolic and inconclusive post mortem. Under the chief inspector's penetratingly suspicious eye the duty sergeant attempted to explain.

"We were moving some prisoners and then we had a whole lot of fresh prisoners brought in by..."

"Moving prisoners? Moving bloody prisoners, what for?"

"Well, sir, when I went..."

"Where were these new prisoners, where did they come from?"

"There'd been a disturbance in the market, I'd sent two constables to..."

"How many were there, these new prisoners?"

"Well, I should say there were six, no seven, no er..."

"Never mind what *you* say, sergeant, how did *my* prisoner get away?"

"It was very crowded in here, sir and very noisy. I was calling out names. There was some confusion. Your prisoner, Usworth, when I called his name he wasn't here. It seems, when we checked later, he'd answered to the name of another prisoner who was being discharged..."

"Discharged, bloody discharged," Jenner muttered irritably.

"...the other prisoner was still in the cell..."

"So, you released my suspect out onto the bloody street, a potentially dangerous and violent man, not to say absolutely vital to my enquiries, as if he'd just had a bloody ticking off for dropping a fag packet on the pavement?"

The poor sergeant, crumpled in the icy track of Jenner's piercing stare, stood almost to attention, somehow desperately maintaining a semblance of professional dignity.

"It seems so, sir."

"Quite. It seems so, sergeant."

Jenner continued to glare at the sergeant for a time and then, without another word turned and went back upstairs, muttering 'when we checked later' and 'it seems so' under his breath. Leaning on his uniformed opposite number, he dragooned as many officers as he was able, to try and catch Sam, but as he kept saying to himself, they were probably only 'shutting the bloody stable door.' Jennifer thought they should join the search, but he disagreed saying 'two or three more plodding round the city centre like aimless tourists without a guide' was a waste of their resources. Ettie tried to assist with suggestions on the best places to look, but he was too preoccupied and wouldn't listen.

"Not now, Ettie..."

"I know it's embarrassing, Derek, but..."

He looked at her sharply, surprised at the use of his forename.

"No, it's not that. I have to find him, but *who* am I looking for, is it Sam or is it Matt?"

"That's precisely my point, if..."

"Leave it to us, we'll talk later, this is police business."

Before she could say anymore he stomped into the main office, apparently to direct operations. Ettie called after him, but he didn't reply. After a few minutes, Jennifer followed, but couldn't find him in the main office or in any part of the building. He'd left without telling anyone of his whereabouts.

"What were you going to tell him?" Jennifer says.

Temporarily crushed by Jenner's rude dismissal, Ettie soon recovers, shrugs and jumps up.

"Doesn't matter now," she says, donning her hat, "I've wasted enough time as it is."

Jennifer is puzzled and disappointed. Not wanting to add to her troubles, Ettie sits down again, though rams her hat down stoutly as if to say 'but I'm not stopping.'

"It's as the chief inspector said, the importance of finding Sam is very much who he is and why he escaped."

"It's not Matt."

"If it was, I'd be less concerned. It's Sam alright and he has to be found. He's from the past. Acting as if he's still in his own time, he's trying to return. He lacks the skills to do it, which makes him extremely dangerous."

"How so?"

Ettie gets up again. She won't speculate, for even she's not sure.

"Of course, Sam will be unaware of this. Believing he's still in 1842, my guess is he'll go in search of Doctor Foxley."

"We know where Foxley's surgery used to be, but that means he'll have to go..."

"Sergeant, where is chief inspector Jenner?"

Emmins has crept unnoticed through the main office and now stands imposingly behind Jennifer. She turns to him nervously and panics.

"Out sir."

"Where?"

"He...he's... leading the pursuit of the escaped prisoner, Usworth."

"When he reports in, tell him I want a full update."

As his large form disappears along the corridor, Ettie shakes her head.

"Was that wise? You don't know where he is."

"It just seemed..."

The telephone rings. Jennifer takes the call, replacing the receiver with a curt 'thank you.'

"Anything important?" Ettie asks.

"Not really, report of a man creating a disturbance in the Broad Marsh shopping centre."

"Is that far?"

"No, it's only...oh, of course...Broad Marsh is where Foxley's surgery used to be!"

They watch him carefully from the office as he wanders without apparent purpose, clutching the building plans. Several times he's already returned to query particular parts of the site. A few of the field archaeologists are scraping the subsoil in one of their trenches, but otherwise the area is inactive, the few construction workers standing around in moody idleness. Ignoring both these and the archaeologists, he stops at one corner, sits on a newly constructed outer wall and studies the documents. Although engrossed, he's also preoccupied on another matter as he looks up and stares blankly across the excavations. Then he gets up and marches back to the far end of the site, studying his papers as he goes. A younger man arrives at the office and asks after him.

"He's somewhere on the site," the contract manager says gruffly, pointing to the periphery fence, "You'll have to look for him."

John Duggan does, but finds it increasingly difficult as each time he catches a glimpse of his boss, Jenner disappears behind a hoarding or JCB or stack of bricks or even worse into the subterranean depths of the postponed foundations. He calls several times, but either Jenner is too far ahead, temporarily deaf or, more likely, chooses not to hear. John eventually finds him in deep thought, inspecting the hole where the skeleton was recently discovered. He looks up only after John has stood around for several minutes. Then he consults his building plans again and with a faint 'hmm,' gets out of the hole.

"D'you get it?" he says.

John takes out his notebook.

"I've found where the old Great Central Railway used to be," he says.

"Does it fit?" Jenner says.

"The main station was in town, you know the Victoria shopping centre, that's on the site of the original Victoria station. It then ran south towards London. There was a tunnel right under the city centre."

"What about towards the north, where did that run?"

John flicks through his notes.

"Quite close to here."

"Have you got the map?"

John hands it to Jenner, who lays it down at the edge of the hole, crouches down and peruses it carefully. He runs his finger across the paper, grunting with occasional 'hmms" and 'could be' and 'yes' and 'here.' As he analyses the map, he consults the building plans, spreading them on the ground and holding them down with stones against the breeze.

"Look at this," he says, pointing to the map and then waving his hand at one of the plans, "It's as I thought. Now, what about the other one?"

John turns over another page of his notes.

"Around the same time, only a few months apart," he says, "The Great Northern Railway branch was..."

"Show me on the map."

John crouches down next to him and points to the left side of the map. Jenner pulls up one of the building papers and holds it next to the map.

"Aha! Look at that!"

Jenner jumps up.

"A few more things to sort out here. First we have to talk to that archaeologist. Right, anything happening at the station?"

"Bit of a flap on. The chief super was in the main office."

"Where's sergeant Heathcott?"

"Gone out, some trouble in the Broad Marsh centre."

Spurred by Ettie's continual reminders of the 'vital need' to find Sam and aided by a string of green traffic signals, Jennifer gets them to the Broad Marsh Centre ahead of the local patrol car. A harassed receptionist, close to the entrance to the caves, is valiantly trying to make sense of the garbled complaints and jumbled recollections of a group of visitors. They tumble back out of the entrance barely ten minutes after entering it, disoriented and distressed, some people shaking and several children crying. Some are demanding their money back, which the receptionist is refusing to do until the guide appears.

"Couldn't hear him," one man says, "so much noise. I came 'specially to find out about the war."

"More like a war in there," a woman next to him says.

Simultaneously besieged by a security man and several shopkeepers, all demanding to know what has happened to 'the man,' the receptionist is finding it even more difficult to understand them.

"Ran in berserk," one of the shopkeepers says.

"Barged through us he did and knocked the guide to the floor," says the woman from the group, "Then these security men came and said we ought to get out."

"What happened to him?"

"Don't know."

With a universal shaking of heads there's a brief lull in the noise and then the guide staggers out the door. Apart from a bruise on his face, which looks more severe than it is, he's uninjured. As his party had scurried back to the entrance, the security men had helped him from the floor and then gone back to pursue the intruder.

"Ruddy madman," he mumbles, "Knocked me down for no reason."

"Fancy that," says the woman from his group, "What some people will do to get out of paying."

The guide isn't so sure.

"Strange man, odd look in his eyes."

An ambulance has been called for the guide, its siren jerking up the background tension and increasing the number of gawpers gathering near the entrance, their mundane shopping expeditions turning into a more interesting show. Jennifer pushes through the crowd. The receptionist points to the double doors when asked about 'the man.'

"You can't go in there!" she shouts as Jennifer and Ettie sidestep the crowd and the security men. No one follows them.

"You'd better be right," Jennifer says as they shuffle along the first, dimly lit passage.

Ettie is concentrating intently and doesn't reply. They reach the first staircase and then the second, narrow passage where the guide's monologue on wartime Nottingham had been so rudely and violently interrupted. Jennifer strides ahead, but Ettie stops near the bunks and gazes around the confined space, with its evocative 1940s clothes and equipment. redolent of an emergency home to a desperate family sixty years before. She sits on one of the bunks, picks up an air raid warden's helmet and scans a magazine. Jennifer leans against one of the other bunks. Ettie concentrates impassively, her laden stare casting a charged intensity, reverberating from wall to wall in silent reminders of the past. Though she's anxious to move on, Jennifer is momentarily transfixed and pulled by Ettie's plunge into the well of collective memory.

"Do you hear them?" Ettie says.

Jennifer listens, amazed by the silence. No scrape, trickle or breath disturbs the sepulchral stony brown enclosure of the passage. No voices behind, no voices ahead, they could be aground on a deceptively safe sandbank of suspended time. They've travelled only a short distance, yet could be separated from the frenetic mayhem of the shopping centre by the immensity of those sixty years.

"I hear nothing," Jennifer whispers.

"They are here, crowding and mingling, laughing, crying,

playing, waiting, wondering, their sprits secreted into the stone."

"The war?"

"A dull rumbling like the extended belch of a distant giant."

"Bombs."

"A faint whirring sound, it gets louder, more high pitched, piercing now and longer, continuous."

"The all clear, they are safe now."

"Then we can go on."

Ettie gets up, replaces the magazine and helmet and moves on down the passage. Jennifer follows. Ettie quickens her pace and they soon reach the second staircase.

"What was it?" Jennifer says, "Did you feel the people in the war?"

"Oh no," Ettie shudders, "They felt me, or at least the walls did that hold their memories. No words were spoken, but the messages were clear. This place is so powerful. How long has it been used?"

"Hundreds, maybe even thousands of years. The Celtic name for Nottingham means place of the caves, that's long before the Romans came."

"Then they are all here. Tell me about Broad Marsh before the shopping centre was built."

"Broad Marsh and Narrow Marsh, the names derive from land near the river Leen. Eighty years ago it was a pretty rough area, policemen patrolled in pairs."

"And earlier it was where doctor Foxley had his surgery. Sam is looking for that surgery to make contact with Foxley."

"Why?"

"I don't know, but he either got lost or panicked when he came down."

They reach a larger section. Several alternative passages have been blocked off with wooden fencing. Ettie stops, considering which they should take. She listens, waiting for unseen guidance from the high roof or widely separated walls. Then, as if receiving such extra sensory direction, she moves towards the passage that remains open. Jennifer follows, but their progress is interrupted as one of the wooden fences is torn aside. The two women turn round fearfully to see a figure lurking in the shadows. They stand back as he pulls the remaining portion of the fence and ambles in their direction. Ettie and Jennifer press against the far wall, close to another fenced off passage, which might if needed provide a means of emergency escape.

Though it's no longer technically a crime scene, Jenner and John Duggan have commandeered the site office at Best Hill. The construction manager, already thoroughly peeved over the delay to the work and feeling utterly redundant has left for a site meeting with the architect. Neither of them relished the prospect of sharing the office, however temporarily with the two policemen.

"Go over it again," Jenner says, "all the remaining links of Martin Sarwell."

"Obviously the railways," John begins, scanning his notebook again.

"Quite so, railway historian, anorak for disused lines, cuttings and especially...embankments. Yes, I think we've explored that. What else?"

"Two years ago he was seeing Ella Weston. Seems to have ended abruptly with her pretty upset."

"We only really have his friend Banning's word for that."

"Denise Deverall also said..."

"No more reliable. Ella Weston's not been forthcoming other than saying she didn't like him."

"Doesn't seem to fit."

"Not if it was a purely personal relationship, but what if his interest was concerned with something else? That could explain her hostility. Sarwell may have been deliberately circumspect to his friend Banning, who put his own interpretation on the relationship. Then we have his financial difficulties."

"His company was in trouble, he was running out of money for his research. He was approaching everybody for funds – definitely Denise Deverall and Sylvia Darrington – Cressley and perhaps even Matt Usworth."

"Sarwell wasn't a good risk. They could have had problems with repayment."

"An argument that got out of hand, someone loses their temper, maybe an accident, panic, dump the body down an old mineshaft?"

"Perhaps," Jenner says doubtfully, "Finally we have Sarwell's obsession with Doctor Foxley, even to the extent of believing he was a kind of resurrection of him."

"Bit far fetched."

"Quite so, constable, but like tea from China, what's far fetched might not always be without its uses. Which leaves just one more thing to sort out..."

"Chief inspector Jenner?"

A middle aged woman in a long bright green sweater and sporting slightly soiled boots, stands in the doorway.

"They told me I'd find you in here. We've not met, Tanya Farlow, city archaeologist."

Her handshake is firm and vigorous.

"I've already told the site manager, so far as we are concerned he can resume work. I assume that's alright with you?"

"Resume work, what about your excavations?"

"That's the whole point, you see, no value in carrying on. Our people are already packing up. I'd always had my doubts about this location, but we had to be sure. Now it's clinched it."

"Clinched what?"

"Carbon dating of the skeleton. Can't be absolutely precise, of course, but enough to know that it's definitely not medieval, much more recent. It means the site itself is of no historical value to us. Pity, but there it is, in our game it's one of the..."

"How recent?"

"Hard to say, but with other evidence I would guess no more than a hundred years, but could be much less than that."

"How much less, a few years...three years?"

She grimaces, puckers her lips and with an unfolding of her hands says, 'could be, could be,' adding with a laugh 'that would make the body younger than the building!'

But Jenner is not amused.

"Then we need to re-examine the skeleton."

"Yes, I thought you'd want to. Definitely a matter for your skills now rather than mine, eh? Very intriguing."

"Quite."

She closes the door and marches across the site, rounding up her field workers as they pack up their equipment.

"I think she was joking, sir," John says, half heartedly convincing himself.

"Quite so," Jenner says, "but I'm not. We need to get back to the station."

At the door they meet Edwards, the site manager.

"Now we can get started again," he says jauntily.

"Not quite," Jenner says, "This site is now a crime scene."

Jenner is fidgety all the way to the station, constantly re-examining his papers and muttering 'must do that' and 'look at that again.' Sandra Tye meets them at the entrance.

"Matt Usworth, sir, he was seen yesterday."

"Good, so we can..."

"Only problem is, he's disappeared again!"

Running for so long he's lost all sense of time and distance. All he can think about is getting away from the men. So many rock enclosed passages, by now he might easily have reached the bottom of the earth itself, burrowing into the sandstone bowels of the city like some fugitive mole or terrified rabbit. But don't moles re-emerge from a new hole? Maybe, but rabbits usually burrow one way and he can't go back even if he could find the way because he's lost for sure.

He sits on the ground to rest, but keeps alert for any sounds of pursuit as he tries to disentangle the mangled events of the last few days. Unconnected images assail him like an angry mob hammering on the door of his mind. He closes his eyes for relief, but this only increases their intensity. Even when he opens them again the pictures leap across the dusty floor and scramble up the stone walls. Yet they are silent, not interrupting the suspicious, surely artificial peace of the caves. Gradually the disparate memories fall into a coherent order as if some external collator has gathered up the index cards of recollection and dropped them into their proper places in the filing cabinet of his thoughts.

The party, which he'd crudely gate crashed in his search for...for what...he can no longer remember. Running upstairs, running towards or running away. Arrested by those strange constables, dressed for their parts, but somehow speaking lines that didn't fit, then whisked away in that weird and noisy contrivance to be interrogated. Did they believe him? Did he believe himself? All his troubles started when first he left the city. His only thought had been of escape. So long it seemed he'd been escaping. Only a few nights ago, he'd escaped through here. It seems so far in the past now. Escape from a confined space followed by the imprisonment of the open roads, fields and woods. Now he's back. These caves gave him freedom, can he find it again?

He hears voices and footsteps. They are coming! He walks on, deeper into the rock bored sanctuary, illuminated by these strange lamps with no flames. More illusions, fantastic creations of his feverish mind? Is he dreaming? Where will he awake when this tangled sleep is over? Back in that dingy, poor compressed room in the backstreet court of the city? Lying on his back, exposed in a field where one man knocked down another or cowering under a hedge in the woods? Tramping disconsolately in the grounds of Elvington House or brooding his fate in a police cell? Where does dreaming end and waking begin? Maybe he's back on that same night, dozing on the floor, deluding himself about the lights and the noise, all else part of his nightmares.

The men shouting, 'Come back, come back,' force away his delusions. Their footsteps get louder. He must find his way to the western edge of the city. He runs into a longer, narrower passage. The light is very dim, but he can see several side passages. He may not be able to outrun them indefinitely. If they catch him, he'll be back in the police station. He's already told them he witnessed a murder, but the authorities never listen to working men. They'll drag up the accident with Jonathon Cressley. He'll be charged with murder and after a pathetic trial, hanged! He stops at the passages and looks between them. His only hope is to confuse his pursuers. Go down one of the passages, the least inviting and hope they won't follow. One entrance is partly closed off with wooden fencing. He prises it aside and crawls through, replacing the boards behind him. The passage is low and narrow. He slithers forward a few paces and bangs his head on the stone. He gets down and shambles along. There's no light except shadowy streaks from the main passage. After covering about fifteen meters he hears the men behind. He stops, anxious not to let even his breathing give him away. He hears nothing, but knows they too have stopped.

They shuffle their feet, but don't speak. They're considering which way to take, but also listening for the slightest indication of their quarry. He breathes slowly, each tiny intake of air seeming a shrill whistle in the confined space. They move again, but still say nothing. His back aches from bending, but dares not sink to the floor for relief. Another long, aching silence. His knees weaken. He has to grip the side of the wall to stop himself falling. His hand slides on the rock. Will they hear him?

"Over there," one says.

They move again. Sam shudders, waiting for the inevitable and fatal clearing of the flimsy wooden fencing. They stop. Footsteps again, but they recede and then fade away. They've taken another passage! He waits a few moments, his back seared in pain. Then, slowly, deliberately, quietly he eases himself down to the floor and rolls to his side to lean against the wall. Only after a few minutes of definite silence, does he move again. Forward, for he daren't go back in case his pursuers, realising their mistake, backtrack, figure out his ruse and run him to earth. Time is short. He must make the best of it and take this passage, wherever it leads. After a few minutes he wonders if the passage is a dead end. If it is, it's too late, trapped like the rabbit at the end of the burrow. He crawls as the passage narrows still further and almost all light is extinguished. Surely such confinement will end abruptly? He goes on and in the bare flickering faintness, sees a slight widening.

Yet even if he does escape, will he then be in the wrong place, far from the object of his search? How will he find the south side surgery? When he sees daylight again it might be on the far side of town, further removed, without any hope of retracing his steps. He has to contact Foxley, but what does he really know about the doctor? The little he has to go on was on the scribbled note she'd pressed the paper into his hand at one of the meetings.

"He asked after you. You need to see him, this is the address."

It was only the second time Sam had met her. He knew her as Cecily, a middle class woman, sympathetic to the Chartist cause, who helped the local branch with administration and compiling notices. Even now he can see the intensity in her eyes, telling him doctor Foxley would help. No one had ever mentioned Foxley being involved in the movement. Why would he want to see Sam? Then she was gone, as quickly as she arrived. It seemed odd, but with other pressures he'd given it little thought. Until now when finding him seems his only hope. He'd got rid of the paper before they got him to the police station, but can still remember the address.

It gets high enough for him to stand. He stops and listens. Only the dark silence of the walls. There's something familiar about this place. Is it where he escaped before? He should relax and take stock, try to remember the details of that night, figure out where he's gone wrong and what he should do, but his mind can't settle. Who were those people he passed? What were they doing down here? What's this talk of war? Has the campaign turned into a war? He thought they'd lost any hope of forceful means to freedom back in 1839. Has the frustration and repression spilled over into violence? Have events moved so fast in so few days? Why hasn't he heard before? Is it days or months? So many changes, so much he can't explain. Another delusion, has he lost hold of reality? Concentrate, get a grip. Force or persuasion, the perennial argument. Think about them. How many times have they debated their preparedness? Is the other side too powerful or is it more about short term, organisational issues? His mind oscillates. He must concentrate. Find Foxley. The surgery must be close. He must be near the south side of the city. At least he was when he came in.

He walks on, now in almost total darkness, his arms stretched ahead in case the walls or roof should suddenly diminish. He remembers Cecily again. The eyes of fixed resolve, the firm set lips, the auburn hair, the voice of quiet determination, something soothingly reminiscent... something close. The only other time he spoke to her she talked of a stranger at their meetings. Sam never saw him. She said this stranger reminded her of Sam. Maybe if he could find her she might help, but how to find her, he doesn't know where she lives.

He hears noises, muffled, heavy. They could be behind. They are coming! He must be gone. He runs forward and then slows, conscious he might suddenly crash into the stone and injure himself. Then he hears it again. Is it behind or to the side? It could be from the stone itself. They're breaking through! He moves forward again, slowly at first, then runs headlong as he hears a heaving, scraping all around. His hand hits the left wall and instinctively he turns to his right, his feet scrabbling on loose stones. His feet sound slightly hollow, almost echoing as if he's entered a larger place. Carefully he slithers around, counting three separate openings. What to do in the hopeless darkness. The noises again, dull, stifled, but close, very close. He takes the last opening, sliding along in the blackness, feeling, groping, hoping for release. All darkness now. Silence, then the sounds again, scratching, voices. Someone is close, very close as if they're breaking through to him.

Jenner is alone in his office. He's read Ettie's note at least five times and now begins his sixth, slower, more considered reading.

> '...regret not acting on my doubts earlier, but at least now I am certain. I know you'll not want to face it, but I am sure the man you were holding was Samuel, not Matthew Usworth and he has managed (I can't say yet exactly how) to transfer into the present from 1842. I am equally certain that the ultimate answer to

all your enquiries lies in the past. Obviously therefore the danger is not over, in fact the gravest crisis, overshadowing all the others, may be imminent. We must find Samuel. Out on his own, he may do irreparable damage. Jennifer and I are going now to try and locate him...'

Ettie may be sure, but Jenner is not. He struggles to accept Samuel Usworth as a real person, as distinct from Matthew's useful invention. For practical purposes they could be one and the same. Sam is a façade, a humanised suit of clothes into which Matt conveniently slips. His existence is merely an opportunistic device on Matt's part and even if they really are separate, Ettie may be only partly correct. She may be right someone transcends the past and the present, but that may be Matt rather than Sam. What if he's a kind of time jumping spy, mining the past to further his self interested designs in the present, dragging up a real man from that past as his alter ego? Interestingly, Matt reappears just when Sam escapes only to immediately disappear again! Concentrating solely on Sam, Ettie may have underestimated Matthew Usworth, something she may soon regret. She and Jennifer may be in serious danger.

He tries to get them both, but can't get any phones to connect. Should he join the pursuit of Usworth? So far his interventions have not helped, why should his involvement make any difference? He looks again at Duggan's notes on Sarwell. The answer lies there. That damned obsession with railway lines...especially embankments. He looks over the building plans and the maps again, but his concentration wavers. Can she be right, Matt and Sam are not the same person? What if one is from the past or has been in the past? Is it all in his and Ettie's imagination? He should talk it over with her. What must he do? Is he cracking up? Emmins certainly thinks so. The thought unnerves him. The chief superintendent is in the building. He's the last person Jenner wants to see. He must get away. Go down to Broad Marsh? Contact Ettie, finally bottom out this Sam-Matt business. No, before that there's something else he must follow up, which means a journey in the opposite direction.

The man walks out of the shadows. Ettie and Jennifer see his uniform. He's one of the security men who ran into the caves in pursuit of Sam. His colleague emerges from the wooden barrier as Jennifer moves across to them.

They stare for some moments at the two women and then the first says, "You shouldn't be in here."

Jennifer shows them her warrant card.

"We'll take over now, you can go back."

"Best of luck," the second man says.

"What were you doing in that passage?" Ettie says, "Did he go that way?"

"Seems not," the first man says, "We got lost further in and came out that way."

"Does it lead anywhere?"

"Just doubles round on the main one."

The men are relieved to go back. Ettie and Jennifer watch them retreating up the passageway to the stairs. Then, without a word to each other, they continue deeper, along the open path. They turn a corner and enter a narrowing, dark passage, in the distance a dim single electric bulb set into the wall. Just beyond this Ettie stops and leans against the wall as if she might be listening to a conversation on the other side of the rock. Jennifer waits patiently, wondering with these delays whether they have any realistic chance of catching Sam.

"Do you feel his presence?" she says.

"Oh much earlier than his time," Ettie says, "these caves and passages respond to sympathetic presences."

Jennifer steps back a couple of paces.

"Shall I stand away from you, will they make contact better without me?"

"No, no!" Ettie says, pulling her back, "You're sympathetic to the place, you know its history, any contact will be enhanced by your being here."

Jennifer draws closer. She hears nothing as Ettie continues to concentrate.

"Do you smell it?" Ettie says after a few minutes.

Jennifer sniffs the air, but smells nothing except the pervading dry mustiness.

"It's very strong," Ettie says, pointing further down the passage.

Jennifer sniffs deeply again, inhaling great gulps into her nostrils, which quiver and tickle in the dry, dusty air. Nothing. She shakes her head and wonders if she should back away so not to disturb Ettie's contact.

"I feel a large place with indentations in the stone floor, like vats."

Jennifer looks round. Ettie waves towards the passage again.

"No, not here, further on. There are many people working there. The smell, it's so strong. There are things hanging up, flat, drying, men plunging things into hot water in the stone vats. It's so hot and smelly. The things hanging up they are... leather."

"A tannery?" Jennifer says.

"Could be, why do you say that?"

"Because in medieval times there was a tannery down here."

"We will see it, come on!"

Ettie runs ahead. Jennifer is glad to be on the move. Maybe now they might find Sam. The passage widens and slopes downward. As they descend Ettie slows up and cocks her head as if listening.

"It gets louder," she says

Still Jennifer hears nothing, but her imagination, reinforced by Ettie's powerful imagery conjures up both the scene and the acrid overpowering aroma. She's never seen the medieval tannery, but before they turn the final corner and enter its vast chamber, she can picture the remains of the great stone, steaming receptacles and the drying spaces. When they arrive only the people are missing, though as Ettie stares wondrously around, Jennifer feels she may even see and hear them at their laborious tasks, darting between the vats, heaving and immersing the skins, sweating in the pungent, torrid atmosphere. Ettie sits on the side of one of the large stone tanks, her eyes closed, hands gripping the edge tightly. She sways slightly. Jennifer watches and waits, getting gradually more concerned. Responding to this medieval memory may be like continually playing the same gramophone record. Ettie may be distancing herself too far from their vital aim of finding Sam!

"Is he close?" she says at last, hoping to jerk Ettie out of her intensity.

Ettie opens her eyes and gets up.

"Everything is close," she says, "This place is a repository of the past, a storehouse, jammed full of a hundredfold memories. We not only pass along a passage, carved into the rock, but a fissure between past and present. It's a time passage."

Concentrating on their objective, Jennifer is alarmed and irritated.

"Does that make it easier or more difficult for us to find Sam?"

"It's important to find Sam, but finding him may be only the beginning. Sam *is* his past. We have to unravel it all. Revealing his past is how we'll discover answers to the mystery. I know now. We can't do it at arm's length."

"We have to get closer?"

"Much closer."

Ettie walks on.

"This way," she says, leaving the tannery chamber and entering another narrow passage.

They walk for some distance, on either side passing several more open areas and passage entrances. Jennifer assumes the security men must have double backed along one of these. Ettie ignores them, confidently striding ahead even more quickly. It's as if she knows every minor turning and corner though she's never ventured down here before. They reach a fork. Ettie hesitates and then turns to the left. If they were to follow the standard tour route they should soon start the ascent to the exit, but they are still descending. The passages they follow are still lit by electric light, but the lamps are spaced further apart and they frequently pass through sections almost in darkness. The sound of their feet on the stony floor reverberates through the still air. No other sound disturbs it and the jagged, brown wall absorbs and dulls their footfalls.

They are now deep into the rock beneath the city. Suddenly aware of the immense depth, Jennifer likens it to the ancient vaults of the Great Pyramid, conscious of the hundreds of tons of dense rock, massed above them. Whether it's the ponderous silence, pierced only by their movements or the weighty superstructure above, her mind, so long intently focused on finding Sam, begins to wander. For the first time flickering fear nags and in the shadowy gloom irrational images penetrate with doubt filled foreboding. She approaches each corner with trepidation as her pace slackens to a heavy listlessness and she has to forcibly quicken her step to keep up with Ettie.

Ettie's conviction contrasts with Jennifer's uncertainty as she repeats those pithy phrases, 'arm's length...much closer.' She stops where the side of the passage has been partially bricked up and peers over the edge into the blackness. Jennifer catches up and takes her arm.

"Ettie, how is finding Sam only the beginning? What did you mean, we can't do it at arm's length and we have to get closer? How do we get closer?"

Ettie turns back, dislodging one of the bricks as she does.

"We'll not release the secrets of the past by only working from the present. I thought it might be done, but this place has made me realise that's not possible. It may also be the means to do it."

"Because it's a time passage?"

"When we find him, I have to find the power to go back with Sam."

Suddenly Jennifer feels very insecure. Ettie sees her fearfully drawn face and takes her hand.

"Your local knowledge is vital."

Then she leans back, her head filled with deep, intermittent reverberations. Jennifer notices.

"What is it Ettie?"

Ettie strains to listen.

"Don't you hear it?" she says, "Listen!"

Jennifer hears it too, rumbling, accelerating, getting closer.

"What is it?" she says.

"It could be...but no, it can't...this is a closed opening... but is it?"

"A train?" Jennifer whispers unbelievingly.

Ettie nods.

"Do you know where we are?"

The sound recedes. Jennifer looks over the brick wall. Some wooden fencing lies beyond.

"I think this is the original Great Central Railway tunnel that ran under the city centre. This could be a closed access to it."

"In that case get that loose brick and help me knock a hole in this wall so we can get through!"

Jenner asks after everyone when he returns to the station. He's particularly concerned if any messages have been received from Ettie or Jennifer. John Duggan shakes his head.

"I keep trying their mobiles, but there's nothing."

"But the chief superintendent..." John begins

"Is he in the building?" Jenner replies aggressively.

"No sir, but he..."

"Quite, now come on constable, there's work to do."

With that he rushes into his office and throws a pile of papers at John.

"Look at the statements of Jon Cardington and David Underwood again and then tell me what you think."

"What am I looking for, sir?"

"You're not *looking* for anything, you're keeping your mind open for anything that doesn't fit, anything that should make us *think* again. There's something there. Come back when you've found it,"

Mystified, John retreats.

"I can't trust myself," Jenner thinks, "His second opinion on those statements is vital. He has to spot it."

His trip has been successful or at least fruitful. Now he must pull everything together with the workhouse records. The motive and the means are emerging, but he continues to worry about Ettie and Jennifer. What he's found points to great danger. Every instinct tells him any delay could be disastrous. They must act and soon. John returns.

"Have you found anything in those statements?"

"No, sir, not yet, but I thought you ought to see this."

John hands him the specialist's report on the Chartist handbill, found at the site where Martin Sarwell's body was discovered. Jenner reads one telling passage several times.

'...print and paper texture are consistent with a document of the mid nineteenth century. Even if it had been stored in a protective environment, the condition of the handbill indicates an incredible state of preservation, whereas it was actually discovered in the open in a situation, which should have led to rapid decay. There is the possibility that it was deposited at that location after being stored elsewhere, but other factors indicate that even with careful storage over a period of say a hundred and fifty years, it would nevertheless show signs of ageing. Such signs are not present. The handbill, although authentic (ie. it is not a facsimile), seems remarkably 'modern.' Obviously, in these circumstances you may consider it necessary to subject the document to further analysis in order to resolve this paradox. If so, then there is...'

But Jenner does not feel it necessary. Such signs of ageing are not present. The result, though bizarre is not at variance with his other discoveries. Indeed, it vindicates them. There can be only one inescapable conclusion. The Chartist handbill, was picked up in 1842 and then deposited, accidentally or otherwise, by someone who had recently travelled from that time into the present. How can Jenner now deny Ettie's belief? Is it Sam? It could be Matt. After all, it was him that 'revealed' the genuine Chartist newspaper. He has to set this against the information from the workhouse records. All is coming together and he should feel some satisfaction all the mysteries might be soon resolved, but he's apprehensive. For all is closing in on him just as much as on the perpetrator. He fears for Ettie and Jennifer and must find them.

Sam twists and turns fearfully. The hammering is as if the very wall of stone is being broken apart all around him. The pounding increases, though the sound changes, now more hollow with a heavy tearing, less like stone being beaten, closer to...brick. He listens carefully as he slinks into the blackness and back against the stone, trying to locate the source of the incursion. There must be many passageways in the darkness for the bludgeoning attacks echo and rebound making it difficult to pinpoint the direction. It gets louder with soft splintering as if shards of rock or brick are being snapped. Then the breathing, hard, short, gasping, at least two people ripping into the fragile barrier. Still he can't be sure where it comes from, his ears fooled by the concentrated mass of surrounding stone. Then, a faint streak of flickering light strikes the stone, released by some tiny punctured hole. He looks left, towards where the light must have come and sees a small hole cleaved through a small section of rough brickwork. It widens as fingers grapple and wrench the mortar, pushing more brick outwards.

It's them, the men who chased him. Now they have him, cornered like a rat in the bilge of a sinking ship, faced with the grim choice of drowning or battering. Two hands grasp the remaining bricks and force them aside. More light hits the wall, further increasing his tension as it reveals his precipitous position. Now he fully understands the echoing enormity that assailed his ears. He leans against a slender, straight sided rock. To his left is the opening of the narrow passage, down which he came. Further along on the same side is another passage, littered with broken bricks and friable splatters of mortar. Two faces peer grimly through the brick flanked space. Women's faces, their hair tinged red with brick dust and streaked white with fragmented mortar. Not noticing him at first, they stare through the gap with the same apprehension. He's trapped. To his right, a sheer drop into a rounded chamber with a flat bottom filled with debris of loose gravelly grey stone. The walls and roof are brick lined except for each end, where the chamber seems to stretch into a black distance. He cannot tell how far it goes for the light is too dim. A few more centimeters and he would have fallen, at the very least breaking his legs from the drop onto the stones. The women crawl through the hole and lean against the brick, gaping into the same cavernous expanse. The ledge is so narrow, their legs dangle over the edge. Then they see him.

"Sam!"

He starts at the mention of his name. A woman he's never seen before, though she seems to know him. He shifts uneasily, in the restricted space only able to shuffle his shoulders in a futile gesture of escape. Even if he had time to get back into the passage, he knows it leads to disaster. Then he recognises the other woman. It's her from the police station. Ettie notices his fear.

"Don't be afraid," she says, "We are your friends."

He looks down at the stone strewn floor and then, warily at them.

"If only we knew where we were," Ettie says.

Jennifer nods at the broad space in front of them.

"It is the railway tunnel."

"Is there a way out?" Ettie says.

Jennifer shakes her head and points to her left where the ledge ends at the opening to a third passage.

"That's the only way."

Sam follows Jennifer's finger.

"Trust us, Sam," Ettie says as she and Jennifer sidle along the ledge towards the passage, "there's no other way."

Sam looks down into the Victorian railway tunnel. For a moment he fancies he hears a train. He listens more intently, but hears it no more. Then his nostrils quiver as if assailed by a sudden smoky aroma. But this too passes. Brief, detached remembrances like leaves caught on the wind, dancing for a few moments only to be blown away forever.

A railway under the city centre? It's ludicrous. The railway is to the south of the town, everyone knows that and what is this *Great Central* anyway? There's no such line. She said it was *closed*. Why build a railway tunnel only to close it and not run trains? Another delusion? What if she's wrong? He could shin down at the edge, maybe drop down without hurting himself, then make his escape through the railway tunnel. What about the trains? On a railway with no tracks, whoever heard of such a thing? If so, better not make it worse by running along a railway tunnel that doesn't exist. The two women have almost reached the passage entrance. They seem not to threaten him, but he hesitates. Then he hears, soft but distinct noises from the passage he has just left. They are back with others!

With no choice, he pushes gently off the wall and levers along the edge, entering the dark passage behind Ettie. Silently except for their combined grunts, slitherings and occasional bumps into the rock, they journey along the unknown passage, hoping it won't lead to impenetrable rock, another underground hazard or into the dubious clutches of insensitive authority. Each is accompanied by their particular thoughts.

At the front, Jennifer balances her duty as a police officer to apprehend a fugitive with her sympathy for Ettie's desire to save Sam. But first she must find a way out. Scrabbling through the darkness she has to reconcile knowledge of the city above and their jumbled underground wanderings. If she succeeds they might possibly find a way out.

In the rear, Sam oscillates between equal fears of a frightening reality and the terrifying nightmare of an unreality, not knowing which he inhabits. In the blackness of the caves every sound is magnified and every smell deformed. He's unsure whether the musty draught of stale air marks the onset of some new, unimaginable apparition or the scratch of his feet on the pebbles heralds the arrival of another threatening invader. Yet these physical distortions are nothing to the tortures in his mangled mind. Just as he manages to grapple some understanding of what's happening the explanation floats away on flitting nonsense impressions.

In the middle, Ettie thinks about Sam, rehearsing how she can reassure him while being honest about his predicament. It must be him who whisked past her in that ethereal wafting force in the canal tunnel. How or why it happened she doesn't know, but he may no longer fully believe he's still in 1842.

There's some dim light ahead, which gradually increases as they move along the passage. It's wider and higher, the sandstone rock glinting slightly in the sombre, gloaming half light. They reach another, even wider passage with electric lights set into the walls. Clearly now they must be back on the main tourist route, though some distance from the entrance in the shopping centre. Jennifer skirts the sides, computing their whereabouts and assessing which way to follow. Sam stands slightly apart, but makes no attempt to get away. Ettie faces him, explains who they are and reassures him again of their good intentions.

"I'm sure Jennifer will find the way out."

Sam glances at Jennifer, who continues to pace along the wall. Ettie risks a direct approach.

"I know how you came through the canal tunnel. I was there. You passed me."

The kindled interest in Sam's eyes tells her she's right.

"You must believe me and not be alarmed, but when you came through the tunnel you also passed through time."

His eyes burn with anxiety, but he doesn't flinch. There's also a curious, puzzled eagerness.

"It might help if you told me what happened before you got to the canal."

For a moment Sam considers running, but something in Ettie's voice and her open expression convinces him whatever he fears, the greater fear must be continuing alone in this strange, inexplicable world. Wearied and bewildered beyond endurance he tells her everything, releasing his burdened mind in a stream of disjointedly exploding stories. He tells of his first escape from the city, his wanderings and eventual return. He tells of the party at Elvington House, his arrest and questioning and his next escape back into the city. After gentle coaxing he tells of the death of Jonathon and the earlier murder he witnessed in the field.

Ettie listens patiently, unperturbed and except for occasionally nodding her head, almost unresponsively. Jennifer leads them along the lighted passage, now satisfied she has a measure of their whereabouts. Sam is relaxed beside Ettie and confident Jennifer will get them out safely. No longer feeling threatened, he tells more. It's good to talk of the movement, of hopes and fears, trials and triumphs, danger and contentment, achievements and aspirations. He hesitates when she asks about his contacts in Nottingham.

Can he really trust her? Will she betray him? Is this a careful charade leading to a trap? With the fateful acceptance of one whose options are almost exhausted, with little to be gained in resisting the inevitable, he goes on, though some names he conceals in a last vestige of caution. She shows no especial interest in Cecily, but he gets her attention when he mentions the stranger.

"You'd not heard of him before?"

"Never."

"Where did he come from?"

"I don't know."

Ettie wants to know more, but Sam can only tell what Cecily told him. As he talks he realises how much more he should have questioned and how much remains mysterious.

"Was he well informed of the Chartists?"

"Very well," Sam says, again conscious he should have queried that intelligence earlier, "Some things Cecily said he knew, it was...oh, it doesn't matter."

"Go on."

"It's just that some things she said he knew it was as if...he already knew what might happen."

In Ettie's face he reads a peculiar understanding. It reminds him of the oddity of his own situation in another time. He shudders. Ettie tries to distract him.

"Tell me of your life before the Chartists."

The passage climbs upwards. Maybe the prospect of getting out will release and invigorate his spirits. At first, Sam can only comfortably talk of his days as a shoemaking apprentice, but gradually he moves back to his obscure origins, though 'workhouse' is uttered quietly as if the word itself might spit out the pain of his upbringing. Ettie is thoughtful for a few moments, just as she had been when Jennifer explained about the railway. They reach some stone steps.

"I know where we are," Jennifer says with relief.

They turn a corner on the steps and light streams down from above. Ettie looks up and understands. The stranger was Matt. Could he also have been the murderer in the field? At the head of the steps there's a wrought iron gate. It's not locked, but very stiff from under use. They pull it together and after loosening, it scrapes noisily along the top step as it swings open slowly.

They emerge onto the gardens in the lower slopes of the castle rock. People are moving down towards the entrance and don't notice them. In the distance they hear police sirens from the Broad Marsh area. Jennifer leads them in the opposite direction, away from the city centre past the old hospital and through streets of once elegant Victorian houses, long since consigned to student bedsits and offices. Always they tramp against the flow of people, who are drawn towards the sirens and the unfolding drama at the shopping centre. Jennifer finds her car and they speed away into the western suburbs. Utterly disorientated and confounded Sam sits in the car, trying not to look out the window. Ettie keeps talking to him, always about the past and things familiar, though by now he cannot doubt that *this* world is not *his* world.

The last visitor has left the Broad Marsh Shopping Centre. The wide aisles and units deserted, as electrical goods, toys and clothes, devoid of both sellers and buyers, stand forlornly like inanimate accomplices to some disaster that's blasted away their human companions. Understandably, the retailers are extremely doubtful about the operation and rumours abound. A bomb has been discovered. The caves, safe and secure for hundreds of years have partly collapsed. Long dormant subsidence from a worked out mine under the city threatens the foundations of the whole Centre. An underground river has bubbled up to flood the caves. A crazed and desperate gunman is holding a group of tourists hostage, deep under the city.

Yet that particular group of visitors long ago surfaced from the caves, fuelling most of the other rumours with their lurid accounts of the strange man who'd interrupted their tour. Bursting onto the shopping concourse, in their excitement they caused the initial panic resulting in the alarm being raised and the police alerted. Soon after Jennifer and Ettie had gone in, the security staff emerged, providing further elaboration to the now rapidly growing story. No match for Sam's older, perhaps more instinctive understanding of the caves, their modern knowledge had failed them. In the dark, complicated passageways he'd successfully relied on his good memory from his one previous journey and been able to hide and give them the slip.

The exaggerated experiences of the visitors, the guide and the security men galloped like a racehorse round the city. The first task for Emmins when he arrives is to placate the melee of press while keeping them away from the Centre. He issues a brief statement, but his unhelpful answers to their questions only exacerbates the press irritation. Extricating himself from the throng, he finds the situation almost as confused inside the Centre as outside in the street. With the public out the way, everything is orderly and subdued, but also inactive. A further witnesses reports the fugitive has a gun and the armed response unit has been requested, though her description bears no relation to the odd character seen in the caves.

One persistent rumour is of two women who entered the caves after the main evacuation. A security guard said one was a police officer who'd made them leave. At first this isn't taken seriously as all officers appear to be accounted for, but as he waits for the armed unit, Emmins isn't so sure. What about Jenner's team? Then he sees John Duggan and Sandra Tye.

"Where are sergeant Heathcott and chief inspector Jenner?"

Both constables are nervous and hesitant. John eventually replies.

"Sergeant Heathcott came down earlier, sir when the first call came in."

"Where is she now?"

John hesitates and then says quietly, "She could be inside."

"Bloody hell! And what about Jenner, where's he?"

John is silent. Sandra replies.

"We don't know, sir. He left the station. He's disappeared."

They arrive at Ettie's hotel and go straight up to her room. Sam is cold, hungry and dirty. They arrange for a meal to be sent up. While he washes (in the washbasin as he's afraid of the shower) and tucks in ravenously, Ettie and Jennifer talk.

"The stranger he talked about," Jennifer says, "Is it Matt?"

"There's no doubt," Ettie says, " I suspected he'd found a way to go into the past, probably by the same route Sam came from it. The campaign to reopen the tunnel, opposed so strongly by Matt, led to an unexpected opportunity for him. Somehow he discovered the canal would operate as a time conduit between past and present and so made good use if it."

"Where is he now?"

Ettie looks across at Sam, temporarily oblivious to the menacing forces surrounding him. She knows what must be done. The dangerously potent brew of past and present, which he's unwittingly caused, cannot continue. Sam must be returned to 1842. Ettie faces the prospect unwillingly, reluctant to state it bluntly, yet sure both in their different ways will accept the conclusion. He with the faith of the ignorant, she with the resignation of the perceptive. She begins with Jennifer.

"The chief inspector's inquiries will have frightened Matt. He really has only one place to go."

"To the past?"

"We have to act quickly. I'll change into my 1840 party dress and return to the canal with Sam."

"I have no clothes," Jennifer says, flustered.

"You'll not need them," Ettie says, touching her hand.

"I don't understand, surely I have to..."

"You can't come with me. Someone must remain and link up with the chief inspector."

"You can't do this alone."

"I must. Besides, there are other things that have to be done."

They part in the hotel drive. Sam waits in Ettie's car, brooding, expectant, but slightly less tense. Ettie is dressed for his period. On the way she will tell him of the perilous enterprise she plans. With little understanding and much trust in her he'll not demur. She turns to Jennifer for a final briefing.

"Remember, you must find Denise Deverall."

Reluctantly and with considerable misgivings, but unable to combat Ettie's determination, Jennifer leaves. Ettie watches until her car is out of sight before going on to the canal. All is quiet when they arrive. No one crosses the fields, no one is on the towpath, no one is near the tunnel. As they walk towards its entrance, Ettie is struck by the unnatural silence. No birds in the trees, no distant car engines, no voices, even the afternoon breeze has calmed. The air is still, yet charged with a curious anticipation. As they reach the tunnel mouth, sinister sensations multiply and she feels a distinct presence.

- 12 -

Her agitation becoming intolerable, Ettie has drawn away from the tunnel. She fidgets while dragging Sam back along the towpath. His feet scrape noisily on the stone and he stares blankly into the water. Ettie stops and slumps down on one of the seats. Sam sits beside her. He still concentrates on the water. She glances furtively towards the tunnel. It has to be faced. Someone is in the tunnel, but there's no other way. He turns from the canal and looks at her, silently, questioningly.

"Do you fear the tunnel?" she says.

"No more than you."

"We all fear what cannot be avoided."

He gets up.

"Must I return the same way I came?"

She nods.

"Then..."

He takes her hand and together they walk back. With each tread, Ettie's foreboding increases, but her step doesn't falter. Sam senses it and grips her hand even tighter.

"I have faced things much worse," he says.

"So have I."

Such memories reinforce her and she moves more confidently, though perhaps with the abandon of a reckless walker approaching hot cinders, constantly reminding herself, with doubtful certainty, that everything will be 'alright.' They reach the tunnel entrance and pass through. The immediate loss of brightness seems much greater and sudden than it really is. Sam stares at the water again, but repelled by its glinting coldness, quickly looks away. They've not come far, well short of the point where Sam had stumbled through from the past. Ettie's uneasy and stops. Sam follows her gaze into the tunnel. In the dim light a short distance before them, a stark figure stands on the path. Ettie glances across at Sam, looking for signs of recognition. The man seems familiar, though Sam is sure he's never seen him before.

"Matt," she says.

His clothes are similar to Sam's and he wears an almost identical hat.

"I see you've come dressed for the occasion," she says.

"As have you," Matt says, "The same outfit you had at the party, I believe."

"You haven't asked about my companion."

"I know who he is."

Sam studies Matt's face as he walks towards them.

"Do you know him?" Ettie says.

"I can guess," Sam says, "Is he the stranger Cecily mentioned?"

"He could be."

Matt stops just short of them, leering like the cheeky schoolboy, silently defying an admonishment from his teacher.

"What are you doing here?" he says.

His and Sam's eyes meet in mutual incredulity and some fear.

"Much the same as you, I imagine," Ettie says, "though at least I respect the power of the forces and understand the dangers. Like a child with matches you stupidly play with things beyond your understanding."

He laughs.

"You are the child here, because you can't possibly appreciate the significance of what I've discovered."

"You can't *discover* the past like some unknown continent. It's already been, it *is*. It's not the same as trawling through a hundred year old newspaper and presenting *new* facts. The past isn't dead, you can't pick through it as if it's a pile of old clothes. It's *alive* and what's living can be dangerous."

He laughs again, wagging a pointed finger at her contemptuously.

"You're the one that doesn't understand. How can the past be alive, it's gone, it's raw material?"

Ettie shudders. Sam looks frightened.

"So you admit to involving yourself in the past?"

"How quaint? *Involving yourself,* not your usual language. Don't you call it *time linking?* If so, I admit it. I've linked myself in time to the 1840s to further my researches."

"Hence the production of the authentic and oddly *contemporary* Chartist newspaper?"

He shrugs and smiles.

"An attractively simple illustration of what can be achieved."

"But it's not all attractive," Ettie says angrily, "An 1840 penny in remarkably good condition dropped on the floor in the police station and that Chartist handbill found near the body of Martin Sarwell."

Matt explodes, angrily moving forward, though halts as Ettie puts up her arm and Sam cowers beside her.

"That handbill wasn't mine. I had nothing to do with Martin Sarwell!"

"Of course not," Ettie says doubtfully.

"I had no reason to kill Sarwell," he says, less vehemently.

With its implied scepticism of his sincerity, Ettie's silence irritates him, especially as she persists in references to death.

"If the past is raw material as you put it, then it's a corpse on the mortuary table, ready to be cut up and dissected?"

"If you like."

"I don't like."

"What I've done has harmed no one," he says, anxious to reiterate his declared innocence.

"What you've done has probably imperilled us all! I told you the past is dynamic, not a collection of crusty old relics from which you take the bits you like and throw away the ones you don't."

"Then why are you here?"

She turns to Sam.

"I've come to get this man back to his own time. As you well know, it has to be done here because this is where he came through."

Matt moves forward.

"Not yet. There are things to be done."

"No, you'll do no more mixing of past and present."

"One advantage of looking backwards is you know what will or *might* happen. Sam is the lost local leader, a forgotten man, dissolved into the mists of history, but now I *know* what could have happened to him."

"*Could* have happened?"

"My researches imply he got away. The sources are vague, but I believe he escaped the authorities."

"Then you'll assist in helping him."

"In good time. First we have to rehabilitate Sam, matching his achievements to his reputation. To do that he has to stay in Nottingham."

"I don't understand."

He laughs again, a little more relaxed.

"Exactly, that's my point. Taking him back your way, without any direction, means he'll run away, as my sources indicate."

"How do you know all this?"

"There's a reference to Liverpool, after that it dries up, presumably because he either didn't make any further contact or it was safer not to record it. He must stay in Nottingham."

"But then he'll be caught!"

"No! I won't let that happen. I'll look after him, but *my* way, after he's fulfilled his true role and his exploits are properly recorded."

Matt moves forward again towards Sam. Ettie puts her arm around him and shouts at Matt.

"You fool! You still don't understand. You've not thought it through. You can't change history. You'll not take him. I won't let you!"

"In which case the three of us will have to travel back together."

As she drives away from the hotel, Jennifer wonders whether she'll ever see Ettie again. Having taken so long to accept Sam's origins, now she has grave misgivings about Ettie's plan. Getting him back is one thing, getting herself back is another. Even if Ettie can use the canal tunnel as a 'time conduit,' will it work both ways? Such unnerving thoughts strike at the foundations of all Jennifer takes for granted. A rational basis for events, evidence based on facts that can be tested against objective assumptions. Now, almost without question, she's swallowed or been swallowed by, practices founded on subjective premises and vague feelings. The pendulum in her mind swings continually between growing concern for Ettie and incredulity with the basis for that concern.

Ettie had been insistent. Denise had to be contacted without delay. She isn't at her house and neighbours haven't seen her for several days. Jennifer goes on to the distribution depot where Denise worked, but they haven't seen her either. Her boss says she'd taken a few days leave, but that had run out and she'd not returned.

"Is there anyone who might know her whereabouts?" Jennifer asks.

He shakes his head, "She worked closely with Amanda, but she knows nothing. I've already enquired."

So now Denise has also disappeared and Ettie's fears are justified. It's almost finishing time and the staff leave. Jennifer hovers until Amanda comes out. She's not keen to talk and only opens up when Jennifer gets her away to a nearby cafe.

"Gone missing has she?"

"Why do you say that?" Jennifer says.

Amanda shrugs her shoulders.

"Dunno, just thought she might."

"What do you know?"

Amanda leans forward across the table.

"Didn't want to say anything to him, you know, the boss, 'case Denise got in trouble."

"For staying away, you don't seem surprised?"

"Just the way she was talking...before..."

"What was she saying?"

"She's usually easy going, nothing seems to bother her, especially him, the boss, you know, nothing at work anyway."

"Outside work?"

"She's been a bit distracted."

"Perhaps she's still upset over the disappearance of her boyfriend, Bernard Weston?"

Amanda is unconvinced.

"No, I think she's over that, well, as much as you can be, you know. This was something more recent."

"A new boyfriend perhaps? What was distracting her?"

"Old clothes."

"Old clothes?"

"I'm dead serious or at least she was. Kept talking about old clothes. I know she was always designing clothes, but this was different. She kept saying as how she'd got to find out more, got to do...what was it... research, yes that's it, research."

"And she didn't say where she might have gone?"

Amanda gets even closer and even more conspiratorial.

"You won't tell him, will you, the boss, nowt to do with him anyway. I'm sure she'll be back when she's ready, but maybe she's got things to work out, you know."

"What did she say?"

"Couple of times she mentioned a new clothing museum that's just opened, said they'd know, they'd be able to help her."

"Where is it?"

"Down south, Tambleford."

After the closure of its two clothing factories and main reason for existence, Tambleford tried to reinvent itself. Like trains at its abandoned railway station, much of the promised alternative means of employment failed to arrive. What did has been inadequate to haul the south midland town out of its commercial doldrums. Modern day cottage industries such as tea rooms, antique shops and the revival of newly invented 'old crafts' have only marginally stemmed the ebb tide of economic recession. The clothing museum has been more successful than most. At least its raison d'etre has a loose connection with the town's industrial heritage even if its clientele is hardly typical of its erstwhile workers. Tucked down a side street, it's surprisingly large, the narrow, obscure entrance concealing the lengthy interior stretching deep behind the adjacent shops and its two upper floors. It's not busy and no one is at the desk. Jennifer waits a few moments and then wanders around. At the back of the first floor, she reaches the mid nineteenth century exhibits and lingers. A middle aged woman approaches. Jennifer shows her card and asks about Denise.

"We have no one of that name working here."

"She may not be staff, perhaps a visitor."

"We have many visitors... (Jennifer looks around dubiously) ...at our busy times...at the weekends."

"She wouldn't have been an ordinary visitor. This woman is an expert on dresses, especially the nineteenth century and a designer in her own right."

"Now that sounds like Miss Cantrell, Georgina Cantrell. She's been here several times."

Her description matches Denise.

"Has she visited recently?"

"Oh yes, she came a few days ago, but it must be a mistake. Miss Cantrell has no interest in dresses at all, she's researching *men's* clothes."

"1840s by any chance?"

"Yes, how did you guess?"

"Is she here now?"

Denise Deverall, alias Georgina Cantrell has put up in a modest hotel at the cheaper end of town. It's clean, orderly and very small. Jennifer finds her in the lounge, sipping a cup of tea, which she suspects she's been cradling for at least an hour. She's dressed tidily, but plainly and her face, pale and tired, seems to reflect the same depressed mood, so different from her usual confident, almost arrogant manner. She picks her fingers nervously and her eyes wander to the window as if she might be looking for someone. At first she doesn't recognise Jennifer and slow to appreciate the significance of her visit, being more concerned with the mechanics of discovery.

"How did you find me?"

"It wasn't difficult, but why the subterfuge, why the false name?"

Denise brushes it off with a wave.

"A whim, a passing fancy."

"Naturally and that's why you've chosen to stay down here long after your ...researches...are completed."

Denise turns towards the door.

"I'm having more tea, want some?"

"No thank you. Why are you running away?"

For a withering second the beginning of defiance, an embryonic clever put down, a refusal to admit what can be plainly seen flickers, but it passes abruptly, unable to get beyond its starting block. The tears well in her eyes and she pulls out a crumpled handkerchief just quickly enough to dab them hurriedly.

"Couldn't stay, had to get away."

"Who are you running from?"

"Matt."

"What's he done?"

"Nothing, but he talks, always he talks and talks. Never stops, couldn't take any more."

"What about?"

"The past, always about the past."

"Is that why you were looking into men's clothes in the 1840s?"

"He wanted to know everything, had to be perfect. I've made up so many things."

"So he has many Victorian clothes?"

"Bit of a laugh at first, a challenge, a change from dresses, but he takes it all so seriously."

"Odd maybe, but hardly dangerous, a few clothes."

Now Denise does cry as the repressed tension is released. The tea arrives and she hides her tears. Jennifer takes charge and asks for a second cup for herself. The waitress leaves.

"There's more, much more," Denise says, "He kept asking me about people, dead people, what I knew about local people. Always he wanted to know about somebody called Cecily. I'm really frightened."

"Because of these dead people?"

"Because of Matt and Bernard and why Bernard died. There's something I need to show you and something I need to tell you, something I've known for a very long time."

Lunging forward, Matt grabs Sam and pulls him along the path. For a few seconds Ettie retains her grip and tries to hold him back, with Sam's flailing arms stretched between them, like an elasticated scarecrow in the wind. Then, as Matt's strength prevails, her fingers loosen and Sam is suddenly jerked forward. Matt starts running, still hauling the startled Sam along as a bobbing and rolling jolly boat tied to the back of an accelerating pleasure cruiser. Following behind, Ettie cries to Sam.

"Don't let him take you! Break free!"

Physically as strong, but wearied and traumatised, Sam is weak against Matt's heady vigour and seems incapable of releasing himself. They reach that part of the tunnel, which once led directly into the mines and close to where the time rent brick had yielded to Sam's breach from the past. As if sensing its significance, Matt pauses. Seeing Ettie reaching them, he shouts, but the words, merge into the wall, echoing incoherently through the tunnel, so she can't understand them. Still holding Sam, Matt speaks again. Then he turns right round, away from the water and faces the canal as a wildly rushing sound like the sweeping through the forest of a million leaves comes through the rigidly still air. Reminiscent of those unknown and malevolent forces that pressed on her, it terrifies Ettie, but like the snapping of falling timbers in a firestorm it wrenches Sam from his petrified reverie and he pulls away from Matt. In the same second Ettie grabs Sam, while Matt, thrusting out his arm in a pathetic effort to pull him from her, steps straight into a vibrating opaque flux before being swallowed by the canal. Then stillness in the air and smooth, undisturbed emptiness on the surface of the water, no sound, no image, no movement, no Matt.

The suddenness of Matt's leaving rips Sam from his torpor. Wide eyed and still frightened, he jabbers all the way back to the car and continues for the next hour. While he rattles on and between placating him as best she can, Ettie concentrates on what she has to do. If Matt's amateurish time linking exploits are successful, he is now, in the short term safely and in the longer term unsafely, positioned in 1842. She's resisted his attempt to drag them with him in his perilous plunge into the past. This has gained her valuable time, but she'll have to move quickly. In the longer term his unpredictable machinations in the past could threaten everything. Whatever else he said, Matt has to be right about what *could* happen to Sam. He's also right Ettie hasn't thought about the *where* as well as the when of Sam's return. Unknowingly, Matt has helped. The vague reference to Liverpool has to be based on real events. What *could* happen has to be turned into what *will* happen. Staying at the Cross Cut is not an option. Matt has used it before her, making it too problematic. If she takes Sam that way, they'll probably walk straight into Matt's carefully laid trap. If they hang around, waiting for a better opportunity he might return and cause further mayhem. He may also have damaged the canal as a time conduit. They have to get to Liverpool. At least then they'll be in the right place if not yet in the right time. Matt will guess her intentions, but if he's in 1842 his movements will be slower and staying in the present she should get Sam to Liverpool quicker. They have to get there first!

Sam sleeps, rapidly induced by the combined effects of the rolling of the car and his physical and psychological exhaustion after they left the canal. He no longer seems frightened of cars. He may have become accustomed, but more likely he's deliberately suppressed his fear, perhaps hoping he'll suddenly awake into a world where they and all the other nightmares no longer exist. Either way, Ettie is content. A much stronger man would have been broken by a fraction of what he's been forced to endure. It's better he sleeps. She doesn't have to explain the inexplicable, listen to his lamentable, repetitive cries of despair, or field unconvincing reassurances in response to his barrage of questions. It all saps her energy, which she needs to conserve for the struggle they have to face.

Ettie stops at a service area to consult the map. Anxious not to disturb him, she slows down as gradually as she can. He doesn't stir. The map is spread out across the steering wheel. Ettie is engrossed in the vagaries of Cheshire roads for a few minutes until she has the uncanny feeling of being watched. The obvious reaction is to look up at the windscreen over the top edge of the map, but instead she keeps studying, ostrich like. Without looking up, she bends her head slightly to glance over to Sam. He's unmoved. The feeling gets stronger. She commits the route to memory, but folds the map and stuffs it into the side of the door without looking directly at the windscreen. The car park flits in her peripheral vision. If anyone is there they've seen her anyway. She turns to face it. Nothing.

She gets out, locks the car behind her and dons her coat over the Victorian dress. As she goes over to get sandwiches and drinks, the sense of being observed persists. She stops several times and scrutinises billboards, trees, railings, anything that might hide a watcher. There are plenty of people around, but she knows it won't be one of them. At the entrance, she looks back to the car, suddenly aware of Sam's vulnerability. She even considers going back, but then goes in. She'll be quick.

The shop is crowded and there are several aisles allowing plenty of opportunity for someone to lurk behind the shelves. There's a crush at the sandwiches. She has to wait. As she turns to look at the drinks she fancies she sees a cap bobbing above one of the shelves. Not a contemporary cap, squarer, peaked, the sort of cap worn by a working man in...she looks again, there's no one. She gets the sandwiches and moves on to the drinks. Someone is behind her. She turns round fearfully. A young girl with a stud in her nose, nothing Victorian about that. She picks up the drinks and goes to the cashier. Another queue, she waits nervously. At last she's served and hurries back to the car, half expecting to see it empty. Must it be someone from the past? What if Matt has returned to harass her?

The next twenty miles are uneventful until she has to make a detour due to road works. Still Sam sleeps as she follows a secondary road through small villages and skirts lonely farms. The signage is poor and she slows down on entering one place, sure she's taken the wrong turning. She stops and asks the way at the village store where she's given directions back to the main road and told to ignore the misleading signs! In the car Sam is stirring, but sleeps on. As she drives away the feeling of a predatory presence returns. She tries to ignore it, taking corners too fast and accelerating on the straight sections until almost colliding with a tractor, she has to slow down.

She reaches the main road and manages to shrug off her nervous unease, though now other nagging thoughts undermine her. Even if she reaches Liverpool safely, with all this confusion and interference, will time and space coordinate? How much has been distorted? Is the *right* place now, the right place *then*? Time linking is one thing, but this degree of time movement is outside her experience. Even if she gets into the past, will she get back? She's even unsure whether this running to Liverpool is correct and whether her plan will work out. One thing ought to be checked. She could ring Jenner, but his state of mind worries her. Better to contact Jennifer. There's no reply. She leaves a message.

"...okay so far, on my way to Liverpool. There's also something I need to know. If you can find it out and then let me know as soon as possible. There's not a lot of time..."

Sam wakes up as they reach the outskirts of the city.

"Not like I remember it," he says when she tells him where they are.

"You've been to Liverpool before?"

"A meeting, near the docks, a couple of years ago."

"That might be useful."

His foot kicks against her bag on the floor and various items spill out.

"What's this?" he says, picking up a necklace and two brooches.

"Things to pawn when we...to get money...what I have will be no use in 1842."

He puts them back.

"You're very generous, to give up these things for me."

"They're replaceable."

"I know a pawnshop in town. I ought to give you something, but I have..."

"It doesn't matter."

"I have so little."

He ferrets in his pockets and drops some coins into the box on the dashboard. She heads for the city centre without any clear idea of their exact destination. Everything is too changed for Sam to be of much help though he senses the general direction of the river and several times indicates the correct road to take. Ettie senses other things and the closer they get the stronger are her apprehensions. They are not alone. She's glad of Sam's instinctive antennae. Alone she might succumb to deliberate misguidance. Has Matt returned? How can he know where they are? If it's not him...then who?

They stop and park near the old docks. From here it's only possible to continue on foot. It's getting dark. She remembers the phone, which has been turned off. There's one message from Jennifer. Ettie takes Sam's coins. The whole area, regenerated and transformed in the last twenty years is utterly unlike a nineteenth century dockside, yet it retains enough to recreate that era. The old warehouses may now be restaurants, bars, arts centres and museums, their walls sandblasted out of the smoke and soot, but the hard shell of the past is still there, guarding, protecting an inner soft yoke of a contemporary world, long gone. Perhaps it's not entirely lost, only needing a catalyst to energise its core and wake it from a long sleep. Ettie needs that catalyst. A neutral, indifferent, unknowing spectator, but one that enlivens more than the walls, invigorates more than the stones on the ground or the pulleys and cranes and doors in the roofs. It must be here.

She walks quickly, purposefully around the edge of the dock. Sam follows dutifully, carrying her bag, staring unbelievingly at the smart boutiques and the laughing visitors, sitting outside the bistros. Ettie is absorbed, apparently intent on some clear objective, but really covering up an inner turmoil, close to panic. She's drawn to water, to the dock, but has only a vague sense of how it might fuse them with the past. Something has to forge the link, but it eludes her. They reach a footway where two of the docks connect. It's a bridge between the two sides across a narrower inlet where ships originally passed between the docks. Ettie hesitates and grips the chain at the edge. Sam comes up beside her.

"What is it?" he says.

She shakes her head. He looks ahead and shrugs, suddenly more confident.

"We have to go this way," he says, "Come on, there's no one there."

He strides ahead. Ettie holds back, shivering. Here on this slender, vulnerable span, with water before them, behind them, to their left, to their right and below they have to be closer, nearer to whatever will ease their way, but she's afraid. Sam reaches the middle of the bridge. He turns back. It's then she sees. A slight, hazy, shifting form gradually solidifies, assuming recognisable shape, depth and colour. A man dressed in working clothes, the unmistakable hat of the time, a heavy coat and coarse trousers, intent eyes and a mouth set in defiance and expectation. A familiar face. Matt.

"No!" Ettie shouts.

Sam turns as Matt advances towards him.

"Come back!" Ettie shouts.

Sam steps back slightly, but he's mesmerised by Matt and cannot move further. Matt grabs at him. Sam tries to fend him off with Ettie's bag. As Matt tries again to get hold of him, he takes the bag from Sam's hand. Furious, Sam pulls it back, but it slips from his hand and is sent hurtling back towards Ettie. As she catches it, Matt drags Sam further over the bridge.

Jenner has gone back to the Best Hill site, ostensibly (he tells the consternated site manager) to follow up certain 'issues relevant to the enquiry,' but really to provide a backdrop to his troubled mind. The DNA test result on the skeleton had come in just before he left. There's no doubt. The comparison with samples taken from Ella Weston is conclusive. A clear match. The remains have to be those of her brother, Bernard Weston. So the mystery of his whereabouts has been finally cleared up, but not yet the precise details of his fate. Jenner is sure, but afraid of the implications.

He wanders around aimlessly, hoping physical activity might free his mind, but it does nothing to stabilise his nerves. He stays a quarter hour, but it seems much longer. Then his phone rings. It's rung before and he's ignored it, meaning to turn it off. Now, before prudence kicks in, he answers. It's Emmins.

"Where the bloody hell are you? We've got a full scale emergency unfolding here, all revolving around that escaped prisoner of yours!"

"On my way, sir."

"I'm sure, but where *are* you?"

Jenner rings off. If he stays Emmins will surely track him down. It's time to get away, escape, anywhere. Mumbling some meaningless excuse to the bemused site manager, he scuttles off. The last place he wants to be is the circus at Broad Marsh. *Your* escaped prisoner! Jenner had nothing to do with the careless loss of Usworth! He blamed Jennifer for the foolhardy pursuit of a suspicious man, though Ettie may well have encouraged her. That's not fair. They could be in great danger, even more so with Emmins embarked on a full scale siege. Who is this man anyway? Sam? More likely Matt.

He stops the car at an unoccupied lay-by. He'll think through the evidence again. Yet already it seems a failed investigation. Doubt overwhelms him, but is the doubt about the evidence or about himself? Ettie and Jennifer were last seen going into the caves under the city centre. Maybe he ought to be there, giving his support. Yet, he'd only be in the way, Emmis way, pushed around like all the others, achieving nothing. Besides, what will it achieve? If it really is Sam, then Ettie will handle things better than he can. Perhaps anyone will handle it better than him.

He turns on the car CD player. Miaskovsky 21st, no skip that, too strident, try something else. Borodin, 3rd, pastoral, lyrical. Yes that will do, but unfinished, very appropriate, unfinished music, unfinished investigation. Unfinished or finished...a finished policeman. He thinks of his wife, dead twenty years. He doesn't often think of her, even when he listens to her music, a lasting legacy, Russian symphonic music. She lives on in the music, in what will he live on?

How will he convince anyone? Even if Ettie is right (and the DNA evidence is pointing strongly in her direction) how can he explain? No one will believe him. Bloody laughing stock. That's what he'll be. Bloody laughing stock. What future is there for a detective who believes in spirits and time travelling murderers? Ettie and Jennifer in those caves, pursuing such a man. He feels the danger. He tries to ring. Nothing. There'll be no signal down there. Yet the evidence stacks up. He must do something. He can't stay here!

As Ettie grabs the flying bag, it twists over and some items of jewellery fall out, clattering on the boards of the bridge. Afraid they'll roll over the edge and into the water, she stoops down to pick them up. One brooch rolls. She gets down on her knees, quickly scoops all the pieces in her hands and lobs them back in the bag. She glances up and sees Sam struggling. Although Matt still has hold of him, his image wavers. Ettie blinks to clear her eyes, but it's no illusion. Matt's form is less distinct. He's taking Sam away into another time! She has to do something! She gets up on one leg and looks round anxiously. Feeling Sam's coins in her pocket, she takes them out and angrily throws them at Matt. They hit him in the forehead and instantly he loosens his grip. Sam pulls back and turns from him.

"This way, come back!" Ettie shouts as she gets up.

Sam runs back. By the time he reaches her Matt has gone.

Ettie and Sam hurry along the dockside. Continually jostled by seamen, dockers, clerks, passengers and the vast army of dockside protectors, parasites and predators, they have to dodge pickpockets and prostitutes and avoid the rowdy temptations of publicans. The gas lamps twinkle in the twilight, their flickering light reflected in glistening pools in the water and piercing the evening mist in silky yellow orbs.

The air is smoky and thick from many fires and filled with the sound of ships and sailors. Masts and rigging criss-cross the pinky grey sky like huge spiders' webs. Furled sails are roped in neat rows like corpulent washer women while others, waiting for the tide, flap and billow in the breeze. Cranes wheeze and slash the air, pulleys squeal and complain as many loads are lifted and lurched into position, passengers wait and wonder, sitting on their luggage or wandering endlessly along well worn paths at the dockside. Always there are the late arrivals, puffing their bodies and pulling their belongings in their anxious sprint from the ticket office to the ship.

Plunged now into his own contemporary, if not familiar, environment, Sam is leading, confident he can remember the way. They turn into a dark and narrow side alley, the single dockside lamp at the near end casting a dismal, diminishing light. Ettie is reluctant and hangs back. Sam pulls her clear of a passing drunk.

"It's not far, only a few yards."

They enter the alley, Ettie skipping to keep clear of the puddles. Half way down Sam stops beside a window, filled with many articles. He waits at the door and points to the tell tale three balls above him.

"Told you'd I'd find it," he says triumphantly.

They enter the pawnbrokers.

"Do you want me to do the talking?" he whispers.

"Yes," she says, handing him her bag.

The pawnbroker, a small man with dark, deep set eyes picks up all the pieces, giving them a quick, cursory examination before getting out his eye piece and scrutinising each of them more rigorously. He glances at the two of them, maybe wondering how they are related. Mother and son, Ettie thinks. Perhaps she exudes a maternal protectiveness. The pawnbroker will never know how close they came to not being here at all. He completes his examination, then looks at some of the items again as if needing to satisfy himself of their real worth. Ettie is nervous. Jewellery should be ageless, but what if he's so intrigued by their unusualness he won't take them?

Without money what will they do? He puts the pieces

down, scribbles some calculations and then slides across the total amount on a paper. Sam looks at it and then hands it to Ettie. The figure in 1842 terms is meaningless to her, but Sam nods to indicate it's a fair price. The deal is done. The pawnbroker puts the jewellery in a box and hands over the money. They hurry back down the alley to the comparative safety of the dockside. Neither of them looks back, but Ettie is sure the pawnbroker watches them all the way until they've turned the corner.

The dockside is more crowded than earlier. It's getting late. Ettie is surer of her intention even if less sure of her ability to carry it out. Jennifer's message confirms it. They must reach the ticket office before it closes. The mist is heavier. Away from the lights, a syrupy grey soup hangs over the water. The ships loom ghostly, like hanging shrouds, their sombre silent resting, broken only by the heaving of heavy timbers and the lapping water. Beside them a constant babbling rattle of people, interspersed with the whoops and wails of the excited, the expectant, the dejected and the forlorn. Ettie and Sam struggle through.

Unwittingly, it seems Matt was the catalyst, his desperate, crazy attack forcing them back in time, yet out of his immediate control. It must have been the water, the eternal channel between worlds, surrounding them, drawing them. Yet in itself, it was not enough. Water is a channel, not a vehicle. There had to be other, more dynamic forces at work. Matt is a dangerously uncontrollable player in what he sees as a foolish game with time. He was the catalyst, but not the agent of change. Which leaves only Ettie and Sam themselves. What did they do?

Ettie knows their escape from Matt is only temporary. Somehow he was able to track their movements from the past and briefly return to the present to try to carry Sam back with him. They thwarted him, while also pulling themselves back to 1842. What they can do, he may also do especially if he can detect how it was done. By pulling themselves back, did they also pull him back? They may have cast him aside in space, but not in time. Briefly ejected from the dockside, he may return later and that return may be quick. He could be lurking around one of these corners, hidden in any one of these milling groups, ready to pounce!

How was it done? If she knew she may be better able to protect them from his next attack. She might even find out how to get herself back. The bag, it has to be the bag. Matt touched the bag and then Sam threw it and Ettie caught it. The jewellery fell out, jewellery from the present to change into money in the past. Jewellery held by Matt and then thrown by Sam, a man from the past, holding something from the present, caught by Ettie, a woman from the present...who then...picked them up...so what ...no, who then threw Sam's coins...coins from the past thrown from the present...to strike Matt, a man from the present who had been in the past, now trying to pull Sam back to the past...Ettie's head spins. Past, present, things from the past, things from the present, coming from the past, going to the past.

They near the ticket office. More crowds, more queues, more noise, more acrid, salty, sweaty smells. Sam has the money and will transact the business. They enter the office. It's small and dark with only a few oil lamps. Two harassed clerks, one short and chirpy, the other tall and dour, are battling manfully to clear the congestion. Sam has to wait, standing behind a family, mother holding a baby, father and five other children. The man struggles with various bags and boxes. Each of the children also carry something. All their worldly possessions, probably mostly clothes, rammed and stuffed into what they can carry. A new life to be built on the wreckage of the old. Ettie stands by the door, staring across the dock, the lights from the ships gleaming through the fog. Muffled, rumbling sounds, from all or no directions converge. Clinking chains, splashing anchors, whirring ropes, heavy loads hammering on boards, clanking gangplanks, the running and shuffling of many feet, the windy winding of widening canvas and all the while the creaking, cracking, splish splashing. Now a new sound, the distant watery wheeling purr of a steamer. Ettie sniffs the air. The congealing cocktail of smells joined by the smoky, steamy whiff of its funnel.

Sam is still behind the laden family. Ettie steps onto the dockside again. Her outfit must be effective for none of those passing give her a second glance though some, as if caught in her invisible beam of concentration, boring across the dock, glance at her wonderingly. Most hurry by, entwined in their world weathered cares. They do not notice. Oddly, her apprehensions subside, mixing now with an acceptance they've reached this brief spit of relative security in the whirling sea of time and place. She has to remind herself of the where and the when. She is *in* here, not some distant, safe spectator, able to instantly disengage and return to her own real world. *This* is real. She mustn't be complacent or allow herself to be sucked into an artificial comfort zone. Not her place, but her time. Surely now she can summon up a benevolent contact? She must remember and not be distracted, honing all her attention on Lizzie. She stares intensely into the murky night, her eyes fixed yet unfocused, her mind vacant yet receptive, her only thought being that bare room in that lonely cottage, but Lizzie will not or cannot respond.

Past and present with the jewels between them? Ettie sees it now. By throwing the jewels Sam reinforced his bond with Ettie. By touching those jewels, Matt was fixed, at least for those moments into their power. That power was released when Ettie threw the coins at Matt. They became the wax, setting the seal between past and present. Simultaneously it released Sam from Matt and pulled both he and Ettie into the past where Matt had sought to drag him.

Sam comes out of the office clutching his ticket.

"Put it somewhere safe," Ettie says, "Which ship?"

"The *Sylvania*."

The right ship. Ettie is pleased. It's a long walk, but there's time if they're brisk. The crowds thin out as they get nearer, but it's also lonelier and darker. Half way there Sam stops.

"I'm running away," he says, "I've let down so many and without you even this would be impossible."

"You let down many more if you don't go."

"How so? I cannot fight from far away."

"Your fight is not over. Believe me. I know."

She takes his shoulder and they go on, but while Sam is reassured, Ettie is not. Her concerns about Matt and his persistent interference in the precarious relationship between past and present continue to grow. As they near the *Sylvania* those concerns become two worrying alarms. She knows he must be close and unless she can ward off a further attack she may not be able to hold Sam much longer in 1842. Unfortunately her fears are only too quickly realised. They must turn a blind corner to reach the side dock where the *Sylvania* is berthed. Ettie approaches with grave misgivings, unsure what to do, wondering whether to call Sam back, but it's already too late. He rounds the corner and with a cry stops abruptly. Ettie joins him to find Matt standing in their path. No one else is around.

"You won't escape me this time," Matt says, "I'm prepared."

"Let us pass," Ettie barks.

"What and let the opportunity of a lifetime slip away?"

"You cannot stop us."

"Ah, but you see, I have no choice. I have to talk to Sam about Doctor Foxley."

"What do you know about Foxley?" Sam says aggressively.

"I know you were after him. You had to be because of what Cecily Stacey told you."

"I've never met Cecily Stacey."

"That's not my information."

"Is this true?" Ettie says to Sam, "Did you meet Cecily?"

"No, no, no!"

"No matter," Matt says, "You knew anyway, that's why you were after Foxley!"

Sam is silent.

"I thought so," Matt continues, "Foxley had something to tell you or better still show you. It's vital to the history of the movement. We have to track it down."

"I don't know what you're talking about."

Matt gets closer to Sam.

"You do! You do!"

"Get away from him!" Ettie shouts.

"I have to get him back to Nottingham."

Ettie gets between them.

"How do you know all this?" she says.

"Because it's in the minute book, the one Denise found. Cecily wrote it down. It's in there. I know it's there, but he knows more, much more!"

Matt moves again towards Sam and puts out his hand. It's as if he tries to grasp a mirror, an image almost of himself.

"Get away!" Ettie shouts, "He has to get on the ship."

"He's not getting on any ship! He's got to come with me!" Matt grabs hold of Sam's collar.

"Tell her!" he shouts, "Tell her I'm right!"

Sam lifts his arms to push Matt away. Ettie comes over, but as she does Sam stumbles and is dragged along by Matt to the edge of the dock.

"You're too close!" Ettie shouts.

Sam tries to free himself again, but slips on the wet stone, loses his balance and goes over the side. Matt puts out his arm, but is unable to catch him. With a tremendous splash Sam falls into the water. Ettie runs to the side. She shouts to Sam, but there's no reply. In the dim light she scans the surface. The rippling water clears and is soon calm again. The reflection of a distant light reappears. Nothing disturbs the flat water. Ettie looks round, but Matt has gone.

The operation at Broad Marsh is called off. With armed back up, Emmins orders the caves to be entered, but a thorough search reveals nothing. Jenner returns to the station the next day, thankfully managing to avoid Emmins and any debate about either his or Jennifer's movements. She's left several garbled messages on his mobile.

"Just to let you know I'm okay, will report in later... following up a lead, will get back to you...interesting information, will explain at the station."

No mention of Ettie being okay. What lead? What interesting information? Then comes the summons to Emmins.

"Pretty poor performance, Jenner, pretty bloody poor."

"Quite so, sir."

"Incommunicado, letting one of your officers engage in a dangerous operation without any reference to me."

"Quite, well actually sir..."

"And now she's gone missing with a civilian…"

"Not exactly, sir, you see…"

"Then there's the matter of a dangerous escaped prisoner, who was in your charge."

"I wasn't respon…"

"Not bloody good enough, Jenner. You're an experienced officer and despite, certain er…unconventional activities… with a good record. Got to be an improvement, pretty bloody quick. Get me?"

"Quite so, sir."

The more than usually one-sided conversation is terminated as suddenly as it began with the chief superintendent nodding to the door with the clear intimation Jenner should be rapidly on the other side of it. Yet this peremptory, slightly unjust drubbing has a salutary and not wholly unwelcome effect. Misfortune is sometimes a catalyst to recovery. As he nurses injured pride and suppresses profound anger, Jenner's spirits are jerked out of depression. Despite the mistakes, his gut feeling about the case hasn't changed. Beating himself up with his inadequacies won't alter what he feels. Lessons should be learnt from mistakes. He'll not be thwarted by the rules, thrown at him either by Emmins or the less merciful attacks of his own high standards. If the case cannot be wrapped up by conventional means, then…and Emmins acknowledges his experience in this area…then it must be closed by unconventional ones. Somehow he has to *prove* what he believes. Using such tactics, even more than in the past, may mean changing the routines of a lifetime. A very different case might produce a very different sort of policeman.

Jennifer's return is almost as clandestine as Jenner's. She creeps through the station, reaching his office without attracting undue attention. His relief is mixed with irritation.

"Your disappearance has brought down the wrath of the powers that be on me, sergeant. Where have you been?"

His concerns are only partly relieved after she explains her movements.

"So Ettie got away with Usworth, but where are they now?"

"I left them at the hotel."

"What have you got from Denise Deverall?"

She recounts Denise's fear, verging on terror.

"Matthew Usworth," he mutters, "I knew it."

Jennifer tells him of the long held memory Denise has been bottling up. Then she asks him about the Chartist minute book. He gets it out and she flicks through, reaching where a page has been torn out.

"I never noticed that," he says.

Jennifer takes out the page Denise gave her.

"The missing entry that Denise kept until now!"

Jenner studies the brown aged ink carefully and then takes out his notes.

"Look at this," he says, "it's what I found in the workhouse records."

Jennifer compares the information.

"Now, we're really getting somewhere."

He nods gravely.

"Indeed so. What we've found, what you've now told me and all our other information means we have to be very concerned for Ettie's safety. You're sure this man really is Sam Usworth?"

"Yes I do and I think he's safe. From what you've said, it looks like he really did witness the murder of Bernard Weston."

"Quite, but while he may be safe, his position is not. What does Ettie intend to do?"

Jennifer hesitates.

"She's spoken to you, hasn't she, since you left her at the hotel?"

She tells him of the telephone message.

"You've checked this out?" he says.

"Yes and I left a message on her phone. Ettie wants to return him to the past."

"That's what I was afraid of. Getting him back may expose her to even greater danger...from others!"

He gets up. Jennifer goes over to the cupboard and takes something out.

"I'm going out," he says.

"You'd better take this," she says, "you might need it."
She hands him the 1840 police hat he wore to the party.

Ettie waits on the platform for the Birmingham train. Only twenty odd miles from Liverpool and she's already had to buy another ticket and change to another railway. It sounds very impressive. *The Grand Junction.* Somebody had said it was the longest line in the country. The platform is crammed with people. She bought a second class ticket, which should ensure a reasonable seat. She'd unwisely travelled third class from Liverpool in a draughty carriage with very hard wooden benches. The train approaches, the locomotive spluttering white steam and billowing huge quantities of grey black smoke from its enormously tall chimney. She can see the driver as it slows. He's perched over the far end of the boiler. The fireman is beside him, holding the side rail and resting against the tender, which is piled high with coal. They stand in the open. The locomotive has no cab. Fortunately for them it's a dry day. They must get drenched in a storm.

She finds a seat by the window and settles down. She's made an early start for a journey, which will take many hours. She's still tired. Last night, after such a frenetic day and a hearty meal at the Liverpool hotel, she was exhausted, but at first had been unable to sleep. The bare room with its green washed surroundings imploded on her. The flickering candlelight played monstrous figures on the wall, assuming the shape of the loud and leering people at the docks. Clattering wheels and clopping hoofbeats from the street disturbed her peace until very late. Eventually she'd slept soundly, waking just in time for a stout breakfast and a dash for the first Manchester train.

The locomotive hisses long and loud, as if to gather its breath, then with throaty thuds lumbers forward, jerking them away. The barren station recedes. She leans back, watches the unfolding landscape for a few moments as the train wearily increases speed and then closes her eyes, only to let the previous day's events inevitably intrude.

She had to get away from the dockside as quickly as possible. Her brisk walk turned into a run. She tripped a few times until she got used to the long dress though the hem was spattered and wet. When she got back to the maze of alleys the crowds were thicker than ever. The packed and heaving pubs rang with jangled and raucous carousing, ladling their inebriated overspill out onto the footway. She had to pick her way carefully to avoid trampling on the prostrate drunks on the floor or hustled by those still standing. She lost her way and panicked, several times wandering into alleys even darker and more sinister than that of the pawnbroker's shop. Would she be marooned amidst this human flotsam, consigned to live on the fringe of a perpetual mass drinking bout? Every face darting out of the mist, springing from corners or leaping out of shadows seemed more threatening. Even the children, ragged, rough or reticent were frightening, scampering everywhere, bursting from nowhere, hollering from somewhere. Along alleys and more alleys, each one darker and dingier than the one before, courts and crevices, tiny houses nestling against warehouses and factories, gradually she lost the sights and smells of the port.

Just as she abandoned all hope of escaping from the cramped and teeming hordes, pressed and crushed in their brick lined labyrinth, she emerged into a wider, lighter, open street. Unsure, but calmer she slowed down and followed the direction of the people and the cabs, towards a bright square. She must be close to the centre of the city. How to get back and which to choose, time or place? As the unanswered question wandered around her mind she wandered aimlessly around the square, circling it twice before turning into another wide street.

She glanced down the next street. A clutch of bustling people were gathered at a turning point for cabs. A familiar smell was in the air, reminiscent of the dock. Smoke, steam. The railway station. She checked the coins Sam had insisted she keep. There ought to be enough though she had no idea of the fare. She could go back in place if not in time. She asked about trains for Nottingham and got a blank look. This is 1842. Nottingham is a long way. There are no through trains and no through tickets. Will she get there today? Today, how fast does she think they go? First train in the morning. Spend the night in a hotel.

She knows that was how it was meant to be. The records show Sam disappeared. History cannot be changed. That was Matt's mistake. It was always intended each would play their parts. This was hers. Sam is back in the past. His fate is clear even if his legacy lives on. A matter she will have to sort out with Jenner, but how will she talk to him? This is 1842 and this is an 1842 train! Jenner is a hundred and sixty years ahead!

Jenner's normal placidity is shattered, his worries compounded by not knowing if he can trust his own judgement. Whether or not he was right in not immediately following Jennifer and Ettie, is nothing compared to making the right decision now. Knowing Ettie is in danger goes beyond normal concern while Jennifer's cryptic intelligence has deepened rather than assuaged his apprehensions. His 'logical' mind tells him to restrain his wilder thoughts. His 'feeling' mind tells him otherwise. This *other* mind hadn't really existed before or at least he'd not been aware of it. He'd always had hunches, gut feelings, good coppers always do, but this is more. Now he senses things he cannot explain, almost as if he's only the receiver, the instrument of sensations, the mouthpiece of messages. He's dismissed them as foolish many times, but they creep back, gnawing persistently, like a reckless, but tenacious mouse ever returning to a piece of cheese in full view of the cat. The result is a spiralling inner conflict, a mental badminton with himself as the shuttlecock. But the fact remains, demonstrable or intuitive. Ettie is in danger and needs him.

Yet how can he help when he can't be sure where she is in either time or place? The conflicting strands whirr through his mind. His senses tell him she'll not stop until she returns Sam Usworth to his own time or...fails in the attempt. Better not think of that. If she succeeds, then *logically* she must try to return. That at least makes it easier for him, but where exactly and in what time? How will she get back if she's still in 1842? Will she be in time, but not in place or in place, but not in time? Time, which time? Which place? What is the right place in the right time? His head whirls. He can't cope.

But he must. His senses tell him there is a way. He can help, if he can only find the answer.

The train reaches the outskirts of Birmingham. There are three other people close to her in the carriage, a couple and an older man. Ettie's nervous of speaking too much, conscious of her strange accent, which she tries to disguise. She's managed to avoid more than light and occasional conversation. In between snatches she's worked on her story. A widow, visiting her daughter, recently removed to London. Her first such journey, hence her ignorance of the ways of trains. So far it's worked. None of them is travelling beyond Birmingham and none ask where her daughter lives in London. They might give her directions in Birmingham to the London station. She might better have said she was travelling to Derby

Yet in the last half hour, she would have welcomed their talk. It might have diverted her mind from other things. An odd coincidental thought comes into her mind. Sam fell into the water just like Jonathon Cressley. Despite the three other passengers she feels an uncanny loneliness, as if she's in the carriage on her own, they are not really there and cannot help her. Yet she knows she's not alone in the train. There is another, maybe more. All the hundreds of people in this travelling box are oddly unreal except…one, maybe more, perhaps not of this time…who are real. This insidious uneasiness, coming and going at first, has been growing on the approach to Birmingham. For here she must change trains and leave the comparative security of the carriage. She must not hang back nor stride ahead, but merge with the crowd, mix in the swell, not stand out. She must find her connection quickly.

The train stops. The locomotive heaves a huge sigh of steamy relief, the high chimney flakes its grey smoke up to the roof, dozens of doors are flung open and the train disgorges its bursting load. Ettie tries to join the throng, but it fragments. She feels too exposed to join the wispy trails of stragglers making for the exit. Instead she stands by one of the clumps of passengers waiting for their luggage to be unfastened and handed down from the roof. She looks round nervously.

"Anything to come down, missus?"

She shakes her head to the porter and he moves further down the platform. She follows him with her eyes, scanning past the scurrying children, the laden trolleys and the jumbled groups for a face staring back with the same intensity. It's difficult. Even as people disperse, they obscure those at the far end, concealing perhaps those that prefer to be hidden. After retrieving its belongings, her own group moves off. Turning to join them she glimpses in the corner of her eye, what could be a familiar face, but when she looks back she sees only a mass of strangers crawling towards her. A trick of the sunlight, dancing along the train, glinting on the trolleys, shining through windows, darting between hats and caps. She turns away again. She reaches the front of the train. As she passes, the locomotive spits steam irritably like an old woman sucking bits of meat from her teeth. The driver is checking his instruments, perhaps afraid the old girl will suddenly erupt uncontrollably. The fireman is down on the track, unhooking the tender from the first carriage. As Ettie reaches the exit she feels unseen eyes watching her. She looks back, but only sees the locomotive firing a searing jet of steam up into the roof as a parting call.

She hurries on, asks the way and is directed to the ticket office of the next line, no longer *Grand*, merely the *Birmingham and Derby* Junction. She sees no one suspicious, but always it's as if someone is at her side. Many times she turns, but no one is there. The feeling persists. She's not alone. Nervous, fearful, frustrated. Another line, another ticket, another train, another wait.

Jenner is waiting. He wonders whether that is the real lot of the policeman, happy or otherwise. Waiting. Waiting for things to happen though more often waiting for things that don't happen. Usually there's no choice just as there's no choice now. He must wait and hope. Hope his feelings are right and he's in the right place at the right time. Hope Ettie has been successful and will also get to the same place in the same time. A lot to wait for. A lot to hope for.

The turbulence in his mind only ceases when he starts remembering. Remembering what Ettie said, remembering what she'd done, remembering what he'd done. He remembers how they'd met. The warring forces of past and present threatened to engulf them. How had they come through? The obstacles seemed insuperable. Yet they'd overcome them. Despair and desperation can be the springboard to remedy and release. The super-physical barriers they faced seemed impenetrable, their enemies superhuman, but common sense challenges prevailed.

He remembers the most powerful conduit for time linking is water. Whatever he must do, it must be close to water. He remembers that recurring element in the enquiries. It could still unlock the mystery and could be important now. Finally, he remembers the last place Ettie and Sam had been. Now all that remains is to pull all these things together. He will go there, but not alone. There must be back up. He rings Jennifer and tells her his plans.

"...and before you come I want you to interview David Underwood and Denise Deverall again. Also, get a message to Ella Weston..."

Ettie says all time is co-existent. The barriers between past and present are illusions. Breaking through those barriers is how all time links are forged. It gives him courage. He must remember it when he faces those challenges again. And things, he must have things. He can't get that old rhyme out of his head. Something old, something new, something borrowed, something blue...

Ettie watches each new arrival with mounting tension. Each time she expects to see Matt. She moves further and further away from the entrance, distancing herself from where he might appear, but also cutting herself off from potential help. She reaches the end of the platform and stares into the receding steel lines, wishing them to spring back, grab her and fling her down the track. It starts to rain. She buttons up her coat, pulls down her hat and walks back. It's like it was in the tunnel, when Sam came through. An overwhelming sensation of lack of control, of being watched, of being unable to escape wherever far she runs and the unshakeable pressure of constant close presences. Matt and his chasing. He stirs the havoc of disjointed time, but there are more than him. The others, near but untouchable, far, but with long reaches.

The train arrives at last. It connects with another from London. Most of the carriages are crowded though she manages to find a seat. The numbers ensure anonymity. Plenty of animated conversations making it easy for her not be drawn in, but she's not relaxed. The rain gets heavier, beating loudly against the window. Even though she avoids attention her apprehensions increase. Any moment anyone could suddenly ask some obscure question, remark on the topical politics of the day, some fashion trend or any of innumerable minor issues unknown in her own time, but known to all in this one. She looks around. All these people. What will she say? Will she give herself away? All from another time, another world, not her time, not her world. Exchanging neutral, polite looks with the faces, she wants to scream, but amidst the noise she's confined in her silent anguish! Her fearfulness grows as that feeling of another, others, returns and she feels detached in place as well as time, not part of where she is.

The train picks up speed on the long straight run towards Derby, the hammering of the locomotive, the clouds of smoke and the clattering and rolling of the carriage only intensifying her wretchedness. Fearful her journey will soon end, irrationally she doesn't want to leave the train at Derby. But she must. Another line, another ticket, but not another wait. The *Midland Counties* train for Nottingham is there. The last, short stage of the journey, at the end of which...somehow a return to the present or...remaining here! The trembling and bubbling of the locomotive mirrors her feelings. She boards with trepidation and hovers at the door, looking back along the platform. A movement near the ticket office, a man is running along to catch the train, something familiar, sinister about him...she gets in quickly and shuts the door.

"Have you brought them?" Jenner says.

Jennifer hands him the paper and the book.

"Have you the hat?" she says.

He nods to the back seat of the car. She picks it up and hands it to him.

"Come on," he says, "there's a train due."

They get out and walk towards the station. He has the paper and the book in one hand and the hat in the other.

"How close do you want me to be?" she says.

He stares at her, looking for approval or disdain, but her eyes seem neutral or perhaps just accepting, for even bewilderment is no longer unfamiliar to her. He looks at the paper and the book. Something old, something new, something borrowed, something blue. He has the things. The Chartist handbill, found near Sarwell's body, old from the past, pulled forward in time and found in the present is both old and new. The Chartist minute book with its blue cover, 'borrowed' from Denise.

"Fairly near," he says, "but not too close...it might be dangerous."

She follows cautiously as they enter the station. He checks the arrivals. This has to be the place. Sarwell's railway obsession has recurred throughout the investigations. It's close to water with the Nottingham canal just across the road. It's also a stone's throw from the Broad Marsh centre, where Ettie 'escaped' from the city with Sam. It has to be here, but how long will it take? He walks down the stairs. Jennifer follows at a discreet distance as if to avoid heavenly retribution in the form of unholy lightning suddenly striking Jenner down. Will she think he's finally cracked up? Yet she was with Ettie, she accepted Sam and the need to get him back to his own time. If he's cracked up, so has Jennifer. What a prospect for Emmins, two barmy officers on his patch! He stops on the platform. She almost reaches him and is within earshot.

"I am sure," he says, partly to reassure her, partly to convince himself and then uncertainly, "though it might be a long wait."

Initially, he's right. A train arrives from Norwich, en route for Liverpool. The London train departs. Jennifer sits at the other end of the platform. She says nothing, but he senses her frustration. Is this an absurd vigil? He sits down and stares at the blank wall beyond the tracks. He can only be sure of what he feels and this *feels* right. He ought to concentrate on that rather than how it fits with conventional techniques. After all if he...a fleeting, jabbing vision on the far wall, an old hoarding in outdated lettering, a smell and a sound and an image. He's in that past, he sees and hears and smells the people, the smoke, the approaching train on the rails...it goes...but then there's more...a feeling of distress, someone calling voicelessly across...time? He looks around and then towards Jennifer. She's not stirred. Did she feel it, hear it, see it, smell it? She returns his look, but with no answering recognition. She's not heard nor seen nor smelt. Only he has.

Perhaps he didn't. He only *thought* he did and where did thoughts ever get him? But it stays. Though he no longer hears nor sees nor smells, it stays. Ettie is near and she's in peril. He knows it. He must help her, but how? Is she trapped, beyond his reach in another time? Is Sam with her? Is that why she can't return? No, she's alone. Alone, frightened, pursued, imprisoned and heading here, where if she's not released, she'll remain *there* forever.

He can see a train approaching from up the line. The board indicates it's from Derby. As he watches he senses those pressures moving on him, but only sees and hears what he's sure others see and hear. Jennifer also stares into the distance, but no baffled disbelief crosses her face. She cannot smell what he smells. Smoke, steam, yet the train is square and squat and very modern. He grips the handbill and the book tightly. It cannot be. It cannot be happening to him. All his experience, his training, his duty, his *logic*, all tells him this cannot be. But it is, for now he sees the smoke and steam, clouding the square, squat...not quite modern train. He glances across to Jennifer and the others standing on the platform. No one is in the least perturbed. They cannot see, they cannot smell and now...they cannot hear what he hears, that bellowing, slow shrieking hiss that is no modern train. Now he smells, he sees and he hears. Yet these things are not for him, they are meant for others to interpret, to analyse, to manage, to grasp and control. But there are no others. No one else smells nor sees nor hears. He looks round again. People move forward to meet the train. Why do they do that? Why don't they smell and see and hear this apparition from the

342

past! It isn't real. It isn't here. But it is, why else would they go towards the doors? It's him. What he smells and sees and hears, *that* isn't real.

The train stops. People are alighting. So oddly dressed, yet their modern counterparts don't seem to mind. Can't they *see*? No, they can't. Only he sees, only he is in this time chequered limbo, half in the past, half in the present. Instinctively he rams the old hat hard down on his head and closes his eyes. When he opens them it will have gone and he'll no longer see what shouldn't be there. But eyes tight shut, still he smells and still he hears and knows his eyes cannot contradict his nose and his ears.

A gust of wind carries the locomotive smoke back along the train, momentarily engulfing the platform in a grey fog. A few hurrying figures remain, emerging from the puffy vapour as they make for the stairs. The wind switches again and the smoke disperses. The platform is almost deserted except for someone, standing about half way down, looking perplexed and frightened. This is no ghostly concoction of a beaten up mind, no phantom fabricated by a washed out bit part player, fantasising as he descends into investigative idiocy. He knows the face and it's not used to steam trains and long black dresses.

He calls out. She turns as if she hears, but seems unable to respond. Then he sees another figure, a man, further along the train, get out and move towards her. Another familiar face, though at first he doesn't recognise him. Jenner calls to Ettie. This time she opens her mouth as if she speaks, but he doesn't hear. He calls again. The man, hugging the side of the train, gets closer. She glances around and then turns back to Jenner. If she speaks, still he doesn't hear. He walks towards her. She doesn't move. He sees the fear in her eyes. Then the whiffs of smoke no longer waft along the train and the smell of steam is gone. It's going. The cross merged linking of past with present is closing. Soon the present will cut the past and Ettie will be lost. He takes his hat and gripping it tightly shouts again.

"I know about Foxley!"

She looks as if she understands the words and shouts back.

"So do I!"

He hears, but the windows of the train seem to widen and change colour. She's going! He walks faster. The man also comes closer. Jenner now recognises him. It's Matt. Ettie puts out her hand, but also seems to recede even though she doesn't move. She's being pulled, drawn back into the past! Matt is very close now. Glancing back, Jenner sees no locomotive at the front of the train and the carriages are all modern. He tries to step forward, but his legs are rooted as if he's reached the edge of the present. Only the past is before him though it seems to fade and he can't cross over. Matt is just behind Ettie. In desperation, Jenner takes the hat and flings it forward, aiming to stop him.

The old train is gone. Jenner hears the voices of the other passengers as they trek up the stairs. He glances round and sees Jennifer striding towards him. He looks back. The train doors are closing. Everyone is on board and it moves away with that familiar rumble of diesel engines and blast of acrid exhaust. No steam, no smoke. He turns back anxiously. Ettie stands alone on the platform. Matt is not there. He lifts his leg and finds he *can* move. The past is gone.

Jennifer gets to her first. Exhausted, Ettie collapses into her. Jenner joins them, stepping along with measured steps as if like a child he's just learnt to walk. He stands and leans slightly from side to side, making sure he can really ease the weight between his legs. It seems so unusual. Jennifer leads Ettie to one of the seats. Jenner turns to the stairs and sees a familiar shape pushing and shoving his way towards the exit as if escaping from some unseen threat on the platform. Jenner considers giving chase, but the man has already turned the corner at the top and disappeared. He looks round for his hat.

"You won't find it," Ettie calls.

He goes over and stands just in front of them.

"It's on a railway platform in 1842," she says, "along with Matt."

"Not Matthew Usworth," he says, "I've just seen him on the stairs."

Ettie grimaces.

344

"Then we'll have to build that into our plans, first I need to..."

"First you need some rest," Jennifer says.

"But he doesn't know what he's doing. On the loose he'll release powers to..."

"We know," Jenner says, sitting beside her, "We've already set the plan in motion."

"So Sam is no longer with you," Jennifer says, "is he in his own time?"

"He's not in this time," Ettie says

"We conclude it all with Foxley then?" Jenner says.

Ettie nods.

"David Underwood and Denise Deverall have already been seen. Fear and loyalty, each to their own will be our accomplices."

- 13 -

In the long wait Jenner begins to doubt the wisdom of the operation. Inactivity feeds his growing unease until he feels *any* movement will be better than this debilitating empty silence. The quietness of the street grates against his need for action. Yet not any action, for as he waits his mind fills with the many unwanted permutations that might flow from the well laid bait. Even now he cannot be sure. His assumptions could be false. They could chase up blind alleys while the real culprit escapes along a route they've not envisaged. Yet no. He's provided for them all. But they're stretched. Just four officers, the chief superintendent refused his request for additional resources until 'something like a positive outcome' seemed likely. Sandra Tye waits in another car at the opposite end of the street, Duggan is watching Usworth and Jennifer is with Ettie. Almost all possibilities covered, but they're so thinly spread and he can't be sure which direction... should he have sent Sandra elsewhere? No, he may need her here and besides it would only have drawn attention to...

A car pulls into the street. It passes Sandra and comes towards Jenner. He leans down, a newspaper shielding his face. The car stops short, as expected, but who will emerge? A young man in casual clothes walks to Ella Weston's door, rings the bell and is admitted. Sandra phones Jenner.

"Do we go in, sir?"

"No, not yet. It's too soon, we have to wait, see what he does."

"But sir, she could be in..."

"*Wait*, constable!"

She could be right. Even with a built in safeguard for Ella, it could still go wrong. The minutes pass. What's she saying? What's *he* saying? Should they move in? But if they do, what of the other? Sandra calls again. He reiterates his instructions.

"Just be ready, constable, just be ready!"

More minutes, fifteen, twenty, maybe, they should...? Another car enters the street. It glides down slowly, almost stopping at the house, then moves on, finally stopping some way behind Jenner. He observes the driver through his mirror. A third car stops at the end of the street, just in front of Sandra. The house door opens. Ella Weston, looking tired and distressed emerges, cradled by David Underwood, leading her towards the car. She looks up and down apprehensively. David also surveys the street before quickly getting her into the car and driving away. Neither notice those watching.

"Now," Jenner thinks, "let's do this in the right order."

At a discreet distance, the car pulls away and follows David and Ella. Then, at a further discreet distance, the third car follows. Sandra drives up and Jenner leaves his own car.

"Good," he says as he gets in, "Don't get too close to Duggan, let him do the work, but don't stay too far back, in case we all need to act quickly."

"As we thought," Sandra says, "forewarned by Denise, Matt Usworth came to see Ella."

"Quite, but he didn't expect to see David Underwood's car here. Notice how he hesitated. It'll be interesting to see what happens when they arrive."

So the procession proceeds. David heads out through the western suburbs, followed by Matt, in turn followed by John Duggan, who's been observing him since before dawn. Further back still, Sandra brings up the rear with her fidgety passenger.

"Give us plenty of warning if Usworth takes another road," Jenner reminds John, "Remember, if that happens you stay with him. We'll tail Underwood."

Jenner's precision and discipline would credit a sergeant major. Drilled like Sandra, John understands well his boss's nervousness and answers him with deadpan, sympathetic acknowledgement. Sandra is impassive, but mildly amused, her eyes firmly on the road, avoiding Jenner's mixed glance of enquiry, part reproving, part quizzical. Does she too need reminding? He turns his attention back to the road. They get caught in the congestion leading to the motorway and can only see John's car. Not knowing David or Matt's whereabouts makes him uneasy and he asks John for an update.

"Still together, heading out to the motorway."

The traffic disperses. They have a clear view ahead and can see David, followed by Matt approaching the roundabout.

"Not here," Jenner mutters, "don't bloody lose them here."

"Still heading west," John reports.

"Both of them?"

"Both of them."

Jenner breathes easier. It seems the plan is working.

"Underwood's taken the Creston road," John says.

What? It can't be!

"What about Usworth?" Jenner barks back.

"Also taken the Creston road, I'm in pursuit."

Not yet. They shouldn't be going that way yet. This is not according to the plan!

"Hang back, it's a minor road, don't let them see you."

Sandra also turns into the Creston road. Where are they going? Why aren't they going towards Ettie and Jennifer? The road leads to the reservoir and Jenner realises where they might be heading.

David drives to the top of the drive and parks close to the front door, jumping out quickly to open the passenger door for Ella. She climbs out slowly, dazed, gripping the side of the car as if needing its leverage to raises her legs. David helps her. Half out, she glances around apprehensively, looking lingeringly towards the main gate as if she identifies something protective or perhaps threatening. Her eyes peer at what she suspects is some slight movement at the bottom of the drive and for a moment hesitates, ready to climb back into the car. David, following the direction of her stare, but seeing nothing, gently pulls her away from the car. As he moves towards the front of the house a car enters the drive, the one that's followed them from the city. It slows, but continues towards them. Ella shudders, recognising the driver. David hugs her reassuringly and then puts himself between her and the intruder. The car stops. Matt Usworth gets out and approaches.

"What are you doing here?" David says aggressively.

Cowering, Ella turns to his side and looks away, as if in doing so Matt may not see her.

"What are you doing with Ella, why have you brought her here?" Matt replies.

The two reproving questions, incisive spears, pierce their targets without expecting or receiving any immediate answer. Menacingly immobile, the two men scrutinise the other with lidded hostility, each ready to erupt, but wondering if the other might make the first strike. Then Matt moves two paces forward. Pushing Ella towards the door, David shuffles to meet him.

"She's here under my protection."

"Captivity more like. What are you protecting her from, the truth?"

"From you."

Matt laughs.

"So you interfere with her appointment with Ettie Rodway, taking it from her as soon as the truth is revealed?"

"I don't know what you're talking about. Ella told me of her meeting with Ettie Rodway, but she was afraid *you'd* try to stop her. She needed somewhere secure to meet. Neither her house nor the hotel would be safe from you."

"So you decided to bring her here?"

"I did."

"What about Miss Rodway?"

"We'll contact her in due course, just as soon as..."

"We're rid of you!"

Sylvia Darrington – Cressley bestrides the front door.

"Come in dear, quickly," she says to Ella, who dutifully runs across the threshold, around Sylvia and into the house. Matt eyes her carefully before responding.

"You! I might have known it!"

"Indeed," Sylvia says, "David has told me of Ella's fears. We suspected she'd be in danger when you found out."

David joins Sylvia. Together they block the doorway, but Matt advances.

"And here she'll be safe with you?" he sneers.

"Until she's met Miss Rodway and you cannot get your hands on..."

"You'll not stop me!"

David hunches up, ready to leap at Matt. Sylvia restrains him.

"How did you find out, anyway?" she says.

"I might ask you the same."

"Ella confided in David. She didn't tell you, so how did you know? Someone who confided in you, perhaps?"

Matt's silence confirms her suspicions.

"Yes, someone you've been seeing a lot of lately. Someone who has her own reasons for getting hold of Doctor Foxley's memoirs, Denise Deverall!"

"It doesn't matter how I know."

He moves towards them, but Sylvia pulls David round her and into the house. Matt rushes at the door, but Sylvia is too quick for him, banging it shut in his face, turning the lock and ramming hard the stout bolts on the other side. Matt curses, turns back and kicks the gravel impotently. Undeterred, he walks along to the east wing of the house, avoiding the grounds staff as he searches for another way in, as yet unaware of the surprise awaiting him.

Jenner's frustration is at boiling point. Two hikers have stepped into the road on the opposite side at the corner by the reservoir. Matt's car had just passed, but a lorry on the other side had to swerve to avoid the pedestrians and slithered over in front of Duggan. Sandra had to pull up very sharply to avoid crashing into him. Having successfully jack knifed, the lorry had great difficulty righting itself. Jenner leapt from the car and chased the two shocked and bewildered hikers, cursing and berating them while Duggan tried to get the road clear. Afraid Jenner was about to toss them into the reservoir, Sandra managed to free the two unfortunate walkers from his clutches and steered her fuming and enraged boss back to the car. Fortunately a patrol car had arrived and was able to help Duggan, but the delay could be disastrous.

They resume their journey. There's no sign of either David or Matt, but as they climb the hill towards that familiar bend, all Jenner's instincts tell where they must be going. Now he has a new threat. David Underwood. He tells John to make for Elvington House. They stop just inside the gate. With the top of the drive obscured by trees, they don't see the parked cars or witness the altercation between David and Matt. Though he knows they must act quickly to protect Ella and expose the culprit, Jenner hesitates. The two constables wait impatiently, but they can't know the intensity of his agony. If he's wrong, then the little time left after the infuriating delay will be the least thing they lose. He sees a familiar figure standing near the wall and calls to him.

"Have you seen two cars just arrive?"

Jon Cardington ambles across with the lugubrious reluctance of one whose priorities will never equate with those of a policeman. His stance gives him the air of a picket, an outposted sentinel, deployed to waylay or deceive any unwelcome visitors, especially perhaps, policemen.

"Come on, man!" Jenner snaps as Jon, slowly, achingly gets nearer, "we need to know. Have you seen Matthew Usworth?"

Jon remains silent until he almost reaches Jenner, only then, guardedly responding.

"Ar, I've seen 'im."

"They've gone up to the house?"

Another painfully extended pause.

"Yes and ..."

His momentary doubt whisked away, Jenner runs back and the cars roar up the drive. Jon shakes his head and staring fixedly, follows them from behind a row of bushes.

In the house Sylvia has directed the pair to her private refuge, the library, seating them together across from the desk. Ella is nervous and asks about Matt.

"He'll not get in," Sylvia says.

Ella seems reassured and stares admiringly at Sylvia's graceful green dress, remarking on its elegance.

"The style," she begins, "it reminds me..."

"...of when you were last here, at the party?"

Ella nods.

"A dress specially made for my 1840s party," Sylvia says, arranging her lace cuffs carefully, "I wore another that night, but as you say, it's so stylish, I thought I'd put this one on today."

Ella's wandering eyes fasten on Sylvia, quizzically examining every detail of her clothes as if searching or trying to understand a perplexing aspect of the 1840s dress.

"Now, my dear," Sylvia says, adopting her most kindly and aunt like tone, " we really must get to the bottom of this terrible burden you carry, and protect you from Usworth."

Her smile, expansive and gleaming, is held like the firm grip of an adult to the hand of a vulnerable child. She has the same intensity in her eyes, but less warmth. David, beaming in the glow of his employer's benevolence, squeezes Ella's hand reassuringly.

"You know of Martin Sarwell?" Ella says.

Sylvia clasps her hands together in appalled solidarity.

"Terrible business."

"Before he...before he was killed, he felt he could trust me, confide in me."

"He told you something?"

"He gave me something."

"And you feel this, whatever he gave you, may have been connected to his death and that's why you're frightened?"

Ella nods.

"A burden shared, my dear is a burden lifted. You must tell us about it."

"Martin had been very interested, well he was obsessed, with a local doctor who mysteriously disappeared around 1842. He was called Doctor Foxley."

"Disappeared?"

"That's what Martin said. He couldn't find anything about him after that year."

"Even so, he may not have disappeared as you put it, perhaps there were simply no records. Finding out about people so long ago must be very difficult."

Ella, who until now has been staring at the table, suddenly glances warily at Sylvia, to receive another wide, glinting, seemingly innocuous smile.

"Oh it is, but Martin was very thorough."

The smile narrows slightly.

"And this thing he gave you, what is it?"

"A letter."

"A letter from this Doctor Foxley? To whom?"

"I don't know, it's a draft with no name at the top. It was never sent and is unfinished, just a single page and not much on that."

Briefly, the smile widens slightly again, only to contract quickly.

"What does this letter say?"

Ella wrings her hands.

"It mentions another document."

"Doctor Foxley's memoirs?"

"Yes, that's what the letter calls them. Martin said they were very important. They contained secrets and in the letter Foxley wants whoever it is to know where he'd left them."

"These memoirs are not with the letter?"

"No."

"But he says where they can be found?"

"Not really. He mentions where he's put them, but the problem is it doesn't make much sense. It's a mystery. The language is so old fashioned and it looks like it's written in some sort of code. That's why I mentioned it to Ettie Rodway. I thought someone who was used to examining things from the past might be able to help. She said she'd come across messages of this kind before and they sometimes needed to be unlocked by an interpreter of the past. So I arranged to consult her today. I ought really to…"

"Well I'm sure Miss Rodway is very experienced in these matters, but there's another interested party who must be kept away from this letter at all costs. We must act quickly. He already knows about it and is determined to get it from you."

Ella shudders.

"He'll be outside, waiting for me!"

"You're quite safe in here, but you'll be in real danger if you leave to keep your appointment with Miss Rodway."

"Ettie can come here."

"Of course, later. You have the letter with you?"

"I would rather wait until she arrives."

Sylvia sighs deeply.

"He remains outside. You're safe here, but for how long? Miss Rodway is not the only person with links to the past. There are others with such skills."

Ella turns anxiously towards the window. David gently pulls her arm and motions her to Sylvia, but she ignores him.

"Naturally you are concerned," Sylvia continues, "I've long suspected Matthew Usworth of indulging in, what we might call interference with the past. He's a clever operator, but his interests are extremely dangerous..."

Ella looks around nervously. There's a noise from the corridor. David turns towards the door, but Sylvia remains detached.

"It's nothing," she says, "just some of the staff about their duties."

Further noise, a scuffling and then silence.

"We can forestall him, but must act quickly," Sylvia booms and as she regains their attention, leans forward, her tone becoming stridently demanding, "Let me see the letter. We can do nothing unless we see it. I have also studied the past. Ettie Rodway has no monopoly on these things. We can't wait for her to come. In any case, Usworth could attack her, stopping her getting to you. Then where would we be?"

"Do as Sylvia says," David interposes, "Let her see the letter."

Ella draws back from him and looks nervously at the door.

"Are you expecting someone?" Sylvia asks.

Ella gets up.

"Stop her, David, don't let her get out, it's not safe!"

David gets up. Ella turns and moves closer to the door.

"I have to get out," she says.

"I can help you, believe me," Sylvia persists.

David lurches across at Ella, but she edges away from him and steps away. Sylvia gets up. David bounds towards Ella. As she reaches the door it's thrust open from the other side, the lock broken forcibly and Ella falls into the arms of John Duggan. Jenner and Sandra follow him.

"How precisely do you intend to help her?" Jenner says.

Sylvia moves back to the window, away from them all. Ella has collapsed.

"Get her on the couch," Jenner says, "and get him!"

John lowers Ella onto the couch in the corner by the door and then moves across to David, who stands, goggle eyed, offering no resistance.

"You do choose your moments, chief inspector," Sylvia says, recovering her composure, but still standing by the window.

"You didn't answer my question?"

"I don't know what you're talking about."

"You understand very well. How will you help Miss Weston with Foxley's letter?"

"Foxley? Letter?"

David glances across at Sylvia, who avoids his gaze. Sandra is tending to Ella, who now comes round. David moves to go to her, but John restrains him. Ella mumbles something incoherent before looking first at John and David, then at Sylvia and finally at Jenner.

"You took your time!" she says.

"You knew they were coming?" David says.

"Indeed she did," Jenner says, "unfortunately your movements were not exactly as we envisaged and we were a little delayed. However, we've heard enough. So, Mrs. Darrington – Cressley, tell me about your interest in Doctor Foxley's letter."

"I have no interest in Doctor Foxley's letter."

"More interested perhaps in his *memoir?*"

"I know nothing of a memoir."

"Yes you do," Ella shouts, sitting up and pointing, "You mentioned it when I mentioned the letter."

"Nonsense!"

"That's right, Sylvia," David says, " you mentioned it when..."

"Shut up, David! You don't know what you're talking about, stick to your administrative duties."

"Sylvia, I..."

"What do you think you'll find in this memoir?" Jenner says, "something connected to how you were going to *help* Miss Weston? Something, perhaps to do with your friend?"

"Friend? What friend, what are you talking about? Instead of berating me with these ridiculous accusations, you should be apprehending Matthew Usworth!"

"On what charge?"

Sylvia hesitates.

"Interference with the past, perhaps, as you so eloquently put it?"

David looks across again at Sylvia.

"What did you mean when you said that?" he says.

"Merely a figure of speech. I wanted to help Miss Weston and protect her from Usworth!"

"Much more than a figure of speech," Jenner says.

David's impatience erupts and he tries to push himself away from John, who holds him all the tighter.

"Stop messing around," he shouts, "Either explain or leave us alone. What's this all about?"

Jenner turns to David, motioning John to relax his grip.

"What this is all about, Mr. Underwood, are the murders of Bernard Weston and Martin Sarwell, carried out by Mrs. Darrington – Cressley, assisted by her *accomplice!*"

David recoils at this last word, but Sylvia is adamant.

"I was hundreds of miles away at the time of Bernard Weston's disappearance," she shrieks, "I couldn't possibly have had anything to do with his death!"

"But you weren't away, were you?"

"I was seen in..."

"No, someone *like* you was seen."

"How could you possibly know..."

David stares horrifically into Sylvia's sudden silence. Jenner continues.

"Quite. It took a little time, but really the evidence was there from the start. It all began with a penny. An innocent, ordinary penny, but a very old one. An 1840 penny, in almost pristine condition dropped in the interview room, that no one claimed. Suspicious in itself wouldn't you think, an old coin in such good condition? Yet no one wanted to own something fairly valuable? Why did someone not want to admit it was theirs? Something to do with how they acquired it perhaps? We couldn't link it to anyone, but I knew it had to be one of six people. It set me thinking. Its condition was intriguing, almost as if someone had picked it up only a few days before in almost mint condition, yet those few days before were a hundred and sixty years ago. It didn't make sense and I didn't want to contemplate the unbelievable implication.

'I'd picked up the penny's potential significance, but at first missed the importance of the next pointer completely. A chance remark, so often they are like undiscovered diamonds, buried in the ground for hundreds of years, real gems waiting to be dug out and polished. During an interview with Denise Deverall she spoke disparagingly of this house and of you Sylvia. I put it down to her jealousy particularly when she said there was something about you that seemed reminiscent. She believed it was seeing the house again and not you that was reminiscent, but then she mentioned the room with the paintings, which she'd seen as a child when she visited the house. You know the room, you showed me the pictures of your ancestors? Even then I didn't connect, though inadvertently Denise had done. All those years before she'd seen the painting of your great, great grandmother, Charlotte that you so admired, and subconsciously she saw the amazing similarity between the two of you. I didn't immediately grasp it when I saw the painting. Only later when I was thinking through so many inconclusive strands, I realised how similar you were, you could be twins, exact doubles of each other. But so what? Then the picture was removed. That seemed odd. Had you picked up on my suspicions and didn't want me further reminded?

'By then I was wondering about the connection with your ancestor. Snatches of conversation we'd had, unimportant at the time, but now bugging me. There were strange inconsistencies between our meetings. I remembered when I visited this house on the second occasion I'd had the uncanny feeling of being somehow caught in the past. Again, so what, but what was significant was not so much *what* was said at that meeting, but *how* it was said. You offered me *refreshment* and referred to *luncheon,* expressions consistent with an earlier time. You talked about work in the house providing much needed employment for local *hands,* a very nineteenth century expression for workers."

David explodes.

"This is preposterous! I don't believe I'm hearing this from a policeman. You're not seriously basing a charge against Sylvia on such incredibly... let me be polite....*subjective* evidence!"

Jenner remains calm and turns to David firmly.

"Quite so, Mr. Underwood. You might do well to consider your own position if you are so sure she is not involved, for there is more to hear."

David puffs aggressively, but subsides as he glances across and receives a cold rebuking stare from Ella. Sylvia is silent, clutching the arm of the chair by the window. Turning to her, Jenner continues.

"On my first visit you expounded at some length on your 'Moral Power' organisation. It was most...illuminating, but when I returned I received a dead, bland statement, delivered with the feeling and commitment of a pet parrot. Later on I found the exact words in one of your leaflets. The day before you talked about the work on the house right up to 1855, particularly on the Amber Room, but now you seemed not to know about it. Yet you talked about earlier work in greater detail as if it was *contemporary,* but nothing about work done *after* 1842. That's when I first started to realise how crucial 1842 was, the year of the Chartist Plug riots, the year of so many things that were to crop up later. You were interested in my work as a policeman at that second meeting. You referred to me as a police *officer.* Perhaps not all that significant in itself, but it was the tone, as if the expression was quite novel. Then you said the police were 'a great power for good.' Nothing I could challenge there, but it was an unusual, even *quaint* phrase. Then you referred to the police force beginning *in the capital*. Only later did it come back to me, when I followed up the records into the death of Jonathon, your other ancestor. At the time provincial police forces were very new and largely modelled on the earlier force in London. All this led me to the inevitable conclusion that at my second meeting in this house I was not talking to you at all, but to your great, great grandmother, Charlotte!"

He pauses and in the silence that follows that auspicious name seems to reverberate across the room, bouncing from wall to wall, ceiling to floor in condemnatory echoes. Even David, struggling to comprehend the immensity of Jenner's conclusions, is silent, but then Sylvia starts to laugh until she shakes with apparent mirth.

"Absolutely ludicrous!" she cries, "Even if all this is true, why should I possibly want to kill Bernard Weston?"

"Which brings us neatly to your relationship with him," Jenner says, "I was never convinced it was a purely professional one, a common interest in the reopening of the Cross Cut. Let's say there was enough of a smell around to indicate something more personal, but as with all close relationships they can get very nasty when things start to go wrong. Besides, such a liaison didn't fit well with your Moral Power activities, did it? But then, how much of your real life does?"

"You can't prove any of this, " she sneers.

Jenner ignores her.

"Bernard Weston and Matthew Usworth disagreed over the reopening of the canal. Bernard sided with you and was part of the campaign that led to its reopening. I couldn't understand why he disagreed so strongly with his friend until I stopped thinking about the present and concentrated on the past. Your ancestor Charlotte had pressed for the early closure of the canal because of its association with her brother's death, but what if the canal had some other connection with the past? What if the canal and particularly the tunnel could be the link between you and Charlotte? What if you and Bernard had also discovered something about Charlotte of great significance, which he took very lightly and even maybe threatened to expose? Then you'd want Bernard out of the way and you might need Charlotte's help. You'd then fight very hard to get the canal reopened."

Sylvia laughs again.

"Instead of wasting your time in here, you should be outside arresting Matthew Usworth. I've long suspected him of being 'caught in the past' as you put it. Everything you've said points to him and is much more important than all these ridiculous suppositions about Charlotte."

Jenner is undeterred.

"You're right, a great deal did point to Usworth and there's no doubt he's been undertaking some unconventional research activities in connection with his Chartist interests. Hence the Chartist newspaper presented at one of his meetings. He didn't get that grubbing around dusty archives."

David is incredulous.

"He's actually gone back to the 1840s to find his material?"

"Quite so, Mr. Underwood, but he's not been alone in such ventures. While he's been foolishly meddling with forces way beyond his understanding and spicing up his reputation by adopting methods perhaps akin to an athlete boosting his performance with drugs, I don't believe he's done anything malignant. He..."

"You're the fool, not him!" Sylvia shrieks.

"Maybe we're all fools, dabbling by design or by default in such things," Jenner says, "but the essential point is what was the *motive* for getting rid of Bernard Weston! That baffled me. Then we found the body of Martin Sarwell. I was sure the two murders were connected and the explanation had to be found with Sarwell himself. He had this obsessive interest in Dr. Foxley, but that didn't get us any further. We'd reached an impasse, until another gem, though of an opaque and rugged kind appeared in the shape of a witness to one of the murders."

David is stupefied. Sylvia, apparently impassive, her eyes project a nervous apprehension. Jenner turns to David.

"He didn't know the identity of the victim, but it had to

be Bernard Weston. While he convinced me his evidence was authentic it presented two difficulties, one because it was specific and the other because it was vague. Even from a distance he was sure the murderer was a man. It had to be because he wore trousers, which in 1842 meant it could not possibly have been a woman."

"1842?" David says.

"Quite so."

Jenner glances back at Sylvia. Her face, inscrutably drawn, is unmoved and she shows no surprise at Jenner's incredible suggestion.

"But if it was Bernard Weston, how could it...?" David says.

"Once I'd accepted the *possibility* of some kind of diabolical time transference it followed that somehow Bernard Weston might have been transported back into the past and killed. Within this wild speculation, it was conceivable Charlotte had murdered him. But how could it be? My witness said it was a man. Then came another of those little prizes that are so often mislaid. A remark by one of the staff, complimenting Mrs. Darrington – Cressly on her trouser suit first laid in my mind the unbelievable seed that would eventually germinate. Today, women frequently wear trousers so that observation in itself would not necessarily rule out a woman. It would rule out Charlotte, but what if Sylvia had taken Bernard into the past and disposed of him? The evidence of my witness would then be consistent. However, we still had the problem of the location. He'd been frustratingly vague as to his whereabouts at the time. We searched everywhere to no avail. It seemed my wild idea was just that, wild and impossible. Yet the seed had taken root.'

'With no obvious link I went back to Martin Sarwell. If the two murders were connected the answer had to be with him. There had to be something. I found it in the interview I'd had with his friend, Alan Banning. They were both railway history buffs, but they'd disagreed about a particular line. Some obscure point about why it was closed. Like the Cross Cut canal a generation earlier, it was made redundant by the building of another railway. I took no notice until we discovered where that old line had originally run, right through the Best Hill area and straight across the site where the skeleton had been found. Built across the valley, the railway required the construction of an embankment. Hundreds of tons of material had been deposited to provide a level track for the line. After the railway was closed the embankment had remained, a vegetated relic, totally out of character with the surrounding area. Then came redevelopment in the 1960s. All those hundreds of tons were taken out again and the contours of the land cleared back to what they'd been before the railway. That's why we couldn't connect it together. Until we realised the body had been placed in ground deep below the original embankment. As constable Duggan remarked at the time someone had gone to considerable trouble to put it there. Or had they? If the murder had taken place in 1842, it was before the railway had been built, before the embankment, before it would be necessary to excavate down. What if someone knew all that? If they killed Bernard Weston in 1842 they would know a railway embankment would shortly cover up the evidence. That could only be done by someone from the present, not someone from the past. Then came the clincher. The archaeologists had carried out their tests. The skeleton was relatively new. Not only was it not medieval, it wasn't even nineteenth century. Yet it was found beneath a forty year old building and previously had been at least twelve meters below ground level since the 1850s. Now, the archaeological evidence strengthened my fanciful prospect. A three year old murder committed a hundred and sixty years ago!"

"Assuming, of course, it really was the body of Bernard Weston," David says doubtfully.

"There's no doubt," Jenner says, glaring at him, "DNA comparison with that of his sister makes it irrefutable."

David looks across accusingly at Ella, but she avoids him as she stares hard and probingly at Sylvia, who in turn points at Jenner.

"You can't prove any of this," she says, "The very idea's absurd, as if I and...my great, great grandmother have somehow been floating around together."

"Quite so, that's exactly what I am saying. While you

removed Bernard Weston to the past and disposed of him there, Charlotte created your alibi, posing as you and conspicuously appearing in Scotland."

Sylvia laughs.

"That's just speculation," David says, taking his cue from her.

"Is it?" Jenner says, turning to him, "Not if we consider your own evidence."

David looks uncomfortable.

"On the night of the party, both you and Jon Cardington were in this house. You both gave statements of your whereabouts around the time Miss Weston saw a mysterious stranger approach her."

"You were with me, I had nothing to do with that!" David protests.

Jenner waves his hand and continues.

"At the time I was too concerned to place Matthew Usworth on the scene. I believed he was posing as *his* ancestor, Sam Usworth..."

Sylvia breathes in quickly and forcefully, then coughs loudly to try and disguise her sudden unsettlement.

"...it was some time before I appreciated they were two separate people. In the process I'd missed an important lead. When I compared your statement with that of Jon Cardington they appeared contradictory. I double checked where the two of you said you were when Miss Weston screamed out. Then I checked the distance between those two places. You wanted to speak to Mrs. Darrington – Cressley and therefore went after her *in the direction of the stairs*. At precisely the same time Jon Cardington had a conversation with her just outside the kitchen and she left him and *went towards the hall*. This meant that at the crucial time she was in two places and heading in utterly opposite directions!"

"Jon Cardington could have been mistaken," David says aggressively.

"Quite and so could you, but I don't think so. In your different ways you're both very precise people. I believe both your accounts are correct and exact. Sylvia Darrington – Cressley could not be in two places at the same time. It meant Charlotte, who is clearly her exact double and dressed identically, was also in the house."

Ella sits up. Gazing wide eyed at Sylvia she speaks slowly and dolefully.

"Just as she's dressed now."

Sylvia laughs again.

"You're becoming demented, chief inspector. Jon Cardington went home without permission. He's making it up. I don't recall talking to him."

"Perhaps it wasn't you he spoke to at all. Despite his crusty exterior, he's a sensitive man. Perhaps there was something about whoever he spoke to that unnerved him and he wanted to be out of the house as quickly as possible."

"Indeed, to skive off to the pub."

"He wasn't skiving when he saw Bernard arrive unexpectedly one day for a meeting with you. He also saw the two of you arguing. The day Bernard came to see you was the day he disappeared. You were here and it was Charlotte in Scotland covering for you."

"But he left..."

Another silence as they all look to Sylvia.

"I mean he *must* have left. No one mentioned his visit when I returned."

"You followed him, trapped him, conveyed him into the past and murdered him. You also arranged the murder of Martin Sarwell."

"Ridiculous, I hardly knew the man."

"You knew him very well. He was desperate to try out his wonder food and you were only too willing to oblige. If successful, such a product would be a winner for your company. Sarwell was in deep financial crisis. He needed a breakthrough and he needed it quick. But he had other interests. He had a fixation with Doctor Foxley, even believing he'd lived before as the doctor. At first you didn't take all that seriously, but he was a tenacious ferret and his interest resulted in him figuring out what had actually happened, partly from his researches, partly from clever guesswork. His interest in the past and his growing belief he was in some way reliving Foxley's life led him to confide in you as a fellow traveller in exploring the past. That was his downfall, for his other interest in old railways had enabled him to work out the significance of a particular place where Bernard Weston had been killed. Stupidly he may even have tried to blackmail you. He had to be disposed of."

Sylvia watches Jenner, occasionally casting furtive glimpses at the others, the window and the door.

"I have an alibi for the time of Sarwell's murder."

"Indeed you do, but where was Charlotte?"

She laughs again, but now it's hollow, forced, desperate.

"Even if this is true, even if I have dabbled in the past, someone else has done much more than me. Everything you've said points to Matthew Usworth, not to me. He's been the dubious scholar, basing his dramatic revelations on dangerous forays into the 1840s. He had to be stopped. Bernard knew what he was doing. He was determined to stop him and sought my help."

"Why then did he oppose the reopening of the canal?"

"Because...he didn't...yes, he did...it was...because he knew it provided a way for others to block him, to stop his moving ...transferring."

She stops suddenly, increasing her grip on the chair.

"So you admit the canal tunnel is a means of time transference?"

She shakes her head desperately towards the window and then turns back to Jenner.

"At his meeting he held up that contemporary Chartist newspaper, what was it called, 'The East Midland Working People's Examiner?' It was him that dropped the penny, but it wasn't just that, what about the Chartist handbill that was found by Sarwell's body?"

"What indeed? How do you know about that? We've not divulged that information."

David, at last accepting Sylvia's involvement, stands ashen and shocked into an impotent rigidity. Sylvia will not look at David and, ignoring Jenner's question, accusingly points at him again.

"Why should I have done this?"

"Because of what they found out. Just as now you're

desperate to find Doctor Foxley's memoir and what it might contain. For in such a document there is…"

"It's her, it's her, she's Charlotte!" Ella screams, jumping up and lunging towards her. Instinctively, Sylvia steps back, closer to the window. Ella kicks the couch from under her and it slithers along the floor, hitting Jenner in the knees. Stumbling, he tries to grab a chair, but flails helplessly against the wall and slumps down. Sandra also tries to stop her, but also collides with the couch. David moves towards her, breaking free from John, but she thrusts him aside. Shaking and springing towards Sylvia, she shouts

"Charlotte! Charlotte!"

Sylvia is at the window. Footsteps on the terrace outside. She looks out and after a quick glance at the others, wrenches open the French door, banging it forcefully behind her into Ella's face. David and the others scramble after her, crashing and bumping as they try to negotiate around each other as well as the couch, the desk and chairs. Ella gets onto the terrace, but Sylvia has already got some way along. Two other figures are running towards her, a woman and a man. Ella stops in amazement. The woman is Sylvia's same height and build and dressed in the same green dress. The man, chasing after her is Matt Usworth.

"Stop her, Ella," he shouts, "Don't let her get…"

His words abruptly cut as he sees Sylvia and like Ella is struck by the unbelievable similarity of the two women. They are exact doubles and it is impossible to say who is Sylvia and who is Charlotte. As they meet the newcomer hands the hat she's been carrying to the other. The one closer to Ella, looks back. In their panic and confusion, the others pile up against the door with Jenner shouting "Get out the bloody way!"

The two women exchange a few words, nod to each other and then run back towards Ella. Before she can object or the others stop them they frog march her along the terrace. Matt, dumbfounded, gapes at the three as Ella is roughly lifted and rapidly slithered along. Unsuccessfully trying to distinguish between them, his eyes dart between Sylvia and Charlotte. The same clothes, the same features, the same gait, but most frightening of all, the same hard, ruthless expression. One of them holds a small object to Ella's throat, while the other picks up something lying beneath a bush at the side of the terrace. It's wooden and long, probably a spade handle left by one of the gardeners. Ella opens her mouth to speak, but her breath is voiceless as something unseen, beneath one of the dresses is pressed into her side. She stares at Matt, her eyes part pleading, part querying, part fearing as if propelled by one set of enemies into the questionably uncertain clutches of another.

He moves forward, but the mirrored maulers march on, quickening their pace. Behind them Jenner's group have at last extricated themselves from the library. Matt can hear Jenner's voice, barking instructions, but he sounds faint and muffled as if an invisible barrier separates them. The desperate trio gets closer, advancing cruelly while its pursuers seem oddly leaden footed and terrifyingly delayed. Matt wants to shout to them to hurry but his voice, like their feet, seems weirdly retarded. Ella's eyes have lost their ambivalence. Any fears she may have had for Matt are lost in her overwhelming terror. Her fleet footed abductors are undeterred, whisking her lightly, but with the unstoppable strength of a frightful dual juggernaut. But stopped they must be. Matt positions himself ready to free Ella, but as he raises his arms, the spade handle is now deployed with merciless precision, hammering into his stomach and thrusting him aside as a rag doll is lifted by the wind.

Crushed and crunched, he falls into the bushes. He scrabbles to get up, scraping his hands on the stones and snagging his arms on the twigs, but stumbles down again. Jenner and the others run towards him, but still they seem oddly lethargic, caught in some grotesquely slow and ineffectual masquerade, dancing forlornly along the terrace. Matt looks the other way. The horrific pair and their captive scuttle away like two monstrous green insects carrying off their prize to a devilish nest. He turns back. John Duggan and David Underwood, followed by Sandra and Jenner seem at last to have escaped from their odd sleepwalking pace and are almost up to him, but valuable time has been lost. Jenner shouts something. Matt cannot make it out, but he follows

Jenner's pointed finger, alarmed to see only one green figure. One of them, Sylvia or Charlotte, has Ella, but cannot be seen!

He gets up and still in some pain, goes after her. She runs quickly along the whole length of the terrace, turning the corner at the end and darting towards the drive. As he squirms on the ground, Jenner and the others see what Matt misses. Grabbing Ella, the other springs away from the terrace, drags her down onto the lawn, pulls her away into the bushes and through a tall hedge. Jenner stops at the edge of the grass, watching Matt racing along the terrace.

"God damn it, which way," he shouts and then to John, "After him!"

As John follows Matt, Jenner looks back to the lawn, but Ella and the other cannot be seen.

"No! No!" he shouts in frustrated despair and then turns to David, "Do you know the grounds?"

David stares at the hedged conifers.

"It's a mini maze."

"Does it lead anywhere?"

"Only to the East Garden."

"Nowhere else?"

David shrugs.

"I don't think so."

Jenner looks at him contemptuously, but there's no time to argue.

"Sandra, cover the left side and take him with you. I'll go to the right. She'll have to come out one way."

They go their separate ways. The clump of hedges is small, but the trees are nearly three meters tall, making it impossible to see into the centre. Jenner reaches the entrance on the right and peers between the trees. Neither seeing nor hearing anything and not trusting David, he wanders along the side and round to the back. To his alarm, he finds a third entrance and, looking beyond towards the wide expanse of the East Garden, sees at its far end a hatted, green figure, pulling her struggling captive. He shouts to Sandra and she and David join him.

"You said there wasn't a third exit!" he bellows, "Where does that garden lead to?"

But before David can reply Jenner sprints across the lawn towards the garden, though by now their quarry has slipped behind another hedge and is out of sight. As they run towards it, they hear a car starting up in the distance. As the others run on, Jenner stops and turns towards the sound of the engine.

"She's getting away, sir," Sandra shouts.

He catches her up and sees Sylvia/Charlotte still wrenching Ella as they reach the perimeter wall and a small gate, overgrown with ivy. A car, driven by the other, waits to pick them up. Ella is bundled into the back and they drive away.

"Damn! Damn! Damn!" Jenner fumes.

They stand, helpless and bedraggled on the roadside outside the gate. Another car comes out of the drive and accelerates towards them. Jenner recognises the driver as it passes. It's Matt Usworth. John Duggan is in futile pursuit on foot.

"Couldn't catch...him, sir," he blurts out between breaths, "...we left...the car...too far away."

"Not your fault," Jennner says, "Quickly, back to the cars and get after them. How could we have been so stupid? One of them gets away with Ella, losing us in the process while the other gets the car."

"They knew the grounds," Sandra says.

"Yes," Jenner agrees, casting an angry eye towards David, "There can be only one place for them to go. Let's hope we're not too late and can get there before Usworth makes matters worse!"

- 14 -

It has to be today. Another day will be too late. Ever since her 'escape' from the past, Ettie has felt this constant cloaking sense of closeness. It cannot last another day. There has to be a resolution, a coming together or a cleaving apart. It will be today. While Ettie's mood is cautiously balanced, Jennifer is constantly on edge. Unconvinced by Jenner's insistence he couldn't leave Ettie with a mere constable, she feels detached from the main action. She sits still for no more than a few minutes at a time, forever fidgeting, pacing purposelessly or patrolling the perimeters of their confine. None of this is helped by her not knowing *where* the action is taking place. Since their arrival, the mobile phones have inextricably failed. Even with her constant movement she's been unable to get a signal. While Ettie's apprehensions are driven by unknown, yet to her, almost palpable forces, Jennifer's centre on their physical isolation.

At first, they're accompanied by the usual collection of dog walkers and indeterminate strollers, but as Jennifer wanders in pursuit of the unattainable telephone link, the place empties. Not a person, not a dog, not a car and eerily quiet as the birds and animals quietly quit, as if to prepare for a storm. Yet the sky is clear and the sun is bright. Whatever storm is coming it will not be of wind and rain and static electricity. When Jennifer complains about the telephone,

Ettie nods knowingly. When Jennifer mentions the lack of people, Ettie nods again. When Jennifer says the unnatural silence feels like an invisible barrier shutting off the sky and enclosing them on all sides, Ettie doesn't comment.

"It's as if we're trapped," Jennifer says nervously, seeking, hoping for some reassurance, but Ettie's reply only increases her restlessness.

"Not just us."

Jennifer prowls the edge of the canal again, venturing into the tunnel.

"I wouldn't go in too far," Ettie says grimly, without further explanation.

Jennifer backs away. Ettie needs to be still. She hasn't moved from the seat on the towpath, about fifty meters from the tunnel entrance. Her mind must be focused and her body not distracted, even by the movement of her limbs. If it has to be here then she must be prepared. The presences have been growing stronger. As they wait their drawing power advances and is most pronounced at the canal. Jennifer returns and sits beside Ettie, feeling safer in closeness. She tries the telephone again before stuffing in her bag in frustration.

Ettie watches and listens. The stillness frightens her too, but she suppresses her anxieties. Outwardly calm, she scans the surrounding country. Even the leaves on the trees seem fixed as if time has wound down and everything must wait, motionless until an unseen hand wielding an ageless rhythmic key, noiselessly releases it again. But what if the key, stiff from ill use, jams in the corroded lock? Even worse, what if the unseen hand, through inexperience or recklessness, turns it too far or too little? A naive meddler like Matt Usworth perhaps? Worse still, a vicious, grievous menace, intent on mischief. For now, all pretence has been discarded. All know about each other. All are intent on swiftly concluding their ends.

This is the place and this is the time. It must be decided here and soon. They haven't long. A hazardous carrot has been dangled in front of dangerous forces. Ettie must prepare herself and reinforce all the strength she can muster, protecting themselves from the past mastering the present, and the present intervening in the past. Those seeking to unbalance the finely taught wire separating them must be stopped. Can they be controlled? She shudders. Ettie may need to walk that wire.

On the way to the car Jenner collides with a burly figure, hovering at the corner of the house.

"Thou needs to look where thou's going," Jon Cardington bellows.

"And you need to make sure you're not obstructing police officers," Jenner says gruffly, levering himself by the wall, away from Jon, "Did you see Mrs. Darrington – Cressley?"

"Ar, ow went to ge'er car."

"Quite, anyone else?"

"Only 'er friend."

"What friend?"

"Friend who was at'door wi'all that cafuffle wi'that Usworth feller."

"She was at the door, arguing with Usworth and Mrs. Darrington – Cressley was outside?"

"Ar."

"So there were two of them?"

"'Course," Jon looks at him, wondering why it's necessary to restate the obvious, "When t'others went inside, that Usworth went after 'er. They were arguing, then she shot off, went round corner at'ouse. Didn't see 'er after that."

"Did you see this friend before?"

"I saw two women, dressed in green walking int'grounds earlier. Long way off, difficult to tell, but I reckon one was Mrs. Darrington – Cressley."

"Could you tell them apart?"

Jon rubs his chin thoughtfully.

"Could be, t'other wa' different...she had a bonnet on..."

"Why didn't you tell us this earlier when we arrived?"

"Nob'dy asked me."

In the car, Jenner tells Sandra to get to the canal.

"You're sure, sir?"

"No constable, I'm not *sure*, but it's all we have to go on."

Sandra drives as fast as a slim respect for safety will allow, but consumed by his fear and anger nothing less than the speed of light will satisfy Jenner. Jon's words reverberate.

T'other had a bonnet.

The woman who dragged Ella through the old gateway had a hat. The other had given her the hat when they met on the terrace. Jon had seen the 'other' arguing with Usworth. Only the hat distinguished them and would be an immediate giveaway. If he was right, Sylvia had kept the hat when she was outside and then handed it to Charlotte. He had to be right. Only Sylvia would collect and drive round the car to meet her. Which meant Ella was right – it *was* Charlotte in the house! Just as before when he visited though now there's no doubt. A clever act, which fooled everybody except Ella.

Ella! What danger she was in and not just her. What of Ettie and Jennifer? Thanks to him underestimating the Darrington – Cressleys' foresight and planning they'll be delayed no matter how fast Sandra drives. He should have anticipated this diversion, but how could he know David would acquiesce so foolishly to their designs? He must warn Ettie! But the phones are dead, as if a malignant force is blocking them!

Ettie leaves her vigil at the seat and walks towards the tunnel, its brick arched entrance guarding the grim, gaping hole. Close to it, she senses danger. She peers into the hollow darkness. The tunnel seems menacing, but can they harness it to their needs? The dimly receding walls and water seem innocently blended of solid and liquid, soft and hard naturally balanced, rough and smooth, fused into delight, peace, support. But merging such extremes is dangerous. If the hard walls and roof become supple, would the guile of an unknown force also make them malleable to its will? If water assumes an inconceivable firmness, then it would become fixed and an obstruction for the unwary. Things are not just merged, but transformed. Nothing is what it seems.

The canal in the tunnel, its yielding and enclosing water, wrapped in a defensive shell of bricks and stone and earth, connects more than places. A link for voyagers to travel across time, but how to predict or control those making use of the waterway between past and present? When Ella gets here she may encourage Lizzie to intervene and help, but will she be reliable? Her erratic and confused outbursts may mystify, even frighten Lizzie.

Ettie must breathe warming breezes of courage across the decades. Lizzie must be strong. Silently, Ettie appeals to the walls, declares to the roof and supplicates the waters. She stares deeply into the tunnel's contracting light. Beyond the limiting depth and breadth of its funnelled chasm, an unbroken spiritual chain has to be forged and held tightly between them. She waits a moment, wondering, hoping, believing she can catch some slight soft shade of Lizzie from the distant remoteness. In line with the rim of the roof arch, she steps across the unmarked towpath threshold, Then she steps back as if getting too close to the red hot embers of a ground fire. Yet not to step forward might be to deny the help she desperately needs, for it will only come from within the darkened portals. She looks back. Jennifer is standing, surveying in all directions, guarding all approaches. She cannot guard this, the most dangerous of all. Only Ettie can do that, but guarding is not enough. This is no time for defence. To make contact she must advance and thereby risk attack.

She walks on a few meters and then stops, listening, watching, smelling the dank air and caressing the brickwork as if it might be stroked into releasing precious messages. As she stares into the diminishing tunnel, her eyes gradually adjust to the increasing darkness, but all is less distinct as walls, water and roof meld in the gloomy distance. There she *sees* nothing unusual, but *feels* enough to make her fearful. She averts her eyes from the distant vortex, bouncing her attention between immediate walls, roof and water. All still, but she neither sees nor hears anything unusual. The *feeling* is different, benign, not like the malignancy emanating from further within. There's a presence, but no contact is made.

A few drops of water fall from the roof onto her head. As she brushes her hair and slips on her hat, she feels the closeness of a presence. She adjusts her hat, pulling and poking it as the power is ratcheted around her. Glancing into the tunnel, its end seems even murkier than before as if enshrouded by mist from the water, a dull cloud, covering anything more than ten meters ahead. Yet she no longer feels threatened. This is no advancing miasma, but a protective veil thrown up to shield her from time wound arms thrown out by the advancing clutches of the past.

She waits expectantly, confident whatever is near won't harm her. She leans against the near wall and watches the far side and the intervening water, which has become motionless and unblemished. Its apparent solidity might invite the unwary to try and walk across. She stares, but is not tempted. The far wall seems unnaturally sleek as if bricks and mortar have been painted onto a totally smooth surface, gracefully winding upwards, unwrinkled by the slightest crack or ridge. Out of this near perfect texture, the outlines of a familiar face appear. Ettie steadies herself against the wall with one hand, holding her hat with the other. Immediately the features sharpen as if cued by Ettie's involuntary signals.

The enormous mouth opens to speak. Lizzie's image is starkly sharp and her words are delivered with a clarity Ettie has not heard before. In a few, curt, but succinct sentences she unburdens herself of those age held secrets that so long also consumed Doctor Foxley's energies.

"As a midwife you learn many things. Most make you happy, some make you sad, a few you wish you'd never learnt."

Ettie lifts her hat slightly to scratch her forehead. As she does, she notices Lizzie's image wavers. Pulling her hat down again, Lizzie's features return to their sharpness. With a heart felt sigh, Lizzie continues.

"You are defended by what you already know and by what you will discover. Already you have achieved half of what you need to do. By your enemies you may be beaten black and blue, but in being so beaten, blue between black is your strength."

Ettie repeats the advice to herself. Achieved only half and so little time to learn the other half? She has to know more. She must risk asking the vital question. Then Jennifer calls. Lizzie's image flickers. Jennifer calls again. The flickering becomes a withering shimmer. Ettie looks towards the tunnel mouth. Jennifer is walking towards her. She's agitated and waving her arm. Ettie looks back into the tunnel. The dark form is almost gone. She half turns and, without thinking moves her hand to her hat. She nudges it and then stops, but too late, the image folds abruptly, the walls and roof recover their genuine consistency and the defensive cloud evaporates. For an instant she stares at the emptiness of the tunnel and the limpid indifference of the water. Nothing now to be gained from delay. She walks quickly to the entrance.

Once outside the tunnel, Ettie is surprised how cold it's suddenly become, the air heavy with the malevolently expectant chill of an imminent storm. Yet still bright, the clouds fluffily scampering across the sky without any darkly, hanging precursors of wind and rain.

"There's a car," Jennifer says as they meet.

Between the hedge she points out a vehicle, a lone deposit in the otherwise empty park. It's too far away to make out the number, but there's something familiar about it.

"You know it?" Ettie says.

Jennifer nods. A figure emerges from the front of the car. It goes around to a rear door, from which a second figure emerges, apparently pulling out a third. The first two are dressed in green. The three of them walk quickly towards the canal, the third figure dragged between the other two. As they get closer, Jennifer stares incredulously at the three women, the first two clad in long flowing dresses. She continues to watch them, transfixed. Ettie reads her thoughts.

"Yes," she says, "There are two of them, as I feared."

"Where are the others?" Jennifer says ominously as she tries one more time to get her phone to work.

Ettie shakes her head.

"Nothing will work."

Jennifer stuffs away the impotent phone.

"I'll have to stop them, they've got Ella Weston" she says, moving away from the hedge.

Ettie puts a hand on her arm.

"No!"

"But I have to do something. I can't just let them take her like that."

"There are other issues which have to be resolved first and they can't be tackled that way. Besides, they will be strengthened now in ways beyond your imagining."

"It's all going wrong!" Jennifer says in angry frustration, "Where are the others?"

"The chief inspector will know where to come," Ettie says calmly.

"We have no back up."

"All the more reason to do as I say. We must conceal ourselves."

"Hide away?"

"Make ourselves secure at least until we, or they are able to resolve the issue."

"*Resolve* sounds so neutral."

"If only it were."

Ettie points to a tree close by the seat on the bank.

"Get behind there and wait for my signal."

"Where are you going?"

"Up ahead, closer to the tunnel mouth."

"Alone? We're splitting up?"

"You have to close off their retreat before I show myself. It's the only way. Trust me. In this place, we have to operate by other rules now, for the usual ones no longer apply."

Ettie turns and walks on towards the tunnel. She stops just short of it and pokes around in the undergrowth. Jennifer anxiously glances towards the advancing trio.

"Quickly, they're almost here," she shouts, lowering herself behind the tree and then as an afterthought, "Are you sure that's the best place?"

"It has to be here," Ettie says, "We have to be unseen when they approach, but also close. Above all they have to be kept out of the tunnel."

Jennifer is still unsure, but it's too late to argue and she motions Ettie to get hidden. No sooner has she crouched down and flattened herself at the base of the tree than the three pass her and reach the towpath. Unaware help is near, Ella allows herself to be hauled along by the two Cressleys. The air gets very cold even though the sun remains high and bright. Ella shivers, as does Jennifer. They stop some ten meters short of the hideaway where Ettie waits.

Sylvia releases her grip on Ella as she pushes her closer to the water's edge. Ella rubs her arm, but Sylvia remains close and any slight attempt to escape will be answered by a ruthless jerk into the canal. Charlotte keeps hold and, from beneath her bonnet, coldly and menacingly stares at her. Ella glares back.

"I know who you are. You don't fool me, I can tell you apart. You are Charlotte."

Charlotte ignores her, transferring her riveted gaze to the tunnel mouth. Something there unnerves her. Sylvia touches Ella's arm.

"As we all know each other, it's going to make everything a lot easier, isn't it? Let's stop all this wasting time and give us Foxley's document."

Ella leers defiantly. Sylvia grabs her arm again.

"Mess us around any longer, my girl and you'll find those cold waters down there a little closer to you."

"I knew it was you in the house, " Ella says to Charlotte, "That dress couldn't be new, not a copy, I knew it was authentic, the real thing, so you couldn't have been *her*."

'Her' grips so tightly Ella cries out. Charlotte half turns in response, though her attention is still rapt on the mysterious unknown at the tunnel entrance. 'Her' speaks again.

"It would be very fitting, wouldn't it Charlotte, to drown her in the same place as poor Jonathon? A kind of justice, wouldn't you say?"

Charlotte starts at the mention of her brother's name.

"Give us what we want," she says in a low, gravelly tone.

"Otherwise," Sylvia cuts in, pointing to the water in case Ella has not yet understood the message, "We'll be leaving you here."

"You'll be leaving her anyway!"

Jennifer's patience has run out and fearing for Ella, can wait no longer for Ettie's signal. Sylvia turns to face her, pulling Ella around. Charlotte steps back and then moves nearer to the tunnel. Jennifer advances towards Sylvia, who puts the knife at Ella's throat.

"One more step and she gets it," Sylvia says, shuffling closer again to the water.

"We have to get away," Charlotte says edgily.

"Not till we've got that paper," Sylvia says, "Then we can get away."

"There is no paper!"

Ettie emerges from the bushes and guards the path at the tunnel. Charlotte stops and steps away from the canal, to stand with her back to the hedge, keeping her eyes on Ettie. Sylvia joins her with Ella between them, while she warily watches Jennifer.

"Get out of our way and you won't be harmed," Charlotte says.

"No paper, no document from Doctor Foxley, I don't believe it," Sylvia says.

"A ruse to expose you," Jennifer says.

Sylvia laughs. She and Charlotte resume their progress towards Ettie. Jennifer follows at a slight, but discreet distance.

"I told you to stay still!" Sylvia shouts.

Jennifer stops as Ella cries in pain with the tip of the knife pricking into her neck.

"You won't get away with it," Jennifer says, "It's only a matter of time before..."

"We've nothing to lose," Sylvia says, shuffling even closer to the tunnel.

Ettie stands resolute, arms folded, her hat pulled well down in front of her face.

"What would be so special about a letter from Doctor Foxley?" she shouts.

Charlotte responds to the challenge, laughing as she pulls her bonnet firmly down. She and Ettie glower at each other, defiant and dangerous, green and black tigresses, watchful, intransigent, ready to pounce.

"I should have known that fool would eventually mock us from the grave," she says.

"He's dead?"

"Of course he's dead..."

"I meant..."

"Foxley had an unfortunate and untimely attack of conscience, which necessitated his removal. He was lured away from his practice and disposed of. I never liked him despite what father said."

"He had to be got rid of, because of what he knew?"

"Because of what he might say. Men with consciences never keep secrets to themselves. His loose mind threatened to loosen his tongue."

"He wasn't alone though, was he?"

Charlotte clicks her tongue disdainfully.

"You mean the midwife, Lizzie Traynor. She never said anything, but she always had a disapproving *look*. I wanted to, but...anyway she disappeared at the same time and was never found. Even her children didn't know what became of her. Now, let us pass."

"Why did you kill Bernard Weston?"

Sylvia laughs again.

"Another who knew too much."

"Always poking around into things," Charlotte says, coldly, "I knew there was somebody interfering with our work. He found out he was descended from Lizzie. He came early for one of his meetings with Sylvia. She was...elsewhere. I was here. When I met him I felt him immediately as...an alien interference from this time. After I sent him away, I warned Sylvia on her...return...I told her that for our protection he had to be eradicated. We agreed Sylvia should do it. She arranged to see him secretly. The fool was so busy meddling into things beyond his puny brain, it was easy for her to get him away into my time and get rid of him there. Meanwhile I posed as Sylvia and established her alibi. Everyone believed he'd disappeared, which of course he had. It was really quite amusing."

"How did you get him away?"

"The same way we get away today, through the tunnel!"

"Leading him to a place he won't be found in his own time at Best Hill?"

"Until that other interfering dolt Sarwell also started asking too many questions."

"Him and his damned railway lines!" Sylvia says.

"He was even beginning to get interested in Cecily," Charlotte says.

"Oh yes," Ettie says, "you're cousin, Cecily Stacey, daughter of your father's sister, Anne who ran off to marry Thomas Stacey, your grandfather's business rival. Grandfather Edward Cressley, the founder of the family business, had three children, did he not, the eldest Arthur, who died tragically young, the second son and your own father, James and Anne, the daughter."

"You're very well informed."

"I've had a good informant."

Charlotte suppresses her fury, but Ettie sees the shock in her face.

"Indeed? Someone I should know?"

"Someone you *do* know and someone who, as you said had a disapproving look because *she* knew."

"Lizzie! you've spoken to Lizzie?"

"She's spoken to me."

"I don't believe it," Sylvia says, "Get out of our way!"

They nudge further forward. Ettie stretches out her arms. Jennifer moves closer. Sylvia pushes Ella between them.

"I warned you, she gets it."

"Let her go," Jennifer says, "There is no letter from Foxley."

"In which case we need to get away."

"Into the past? Won't that wipe out all your plans?" Ettie shouts.

"Don't underestimate our powers," Charlotte says icily.

"You cannot escape, it's impossible!"

Pushing Ella so close to the edge that one of her legs is suspended above the water, Sylvia screams at Ettie.

"You're in league with Usworth!"

"I suppose I am, but not the one you're thinking of."

"Another meddler in the past," Charlotte says, "We are in control, you can't compete."

"Try me."

Ella tries to push Sylvia away and is rewarded with a stout smack across the face.

"No, Ettie, no!" she cries, "They are more powerful than you, don't provoke them."

Sylvia tightens her grip once more and clamps a strong hand across her mouth.

"How right she is," Charlotte says while twisting back Ella's arm until she cries out in pain, "My powers are almost magical."

Ettie stands her ground. Charlotte stops only a few steps in front of her. Strengthening her grip on Ella's arm, Charlotte shakes furiously, her hat rhythmically bobbing in time to her indignantly quivering head.

"I could bring back this day in 1842, cold, wet and with a blackness to match your own miserably swart ugliness."

Jennifer looks up, half expecting the sky to match the coldness she feels. It remains bright and almost cloudless. Any blackness comes from within.

"I think not," Ettie replies, "for you're turned out from bonnet to shoes in the colour of the untutored, green in looks and green in skill, a time unserved novice, an apprentice in the wily ways of the time linked traveller!"

"Out of the way!"

Trusting to the show woman's effect and the debilitating power of her opponent's anger, Ettie keeps her arms high and shouts impudently.

"Your way is barred!"

"You don't fool us!" Sylvia cries, "You can't rely on your ally, Matt Usworth. I sussed him and his vicious ancestor long ago. Relying on Samuel Usworth will only deliver you the same fate as his!"

"What was that? Another murder!"

Sliding down the bank from his leafy vantage near the top of the tunnel, Matt lands beside Ettie. With his ferocious eyes and his arms splayed, he's ready to spring at Sylvia, who backs away slightly. Charlotte remains unmoved, studying him with an indifferent, calculated hostility. He glares with a feral intensity at the two women, time sundered twins, raw and vivid, hovering like two hideous green spiders pulling apart their victim.

"Witch! At the house I thought you'd hatched some loathsome sorcery to be in two places at once. Now I see and hear, the truth is even more repellent."

He rushes at Sylvia. Ettie grabs his arm and pulls him back.

"See!" Sylvia screams, "You can't control your acolyte."

"What did you do to Sam?" he shouts.

"So, you admit to prying into the past? See, I told that policeman, here is your real criminal!"

"What did you do with him?"

"Nothing," Charlotte says, "Unfortunately scum of that kind sometimes get away. The authorities, then as now, were lax and incompetent. I had neither the opportunity nor the means to undertake their duties. In the end it was unnecessary. He ceased to be an irritation."

Contempt for his ancestor as a noisome fly provokes Matt into erupting again.

"You're lying! You killed him. That's why he disappears from the records. I searched and searched. He just vanishes without a trace. You did it and your *authorities* covered it up!"

"This is not helpful," Ettie says, holding him with both arms, "Stay back! If you attack they absorb your energy and use it against you."

Physically Matt is the stronger, but Charlotte is energised by submerged reserves of intangible help. Meanwhile as Sylvia and Charlotte concentrate on Ettie and Matt, Jenner and the others arrive to join Jennifer. Unable to break free, Matt sinks back.

"I was always afraid of the canal's reopening," he says quietly, "what it could unleash. I told Bernard, but he wouldn't listen. When it was opened all my fears were justified. When the bricked up entrance was torn down, I sensed the power of the water released. It was done, it was up to me to make the best use of it, but you can't always control these things."

"You admit, you admit it!" Sylvia cries, almost gleefully.

Jenner and the others creep forward stealthily. Distracted by their movement, Ettie momentarily loosens her grip. Feeling the looser restraint, Matt lunges and breaks free, raises his arms and clatters into Charlotte. Sylvia hammers him with the back of her arm while Charlotte elbows him from the side. Jenner and Duggan crash into Sylvia from behind and pull Ella away. The force of the impact propels Sylvia and Charlotte forward. As they career towards Ettie, Matt is levered aside, colliding with John and pushing him into the canal. Jennifer wrests Ella back while Sandra helps John from the water. Jenner stumbles at the edge, but seeing Ettie vulnerable, he gets up and follows the green twins. Ettie still stands in their path, arms outstretched. They rush between her, simultaneously wrenching her arms down and pulling her back as they march up to the tunnel mouth. She sways on the path as Jenner staggers up to her, both overtaken by Matt who runs on towards the twins. Charlotte reaches the threshold of the tunnel, but hesitates, as if her way is blocked by an invisible barrier. Jenner steadies Ettie and then runs on, managing to catch hold of Matt and stop him getting closer to Charlotte. She and Sylvia turn around, with their backs to the obstacle, facing the others at the base of the arch.

"Hold him there," Ettie shouts to Jenner, "Stop him going further."

Jenner is about to go forward and accost the 'twins,' but he hesitates, long enough for Ettie to reach him and hold his arm.

"Wait," she whispers, "and keep hold of Matt."

Matt is quiet now, standing calmly beside Jenner. They're about three meters from Sylvia and Charlotte. Jenner's blue suit contrasts with the black on each side of him, Ettie's black dress and hat and Matt's black jacket. Ettie remembers Lizzie's words.

"...beaten blue between black is your strength..."

"I wish you no harm, but will if you continue to resist us," Charlotte says.

"It's more than me resisting you," Ettie says, glancing at her two companions, "Why didn't you go into the tunnel, Charlotte, what stopped you?"

"Nothing stopped us," Sylvia cries, "we'll soon be away!"

"Your exit's blocked and even if you do get away, you've failed. You fear Matt as Charlotte feared Sam and together they'll defeat you both. Escape means your inheritance is lost, but it's lost anyway. Your family wealth is built on a cruel deception and you were driven by the threat of your deceit being divulged. First by Bernard Weston, then by Martin Sarwell and finally by me through Doctor Foxley. The family business was bequeathed to Charlotte by her grandfather, Edward Cressley, under the terms of his will..."

"Again you are well informed," Charlotte says dryly, "but the terms of his will are public knowledge."

"...he provided for his fortune to pass on his death to his eldest surviving child, who *at the time of Edward's death*, had an heir of his or her own or, *in the event of them predeceasing Edward,* to the grandchild itself. In other words, the estate passed to the surviving offspring who had produced a grandchild or to the grandchild itself. Edward had three adult children, Arthur, James and Anne. James was the second son and Charlotte's father. Ordinarily therefore he would not succeed, but Arthur, having led a somewhat reckless life was also very ill and died only a few months before his father. By one of those strange coincidental twists, Charlotte was born in 1811 on the same night, in the same house that old man Cressley died, in fact just a few hours before. Therefore, by the terms of the will, *at the time of Edward's death,* James inherited, as the oldest surviving child who had produced a grandchild, his first born, Charlotte. Two outsiders were in the house that night. Both had witnessed the birth and one the death. These two, at the time unaware of its significance were bribed into delaying the announcement of the old man's death until *after* Charlotte's birth. For the truth was that the old man had died a few hours *before* she was born. That meant, *that at the time of Edward's death,* James had inconveniently failed to produce his grandchild. As you said, Doctor Foxley was later to be troubled by his conscience and felt it his duty, when he considered the time was right, to mention it to Charlotte, who by now was the real head of the family. It was Martin Sarwell's later interest in the good doctor that sealed his fate, though his interest in that far off year of 1811 had another dimension."

"None of this matters anyway," Charlotte thunders, "there were no..."

"No other births?" Ettie continues, "Well, not really. Martin Sarwell's other discovery was that one of his ancestors was Thomas Stacey, Edward's penniless business rival. Stacey was very clever and invented a valuable device for improving textile production. Stacey was brilliant, but naïve. Edward easily deceived him, depriving him of the credit, absorbing the new technique into his own production and further enhancing his fortune. Stacey tried, but was unable to recoup his losses. Edward had tied him up in legal niceties and traps. Martin even believed he was reliving his life. In a sense he was and when he consulted me it first triggered suspicions that eventually led me to the truth, but not without the help of someone from those far off times.'

'Ella was desperately troubled by her long recurring dream of Lizzie. By the time I saw her it had become unbearably intense. At first I could offer little help, the contact was too diffuse and muddled, but if a clear path could be cleared through the confusion and interference from other presences, then I knew she would lead me to the secrets. Martin Sarwell, the diligent innocent was also on to Lizzie. He suspected she was the key to unlock the door so long closed on Doctor Foxley's fate. Ella was frightened of him, never understanding why he was so interested in her family. Yet his greater interest lay elsewhere. Not even you suspected, Sylvia. If you had, you would have moved against him even quicker, for by now you were being enclosed by relatives from both sides of your family."

"Relatives, what are you talking about?"

"Martin Sarwell's interests extended even beyond Ella's family or Doctor Foxley. He was beginning to uncover the story of Thomas Stacey and his daughter Cecily. At the same time Matt was stumbling on her significance in the Chartist past and her link to his ancestor Sam. Thomas Stacey died in poverty and Anne soon followed him. Cecily was brought up by her aunt, Thomas's sister. She had no contact with the Cressleys and, conveniently for you, was utterly unaware of the provisions of Edward's will."

Sylvia irritably tries to conceal her alarm.

"So Sarwell was a very distant relative, so what?"

"Neither Cecily's aunt nor her mother, estranged from Edward, realised the significance of Cecily being born a month *before* the old man died. Martin Sarwell was getting dangerously close to revealing he might be descended from the rightful heir to the fortune. That would have given you even more reason for murdering him. But it doesn't end there, for he was not your only lost relative. Cecily and Sam had much more in common than Chartism. Martin was descended from Cecily, just as Matt is descended from Sam, but where had Sam come from?"

"The gutters of Nottingham!" Sylvia cries.

"Is that what you told Bernard when he uncovered the secret or was the truth so dangerous, its messenger had to be silenced? We all overlooked Bernard's fascination with the workhouse. He tracked Sam back and found his parents and his date of birth. For before he died, sickly, reckless Arthur had sown the most dangerous seed of all. Sam was the illegitimate son of him and a millgirl, Rachel Usworth. Sam's father died just before his birth, leaving Rachel alone and destitute. That father was the eldest of Edward's children, Arthur. Even more important, Sam was born in that same year 1811, *before* the old man died, *before* Charlotte and *before* Cecily. Samuel Usworth was the first grandchild of Edward Cressley and therefore the real heir. Without knowing it, Sam and Cecily were cousins, as they were also to Charlotte. When Bernard made the discovery it was even more damning than anything Martin might have found out. Now Martin is dead, leaving Matt as the descendant of the true inheritor of the Cressley fortune."

Recovering some of her vigour, Sylvia lashes out.

"Even if it's true, it doesn't mean *this* Usworth is his descendant. No one knows what became of Sam, he just disappeared."

"I know what became of him," Ettie says and then, turning to Matt, "Do you know about your family, where they came from?"

Matt is awestruck and hesitant. Then, gathering his thoughts says, "I wanted to believe Sam was my ancestor, but it seemed impossible and my forays into the past only confirmed it. I wanted to change everything, for him to stay in Nottingham and lead a new movement, foolishly believing I could change history. I wanted so much to talk to him, get first hand the story of his experiences. It would have been the historical breakthrough of all time, but... you were there...I blew it...you saw him fall, drowned in the dock at Liverpool."

"You frightened him and you frightened me, we had to get away."

"The authorities would have covered up his disappearance. That's why we knew so little about him. He was a major figure in the movement, but it was convenient to wipe out his memory. Perhaps if I'd been more patient...less impulsive... less aggressive...but how could I be descended from him? The name's the same, but the family is not connected. My great grandfather was Canadian. He came over during the First World War and stayed on. I've no connection with the Chartists."

"Sam did fall," Ettie says, "and like you I thought he'd gone, but I couldn't leave. I could see the ship and I could hear the voices. I went over and over in my mind all that had happened, all that was inevitable, all that was avoidable. Hopes and fears, traps and escapes. Then I remembered those like you, involving themselves in the past and I had to count myself one of them. Whether I too had been *meddling* in things beyond my skills I wasn't sure, but I was afraid of failure. I knew from previous experience how precarious is the ledge we walk between past and present, how one interfering, ill chosen, slippery step can jeopardise time itself and plunge the future, my future into chaos. I waited what seemed an age, but it couldn't have been more than a few minutes. Then I heard a gurgling, spluttering, splashing and dimly saw dull white flashes in the black water. Arms, then a head emerged from nearby along the dock. I ran so fast, I almost slipped in myself. Sam was there, floundering and bobbing continuously down, but surfacing again and again and gradually getting closer. I stretched out my arm and hauled him to the side, cold, drenched and shocked, but alive. You were wrong about the authorities, but it was better fewer questions were asked. We might have inadequate answers. We moved on, skirting the chattering groups, sliding behind stacks of cargo, avoiding even the dim light from taverns until we reached the ship. He rubbed himself down with some old tarpaulin and sacks. I gave him the papers and pushed him forward. It was better we were not seen together. I saw him aboard. He looked back one last time and then was gone. I waited until the ship caught the evening tide and watched it steal away down the Mersey.'

'I've checked the records. The *Sylvania* arrived safely in Canada and he was aboard. His grandson, your great grandfather, returned to England seventy five years later and here you are now. I was right to be afraid as I knelt in terrified expectation on that dockside, not even knowing if I could return to the future, my own present, but it was meant to be. Just as Sam was meant to escape, I was meant to help him get away and you are meant to be here now. It's as if Sam is with us. We all have our parts to play."

While Ettie talks to Matt, her attention wavers and she doesn't notice Sylvia and Charlotte. They remain quiet, but nudge closer to the tunnel mouth. Jenner too has listened closely, but as she finishes he sees Charlotte already has one leg across the threshold.

"Just stop where you are," he shouts.

"Too late!" Charlotte says.

She leans across to Sylvia, but as she does Jenner leaps forward and grabs from the other side. Keeping one foot within the tunnel, Charlotte clasps Sylvia. For an instant she's pulled from either side, like some unfortunate insect in danger of being ripped apart by two competing predators. Ettie shouts a warning.

"Hold her, don't let her go, but don't cross the edge of the tunnel yourself!"

Matt joins Jenner. Together they lug Sylvia towards them. Lizzie's words return to Ettie again. *"Blue between black is your strength."* Two labouring soldiers, one blue, one black, strenuously busying themselves in a desperate fight to secure Sylvia. Like Ettie, Charlotte can call up superhuman strength from deep within, deep beyond. Millimeter by millimeter she edges her other leg closer to the tunnel, her strength increasing with each tiny movement. Matt and Jenner hold on. *'Blue and black is your strength!'* The others are close, but cannot help. Their hearts are willing, but their bodies are frozen. By her move Charlotte has brought herself into a time spanned togetherness, neither past nor present and yet uncannily straddling both in which only those immediately at the tunnel mouth can participate. In this time fractured enclosure, past and present merge and minutes become hours as the adversaries achingly, slowly slug it out for Sylvia and their own salvation.

Ettie is also transfixed. Lizzie's other words return. *'Already you have achieved half of what you need to do.'* Already and an achievement. Maybe it's not so dire. Does Lizzie mean you've done much and are now so close? Ettie looks at the two men, battling against Charlotte's superhuman force. *Black and Blue...half achieved...half remains.* One is the half achieved and one is the half remaining, Jenner in his blue suit, Matt in his black jacket. But which is which? Something achieved and something remaining? So far, all Matt has achieved has been to get in the way of Sam's escape, but Jenner's intervention was crucial at the railway station. Two men, one black, one blue, one role achieved, the other yet to come, but what is that role? Jenner threw the old police hat. Something from the past sent from the present back into the past. Yet didn't Matt do a similar thing...?

Suddenly Sylvia is twisted and jerked closer by Charlotte. Jenner and Matt's feet claw the path, but slip slightly. Between pained grunts, Jenner casts a quick, anguished glance at Ettie. His silent pleading goes unanswered. Ettie remains motionless, but her mind races. Matt too hurled something into the past. In his powerless frustration and anger he threw the bag at Sam. It missed, but it's still there on the Liverpool dock in 1842. Something of the present sent into the past. It doesn't matter it was ineffective. These transmissions from the present to the past are more powerful as objects of both past and present. The hat and the bag, the power of the present *to* the past. The black and the blue, already the half achieved.

Charlotte gets stronger. Jenner and Matt are slipping. Ettie remains confused and immobile. If only Lizzie could help her now, but Lizzie is imprisoned in the past, out of reach, bounded by the tunnel walls, where it seems only Charlotte can go. Charlotte is of the past, but the past has been breached before, why not again? Sylvia must be stopped from going into the past, but how? Charlotte's strength increases. Jenner and Matt are losing the fight, while Ettie and the others remain petrified!

Two halves. *Half achieved...half remains*. What half? The past controls the present. Charlotte rules! Soon Sylvia will join her there and all will be lost. Past and present. That's it! At last Ettie understands. Past and present are the two halves! Charlotte is not of the past. Not here. She's cast the place into a time limbo to ease Sylvia's passage into the past, the better to confound Ettie, but ... not yet. Charlotte, I am ready. We are all of the present. Sylvia is already compromised and subservient to your will. She can no longer withstand us! We are stronger. We can beat Charlotte. Jenner and Matt, twin pillars of the present, are stronger than Sylvia, but she calls on the past powers of Charlotte. That link can only be broken by something that breaks through this monstrous deadlocked tug of war. She must act before Sylvia is pulled into the shadow of the tunnel and crosses the cut for ever. If the past is to be stopped from pulling the present, then the present must go to the past!

Matt and Jenner continue to stretch every sinew and tighten every muscle to stop Sylvia's slide towards the brink of the tunnel arch. Now determined, Ettie finds her body will move at last. Ignoring the heaving, time strangled brawl, she trips quickly and precariously along the water's edge, enters the tunnel and sidesteps Charlotte. Surprised, Charlotte turns to face her, but still grasps Sylvia tightly. The next few seconds will be critical and final for them all. Ettie must be quicker and nimbler than Charlotte.

"You can't go on and you can't go back!" Ettie shouts to Charlotte, moving swiftly towards her.

Baring her teeth like a cornered beast and tugging Sylvia behind her, Charlotte tries to haul herself over the threshold, but the effort momentarily weakens her, enabling Jenner and Matt to halt her progress and stand their ground. This gives Ettie the vital second she needs. If she gets to Charlotte faster than she can respond, she may block Sylvia being pulled over the threshold. Effectively penned by Ettie at her front and the men at her back, Charlotte glares ferociously, but remains neutralised in a static imbalance. Ettie bounds forward, but as she draws near Charlotte, still holding Sylvia, strikes her on the shoulder, elbowing her down. Ettie falls perilously close to the water. Unable to resist the opportunity, Charlotte lifts her leg to kick Ettie into the canal, but loses some of her own balance. She puts her foot back down quickly to avoid toppling herself, lurches forward and, struggling to retain her balance as she clings on to Sylvia, berates Ettie with her bonnet. Ettie manages to slide along the edge and back over the threshold of the tunnel as she avoids the well aimed, cutting blows. Frustrated, Charlotte wields her hat again, but with the force of her arm it slips from her fingers and is flung across to Ettie, who instinctively grabs it.

Invigorated by a sudden spurt of released energy, Charlotte heaves against the men's braking power and instantly levers Sylvia over the threshold of the tunnel. But Ettie has the bonnet and in the same moment flings her own hat directly at Charlotte. It hits her on her free arm and falls limply to the ground. Charlotte kicks it away and then, pulling with both arms tears Sylvia away from the men. Jenner and Matt stand back, staring uselessly into the tunnel, apparently petrified as Ettie had been earlier.

"You've lost!" Charlotte shouts as she scampers further into the tunnel, "We are away to my time."

Jenner, crumpled with impotent anger and Matt, his limp arms signalling empty defeat, stand dejectedly as they watch Sylvia slink after Charlotte. She beams with childlike glee, but the struggle has weakened her and she limps with a dragging step.

"Come," she calls to Sylvia, "hurry up!"

Sylvia reaches Charlotte as Ettie rejoins Jenner and Matt just outside the tunnel.

"If we go after her, will we disappear into the past?" Jenner says mournfully.

Charlotte grabs Sylvia's hand again.

"Goodbye, fools!" she calls and steps back into the murk.

Matt groans and Jenner shakes his head. Ettie looks silently into the distance, unsure whether Jenner's fear is justified. She sees the two green harridans, each stretching an arm towards the other. Already they seem far away and she strains to make them out more clearly. Even in the dimness she's sure their fingertips are not touching and then its seems one figure lifts her other arm, becoming less distinct. Ettie blinks to ensure she's not imagining. No, definitely, there's now only one green clad shape. Only one woman and Ettie is sure which one remains. Jenner has noticed too.

"Is it safe?" he whispers, "can we..."

The figure moves towards the water's edge and peers in each direction, into the depths into which her companion has disappeared and then back towards her pursuers.

"Yes," Ettie says with relief, her bold step vindicated, "from here, she's in the present!"

"It's....?"

"Yes, it's Sylvia."

Jenner hesitates and then with the resolution of one about to jump through a flaming circle of fire, he puts forward one brave foot over the threshold. He looks back. Ettie and the others are still there. He's not been thrust back a hundred and sixty years. He runs into the tunnel. Sylvia tries to run on before him, but is slowed by her injured ankle, shouting "Wait for me, I'm coming!"

She stops and looks around her again, her eyes desperately searching the walls and roof for some sign of Charlotte. She turns in a full circle, shaking her head, then pokes the air and the walls, seeking for any vestige of the presence, before wiping the damp from her hands, wringing them and shaking her head again.

"Stay where you are!" Jenner shouts as he approaches, "Sylvia Darrington – Cressley I am arresting you..."

Sylvia throws up her arms towards him.

"Get back! You're not here, you're not of this time. You're an illusion. Go, go away!"

He's almost upon her. She stands motionless and dauntless as if an invisible capsule waits to transport her into the past, but fear sweeps across her face. Gradually she realises she's marooned in an unwelcome and terrifying present and steps aside as he approaches.

"There's no point in resisting..." he begins.

She reaches the edge of the canal, glances forlornly once

more into the tunnel and sways precipitously. Jenner stops. She regains her balance and with the forced, if brief strength of the wretched leaps away from him, backs towards the tunnel mouth, the light and the pervasive present. He tries to stop her, but she gets away and breaks into a run. John and Sandra, also freed by Ettie's unlocking of Charlotte's conjured time lock, now block her way. Seeing them, she stops and turns again, first to Jenner, then back to them, twisting and swivelling in her confusion. Her frenzied turning gets faster until she stops, looks down at the water and says 'Jonathon, Jonathon' repeatedly. Then she slips and falls headlong into the water.

She slides down with the smoothness of an Olympic diver, leaving only a telltale ripple and a few bubbles. Jenner runs to the side, looking back and forth for signs of her re-emergence, but the water is still, black and unmoving. Ettie stares deep down the tunnel, but there's no sight or sound of Charlotte. John gets into the water to search for Sylvia. He dives down a couple of times, but surfaces shaking his head. Jenner and Sandra scurry up and down, kneeling and thrusting searching arms into the canal. John emerges a third time, spluttering for air and spitting out water.

"No sign of her," he shouts.

It's now several minutes since Sylvia so sleekly entered the water, leaving so little trace and with an expression closer to acceptance than alarm. Ettie walks further into the tunnel. She stops and listens, scanning forward, back and side to side. Nothing. Then she notices a dull, long, shadowy shape beneath the surface. Slowly the water clears. The shape is whiter at one end. As the shivering form solidifies, Ettie's suspicions are confirmed. The light, spreading folds of a dress lap and shimmer near the surface and the face becomes distinct. It's Sylvia. Seeing her now, Jenner rushes to the side, but Ettie already knows it's too late. John swims across and he and Jenner haul her from the water. She's laid down, a firm, yet almost contented expression on her face as if she's not struggled. For some minutes John tries to resuscitate her until Jenner tells him to stop.

"Just like Jonathon," Jenner says, recalling her words.

"Just like Charlotte," Matt says.

Ettie clutches the bonnet tightly, shakes her head, but says nothing.

A week later, the investigation is officially over. Jenner's superiors accept his report. Except for one item, it's accurate in every rational detail and silent on every irrational one. Sylvia Darrington – Cressley had confessed to the murders of both Bernard Weston and Martin Sarwell before falling into the canal and drowning whilst trying to escape arrest. Her motive for killing Bernard a mixture of personal hatred from the fallout of their relationship and his blackmail relating to complexities surrounding the rightful ownership of the Cressley estate. Sarwell had simply got in the way. The location of Bernard Weston's body is slightly altered, thereby indicating it could have been buried three years before on open land and not under an existing building. Amazingly and not without some encouragement, David Underwood discovered a previously unknown interest by the Ambro Food Company in the area, which meant Sylvia would have had access to the site. This bending of the truth worries Jenner, but the only alternative would be to disclose some if not all of the *irrational* aspects. Jennifer Heathcott, John Duggan and Sandra Tye corroborate his report. Like him, those other aspects are confined to their deeper memories, to be recalled in introspective moments of doubt and incredulity for many years to come.

Before she leaves, Ettie wants to take a last look at the Cross Cut and arranges to meet Jenner near the tunnel. He's reluctant, but she insists.

"We need to exorcise some spirits," she jokes on the telephone.

"Quite," he says, "If that's possible."

The morning is bright, clear and warm. It's the schools' half term. Children play and dogs are walked. The atmosphere is open, positive, people friendly and relaxed, nature abounding in all its splendour. No one could detect anything sinister. Both are a little edgy as they walk from the car.

"You had to come back?" he says.

"Revisiting the scene of the crime, I suppose," she laughs, "How about you?"

"The case is closed, but it's easier to stow away a file than stop the nagging memories."

"It should pass. That's why I needed to return one last time. It will help."

His expression tells her he's doubtful. They reach the towpath. There's no one else around. He stops.

"Matt Usworth must be pleased now he inherits the Darrington – Cressley fortune," she says.

He shrugs.

"Sorting that out is so complicated it'll probably take another hundred and sixty years!"

"At least that's not your problem."

"I wondered whether we were going to make it. You have a careful plan, make all the right assumptions and think of every eventuality, but can never predict how it will go. When David Underwood took Ella to the house instead of here I was very jumpy. Then they got away from us and everything started getting out of control. The phones being down was bad enough, but when we got here it seemed we'd crossed into another world with different rules we couldn't understand."

"In a way that's what happened. Charlotte was on her own territory. I'd underestimated how well she could harness the power of the tunnel and distort time in an enclosed area long enough to give her and Sylvia an advantage."

"So you were as confused and frightened as me?"

"Probably more so."

"So how *did* we stop Sylvia getting away?"

Ettie glances towards the tunnel.

"By heeding what Lizzie told me and remembering how both you and Matt had used your powers from the present to influence the past. We had the advantage. All we needed was to tip the balance. To do that I had to cross the time threshold Charlotte had created at the mouth of the tunnel. I had to risk returning to the past in order to stop Sylvia getting there!"

"It was an incredible gamble."

Ettie takes the green bonnet from her bag.

"It came down to this in the end and Charlotte herself

clinched it. When she attacked me I managed to get back across the threshold. This bonnet is from the past. When she threw it she was throwing the past into the present. In the same instant she pulled Sylvia over the threshold, but I threw my hat back at her, something from the present into the past. I held the past, her bonnet, but she kicked aside my hat from the present. I had counteracted her force. It cut the present from the past. When Charlotte transferred to the past Sylvia couldn't pass through and was left behind."

"Leaving Charlotte back in 1842, wondering and waiting, knowing that in the future all would be lost. Why didn't she warn the future generations?"

"Because she never gave up hope. Remember what Sylvia said about her great great, grandmother. 'She never gave up believing what she'd lost would return.' We thought she meant Jonathon, but she meant Sylvia."

"Better perhaps for her not to know Sylvia could never return."

"Better too Charlotte couldn't tell Sylvia what would be her real fate."

"It's all still beyond me," he grunts.

"Until the next time," Ettie says, trying to be reassuring.

"Next time, I don't want a next time like this!" he protests and then, quietly, "We never found your hat in the tunnel."

"No, that's gone the way of Matt's bag and your hat, all somewhere in 1842."

"One intriguing detail. Neither Ella Weston nor Denise Deverall could be sure whether the dress worn by the drowned woman was authentic 1840s or a clever modern copy. No other expert could be sure either. So we'll never know *who* was really left behind."

They walk back, Ettie clutching her permanent souvenir, Charlotte's bonnet. At the edge of the towpath, Jenner is anxious to get back to the car, but Ettie hesitates and looks for the last time. On the light, lifting breeze she fancies she hears a familiar voice of farewell, but she sees nothing. Then she turns and joins Jenner. Inside the tunnel of the Cross Cut all is quiet except for the perpetual lapping of the water and the dripping condensation, but deep inside, out of immediate sight or hearing, a presence turns over and sighs. The spirit of Lizzie rests peacefully at last.

from *Cross Cut*
back to *Out of Time*

How did Ettie and Jenner first meet? What was the 'previous case' they both talk about?

Soon to be published, Out of Time *is the fantastic 'prequel' to CrossCut, a mystery ranging over 1200 years in which time itself may be the ultimate victim. Here is a sample...*

They press on, arriving at Clinheeveton about eight thirty. It's a small, quiet place, most of the village grouped around a wide triangular expanse of green with large ancient oak trees at each corner. The hotel stands on one side and they pull in beside it. The others have not yet arrived though Gilbert has already pre-booked rooms for them all.

It's the sort of English country hotel Carla has always dreamed about with genuine low wooden beams and horse brasses. There are even two bars. A few old sots in the 'public' are downing the local firewater, exchanging gossip in a wholly incomprehensible rural twang. Despite his intellectual pretensions, Carla imagines Gilbert being thoroughly at home here, easily able to hold his own in any prolonged drinking bout. The lounge is relatively empty and they find a table beside the roaring fire. After a couple of drinks and a good roasting by the hearth, Carla feels well thawed, both physically and emotionally. Troubles can be easily wished away in the fiery radiance. Ettie is less relaxed. Her eyes move searchingly around the room and she watches the window constantly. She's donned her large black hat, ready to go out again. On the table, her glass of port remains untouched

"Phil said we were to meet at the green," she says.

"Which will have been Gilbert's idea," Carla says, returning to the bar for a further supply, "if we're all staying here anyway, why wait outside in the cold?"

While Carla waits for the landlord to come through from the other bar, Ettie gets more agitated, twitching slightly, totally absorbed in the view from the window even though in the darkness there's almost nothing to see except the distant shapes of the trees. They sit in brooding silence until their vigil is broken just before nine by a car pulling up on the green.

"It's Phil," Ettie says, "We must go to him."

She gets up quickly and grabs Carla's arm. Carla, downs her drink in one hand while she's led away by the other, precariously replacing her empty glass on the bar,

"We must have the security of an open place, Ettie says as they reach the door, "We must be outside now!"

As Carla takes her coat it's almost wrenched from the hook as she's jerked by Ettie's firm hand. Pulling Carla with her, Ettie runs across the road and calls to Phil.

"Get away from the car! Come over here!"

He turns in surprise, but does as he's bid, joining them on the wet grass. Ettie keeps walking until she reaches the middle of the green. Carla, annoyed at being plucked so forcefully from her haven by the fire, tries to talk, but Ettie silences her. Standing together, facing each other in the darkness, she tells them to get closer. They try to speak, but Ettie puts her fingers over their lips and nods her head towards one end of the green, though they can see nothing except one of the trees.

"They must be called now, " Ettie whispers.

Phil and Carla look at each other, wide eyed, but still say nothing. Ettie moves a few paces in the direction of the tree, holds out her hands and then, kneeling down on the grass, bows down. Holding her palms flat on the grass she raises her head again.

"Earth and sky, all powers between, help us now as we will honour you," she whispers.

Carla desperately wants to discover what she's 'playing at,' but Phil squeezes her hand for silence. Ettie gets up, walks back and joins them. Then, the light from the hotel silhouetting him beside the tree, they see the unmistakable beard and brown coat, sword at his side and the large helmet. Wulfstan has found them.

"Oh no," Carla says, "I think we've been here before."

Wulfstan walks towards them.

"Give me guidance to resist," Ettie says quietly, her hands clasped before her as she slowly walks towards Wulfstan. Instinctively holding hands, but against their better judgements, Phil and Carla follow. Sensing what Ettie may have been trying to achieve, Carla says, "Now, if you're there, show yourself."

Guessing the same and, on the basis he has nothing to lose, Phil lifts up his arms and shouts, "Heavens awake! Roll your chariot and fling your hammer at the stars!"

Unaware of their attempts to block him, Wulfstan is now less than fifty meters away. Ettie stops.

"He's here to feed off our strength," she says, "and if we have no power, he could destroy us."

A thin warm draught of air weaves around them. As they feel it wafting around their legs, a soft whistling is heard. Then, a distant rumble of thunder even though it's a clear, star filled night, the warm air gathers momentum and the whistling increases. Wulfstan stops, draws his sword and looks across to his right where, at another end of the green another warrior has appeared.

"Eadred," Phil says, "come to protect us."

Then Wulfstan's attention moves back to his left. They follow his gaze. Over at the third end of the green, another slighter figure appears who they've not seen before, a woman, younger than both Wulfstan and Eadred.

"What's this mean?" Carla whispers.

"Not a spirit," Ettie says, "another like Eadred, but I'm not sure..."

She stops as Wulfstan moves forward again. They look

quickly between the other two figures, but neither of them move.

"Help us!" Phil says.

Unconcerned by either Eadred or the other figure, Wulfstan keeps coming. Another distant rumble of thunder, but this time weaker, then the waft of warm air lessens its intensity and the whistling is softer.

"No, no," Ettie shouts, "the gods cannot desert us!"

The two figures are getting less distinct.

"Not just the gods," Carla says as the images of the two figures oscillate between clarity and fuzziness, "I think they are disappearing."

Wulfstan walks on at a quicker pace. Ettie steps back and the others follow, the three walking back in a grotesque reverse square dance.

"Why did we come out here?" Carla says.

"I was told we were safer in the open," Ettie replies.

"Whoever told you got it wrong. Shouldn't we make a run for the hotel?"

"Even if we made it we'd lose the little power of the forces we have."

Wulfstan lifts his sword high as a deafening hammer of thunder and fork lightning slices through the sky. His sword suddenly burns with startling intensity as its massive energy transfuses its tip and Wulfstan's whole form is illuminated in a bright continuous glow.

"What have I done?" Phil groans, "I called up Thunnor, only to let Wulfstan tap into his energy!"

Wulfstan increases his pace again, his vast bulk shaking from side to side and his long hair waving from beneath his helmet. Walking back even faster, Ettie and Carla collide into Phil. He holds them close, the three of them paralysed to the spot as Wulfstan moves even closer, his dark beard and wild, determined eyes lit up by his ghastly luminous sword.

"If only we had the sword," Phil says.

A car enters the village, the beam of its headlights traversing the green. It stops in front of the hotel and a familiar figure emerges.

"Gilbert!" Ettie shouts, "Quickly, over here!"

Gilbert runs over, carrying a bag. Wulfstan, undeterred by the car headlights, glances towards him, but keeps coming. Running parallel Gilbert gets to about twenty meters from Wulfstan.

"The sword," Phil shouts, "have you got the sword?"

Gilbert puts down the bag. Wulfstan stops and turns towards him. Gilbert takes the sword from the bag, holds it before him and runs towards the others. Wulfstan turns back again and also breaks into a run, quickly gaining on Gilbert.

"Throw me the sword!" Phil shouts desperately.

Gilbert stops, pulls back his arm and throws the sword, hilt down. As it turns in the air, the hilt flies across towards Phil, gradually righting itself. He jumps forward and catches the hilt in his right hand, but its force unbalances him and, staggering back he almost falls. Wulfstan comes on towards him. Phil looks round disoriented. As he stands, looking fearfully at Wulfstan, he feels the warm tingling power of the sword in his hand. Wulfstan stops only ten meters away. Phil is about the same distance in front of Ettie and Carla, halfway between them and Wulfstan. A shimmering figure appears and rapidly clears. Eadred. The sword's strength sears through Phil's whole arm. He's aware of Eadred at his side, but dare not look away from Wulfstan. The same female figure they saw earlier now materialises a few meters to the right of Carla. Glancing across she sees a young woman with strong features, strongly resembling Eadred. She doesn't move and looks ahead towards Phil before turning and smiling to Carla. Sensing the opportunity of the moment, Ettie calls to Phil.

"Take up the sword and challenge him. Move forward! You won't be alone."

Though he looks unflinchingly into the angry eyes, Phil hesitates and in that moment Wulfstan moves forward with his drawn sword. Phil lifts the sword and strides forward, his hand sweating with fear and his arm hot from the transmitted power. Immediately he hears another sword being unsheathed and sees Eadred, resolutely walking at his side. The distant thunder returns and the soft warm rippling air encircles his feet. Now only five meters away Wulfstan, stops. They march on. Eadred lifts his sword higher, swaying it slightly towards Phil who, as if pushed by an instinctive force, also lifts his sword and sways it towards Eadred's. As the two swords touch near their tips, Phil and Eadred are swathed by blinding light and an immense deafening roar. Phil is thrown backwards and rolls uncontrollably on the ground.

The roaring subsides, but the intense white light absorbs everything, only gradually diminishing until the air is cold again and all is blackness. Phil looks around. Wulfstan and Eadred have disappeared. He makes out the stars in the sky, the hotel and the distant trees as his eyes readjust to the dimness and feels the dampness of the grass through his clothes. He lies like a drunken reveller on the village green, his ears tickled by the grass and then hears a soft thumping in the ground. Turning round and resting on his elbows he sees Ettie, Carla and Gilbert running towards him.

"There was an unbelievable lightning strike with bright light all around us," Carla says, "The thunder was so loud I though my eardrums would burst. The lightning forked down and shattered into the two swords. Then the light, nothing but intense light."

"The air got very hot," Gilbert says, "You were thrown back by the lightning and as the light cleared I saw a man in the sky with a hammer."

"Thunnor," Phil gasps.

"And Freya," Carla says, "the heat in the air was Freya."

"Then everything went very black," Ettie says, "Nothing but blackness everywhere. We couldn't see anything. It gradually cleared and we saw you alone on the ground."

Stunned, but relieved they walk over to the hotel. Darkness still pervades the houses and the trees. No one stirs. No new lights have been switched on. There are no groups of people in their gardens anxiously watching and waiting. No one stands at the door of the hotel. It's as if nothing has happened. Phil feels weak and Gilbert helps him across the unchanged green. He limps on his left side where Eadred was with him. They are not objects of curiosity as they enter the hotel and no one looks up from what they're doing. The young receptionist talks to a friend. In the public bar the landlord continues to ply gallons of beer to his clientele.